FILTH

FILTH

A NOVEL BY

IRVINE WELSH

W. W. NORTON & COMPANY
NEW YORK • LONDON

Copyright © Irvine Welsh 1998

First published as a Norton paperback 1998
by arrangement with Jonathan Cape

Printed in the United States of America

Designed by Peter Ward

Irvine Welsh has asserted his right under the
Copyright, Designs and Patents Act, 1988 to be identified
as the author of this work

'Woke Up This Morning' Words and Music by Jake Black, Simon Edwards,
Piers Marsh, Robert Spragg and Chester Burnett © 1996 Chrysalis Music Ltd
and Jewel Music Publishing Company Limited, London.
Lyrics reproduced by permission

A CIP catalogue record for this title is available
from the British Library

Library of Congress Cataloging-in-Publication Data

Welsh, Irvine.
        Filth : a novel / by Irvine Welsh. — 1st American ed.
        p.   cm.
    ISBN 0-393-31868-0 (pbk.)
    I. Title.
PR6073.E47F55   1998
823'.914—dc21   98-22279
                                                          CIP

W. W. Norton & Company, Inc.
500 Fifth Avenue, New York, N.Y. 10110
http://www.wwnorton.com

W. W. Norton & Company Ltd.
10 Coptic Street, London WC1A 1PU

1 2 3 4 5 6 7 8 9 0

For Susan, Andrew, Adeline and Jo.
Thanks for keeping me out of trouble.

I started making up a list of people to thank but it got too long — you know who you are. Eternal gratitude to everybody who's supported the stuff I've done (with their hard-earned cash or through shoplifting) and who can see through all the bullshit, both positive and negative, that tends to surround this sort of thing.

Ta.

Irvine Welsh

'We shall do best to think of life as a *desengano*, as a process of disillusionment: since this is, clearly enough, what everything that happens to us is calculated to produce.'

— Arthur Schopenhauer

'When you woke up this morning everything you had was gone. By half past ten your head was going ding-dong. Ringing like a bell from your head down to your toes, like a voice telling you there was something you should know. Last night you were flying but today you're so low — ain't it times like these that make you wonder if you'll ever know the meaning of things as they appear to others; wives, mothers, fathers, sisters and brothers. Don't you wish you didn't function, wish you didn't think beyond the next paycheck and the next little drink? Well you do so make up your mind to go on, 'cos when you woke up this morning everything you had was gone.'

— 'Love, Love, Love & The Doctor'
(from *Woke Up This Morning* by the Alabama 3)

Contents

FILTH

Prologue

The trouble with people like him is that they think that they can brush off people like me. Like I was nothing. They don't understand the type of world we're living in now; all those menaced souls clamouring for attention and recognition. He was a very arrogant young man, so full of himself.

No longer. Now he's groaning, blood spilling thickly from the wounds in his head and his yellow, unfocused eyes are gandering around, desperately trying to find clarity, some meaning in the bleakness, the darkness around him. It must be lonely.

He's trying to speak now. What is it that he is trying to say to me?

Help. Police. Hospital.

Or was it help *please* hospital? It doesn't really matter, that little point of detail because his life is ebbing away: human existence distilled to begging for the emergency services.

You pushed me away mister. You rejected me. You tricked me and spoiled things between me and my true love. I've seen you before. Long ago, just lying there as you are now. Black, broken, dying. I was glad then and I'm glad now.

I reach into my bag and I pull out my claw hammer.

Part of me is elsewhere as I'm bringing it down on his head. He can't resist my blows. They'd done him in good, the others.

After two fruitless strikes I feel a surge of euphoria on my third as his head bursts open. His blood fairly skooshes out, covering his face like an oily waterfall and driving me into a frenzy; I'm smashing at his head and his skull is cracking and opening and I'm digging the claw hammer into the matter of his brain and it smells but that's only him pissing and shitting and the fumes are sticking fast in the still winter air and I wrench the hammer out, and stagger backwards to watch his twitching death throes, seeing him coming from terror to that graceless state of someone who knows that he is definitely falling and I feel myself losing my balance in those awkward shoes and I correct myself, turning and moving down the old stairway into the street.

Out on the pavement it's very cold and totally deserted. I look at a tin-foil carton with a discarded takeaway left in it. Someone has pished in its remains and rice floats on a small freezing reservoir of urine. I move away. The cold has slipped into my bones with every step down the road jarring, making me feel like I'm going to splinter. Flesh and bone seem separate, as if a void exists between them. There's no fear or regret but no elation or sense of triumph either. It's just a job that had to be done.

The Games

Woke up this morning. Woke up into the job.

The job. It holds you. It's all around you; a constant, enclosing absorbing gel. And when you're in the job, you look out at life through that distorted lens. Sometimes, aye, you get your wee zones of relative freedom to retreat into, those light, delicate spaces where new things, different, better things can be perceived of as possibles.

Then it stops. Suddenly you see that those zones aren't there any more. They were getting smaller, you knew that. You knew that some day you'd have to get round to doing something about it. When did this happen? The realisation came some time after. It doesn't really matter how long it took: two years, three, five or ten. The zones got smaller and smaller until they didn't exist, and all that's left behind is the residue. That's the games.

The games are the only way you can survive the job. Everybody has their wee vanities, their own little conceits. My one is that nobody plays the games like me, Bruce Robertson. D.S. Robertson, soon to be D.I. Robertson.

The games are always, repeat, always, being played. Most times, in any organisation, it's expedient not to acknowledge their existence. But they're always there. Like now. Now I'm sitting with a bad nut and Toal's thriving on this. I've been fucking busy and he's told me to be here, not asked, mind you, told. I got

3

it all from Ray Lennox who was first on the scene with some uniformed spastics. Aye, I got it all from young Ray but Toal of course needs his audience. Behind the times Toalie boy, be-hind the blessed times.

He paces up and down like one of those fuckin Inspector Morse type of cunts. His briefings are the closest to action the spastic gets. Then he sits back down on his arse, petulant because people are still filing in. Respect and Toal go together like fish and chocolate ice cream, whatever the spastic deludes himself by choosing to think.

I got three sheets last night and this lighting is nipping my heid and my bowels are as greasy as a hoor's chuff at the end of a shift doon the sauna. I fart silently but move swiftly to the other side of the room. The technique is to let the fart ooze out a bit before you head off, or you just take it with you in your troosers tae the next port of call. It's like the fitba, you have to time your runs. My friend and neighbour, Tom Stronach, a professional footballer and a fanny-merchant extraordinaire, knows all about that.

Hmm.

Tom Stronach. Not a magic name. Not a name to conjure with.

Talking of timing, Gus Bain arrives, red-faced fae Crawford's with the sausage rolls. He's passing them around and looking like a spare prick at a hoors' convention as Toal starts his brief. Niddrie's looking on in the usual disapproving manner of the bastard. My fart-gas has wafted over to him. Result! He's waving it away ostentatiously and he thinks it's fucking Toal!

Toal stands up and clears his throat: – Our victim is a young, black male in his early thirties. He was found on Playfair Steps at around five o'clock this morning by council refuse workers. We suspect that he lives in the London area but there is at present no positive identification. D.S. Lennox was down at the morgue last night with me, he says, nodding to young Ray Lennox who wisely keeps his features set in neutrality in order no tae flag himself up as a target for the hatred and loathing which floats aroond this room like a bad fart. My bad fart, most likely.

There was a time when we could exempt each other from that hatred and loathing. Surely there was. I feel a bit light, then it's like my brain starts to birl in my head sending my thoughts and emotions cascading around. I sense them emptying into something approximating a leaky bucket which is drained before I can examine its contents. And Toal's high, sharp voice, reaching into me.

This is where he starts to play silly buggers. – It seems to have been a fruitless night for our friend. He was in the Jammy Joe's disco until three a.m. this morning and went home alone. That was when he was last reported alive. We can perhaps assume that our man felt very much an outsider, alone in a strange city which seemed to have excluded him.

Typical Toal, concerned with the state of mind of the cunt that got murdered. Fancies himself as an intellectual. This is *Toal* we are talking about here. It would be amusing if it wasn't so fucking tragic.

I bite into my sausage roll. The pepper and the ketchup I normally have with it are up the stairs and it tastes plain and bland without them. That spunk-bag Toal's wrecked my fuckin day already! Wir only jist in the fuckin place!

As my fart retreats via the airvent I clock Niddrie exiting from the door, improving the room's atmosphere in much the same way. Even Toal's sprightlier now. – The man was dressed in blue jeans, a red t-shirt and a black tracksuit top with orange strips on the arms. His hair was cut short. Amanda, Toal gestures to that silly wee lassie Amanda Drummond, who's doing all that she's good for, a psuedo-clerical job, dishing oot copies of the description. Drummond's had her frizzy blonde hair cut short, which makes her look even mair ay a carpet muncher. She has bulging eyes which always give you the impression that she's in shock, and she's hardly any chin; just a sour, twisted mooth which comes out of her neck. She's wearing a long, brown skirt which is too thick to see the pant line through, with a checked

blouse and a fawn and brown striped cardigan. I've seen mair
meat on a butcher's knife.

That?

Polis?

I think not.

— Thanks Amanda, Toal smiles, and this crawling wee sow
coos back at him. She'd suck his fuckin knob right there in front
of us if he asked her tae. No that it'll do her much good; she'll
be away soon, some cunt'll knock her up the duff and that'll be
her playin at being polis over.

— Our murder victim left the nightclub and . . . Toal continues, but Andy Clelland cuts in on a wind-up: — Boss, a wee point
of order. Maybe we shouldnae stigmatise the guy by referring to
him by such a pejorative term as victim?

You have to raise your glass to Clell, he always hits home.
Toal looks a bit doubtful, and Amanda Drummond's nodding
supportively, completely unaware that he's taking the pish.

— The cunt's fuckin well deid, disnae matter what ye call um
now, Dougie Gillman says under his breath. I chuckle and Gus
Bain does n aw.

— Sorry Dougie? Care to share that with us? Toal smiles sarcastically.

— Naw gaffer, s'awright. It's nothing, Gillman shrugs.
Dougie Gillman has short brown hair, narrow, cold blue eyes and
a big, powerful jaw you could break your fingers on. He's about
my height, five-eight, but is as wide as he is tall.

— Perhaps, craving your indulgence gentlemen, Toal says
coldly, now trying to stamp his authority on the proceedings in
Niddrie's absence, — we might continue. The deceased was probably making his way towards hotel accommodation on the South
Side of the city. We've a team out checking the hotels for someone of his description. Assuming that was the case, the route he
took to get there was interesting. We all know that there are
certain places you shouldn't go to in a strange city after dark,
Toal raises his thick, straggly eyebrows, slipping back into his
showboating mode, — places like dark alleys where the ambience

of such surroundings might incite even a reasonable person to perpetrate an evil deed.

The self-indulgent cunt's on one of his trips the day alright. Thinks that we're a bunch of fuckin bairns tae be spooked by his bedtime stories.

– Now that twisting staircase which is the city's umbilical cord connecting the Old Town with the New Town is one such place, he says, pausing dramatically.

Umbilical fuckin cord! It's a fuckin stair you fucking clown. S-T-A-I-R. I know that spazwit's crack; the bastard wants tae be a fuckin scriptwriter. I ken this because I got a sketch of what he had up on his VDU when he went to answer a private phone-call in the quiet anteroom from his office. He was trying to write a telly or film script or some shite. In police time as well. Lazy cunt's got nowt better tae dae, and on his salary too. That shit-bag leads a charmed life, I kid you not.

– As he began his ascent, perhaps the victim pondered this. Did he know the city? Possibly, otherwise he might not have known of this short-cut. But surely, had he known about it, alone, and at that time in the morning, he'd have thought twice about climbing it. That staircase, too dangerous and urine-soaked for even the most desperate jakeys to crash in. The guy must have felt fear. He didn't act on that fear. Is fear not the way of telling you that something's wrong? Like pain? Toal speculates. People shuffle around nervously, and even Amanda Drummond has the good grace to look embarrassed at this. Andy Clelland stifles a laugh by coughing. Dougie Gillman's eyes are on Karen Fulton's erse, which is not a bad place for them to be.

Toal's so intae his ain shit though, he's totally oblivious tae all this. The ring is his and he doesnae want tae spoil his own fun by going for a knockout punch so early. – Maybe he felt it was all paranoia, distortion of emotion. Then the voices. He must have heard them coming, at that time of night you'd be bound to hear people on these steps.

No, he wants us to throw in the towel. Sorry Toalie, but it's not the Bruce Robertson style. Let's joust. – Nae eye witnesses?

7

I ask, glad that I omitted that term 'gaffer'. That fucker's my boss in name only.

— Not as yet Bruce, he says curtly, upset at having his flow interrupted. That's Toal; have a wank in our faces, never mind those wee practical details that might actually help get whoever topped this coon banged up.

— Then they were on him and they kicked him down to a recess in the stairs where a savage beating took place. One of the assailants, only one, went further than the others and struck the man with an implement. Forensic already say that the injuries left are consistent with those that would be made by a hammer wielded at force. This assailant did this repeatedly, caving in the man's skull and driving the implement into his brain. As I said earlier, our friends in the council cleansing department found the body.

Your friends in the council cleansing department Toal. *I* have no scaffy friends.

— Left him lying like rubbish, Gus shakes his head.

— Maybe he wis rubbish.

Fuck. That slipped out. I shouldnae have said that. They're all looking at me. — Tae the scumbag that did him, like, I add.

— Are you postulating that it was a racially motivated attack Bruce? Drummond quizzes, her mouth twisting downwards in a slow, agonised movement. Karen Fulton looks encouragingly at her, then at me.

— Eh, aye, I say. That starts them chattering, too loudly for them to notice that my teeth are doing the same. This fuckin hangover. This fuckin place. This fuckin job.

8

The Crimes

I'm trying to shake off the bad taste in my mouth caused by the hangover and the presence of a certain Mr Toal so early in the day. Aye, it can still be salvaged, but this necessitates getting the fuck out of HQ for a while. Ray Lennox is thinking along similar lines. Toalie's getting the hots about this topped silvery so it's best we keep oot the road. I've more than enough to do at the moment, my paperwork's in a shocking state and that needs rectified before I go off on my winter's week holly-bags. Lennox is officially on drug squad duty but he knows that high visibility is not an option today. It means that Toal's likely to press-gang him on to the murder investigation team.

So Ray and I are out in my Volvo on a roving commission. There's a bit of a ground frost and the air feels raw and sharp. Winter's digging in alright, and it's going to be a bad one. The car heater's warming up nicely when this spastic from control comes on the radio and asks us for our location. Ray tells them that we're proceeding west in the direction of Craigleith. Control then inform us that some auld crone up in Ravelston Dykes has reported a burglary.

—You want tae check it? I ask him.

—Yeah, keep oot ay Toalie's wey a wee bit longer.

Ray knows the score. —That's the wey Ray, mind what I telt

you aboot that cunt. He's got the attention span ay a goldfish, so if you can keep out of his sight for a while . . .

— . . . the cunt forgets all aboot ye! Ray grins. Ray Lennox is a good young guy. About six-foot tall, brown hair in a side parting, a moustache that's a tiny bit too long and unkempt and makes him look a wee bit daft, and a large hooked nose and shifty eyes. Sound polisman, and he's now starting tae take a mair active role in the craft.

This was really a common-or-garden uniformed spastics job, but we were in the area and it wasted time. One of my mottoes aboot the job is: better you wasting some cunt else's time than some cunt wasting your time.

— Calling Foxtrot, come in Foxtrot, this is Z Victor two BR, over.

— Foxtrot . . . the radio crackles.

— Proceeding to address in Ravelston Dykes. D.S. Robertson and Lennox, over.

— Roger BR. Over.

We pull up outside the driveway of this big hoose. There's an old Escort parked in the street. It looks a bit run-down for Ravvy Dykes.

An old cow with a faraway look lets us in. I get a bit of a whiff from her. Age makes you smell, rich fucker or schemie, it makes nae odds. I shudder in the hallway: it's none too warm in here. This is a big hoose tae heat and I get a scent of old money. The place is crammed full of bric-à-brac, a good lifetime, at least, of memories here. Loads of pictures in silver frames: lined up on the tables, sideboards and the mantelpiece like an army of tin sodjirs. Overkill. This is telling me that loads of little birdies have flown the nest and they've flown pretty far. All sorts of hooses, cars and clathes in those pictures; they fairly glint of the new world. The old bat should cash in, sell this asset and coast out her days in a plush centrally heated and roond-the-clock warden-attended sheltered housing complex. But naw; that twisted pride again. All it equals is a faster and more ragged route tae the grave, but there's nae telling that tae some fuckers.

That old coal fire looks comfortable. The coal is placed in a nice brass bucket. One lump or two, or twenty hundred thousand falling around you? The filthy, dirty coal and the minging cunts that dig it. You dig it baby? You dig that coal brother?

I don't fuckin well dig it or dig the filthy cunts that do.

I leave Ray with the old bat in order to have a better nose around. Some nice auld mahogany furniture here. Some wee opportunistic spazwit's done the brek-in, through a french door at the back, which is a total waste. An organised firm wi a big van could have cleaned up with some bent antiques dealer. The old dear goes away to make some tea and when she comes back she goes aw stroppy on us.

— It's my paperweight! she says, pointing to a sideboard. — It's gone now . . . it was here a minute ago.

It wisnae as if it was any of my fuckin business. We just came here to waste a bit of time. The dopey auld cow; her wizened face glaikit with shock. That bemused look, the great fucking British public; it makes me want to smash the wearer's teeth in with a baton. No much teeth left in this auld cunt tae smash, mind you. The vandalism time perpetuates on the human body. Fuck me, I'm sounding like that arsehole Toal!

— I'm sorry, I don't quite follow you, Ray says.

Fuckin auld spasticworks. You've got to give it to Ray Lennox though; ice cool in such situ's, an auld heid on young shoulders.

— But it was here. It *was* here! she's asserting. Ravelston Dykes. Money talks. Tick tock tick tock. Used to getting their own way. Those tones I know so well. But I'm a servant of the state. I'm in the business of law enforcement. Same rules apply.

I take a deep breath and look her in the eye. She's feeble, frightened and isolated in spite of her wealth. The dominant photo of the husband on the marble fireplace. Top tin sodjir. A wee bit rusty though, aw the more set off by the splendour of the frame. You can see cancer written all over him. A recent photo. She's still in shock, still vulnerable. — I want you to fully understand what you are saying to me here Mrs Dornan.

She looks like a cow being herded into an abattoir. Just at that point where they know that something is up and that it's not good news. Ten-ti-ten-ten . . . ten-ti-ten-ten-ten . . .

—You're telling me that the paperweight was here after the appointed burglary, but has subsequently appeared to be missing, this coinciding with the appearance of the investigating officers, namely ourselves. I want you to be crystal clear about this.

—Well . . . yes . . . I mean . . .

I move over to the window and look out into the garden. I notice that the Escort I clocked is still there. The one which looked semi-abandoned. Semi-abandoned? What the fuck in the name of Jesus Christ almighty is that? Some cunt's Jackie Trent here and nae mistake. I clear my throat and turn back to the ancient cow. — I want you to concentrate Mrs Dornan. I want you to be absolutely sure about what you're saying and the implications of it. Now you've had a bad shock, I lecture her. — Having an intruder in your home: not very pleasant. I want you to be sure about what you mean before I consider the ramifications. This means initiating a second tier of the investigation, implicating the officers who came here to investigate this burglary. I nod towards Ray and then glance down at my own chest. — The same rules have to apply in each and every case. What I'm saying to you is: are you sure that the paperweight was not taken in the original burglary?

Ray comes over at this point, for a bit of back up. — I think we're jumping the gun a bit here D.S. Robertson.

—Well D.S. Lennox, the lady seems to be concerned about this paperweight and perhaps a little confused about what was actually taken during the burglary.

—Yes . . . I mean . . . she stammers.

— She seems to feel it vanished during our investigation, I give a slightly rueful expression. Ray still plays it deadpan.

— I didn't say . . . the old cow whines.

— I think the best thing would be if we turned out our pockets, D.S. Robertson, Ray laughs in mild impatience.

— No! I didn't mean . . . I don't think that *you* took it, not for a minute . . . she bleats, all embarrassed. That was the mistake you silly old fucker.

Ray gives a practised, tired shake of the head. – What I'd like to suggest . . .

I cut in. This cow's irritated me. I want sport. – I don't think you quite understand what the lady's saying D.S. Lennox. She's claiming that the paperweight vanished after the investigating officers arrived, I point at myself and then at him. – The inference is that the investigating officers have expropriated this property.

I curse inwardly, that was a mistake using the term expropriated. Stolen would have been better, for obvious reasons.

– I didn't mean that . . . the dopey cow apologises. She's buckling inwards, shrinking like a crisp packet flung into a pub fire, diminishing before it combusts. She'll be offering us financial compensation for upsetting us soon. Keep backpedalling you old spazwit. I'm savouring this.

– If I could proceed with my suggestion, Ray says, his tone practical, – I think that you should go through the inventory again. List the lot, make sure that nothing's left out.

My pager goes. It's control. Fuck me, Toal wants me. – Excuse me, I smile. I point to the phone. – May I? I dial his direct line. I'm only half listening to him, I'm half tuned in to Ray's performance, which I'm enjoying very much.

– Toal speaking . . .

– It's D.S. Robertson.

– Bruce, good. I'm needing you on this murder case. Busby's put another note in long-term sick. We're stretched to our limit.

– I see.

– *Are you asking me or telling me?*

– *Well, I . . .*

– *I want to be clear about this Mrs Dornan; are you asking me or telling me?*

– *It's just that . . .*

Toal is getting uppity. The bastard's always resented my pull with the lads; my status as Federation rep, but also the fact that I'm more prominent in the craft than he'll ever be. That's what cuts the ice with the boys in the canteen, not fucking name, rank or serial number. The basic fact of it is that *nobody* tells me what to do. I'm listening to Toal rabbiting on about this wog being topped and I'm thinking: fucking great! Another one bites the dust, and then I'm thinking of my forthcoming winter's week's holiday in Amsterdam and my favourite hoors d'oeuvres and I'm thinking of two vibrators, one up her arse and one up her cunt. The technology of love, deployed on a massive scale. I've got a semi; I've got a semi and I'm talking to Toal!

— The last thing we need now's a stiff, Toal sniffs.

— *Evening News* got it yet?

Right up her fuckin hole.

— Not so far.

— So why the hassle? It's just a nigger. Not exactly a shortage of them, is there? I joke.

— Listen, I don't want any canteen culture bullshit on this investigation. I want you briefed properly by Lennox, he snaps. Toal is known for having no sense of humour. He's taking this equal opps bullshit too far.

— What about Lennox doing it? I whisper,
— He was first on the scene.

— *I understand how terrible this is, Mrs Dornan. Especially with something so valuable to you.*

— *I was sure it was there though. I could have sworn!*

— *That's what I always find, Mrs Dornan. Sometimes when the thing that you want most to be there is away, you can't believe it, so you do actually visualise it there in your mind's eye. A classic shock reaction. Burglary can be very traumatic. It might be an idea to call your GP. Shall I do that now?*

— *Oh no, I'm sorry, I'm making such a fuss . . .*

— *Make out the inventory Mrs Dornan. I think that's the best move . . .*

— I can't take Ray off DS, he's close to busting these suppliers at that Sunrise Community. Besides, he doesn't have your homicide experience

— *Yes . . . I'll do that . . . I'm so sorry officer . . . eh . . .*

— I think you're forgetting something. I'm on my winter's week brek in just over one week's time.

— *Lennox ma'am, D.S. Lennox.*

There's a short silence on the other end of the phone. My heart misses a beat. I feel as if I'm listening for the first time.

— All leave is suspended for Serious Crimes personnel, there's a memo coming round today, Toal says.

All leave is suspended.

I can't think straight here. What did he say?

— Look Robbo, Toalie continues, it's 'Robbo' now, — this victim, we don't have a positive ID yet, but it seems he's connected. The Chief Super's got me by the bollocks. We're stretched and the budget is almost exhausted. We've cut back on the OT as much as we can. You're the first one to complain if there are overtime restrictions . . .

I keep silent.

— . . . This fucking stupid departmental reorganisation . . . Anyway, Personnel will be sending round a memo. We're out on a limb here, then this murder happens . . . it's the wrong time for everyone Robbo. We've all got to make sacrifices, to pull out the stops.

— I'm on leave in nine days' time Brother Toal, I tell him.

— Look Bruce, it's *Bruce* now, is it — . . . don't you be bloody difficult . . . Niddrie's got my nuts in a sling, his voice breaks into a pedantic squeak as if to emphasise what he's saying. — Give me a break!

— My leave is booked, Brother Toal, I reiterate, putting the phone down.

Ray has the dopey cow making up an inventory. I finger the paperweight in my pocket. He nods to the door and we depart.

As we go the old boot screeches miserably, – It wasn't as if the paperweight was worth anything. It looks expensive but it's only a low carat gold. It's just the sentimental value. Jim brought me it back from Italy after the war. We were as poor as church-mice then.

Ya fuckin dirty fanny-flapped faced auld hoor! A fuss over fuckin nowt!

– We'll do our best to recover all the goods Mrs Dornan, Ray nods sincerely as I turn away from the decomposing auld bag of fetid garbage soas that she doesn't catch me snorting in exasperation. Fucking auld spastic.

You can kiss ma bacon-flavoured po-leese ass muthafuckah.

Her problem is that she's been too long without a good fuckin knobbin. That always distorts a woman's perspective. Social Services should pay some ay they bored young studs oan the dole a wee allowance tae go roond and gie these auld cunts a good fuckin seein tae. Then they wouldnae be such a drain on resources wi thir phoney illnesses. Every time I go to see my doctor about my rash and my anxiety attacks, there's always loads of the auld cunts holding me back with their trivial complaints.

In the car I produce the paperweight. – Worth fuck all, totally u.s.

– Tight auld cunt, Ray sneers, taking the wheel, then he shouts at a guy who pulls out in front of us, – Fuckin spastic!

– Cunts on the road these days . . . I muse, still looking at the dotty old boot's useless paperweight.

– I should follow that cunt . . . get his fuckin number, run a check on him . . . Ray spits, then he suddenly laughs and says: – Fuck his erse. All set for the Dam? You were saying you had booked up.

– Too right I am. Me and my mate Bladesey. You ken Bladesey? Wee cunt fae the craft. Civil Servant. Registrar

General for Scotland's Office. Took pity oan the wee fucker cause he's no goat any mates.

— I think so. Wee joker wi specs? Really thick lenses?

— That's the boy.

— I had a good crack wi that cunt once. No a bad wee guy . . . for an English cunt.

— Aye, we're booked up: now Toalie's trying to play the fuckin toss-bag. He's got the shits about this coon that's been topped. Trying to suspend all leave. Personnel are sticking a note round today.

— Fuckin spastics.

— Me give up ma fuckin holiday for some stiffed nig-nog? Aye, right. I look fuckin sweet right enough. As if I give an Aylesbury. Every fucker kens that I have my three weeks' summer in Thailand and my winter's week in the Dam. Tradition. Custom and fuckin practice. Nae pen-pushing cunts are stopping that. No siree, I'll be fuckin well shaggin for Scotland come the tenth of this month.

I go to put a tape of *Deep Purple in Rock* into the cassette player, but decide against it because this will precipitate an argument with Lennox over whether Coverdale is a better vocalist than Gillan, which as any spastic knows is a non-argument. I mean, who could compare Coverdale's Purple or Whitesnake output to the original Deep Purple line-up Gillan graced alongside Blackmore, Lord, Glover and Paice? Only an idiot would try. Additionally, Gillan produced in *Glory Road* and *Future Shock*, two classic solo hit albums. What did Coverdale ever do as a solo artist? But I'm not getting into this with Lennox, so I put on Ozzy Osborne's *Ultimate Sin*.

Lennox nods thoughtfully as the Oz struts his stuff. — Tell ye what though Robbo, you've got a very understanding wife. If Mhari had found out I was off to Amsterdam with a mate . . .

Ray's bird. She left him anyway. Probably wasn't giving her enough. Of course, Ray could never give any bird enough. The mouth department and the trouser department are well out of synchronisation in the not-so-superstore that is Ray Lennox, I kid you not.

— It's a question of values Ray. Give and take. Keeps the spice in a relationship, I tell him.

Ray raises his eyebrows. — I'd watch Toal though Robbo. Just play it gently, he'll let ye go. This case'll be wrapped up in ten minutes anyway.

— Ye never know but, eh.

— C'mon Bruce, somebody daft enough to top a silvery in a staircase in the centre ay the toon shouldnae prove too hard tae catch. It'll be some schemie young bloods pished up on the toon and tooled up . . . Toal's probably seeing it as some big political thing cause the wog probably had a rich daddy who plays golf with some big noise doon in London. If it was an ordinary punter from Brixton they wouldn't give a toss. You know how insecure that spastic is.

— Exactly Ray. That spastic's jealous of my status in the craft . . . and he was trying to butter me up about all my homicide experience. Where did I get most of it though? Over in fuckin Australia, which counts for nothing with these spastics when it comes tae promoted posts. Doesnae count for nowt though, when they want somebody drafted on to one ay their fuckin teams.

— Out of order, Ray nods.

— Here, Ray, I shout, clocking a Crawford's, — pull up at that baker's a minute.

I get a couple of bacon rolls and Ray gets another sausage roll, which we scran back and wash doon with hot, slimy, milky coffee. It has the aftertaste of a jakey's lips after a binge on the old purple tin! I take over at the wheel and we drive down by the Water of Leith and I chuck the auld cow's paperweight into the river. I'm writhing in the seat as I drive. I have a rash developing on my testies and my arse. Caused by excess sweat and chaffing, the quack said. The cream he gave me seems to be making it worse, if anything. I suppose it's something that'll have to get worse before it gets better. Fuckin spastics. How do they expect me to do my job under these circumstances?

I cannae

It's getting really fucking itchy and I shift my weight on to one buttock and claw at my arse through my shiny black flannels. She's . . . I need a proper fucking laundry service, that's what I need. It's no good. I stick it out until we get to the High Street where I stop the car at Hunter Square and go into the public bogs. This needs a good claw. I whip everything down and remove the dampness from around my arse with toilet paper. Then I scratch like fuck but it stings as the grease from the bacon roll, I realise, is still under my nails. I claw and claw feeling a delicious liberation as the wound tears and pulsates. I see the blood on my fingers. I wedge some toilet paper between the cheeks of my arse in order to stop them from rubbing together and creating the friction which causes the tissue to itch. My balls are not too bad. I go back up without bothering to wash my hands.

— You down the lodge tonight Bruce? Ray asks, as I pull down the Royal Mile. We'll cruise down to HQ via Leith; kills a wee bit time.

— Nah . . . maybe Thursday, for the pool round robin.

— Quiet night in with the missus?

—Yeah, I say, glowing with pride, — Carole's making a special meal tonight.

— I wish I had somebody to make me a special meal, Ray says, as we motor down Easter Road past Tinelli's Restaurant, an old haunt of Carole's and mine.

—You're no telling me that you've no got something oan the go?

— Nah, since ah split up wi Mhari ah've been daein a bit ay sniffin, but thir no bitin, Ray says, looking doleful, as well the cunt might.

— Mibbee gittin too desperate Ray, giein the birds that I-want-intae-yir-drawers-at-all-costs stink.

Lennox looks thoughtful, and lets his finger rub the side of his nose. Talking of stinks, there's an almighty Judi Dench coming into the car and I'm about to pull up that scummy bastard for letting one go, when I realise that its source is the sewage filtration plant. — Aye, mibbee, he concedes.

— Huv tae fix ye up wi ma sister-in-law again, eh Ray! I laugh. Ray looks embarrassed. He hates tae be reminded of the time we both rode that cow. Every cunt has their Achilles' heel, and I always make a point of remembering my associates' ones. Something that crushes their self-image to a pulp. Yes, it's all stored for future reference.

Wheels Of Steel

Back doon at HQ everyone in the canteen's gaun fuckin spare about the holiday memo. I say nothing. Best to play it cool and let their anger ferment for a bit. Of course, they're all looking to me, as Fed rep, for a bit of leadership but I've got to keep my nose clean as there's the new D.I. post which is coming up soon in the departmental reorganisation. No way would I put my neck on the line for any spastic in this place, although I obviously keep them thinking otherwise.

Toal's shiting it about this departmental reorganisation. I don't know why, he should be well used to it by now. They have one here every six months, and every one they undertake fucks things up even worse than before. So they set up a working party and they go away for ages and when they come back they rec- ommend yet another departmental reorganisation. The best thing aboot this yin is that it puts our good friend Mister Toal on shaky ground as when I get this promotion I'll be on the same grade as him. It's a promotion I should have had long ago but for their stupid fucking rules and Carole's idiocy.

But he's on a wee run right now, is Toalie. He's got us all in for another fuckin briefing, and this new civvy blonde piece is handing oot the notes. I get a waft of her perfume. I give Clell the eye and he nods back in shared acknowledgement of the fact that the blonde piece looks some ride. Ah'd say mid-thirties, body still firm, but jist startin tae git that heavier wey that I like. Well worth one.

Toal's slavering on about this journalist coon that got topped and his diplomat father, but I can't hear a fuckin word of it cause the blonde piece is standing in a light which makes her top look almost see-through and these jugs are fuckin well prominent. Ya cunt ye. Gie ye a fuckin migraine, thon. Thankfully Toal's briefing is short, so I get downstairs for a coffee and a sausage roll.

I force myself to look through the copies of the file that Toal's opened up on the topped silvery. They now have a positive identification: a Mister Efan Wurie. His father is the ambassador for Ghana. He was staying at the Kilmuir Hotel on the South Side. He only checked in a couple of days ago.

A couple of days ago . . .

That means

Shouldnae fuckin well be here.

He should not

A journalist. A diplomat's son and a journalist. That wisnae

Shouldnae have been here in the first place

What sort of a journalist was he?

Only on some commie nigger mag that no cunt reads. Fitba fuckin fanzine journalism.

There's little of note in the file otherwise, so I place a call to the Lothian Forum on Coon Rights, or whatever they call them. Maybe he was up here to meet an Edinburgh darkie. It's engaged. I'm absolutely Aylesbury'ed, so I decide to knock off early, taking the motor out to my pal Hector The Farmer's, who's got some good video tapes.

I'm tearing out of town in the Volvo, the Michael Schenker Band giving it big licks. I'm always indebted to them for saving a crap Reading Festival I once went to. Before we know it, there it stands in front of me: Hector's House.

Hector crushes my hand in a masonic grip, his alcohol-flushed face beaming at me. —Got time to come for a dram, he asks.

— Sorry mate, I'm on a murder investigation. Some daft

nigger's only gone and got himself topped. Still, there's big OT possibilities. Got the goods?

— Aye, Hector smiles and produces a Tesco's bag with two VHS format video tapes in it.

We arrange to meet at the Lodge later that week and I speed off homewards, a strong jab in my shiny flannels every time I pass a piece of quality fanny.

That night I'm home, home alone, although that's my business, not Ray Lennox's or any cunt else's. I've got a large slice of gala pie for my tea. I put it into the microwave and watch the movie I got from Hector. Two hoors are having a good licking and frigging session and the black studs are just about to come and join them . . . no . . . I switch it off. I don't want any black studs. I put on another tape featuring two lesbians and a milkman.

I bite into the gala pie and my teeth ache and send a spasm through my body. The fuckin thing's still frozen in the middle. I eat it anyway. The video is okay but I start to feel uneasy as a fluttering rises and intensifies in my chest. The room looks gaudy with too many rough edges. I go to the kitchen and pour out a large measure of reassuring whisky. I take the bottle with me into the front room. Another glass and the unease passes. I'm not thinking about work. I'm here, at home.

I stay up and sleep in the rocking chair after having had a few nippy sweeties. I'm half-dozing and half-awake, thinking of Carole. She'll be back soon. She knows what side her bread's buttered on.

After a while my guts really begin to ache badly and I'm sweating. I sit writhing in the chair as it rocks in a sickening rhythm but I can't go to bed, not until it gets light. I think I'm going to throw up. I keep it down, trying to breathe in slowly. The thick, stagnant alcohol sweat. My fuckin guts. It'll be from that gala pie. I've a good mind to report the deli spastics to the environmental health, no that those fuckers are any use.

After a bit it thankfully eases off as sleep takes me away.

Sleep 000000000000000000000000000000000000 nd pleasant
dreams th 00000000000000000000000000000000 urbed by the
shite that y 00000000000000000000000000000000 e Toal and his
ilk . . . no th 00000000000000000000000000000 m; he thinks
that he can do 0000000000000000000000000000

No chance 00000000000000000000000000 000

0000000000000000000000000000000100000

000I am000000000000000000 I am a 000

00000000 I am alive0000000000000

000000000000000000I am alive0000000

000000 I am soft and I am weak 000000

00000000000000000I must grow 00000

0000 I must eat 0000000000000000000000

000000000000 I must grow strong 000

0000eat 00000000000000000eat00000

0000eat 00000000000 eat 0000 eat000

000000 eat 000000 eat000000000eat eat

eat eat eat eat eat00000000000000000000

0000000eat00000000000000000000000

000000000 big and strong0000000000

000000000000000000000000000000000

000000000000000000000000000000000

000000000000000000000000000000000

00000000000000000000000000000000

0000000000000000000000000000000

000000000000000000000000000000

. . . still fuck 00000000000000000000000 hungry as fuck
with my guts rumbling away. It's darkness and I'm in bed. I don't
remember going to bed. This is unusual for me. I sense the space
beside me and I grab at her dressing gown and hold it tightly. It
still has her smell. I'd let it go in the night and I had the bad
dreams as a result. I've also been inadvertently clawing at my
balls because they are nipping something terrible.

My head feels broken and weak, like it's been smashed open
and its contents spilt all over the pillow. Despite this, the ten-
dons of my neck feel yanked to their tensile limit, seemingly
unable to support its dead weight. The first sunlight is filtering

insipidly through the blinds making the room look washed out and blurry.

With some effort, I get up and wash and go to have a close shave but I've ran out of blades and scratch the worn one over my face. I decide against the car and head for the bus stop with a strange mixture of liberation and despair, realising that it's only ten-twenty a.m. and I've already decided I'm going to be out drinking tonight.

My stomach is still upset and the stink of bodies on the bus seems overpowering. Too many schemies. Can they not have a bus which runs from Colinton into the city centre without having to pass through Oxgangs? When I alight a jakey holds out a hopeful grubby hand. I shake it and tell the cunt that Jesus loves him. He looks bemused as I move away and I'm doon the road by the time the growls start. If it wasn't coming up to the season of goodwill I'd've gone back and had the cunt pinched.

I go to the newsagent and buy a *Sun*. I also look at the pornographic magazines on the top shelf. I make no apologies for this; the job is one in which it's dangerous to think too much, so the best thing is to channel your energy into something that's the easiest to think about but which does you no harm. For most of us sex fits the bill nicely.

I leave without making another purchase however, and I'm upset at the cheerfulness of the shopkeeper. — The *Sun*, he shouts loudly, — very good, thirty pence.

This disgusts me as I'm not like the rest of the festering plebs who read the *Sun*. I'm more like somebody who writes the thing, edits it even. Know the difference, you pleb, always know the fuckin difference.

The last thing I need first thing in the morning is yet another briefing from Toal about this Wurie murder. As it happens, it's the first thing I get along with Gus Bain, Peter Inglis and three constable spastics, namely: Roy, whom I know through the Lodge, Muir, whom I worked with on Drug Squad and who's acceptably Jackie Trent, and Considine who seems okay. So it looks like Toal's heading up this team himself to work on the topped coon case.

I'm fucking burning inside though when I see that silly wee cow Amanda Drummond here. What the fuck is she daein on a murder team? Wouldnae trust her to pick the fucking curtains for the office.

Why doesn't anybody tell that silly wee lassie that she is superfluous now that we've got that big blonde civvy piece wi the waxed legs and sunbed tan handing oot the paperwork? Yes, and she's here now, coming right into my sights. Phoah! She passes me a briefing note.

— Thank you my darling, I smile at her and she gives me the unfazed measuring look of the game hoor who kens what she's aboot.

— Fuckin doll, I hear a voice in my ear. It's Ray Lennox.

— What the fuck are you daein here, I ask him, — I thought you were on D.S. duty.

I ken what the cunt's daein here awright; he's stalking that blonde piece, that's what he's daein here.

— I'm on my way. Just popped in to say good morning, he smiles, and departs. Lennox has trimmed his mouser, but he's gone over the score. He looks like a fuckin pansy now.

I pucker my lips in the direction of the blonde piece's arse, gift-wrapped perfectly as it is in that tight skirt, but the gesture which was meant for Ray's matey complicity is picked up by the ice-hearted hanger-on Amanda Drummond.

I ignore The Thin White Puke's distasteful scowl. I nudge Dougie Gillman next to me who clocks the blonde piece's erse with an evaluating, approving nod.

Toal's off on one, flapping with only semi-restrained excitement: — As you know, we now have a positive identification of our victim. He is one Efan Wurie and he is a freelance journalist from Ghana who was working in London. We are unaware of his business in Edinburgh and friends have said that he was here on holiday.

A funny time to come up here for a holiday. Up tae nae fuckin good ah'll bet.

— Some holiday, perr boy, Peter Inglis nods.

Yes, vintage form is being displayed by a certain Inspector Robert Toal, or if you like, he's spraffing the same auld fuckin shite as the bastard's prone to do. — We've heard from the Met that our man was recently the victim of an attack in Haggerston, London. On the second of February, this year, he left a bar with two friends. He was set upon by some thugs who came out the back of a van with baseball bats. This was reported but no arrests were made.

— You think maybe one ay they racially biased mobs did the darkie-boy over? Gus asks.

Amanda Drummond winces. Toal looks tired. — We can't say. It might be coincidence. However, this incident must have been in the man's mind as he climbed the steps up to the North Bridge. That makes it even more surprising he wasn't more careful. Toal looks at us for a reaction, but naebody's saying a dicky bird. Then he turns and focuses on me. — Bruce, can I see you in an hour in my office?

I feel a shiver. I don't want anything to do with this case. — Need to make it two hours gaffer. I couldn't stop myself from saying that horrible word which I try never to use in connection with Toal. I hate myself for being so . . . subordinate. Fuck'um. — I've a meeting with the Lothian Forum on Racial Equality. I thought it best from a com rels perspective that we keep in touch, allay fears and what have you, this being a sensitive case and what not.

— Good thinking Bruce, that's the ticket. Make it two hours then.

I feel a rising glow in my chest. I've been out of sorts lately but I've still more than enough gas in my tank to see off the likes of Toal. No way am I going to visit a bunch of jungle-bunnies and their nursemaids. I need two hours for my lunch, minimum requirement. I head out with Gus, but as we're leaving I get pulled up by Amanda Drummond. — Bruce, can I have a word?

— You, my darling, can have a word any time, I smile at her. A waste of time that approach, with such a glacier-hearted dyke, but you have to remember that even glaciers thaw, just as long as you keep the heat turned up. And if there's one thing that Bruce Robertson knows, it's how to do *exactly* that.

She scowls at me, — It's just that I was speaking to Alan Marshall at the Forum this morning, and he said nothing to me about a meeting with you.

— Hmmm, I rub my chin. I'll need to get closer with that razor. A real close shave; that's what's required. — Must be some wires getting crossed somewhere. I'll get back to you on that one later Mandy love, I say, winking and turning away.

— It's Amanda, and it's not love, she hisses, but I've already turned my back and I'm gesturing at Gus to head off, totally ignoring the silly wee trollop's ineffectual bleatings.

You are dismissed, girlie.

We get into the car and head out to Crawford's. In the queue we see two uniformed spastics whom we know but can't place their names. Veteran P.C.s. Myself and Gus look down on them; going nowhere fast in the career structure of the force. When we're in choosing our food, this cheeky auld cunt looks at the uniforms and says, — They'll no be brekin intae this place anyway. Bakers n chippies, the safest places in Edinburgh!

The constables get a big red beamer up the side of their faces. I count my blessings on occasions like this that I'm in a plain-clothed job. The spastics blush and head off, while Gus and I get back into the motor.

— That Drummond lassie. Needs a good fuckin ride, that's what she needs, I tell him, starting up the Volvo and feeling a testosterone rush as I shunt the beast up a gear. C'mon baby, take it.

Gus smiles. He's a nice auld cunt. A bit churchy, but he doesnae push it doon yir throat. — Yir an awfay man Bruce, he says.

— Looks the type that's been disappointed by a man.

Probably frigid, I speculate, as we turn into Raeburn Place. I could go a pint and one of they steak pies from Bert's Bar. Better than that Crawford's shite. But on second thoughts one pint might lead to a dozen and I'm with that auld cunt Gus who won't piss it up on duty. I'll have to tough it out.

— Nice lassie though, says Gus, mildly challengingly.

— Oh aye, she's a nice enough lassie, I agree. Best to back down at this stage. I'll put Gus right about that hoor soon enough.

I switch on the radio. There's some quiz programme on Radio Forth.

— SO MALCOLM, YOU HAVE THREE CHANCES TO WIN THE JACKPOT PRIZE. READY?

— THINK SO!

— RIGHT. WHAT CONTINENT IS PARAGUAY IN?

— EH . . . IS IT EUROPE?

— OOOHHHH . . . SORRY MALCOLM. IT IS, IN FACT, IN SOUTH AMERICA. NEVER MIND, TRY AGAIN. THE CAPITAL OF HUNGARY IS . . .?

— EH. . .OH. . .EHM. . .TRANSYLVANIA?

— OOOHHHH . . . I'M SOREE MAAL-CUM . . . IT IS IN FACT BUDAPEST! YOU'RE THINKING OF THE VAMPIRES AND ALL THAT SORT OF THING AREN'T YOU?

— YEAH BOBBY, AH WIS JUST THINKIN OF COUNT DRACULA AND ALL THAT STUFF.

— NOT TO WORRY. YOU STILL HAVE ONE MORE CHANCE TO WIN THE JACKPOT PRIZE. READY?

— EH . . .YEAH.

— OKAY. THE SEXY SINGER TONY FERRINO IS PLAYED BY WHICH COMEDIAN?

— AW . . . I SHOULD KNOW THIS . . . IS IT STEVE COOGAN?

— STEVE COOGAN IS CORRECT! MALCOLM WIN-TERS OF LARKHALL, YOU HAVE WON OUR JACKPOT PRIZE OF FIVE HUNDRED POUNDS!

I switch that shite off and put in a tape, Saxon's debut album

Wheels of Steel, ~~and for~~ many their best. I'm more into *Denim and Leather* though. I watch Gus's rubber puppet-face twist in distaste as the boys crank up.

— What a din Bruce! Dinnae ken how ye can listen to that!

— It's white man's soul music Gus. We came, conquered and enslaved, I explain.

We get back about an hour later when who should come down into the office but Toal. We agreed two hours; he's fucking up my crossword time, the helium-filled wank-bag. Toal doon-stairs. Toal, here! We are privileged! Normally that spastic never leaves his desk. I never knew the cunt had legs until I saw him one night in the foyer of the King's Theatre when I was taking the wee yin tae the panto. There's that cunt Toal just standing there, and he fuckin cold-shouldered me. I mind the bairn asking who he was and me saying, that's one of the bad men I put away once doll. She frowned at the shit-bag after that!

— Robbo . . . in here, he points to the interview room and shuts the door behind us. — Listen, keep this under your hat, but as you know things are pretty stretched around here, particular-ly until we get the new D.I. post filled in the reorganisation in the New Year.

My post. But listen tae Toal; making out that he *wants* one of us on the same grade as him, when he does nothing. Anyway, as things stand I should be on a much higher grade than that imbe-cile. I would have as well if Carole hadn't made us fuck off to go to Australia for six bastarding years.

— What I want you to do, in effect, is to lead up the team on the Wurie case. I'll be around to oversee, but I'm pretty much tied up with this reorganisation bollocks. I got a note from Busby, he's going to be off for some time yet. I don't know how they expect me to run this division with an inspector short. Anyway, mind and keep me posted. I want this cracked sharpish.

The toss is trying to butter me up because he thinks that if he makes me responsible for this case then I won't want to take my break in the Dam. Fuck his memo; I'll kick up a stink through the Federation and the craft if I have to. Same rules apply. I then have to listen to his smarm about how good an officer I am, and I suppose it's true.

I want that fuckin promo awright, that inspectorship. It's mine, my entitlement, in terms of experience. Any cunt in the service'll tell you that. Fuck me, I couldn't be any worse than the last waster they made up; nobody could. Busby, suffering from so-called stress. He's never away fae the fuckin gowf course. No bad for some, he's goat the welfare spastics twisted roond his finger. I'd gie the useless farting cunt his jotters, then we'd have two inspectorships up for grabs in the division, and it wouldnae cause as much of an atmosphere wi the boys in the cannie. But me: eight wasted years. What did they think I was daein in Sydney aw that time? Playin fuckin tiddly-winks? Counts for nowt, overseas service, under their stupid rules. And cause of her, her that doesn't know her own mind. Edinburgh Carole: ah want tae be oot thair beside ma mother. Sydney Carole: ah cannae settle, ah miss ma sister. Her sister: the only thing I missed aboot her sister was gettin my hole off her.

— I decided that with your homicide experience, Toal confirms, — you were the man to lead the team. Effectively then, you'll be acting inspector. We can't do anything about the remuneration, but if you get a result here it'll stand you in good stead, for eh . . . the future. You'll have Inglis, Bain and Drummond on the team, with uniformed officer support.

I detest Toal, but he knows his job. You have to give the cunt that. He slaps me on the arm and I just nod. We leave the room. — It's settled then Bruce, he smiles.

In the short time it takes to exit thon interview room and stick on the kettle, I realise that the cunt's almost got away with his flattery bullshit. Toal kens fuck all aboot the job. Promotion or no promotion, I'm offski tae the Dam.

I note that Amanda Drummond's been hanging around, making out she's talking to Gus, but really waiting to pounce on Toal. She comes over. — Excuse me Bob, can I have a quick word?

Bob, is it now?

31

— Sure, Toal says, then turns back to me, — Mind Bruce, what I said.

— Aye, I mumble. I move across to Gus, watching Toal's chunky frame and Drummond's matchstick body recede down the corridor. Fuckin Laurel n Hardy right enough. — If he thinks I'm busting a gut about solving this case, he's fuckin mad, I tell Gus.

— The way I see it, this is aw politics, Gus shakes his heid wearily. I like Gus. He looks like a Jim Henson puppet and he's yesterday's man, but I like him. I can afford tae like the cunt. He's in for the promo as well though. The odds against him? Too high to calculate.

— Damn fuckin right it is. I give up my winter's week in the Dam, which the cunt knows I have every year at this time, just soas I can find out who topped this coon and get brownie points for a certain Mister Toal? I do look sweet. I look very fucking sweet indeed. No thank you Mr Toal. No thank you Mr Niddrie.

— He's goat us ower a barrel though Bruce. That inspector's post fae the reorganisation.

— That's nowt tae dae wi it! I snap too loudly at Gus, who looks fretful. I'll have to watch this temper. I backpedal, — He's goat fuck all tae dae wi whae gits that. You think Niddrie or any ay the cunts on the promotion board'll listen tae that tube? What does he ken? He kens fuckin nowt! Sum total: the big fuckin zero, I tap my head.

I leave Gus to think about that. The auld cunt really thinks that *he's* gaunny get the job. Wrong! Saw-ree! He got too soon old and too late smart. I get on with my crossword in the *Sun*.

ACROSS		DOWN	
1	Spider's trap (6)	1	Happen (4,5)
4	Recontinue (6)	2	Trifle, pinball (9)
7	Three Wise Men (4)	3	Muscle (5)
8	Obvious (8)	4	Cables (5)
9	Stain (7)	5	Certain (4)
12	Shilling (3)	6	Tropical fruit (5)

Nope, it's not coming today. I turn back to page three.

— Hi Bruce, Gus says, passing over a bag of Crawford's chips to Peter Inglis, — want tae hear yir stars?

— Aye, awright then. He's distracted me from Alicia from Hull. Fuckin built, that yin.

— What are you?

— Taurus.

— Right: 'You've bitten off more than you can chew and you are having to muddle through as a result . . .'

— That's fuckin right enough! And we all know whose fault that is! I point at the ceiling.

—'. . . Not to worry — this week's solar eclipse should have cleared away some of the uncertainty surrounding your future . . .'

Ray Lennox has just come in: — Sounds like promotion Bruce, he laughs.

— '. . . After that, you're more inclined to relax and enjoy yourself.' Whoah-ho! The winter's week, Peter takes over.

— That must be Amsterdam they're talkin about! I rub my hands together, just as the big blonde piece comes in. She's passing roond some notes.

The mild elation doesnae last long. A fuckin memo fae Niddrie.

I can't believe this. Toal and Drummond. I was up there this morning and fuck all was said to me. Me, who's supposed to be the number two man on this investigation, which, as Toal's formally heading it, means number one. This is back-of-a-fag-packet thinking. She went behind my fuckin back wi another one ay her coon erse-licking Girl Guide projects.

— Waste ay fuckin time! Peter Inglis moans, looking over at me.

— See who's fuckin runnin it n aw, I say, — that fuckin silly wee lassie! What the fuck does she ken aboot polis work? I look at Ray Lennox. He's been sniffin aroond that daft wee tart. He looks a bit guilty and tries to change the subject. — Dinnae ken how we're gaunny solve this murder case if we're aw gaunny be oan a course, he shrugs.

— Bloody nonsense, Gus agrees. The boys are not amused about this. They're looking to me as Fed rep to take the lead. — What dae ye reckon Bruce?

— I think we should just go along with it. As you said Ray, I turn to Lennox, — we're no gaunny solve this case sitting talking tae silly wee lassies, but that's their decision, I shrug.

34

— Toal just wants tae look good wi aw they cunts on the police board, aw they forum bastards, Peter Inglis complains. Too thin for a polisman over thirty is Inglis. Fuckin Aids victim if ye ask me.

— I'd play it cool, just gie the cunts enough rope tae hing thirsels wi, I nod.

Later on I bell my wee Civil Service mate Bladesey and tell him to meet us later up at the Lodge. Then I nip out to Crawford's for an egg roll. It's fucking well freezing out here, although the cold can't block out the acrid Dame Judi Dench which rises up from my flannels. I'll have to get them dry-cleaned. I open my overcoat and flap it to see if the ming is as steadily rancid as I imagine it to be, but it only comes in the odd wafting wave. Those flannels are good for a couple of days yet.

I see a dog-eared envelope protruding from the top inside pocket of my coat. It's the letter to Tony from Chelmsford that I've had in my pocket for a month. Could do wi getting doon there again for a bit of rumpy-pumpy, maybe in the New Year. I'm thinking about that Diana cow and her big bare arse sticking in my face and my flannels again stretch and that familiar bulge is once more in evidence. I button up my overcoat as some women come past. Sorry girls, you don't get a flash of quality meat like this without putting the readies on the table. That Diana, she's fuckin well getting it again though; I can't wait to get back down there. It's those wee breks that keep ye going. Without them all you have is the job. And the games.

At Crawford's they've ran out of scrambled egg. It's probably been nicked by the hard-hatted schemies who should be daein their fuckin jobs rather than fartin aboot in takeaways all day. A waste of fucking police time.

Investigations

It was a good night at the pool round robin. I won the tournament, grinding down Lennox's resistance and emerging 4–3 victor after losing the first two games. The sad cunt took the hump and fucked off. Don't play with the big boys if your cue action isn't up for it and Lennox's sure ain't: at any sport. So now I'm out in the frosty streets with my mate Bladesey, who's coming to the Dam on holiday with me. I fancy carrying on here. Too right I do. It's snowing lightly. I catch a snowflake and marvel at its perfection through a lager haze, before it disintegrates in the heat of my hand.

It's starting to fall heavier as I steer a reluctant Bladesey into a scabby drinking den down in the Cowgate, one of those dives with a late licence which is full of students and pishheids. I stomp my feet to shake the snow off my boots and set up two more pints. We find a seat and I hear some cunt at the next table talking aboot the fitba, he's saying something like Stronach's been a good servant but there isnae a full ninety minutes in him anymair. I'm considering this rather obvious point when out of the corner of my eye I see a completely wrecked auld cunt in faded but clean clathes, noising up some students. The young cunts are lapping it up though, indulging the auld fuckin nobody.

– Isn't that the bohemian chap, Arthur Cormack, you know the old chap who recites the poems? Bladesey's asking me.

I look at him and scoff. — You call the cunt a bohemian, but what does that mean? Tae me that's a fuckin jakey.

— Well actually, he has had a collection of poetry published, and it did win an Arts Council award.

— That's what a bohemian is though, that's the definition: a sponging alcoholic jakey cunt who manages to con rich liberal wankers intae believing that he's some fucking intellectual. He's a fuckin jakey! He lives in the doss-hoose. You can call him what the fuck you like, but tae me he's just a fuckin sponging jakey cunt!

I look across and note that some shaggable wee student birds are making a fuss of this stinking bundle of rags and I detest him even more.

— Actually, I don't know . . . if he lived on the left bank of Paris or somewhere like that, he'd be accepted universally as a bohemian . . . Bladesey says, taking off his glasses and rubbing the lenses with a cloth. One of Bladesey's mince pies is in much worse nick than the other so one lens is far thicker.

— Fuckin froggy cunts, what the fuck dae these cunts ken? A jakey's a fuckin jakey. I point across at the auld cunt. — Ye call that art? Ah've heard um. A jakey mumbling fuckin crap poems at people who dinnae want tae fuckin well hear them. So that's what they call art now, is it? Or some fuckin schemie writing aboot aw the fuckin drugs him n his wideo mates have taken. Of course, he's no fuckin well wi them now, he's livin in the south ay fuckin France or somewhere like that, connin aw these liberal fuckin poncy twats intae thinkin that ehs some kind ay fuckin artiste . . . baws! Fuckin baws! I shout over at the jakey and his student pals.

Bladesey looks a bit nervous. — Bruce, is there anywhere we could, eh actually, ehm go . . .

— Point taken Bladesey. It smells like Scrubbers' Close in here, I snort, looking over at the pishheid and a student with that nigger hair and rags these rich white kids like tae wear. — Come back to my gaff, I tell him. We're both three sheets to the wind.

— Your wife won't mind?

— Naw, she's at her mother's at Aviemore. The auld girl's not so well. Heart disease.

— Oh dear . . . Bladesey looks at me sadly, like that fuckin dug, what's it they call the cunt . . . Droopy, like that dug Droopy in the cartoons.

— Brought it on herself, daft auld cunt, I explain. — You go tae that hoose and the amount of butter they eat, and they fry everything. Sweets, chocolate as well, and fags . . .

— I see . . . I see . . . Bladesey always says in a tone which tells me that, no, the cunt does not fuckin well see. Your best psychologist is the one on the force, pished or no. I'm thinking aboot her mother and I'll give the auld doll this: she always made a good nosh up. Plenty meat. Needed rode though: that was her problem, ever since the old boy kicked it. No enough rumpy-pumpy tae keep the circulation ay blood flowing. Nae wonder her arteries clogged up. The auld boot's ain fault for being sae fuckin frigid. I warned Carole that she'd go the same wey if she didnae lighten up a bit on the shaggin front.

We down our pints and head outside and I flag down a taxi and we're off towards mine. The snow's really starting to lie which means total chaos for the rest of us and serious OT for those traffic spastics who are regarded as the lowest of the low by the Serious Crimes boys. The taxi driver's blethering away sociably, thinking, mistakenly, that this is going to earn him a tip. Wrong! Only an imbecile would think of giving an Edinburgh taxi driver a tip. Sorry, my sweet, sweet friend, but the same rules apply. When we stop and get out of the cab, I work off all my smash on to the cunt, counting it into his hands as his mouth becomes a fraught, shivering gash of disapproval.

— Bladesey, got any two pences? Two twos or four ones is all I need.

— There's a five p, Bladesey says. I take it and drop it into the driver's hand, taking back one penny. — There, I tell the cunt cheerfully, — that's us square. Three pounds sixty pence.

— Thanks very much, he muses.

— Not at all, thank *you* very much, I smile. The fuckwit pockets the coins and speeds off as I open the gate.

— Did you not give the chap a tip? Bladesey asks.

— I would not give that spastic the shite off my shoe, I tell him.

— There's a couple of chaps from the Lodge that drive taxis . . .

— Ah ken that good and well Brother Blades. Just because some fucking cowboy's in the craft, it doesnae make him due a tip in my book. Same rules apply. A tip? These bastards, ah widnae gie them a bad tip oan the fuckin gee-gees. Do we care? Do we fuck!

In the kitchen I pour myself a good measure of twelve-year-old Chivas Regal and I fill a glass with Tesco's Scotch Whisky out of one of these plastic bottles for Bladesey. I'm thinking that it's our national drink and with him being an English cunt, he won't notice the difference and he's three sheets anyway. I could have pished in a glass and he wouldnae have kent any better.

After a while he looks a bit melancholy. — You're so lucky with your wife. She seems to understand you, he bleats.

It looks like he's ready to open up about his relationship with this big piece he married last year. Bunty, her name is. He worships the big cow: it's Bunty this, Bunty that, wi the wee cunt. Of course, she seems to treat Brother Clifford Blades like shite. In my experience this means that the woman needs a good fucking or a better one than Bladesey's capable of giving her. Same rules apply.

— It's all a question of values, I tell him. — I mean . . . it's like what you want out of life. Mind you, I'll need to give this place a good tidy before she comes back! It's like a midden!

— Mmm, you certainly will, Bladesey says, sipping at his whisky. I'm sure the cunt's face screwed up a wee bit. Fuck'um. Cheeky wee bastard.

— What about your daughter Bruce? What school's she at?

— Eh, Mary Erskine's. Still at the primary likes.

— Actually, em, I'm, eh, having a bit of a difficult time with

Craig. Bunty's so protective of him. He's never really accepted me. It's not as if I've set myself up as a father substitute . . . I mean, I thought, play it all by ear . . . your daughter, you never have any problems with her, do you?

– . . . There was a wee incident . . . she was caught telling lies, silly wee lies, it was nothing major, it's all behind us now . . . I tense up. I should not be telling that bastard any of my business. The best form of defence is attack . . . – Listen Bladesey, my auld mucker, do you mind if I ask you a personal question?

– Well, I . . .

– You and Bunty. Are you shagging her?

Bladesey looks at me, then averts his gaze. That cunt's no daein any shaggin, no fuckin way. When he starts to speak, he seems embarrassed, but not offended, no that I gie a fuck. – Well . . . eh . . . actually, that side of things haven't been too great lately . . .

I nod sternly as Bladesey coughs out his humiliation to me. This wanker actually thinks I care. Wrong!

– I suppose I've actually, eh, always been a bit of a loner . . . always had difficulty in making friends . . . that's why the craft's actually been so good for me . . . everybody's accepted . . . Getting this job up here and meeting Bunty . . . well, I thought I'd landed on my feet. I mean Bruce, I don't know what she wants. I never so much as raise my voice at her, even when she's being rather unreasonable to me and I always provide. I mean . . .

I had better straighten the laddie out once and for all. – Listen mate, a bit of advice in the affairs-of-the-heart department. With women what you have to do is shag them regularly. Keep them well-fucked and they'll do anything for you. Well-shod and well-shagged, that's the auld phrase.

– You actually believe that?

– Course I do. All these stupid spastics at the marriage guidance counsellors: a load of fuckin shite. The root of a marital problem is always sexual. Women like to get fucked, whatever they make out. If you ain't fucking the woman you're supposed to be with then that creates a vacuum and nature abhors one of them. Sure as fuck some cunt'll come along and fill the gap. Fill it with several inches of prime beef. And if she's no daein it for you, you go and get your hole somewhaire else. I know that I could just go out now and get my hole like that, I snap my fingers in his face causing him to recoil in his chair, – if I wanted it likes.

— You really think it's that easy?

— Course it fuckin well is. There's fanny gantin oan it, I kid you not. In this toon, in every fuckin toon. Right across this big wide world, I sweep my arms across the room. – All you need to know is where to look. Now me, I'm a detective. I'm polis. A good polisman always knows where to look. And I'm good at my job. I'm maybe not the best polisman in the world, I tell him, waiting for him to nod empathetically, before snapping in dead seriousness, – but I'm certainly one of 'em.

Cause I fuckin well am.

— Well, I'm looking forward to Amsterdam, I must say, he says, looking flushed.

A sad wanker. No self-confidence.

— It'll be fuckin magic Bladesey, I kid you not. Hoors of all colours, shapes and sizes. *Slàinte!*

Carole

The problem with Bruce is that he keeps it all in. I know that he's seen some terrible things in his job and I know that, whatever he says, they've affected him deeply. He's a very sensitive man underneath it all. His hard front fools a lot of people, but I really know my man. They don't understand what a complicated person he is. To know him is to love him and I certainly know him.

What I know for instance, is that Bruce has an effect on women. I know that they find him attractive. I know because I'm aware of the effect I have on men. If you're a sexy person I think you're always very much aware of the sexuality of others. The sexual aura if you like. It becomes a common currency, a code, an unspoken language. Yes, some people just have that sort of glow around them and I know that Bruce certainly does.

I spend a lot of time getting myself ready because I always like to look good for him, and for myself too. There are some women who say that you shouldn't dress to please a man, but when you love someone you revel in their pleasure and I'm guilty of that and I always will be.

I look at my own naked body in front of the mirror. I think, yes Carole, you've still got it girl. I think I'm losing weight. I put on my bra, clipping it at the front, then sliding it round and putting my breasts into it. I take a silky cream blouse from the wardrobe and put it on and button it up. I love the feel of this particular blouse on my skin. There's a navy blue skirt here which goes well with it. I put on the skirt and look at myself in the mirror. Yes, definitely losing that bit of weight I put on; the skirt is hanging well. My face has a wide forehead, but this effect I can neutralise by wearing my fringe long. I admire my full mouth and nice big lips. Bruce always admires my lips, and my small nose and large brown eyes.

I dig out some blue, velvet-effect shoes from the bottom of the wardrobe. I'm thinking about Bruce all the time, about how we play these break-up/make-up games with each other, how these wee absences we take from each other are just a tease, which only make our hearts grow fonder. I feel a need and an aching for him, I'll have to get back to him soon. I wrap my arms around myself and imagine that we're together. In a sense we are together because nothing, space, time, distance whatever, can break the delicious communion between us.

Equal Opportunities

It took me ages to get ready this morning because I couldnae think what to wear. It's Carole's fault; if she was going to shoot off, she could at least have arranged a fuckin laundry service before she went. I came close to just wrapping it and leaving it till the afternoon to go in. However, I discover a black pair of flannels which aren't too bad once I've shaken out some of the dead skin cells.

I'm glad I made the effort though, because my wee girl-friends are in for questioning. I could fuckin well love this wee yin right doon tae her pores. Thir's nothing better than a bird wi these wee lips that curl outwards, highlighted by plenty lip gloss. The classiest young fanny realise this: you can never overdo it on the lipstick and the mascara.

There's a twitching in my flannel troosers and I take a deep breath in order to compose myself. Thank fuck I'm a professional and can rise above any other agenda. – So you didn't see anyone behaving what might be termed suspiciously at the night-club? I ask her. She's a fuckin wee shag this lassie. Estelle, her name is.

– Nuht, she says distractedly. The wee cow's mind's on something else. Gus has her mate next door, I'd like to see how he gets on. I'm about to turn up the heat on this cocky wee slag when I remember that Amanda Drummond's in the same room

44

as us. She's looking at me, and her nose is twitching. I ignore her. Then she says, – D.S. Robertson, can I have a word?

I leave the room, followed by Drummond. This fuckin case. We're making no fucking headway. I've spent most of the morning interviewing some of the punters who were in the club, but very few people will admit to remember seeing Wurie leave. The doorman, that Mark Wilson fucker, I recognised that cunt straight away, and he must have minded of the boy but he's no letting on. As wide as Leith Walk, that cunt. Those two lassies, Sylvia Freeman and Estelle Davidson, I got a vibe off, but that was probably just because they were shags rather than because of any information they had. I'll haul them in again later on. That wee Estelle. Phoah. Mind you, that Sylvia n aw. They can come back. They will come back. When Drummond's oot the fuckin road.

We're out in the corridor and there's a couple of painters splashing cheap institution emulsion on the walls. One of them, I note, is eyeing Drummond's shapeless, bony arse. – We should finish up here now Bruce. There's this afternoon's course, she reminds me. I avert my gaze from the painter to her. One thing I do like about her though: those protruding front teeth which could provide serious fun if they got under your foreskin. No that Drummond would have ever learned how to make best use of them.

– I was trying to forget about that, I tell her. Drummond turns her head away and focuses at some crack on the tiled floor. She's developing a certain expertise in editing out bad news from the airwaves. Well, there will be fuckin plenty tae edit, I kid you not.

This fuckin daft course. As if I give a Luke and Matt Goss. But I have to comply and we dismiss the slags and head down the cannie with Gus for a shorter than usual lunch. The blonde piece is at the table opposite with another couple of civvy shags. I think about going over to say hello, but I see Drummond flapping around like a pelican and Gus and I decide that we won't get any peace until we go up to her fuckin course.

– Ah dinnae see the point ay they modules. Waste ay fuckin

time if ye ask me. Somebody's probably murdering some poor cunt doon in Pilton, and we're poncing aroond here wi some silly wee lassies, I say, during the coffee and enrolment.

— Gie them a chance Robbo, we've no even started yet, Clelland says.

Clell's a wind-up merchant of the first degree. He's a leathery alcoholic guy with short grey hair and a red face. Jowls like piss-flaps. There's the desperate incubating stink of stale aftershave off him. It covers a multitude of sins. I know.

— Listen Clell, think ay the years we've seen in service. Some silly wee tart goes tae college n gets a degree in fuckin sociology and then does some Daz Coupon Certificate in Personnel Management and joins the force on this graduate accelerated programme and she's earning nearly as much fuckin dough as you or me who're pittin ourselves oan the fuckin line tryin tae stoap schemies killin each other! She's never seen past a fuckin desk withoot a real polisman chaperoning her everywhere! Then she writes this fuckin stupid policy document saying: 'be kind to coons and poofs and silly wee lassies like me' and everybody gets the fuckin hots. Then they get this posh wee chinky bird wi an American accent tae come in n tell us how tae dae our job and how tae relate tae the public, with, surprise surprise, another set ay forms tae fill in! Aye right! We do look sweet!

That reminds me. I've a OTA 1–7 tae fill in for my overtime.

— Aye, says Gus Bain, — Scotland's a white man's country. Always has been, always will be. That's the way ah see it at any rate, and ah'm too long in tooth tae change now, he chuckles cheerfully. A good auld boy Gus.

— Precisely Gus. Ah mind when I took Carole and wee Stacey tae see that *Braveheart*. How many pakis or spades did ye see in the colours fightin for Scotland? Same wi *Rob Roy*, same wi *The Bruce*.

— Aye, says Andy Clelland, — but that's a long time ago now.

— Precisely. We built this fuckin country. Thir wis nane ay them at Bannockburn or Culloden when the going was tough. It's our blood, our soil, our history. Then they want tae waltz in here and reap all the benefits and tell us that we should be ashamed ay that! We were fuckin slaves before these cunts were ever rounded up and shipped tae America!

Inside the session, the wee chinky bird, this wee San Yung or whatever they call her, she's standing up wi that business suit oan and she's saying: – Right, I wanna do a free association brain-storming exercise. Just call out at random, any responses you can think of.

She turns and writes a heading on the flipchart: WHAT DOES 'RACISM' MEAN TO YOU?

Clell shouts out first: – Discrimination.

The wee chinky burd goes aw hot n focused and eagerly writes it down on the chart.

Gillman steams in, no like the cunt I'm sure: – Conflict, he snaps.

As she's writin this doon, Clell says, – Might no be conflict. Might be harmony. Gillman ignores him.

Gus Bain says: – You're thinkin of the hairspray.

I chip in and say: – That girl's not wearing Harmony hair-spray. Everybody has a wee laugh at that, well the boys that are auld enough tae mind ay the ad do. Even Dougie Gillman smiles.

The chinky bird raises her voice and says, – I think . . . is it Andy? Clelland nods, – I think Andy made a valid point here. We in policework tend to be conditioned into seeing a conflict-based society due to the nature of our jobs, but in fact race relations in Britain is characterised much more by harmony than anything else.

– It's the leading brand of hairspray, I tell her. Nobody laughs this time and I'm feeling isolated, like a daft cunt.

At least the hoor seems upset, which is what it's all about. She looks directly at me and asks, – What does the term racism mean to you . . . she looks at my name tag, – . . . Bruce?

– It doesn't mean anything to me. I just treat everyone the same.

Bain claps slowly and emphatically, his eyes glazed and his chin jutting out.

– Okay, very laudable, chinky-girl says, – but do you not recognise racism in others?

– Nup. That's thaire lookout. You take responsibility for your own behaviour, not other people's, I tell her. I'm chuffed, that was a good point to make, straight from these cunts' daft interpersonal skills training jargon. I can see that it almost strikes a chord with this Kitchen Sink's fucked up way of thinking. Then Amanda Drummond jumps in with, – But surely in our professional role as law enforcement officers, we have to accept responsibility for society's problems. This is implicit, I would have thought.

You are a silly wee cunt. That is *explicit*, I would have thought. No way are you rocking B.R. spastic fanny. The same rules are applying to the fucking maximum here girlie. – I was speaking as an individual. I thought this was what you wanted. No hiding behind professional roles, I think we were told at the pre-course briefing, we were to respond as human beings. Of course as a law enforcement officer I accept that we have these responsibilities.

The dopey dyke looks fazed by this and deflects the question. Standard tactics. She's acting like a fuckin criminal. Polis? That? Ha! – Good point Bruce, she says patronisingly, – anybody else got anything to add?

– The biggest problem, Gus starts up, – and youse'll no like me for sayin this, but it has to be said, the biggest problem is that blacks cause the maist crime, then he's turning to me, – You worked in London for the Met, Robbo. Tell them.

– Well, I can only speak for my time in the Stroud, I say noncommittally. I look over at Ray Lennox. His face is impassive but there's a tension in his eyes. I'll bet the cunt's suffering. Been on that nostril shite again, I'll wager four to one on.

Chinky-drawers comes in, – What about Stroud Green?

– I think it would be inappropriate to get into the particular problems that one area may or may not have had, I tell her sharply.

– Fine, she says hesitantly. She didnae like that rebuff. But of course, it's no real problem. If we won't talk, then these fuckers are never shy about filling in the gaps. So we listen to a dull lecture, marking time until the coffee break, the heat from the radiator almost making us doze off.

Finally, we adjourn for coffee. Shitey wee fuckin biscuits, that's all they give us with the coffee. I usually get a roll from the canteen or something from the bakers for my piece, but naw, that's all forgotten about with this disruption for their coon-loving course. They think of no other cunt's routine but their own. I take a coffee and stand over beside Clell. I deliberately keep away from Gus. A nice cunt, but he's giving far too much away. Too far into that three score and ten to learn a new script. Careless, and that's food and drink to these cunts. Lennox has the right idea. He's too wide though, that fucker.

We're waiting on our young Mister Lennox. Fuckin sure we are.

Clell, Gillman and I are joined by the wee chinky bird with the toff's English-Yank accent. It keeps fuckin well changing. Probably been tae posh schools all over the world. I hate those privileged cunts. They think that you're fuck all, that they can just use you tae clean up their shite, and in fact, most of the time they are spot-on. What they don't know though, is that you're always lurking in the shadows. The opportunity to pounce usually never comes along but you're always lurking, always ready. Just in case.

Chinko's been giein it loadsay fuckin mooth awright. The particular problems ay the inner city. Aye, right ye fuckin well are doll, you didnae get an accent like that in any fuckin inner city. She's rabbiting on trying to get us tae open up, standard tactics, but we're keeping it tight. Clell's expanding a wee bit, saying what the cunt wants tae hear, but he's on a wind-up. He's jousting with me and Gus; it's just the bastard getting in role. I think the best way tae handle these cunts is just tae keep stumpf. The best cons ken that n aw: just say fuck all. She's rabbiting on though and I'm nodding at her, looking at her eyes and lips moving and I start tae think of her fanny.

I'd fuckin well gie her one awright. No much in the coupon

49

stakes but a tidy body on it. High marks in curvature of arse. Never mind the mantelpiece when yir pokin the fire; that's my motto, and it's stood me in good stead. Same rules.

It's as if she can read my thoughts, cause she sort of blushes and looks at the clock. – Well, she goes, –we'd better be making a move back.

Ah'll fuckin well make a move on you in a minute ya cunt. Probably game as fuck n aw.

Lennox is talking to Amanda Drummond. Most likely trying to slip her a length, the dirty fucker. Although with Lennox it wouldnae be much ay a length. Drummond catches me staring at them and looks away. I'd give her one, if only to pass the time of day. Maybe a knee-trembler in the bogs, if I had a bit of time between finishing the crossword and piece brek. Lennox's index finger rubs the side of his beak. Ice-cool cunt Ray Lennox's give-away that he's telling porky pies, that underneath it all he's a suffering bag of nerves.

Aye Lennox ya cunt, you'll ken.

So we get back into it. Clell's playing the nice cunt, Gus is winding them up, and I'm keeping stumpf. It's hot and I'm start-ing to feel a bit nauseous and shaky. My guts feel sick and heavy. It's like there's something in me, I can almost feel it growing, getting stronger. A tumour perhaps, like the one that did in the auld girl. Prone to it, our family. But she was . . . I'm starting to sweat heavily, a panic attack's coming on.

I'm losing it.

Fuck that.

I'm not like Busby or any of those long-term sick-through-stress saplings that can't handle the big time. The cunts here'll never fuckin know, they'll never fuckin ken cause I'm better than that, better than all of them, stronger than the fuckin lot of those cunts put together.

I excuse myself and go to the bogs. Inside the lavvy I'm shaking and my teeth are hammering together. I sit on the toilet seat. My arse is itching really badly. I want to sterilise those piles: some boiling water, a sharp pain and then that's it. The bog paper is just that harsh council-issue garbage. Fuckin cunts! How do they expect me . . .

I give my piles a clawing until my eyes water. The pain is something to focus on. My breathing is slowing down and the shaking's subsiding. I try to have a wank, attempting to picture the chinky bird, then Amanda Drummond, in the buff, but nothing's coming to me. I should have sneaked out the paper. I don't know who the shag was on page three, I haven't seen her before.

When I get back in, I'm still a bit jumpy. All the eyes are on me.

— You don't look very happy Bruce, Amanda Drummond says, — are you okay? Are you feeling okay?

Attack is the best form of defence. I look her in the eye. — I'd be a lot more okay if I knew what I was doing here. Like several of my colleagues I've been involved in a murder investigation: I'm trying to solve the murder of a man from an ethnic minority group. I've been taken off that to spend time here. I say this in such a way as to let her know that I don't consider *her* to be on the case. — Answer me this if you can: what advances racial harmony most: this course or solving that crime? Cause we sure ain't gonna solve no crime sittin here, sister, I tell her.

— Hear hear! Gus says, and starts clapping, and some of the other boys follow suit. Peter Inglis whistles.

This gies the hoor a beamer and a half.

— It's not a question of one or the other, we need to do both . . . she says weakly, then adds with a bit of gusto, — as the strategy paper makes quite clear.

Oh, the strategy paper is it now? I wondered when we were going to get on to that particular pile of fucking pish. Well I've done my homework, dykeface, thank you very much. — I'm glad you mentioned that because if I could quote a circular from Personnel relating to the strategy paper, and I quote: — 'There are no sacred cows in a modern organisation like the police

51

force. Everything is up for grabs, everything has a priority value.'

— Exactly. The fact that you're here shows it has priority, she snootily retorts.

— Precisely. Conversely, the fact that we are not out there investigating the murder of a young man shows that *that* does *not* have priority.

— Hear hear! shouts Dougie Gillman. Nasty piece of work Dougie, but a brilliant interrogator. One of the few cunts on the force who would make a formidable opponent. Just as well he's not thrown his hat into the ring for the inspector's post. He respects the craft hierarchy.

— And so say all of us, Gus barks.

These spastics are not fucking well getting it their own way the day, that's as sure as the shite on your shoe. By the end of the day they look as bedraggled as a couple of hoors off the back-shift, I kid you not.

At the end of the course I note that Ray Lennox is enjoying a bit of banter with Gus. These cunts seem as tight as fuck. That'll be sorted right out though.

I'm thinking again about the promo stakes on my way down-stairs. It's not a fucking particularly strong field.

GUS BAIN	Too auld and stupid.
KEN ARNOTT	From B division. A straight-down-the-line dull nae-mates-outside-the-force-and-craft polisman. A serious threat if he had half a brain.
PETER INGLIS	No wonder he's crawling up my arse when he's had the audacity to put in for this post. A loser. Something fucking queer aboot that sad loner.

I get to my desk and there's a message saying that a woman was trying to get me, she didn't leave her name. It'll be Carole, nothing surer. Seeing the error of her ways. Getting a bit weepy on her own with Christmas approaching. That is her problem. I have to head off and see the quack. I've an appointment.

I drive out across the city. These cunts have changed the one-way system tae confuse you even further. Trying tae drive from one side of the toon tae the other with aw this Denis Law lying is a fucking joke. If it was up tae me I'd ban all these buses and chop off most of these silly gairdins and get a few fuckin new lanes doon Princes Street.

At Dr Rossi's surgery I'm kept waiting for twelve minutes. I am here at 5.25 for my 5.30 appointment, but it is 5.42 by the time I get seen, probably thanks to some dopey auld cow who smells stale and just wants to waste stamp-payers' money by talking all day to a doctor, the only person who will come near her on account of the whiff coming fae the cunt.

It's okay you fuckin mingin auld bastard, it's only a fuckin murder investigation I'm on. Carry on, carry on, don't mind me.

When I get in, Rossi makes no apology for keeping me late. Instead he asks me to drop my keks.

— Well Mr Robertson, Rossi says, inspecting my testicles and my inner thighs, — this looks like eczema.

— Eczema! But here . . . I mean, people get eczema on their back, or arms or face . . . but no there . . .

Rossi's eyes widen balefully, and a flicker of distaste is evident in them. — Eczema can occur anywhere. There's no evidence to suggest that you might have something additional, certainly it's not an STD.

There's me fucking well disintegrating here and this cunt's just passing it off like it was nowt . . . — I've never had this before. Even when I . . . I mean, I've just never had this before.

— Were your parents prone to it? It can be hereditary.

– No . . .

Parents fuck off parents fuck off

– It's some aggravated skin disorder, probably a form of eczema. I can't emphasise strongly enough that you should keep that area clean. I'm going to prescribe a cream.

I take a deep breath and let the sterile air of Rossi's surgery fill my lungs. I try to remain focused on Rossi without making eye contact. Look at the brows, that's an old con's trick: focus on the polisman's eyebrows rather than his pupils. Haul in a Fyfe a Begbie a McPhee a Wylie or a Doyle and those criminal cunts always adopt the same approach. Eye contact without eye contact. Always fucks the baby polis up, that one. Just formulating a strategy, getting back into the notion of the games feels somewhat empowering and I enquire crisply of Rossi: – What's brought this on?

Rossi's climbing down a bit. His tone's less haughty now. After all, it's just two professional men chatting together in a diagnostic mode. Identify problem and suggest possible solutions. – Well, you may be allergic to a certain foodstuff. It may be part of the stress and anxiety-related condition you've been experiencing.

Stress. That figures. The fuckin job. Toal's caused this! He's fucked Busby and he thinks he'll fuck me. Wrong!

I take Rossi's creams and head away hame. Home is not a good place for me, it never was. I prefer to work all the overtime I can. People like Gus, they lap up the OT. They get in the habit during the summer so that they can accrue as much time to get on the gowf during the day when the links are clear. Me, I can only sleep during the day. I like to keep busy at night. I head home and have a quiet evening in wanking to some of Hector The Farmer's videos. I take a glance at the *Evening News*. There's an article by a spastic who's their so-called 'Chief Crime Reporter' which seems to just offer a sounding board for any bitter coon lover to criticise the service. Then I head out to Jammy Joe's disco: a chance to combine business with pleasure.

It's a bugger to get parked in the town and I shouldn't have taken the motor. Still, I'm going to stay quite sober, I just want to fire into some game tart and take her hame and fuck her until I feel tired enough to get some zeds in.

That Mark Wilson boy is on the door, and the smart cunt's nervously checking me out. Yes, I'm almost positive that cunt used to run with the CCS back in his day. If that's the case, he's bound to back up *0000000eating eating always eating00* hen that whole issue of pe *0000000000000growing00000000000* they basically fucked me *0000feed me my Host0000000000000* There's some tidy fanny i *0000000000000000 I travel through* ettle doon wi a beer and wa *the inside of this vessel, growing,* ce looking and I offer to buy *filling its cavernous voids, to utilise its* Bacardi.

I buy so *space and become one with it. Thank* auld trick ay trying tae ge *you for the home my Host. Thank you.* she asks.

— Naw, I *Thank you for the life.00000000000* it's just that I never ate mu *00000000000 eat more 0000000000000*

— I like *0000000000000000 eat 00000000000000*

— Hear *000000 eat 00000000000 eat 00000000* d I smile, raising my g *00000000000 eat 0000000000000 eat*

We get a t *0000000000000000000 eat 000000000* the light is harsh and I *0000000000 eat 000000000000 eat 000* you got anything to e *000 eat 000000000000 eat 0000000000*

— You ca *00 eat 00000000000000000 eat 000000000* like it hot, she smil *0 eat 00000000000000 eat 0000000000*

I move *000 eat 00000000000000000000 eat 0000* irt. She must have a *00000000000000000 eat 00000000000000* ny and she groaned *0000000000000000000 eat 000000000* as if we were old lov *00000 eat 00000 eat 0000000 eat 00000* fucked harshly tog *00 eat 000000000000000 eat 0000000000* t to get rid off. I st *000000 eat 000000000000 eat 0000000* COMES HEN! I sc *00000000000 eat 000000000 eat 000000* sions and I'm now i *00000000000000000000000000 eat 0000* ng for sleep to take me *00000000000000000000 eat 000000* she's dozing off as well a *00000 eat 00000000000000000000000* t dirty bitch and it was as *00000000000000000000000000000000* ohnny as she's

probably carrying th[e] 00000000000 eat 0000000000000 [w]ith the
fuckin plague – it 0000000000000000000 eat 0000000

00000000000 eat 000000000000000000000
0000000000000000000000000000000000000000
0000000000000000000000000000000000000000
0000000000000000000000000000000000000000000
0000000000000000000000000000000000000000000
000000000000000000000000000000000000000000000
0000000000000000000000000000000000000000000000
00000000000000000000000000000000000000000000
0000000 eat 00000000000000 eat 000000000000
0000000 eat 0000000000000000 eat 000000000
00000 eat 000000000000 eat 000000000000000000

I rin[g] 000000000 eat 000000000000000 eat 00000000 [o]n Lee
Marvin, 00000000000 eat 000000000 eat 0000000000 [ran]ge. I'm
glad I didn[a] 0000000000000000000000000 eat 00000 [i]t hame
via Crawfo[rd] 00000000000000000000 eat 0000000000 [a]nd jam
doughnuts f[or] 000 eat 0000000000000000000000000000
Nobbing[...] 0000000000000000000000000000000000 [...]d to get
away without[...] 0000000000000000000000000000000 phone her
again. If last night was about emptying the bag, tonight, thank
fuck, is Lodge night. The masons is the only place that you can
go to meet cunts that arenae polis. It's different up here tae
down in England. There are, of course, some fat cats and professional types, like down south, but in the Lodges up here it's
mainly tradesmen. It's like the gowf: in Scotland you have
schemie gowf clubs like Silverknowes. Just you try bein a fuckin
tradesman and joinin a golf club in England though.

I personally think that aprons are for silly wee lassies to wear
in the kitchen and no for grown men on a night out. The ritual-
ism of the Lodge has its uses however; it's made me far more
sexually inventive. This helps with the games.

I make myself some toast on the grill, but I burn the first lot
and have to try again. I open the back door to let out the smell.
Outside in the back garden I see that Stacey's bike hasnae been
put intae the shed. It'll rust tae fuck. I stick it inside and then go

to the bottom of the garden on the pretext of pottering, but I want to get a good nose into Stronach's hoose. He'll be at training today, and I could do with a sketch of his bird, see what that wee cow's up tae. She doesnae seem tae be at hame though and it's nippy out here.

The second batch of toast is fine. It's midday and I fill in my overtime from last night at Jammy Joe's on the OTA 1–7 form and head up to HQ in the Volvo accompanied by a tape of Iron Maiden's self-titled debut album, the offering where Paul Di Anno rather than Bruce Dickinson is at the mic.

The recent snows have frozen over. Of course, this means chaos on the roads with the highway cunts unable to cope. As if they werenae used to bad weather. There's a bottleneck stretching from Colinton to fuckin Aberdeen or the likes. THIS HAPPENS EVERY FUCKIN YEAR. I feel like getting out of the car and choking the living shit out of any spastic whose face offends me, which in this case is just about every cunt. Fuckin police force here . . .

Fuckin emergency services

Cunts

I'll fuckin

I park the car outside the shops before Napier College. It's a so-called university now, but every cunt knows it still as Napier College. The punters know a real uni when they see it and this fuckin place for trainee basket-weavers in no way fits the bill. Same rules. There's a decent bakery here and I radio in and tell them that the traffic's scandalous and I'll see them when I do.

When I finally make it in, I start going through the papers on the Wurie case. I'm interrupted by a call from Gus Bain who's up in records. If I didnae ken that bastard better, I'd say that he was sniffing roond the big blonde piece up there n aw. But he's been married tae the same auld boot for seventy thousand light years, the churchy auld cunt.

— Bruce. Gus here. Have you opened your internal mail yit?
A wee present fae the funny felly up the stair.

I rip open one of the pile of sealed envelopes in my in-tray,
the one with the Nid's name on it.

INTERNAL MEMO

To : D.S.s Gillman, Stark, Robertson, McInally, Thomas, Inglis, Clelland, Noble,
Phillips, Lennox and Bain.
From: Chief Superintendent Niddrie.
Date: 3rd December 1997.

Re: Equal Opportunities Module: Racism Awareness.

The course tutors have brought to our attention cases of inappropriate attitudes
and behaviour on the course of which you were a member. With this in mind it
is intended to hold a series of individual debriefing sessions with course members, the tutors and members of the core team of which myself and Deputy
Chief Constable Mathieson are members.

With this in mind, please report to my office on Friday, 4th December at 2.15
p.m., the scheduled time for your debriefing.

I'm sitting digesting it, and snapping open another Kit Kat
when Inglis and Gillman come in moaning.

— That's the fuckin morn, Gillman snorts. — What kind ay
notice is that?

Niddrie must be getting his heid nipped by the top brass.
This case isn't going to go away, more's the pity. The boys are
girning away about it and old Gus has arrived. The auld boy's
fairly up for stirring it as well.

— Well, ah'll tell ye something, he's saying, — ah'm no gaun
up thair withoot a Fed rep. That's you, he smiles, looking at me.

It's patently obvious that the sorry old goat is trying to get
me to wind up Niddrie and Toal and bomb myself right out of
the promo race. He's such a predictable old fuck. It makes sense
to humour him.

– Too fuckin right Gus! What the fuck is this shite? Ah'm straight ontae the blower tae Niddrie. You get roond the rest ay the guys. Tell them: say fuck all withoot a Fed rep. This is a fuckin disciplinary fit up. These cunts are looking tae make one ay us an example just because the papers and they mealy-moothed cunts are kickin up shite aboot this deid silvery moon.

– Right, Gus says.

I sit down and compose myself. I then phone this Marshall guy from the Multicultural Forum on Coon Rights or whatever they call it, the cunt that's been hassling me. – Hello Mr Marshall? D.S. Robertson here.

– I've been trying to get you for ages to arrange a meeting . . .

– Yes, it seems we've been a bit like ships in the night. Two o'clock tomorrow okay for you?

– Yes, that's fine. Shall I come to your office?

– No, not at all, I've kept you waiting, I'll come down to you, I tell him.

I put the phone down, a satisfying glow coming over me. I then bell Niddrie as I catch Gus's attention. I gesture at him to put the kettle on.

– D.S. Robertson here. Re your memo. That date you're giving me, it's not convenient, I tell Niddrie. – I've made an appointment for that time and I can't get out of it.

– Cancel it. This takes precedence, Niddrie sharply informs me. Niddrie hates me calling him direct. Everything should go through Toal. Niddrie believes in the strict hierarchical division of the organisation's reporting structure. The chain of command. He gives newcomers to our division the old 'my door is always open' bullshit, but woe betide the cunts if they ever get daft enough tae try walking through it.

It would be pleasurable to fuck Niddrie about without needing to play the craft card. I know that those New Labour wankers up the City Chambers have been intoxicated with their election victory and are strutting around like peacocks and coming down hard on Niddrie and co. and one of their beefs is equal opps. –

I'm meeting people from the Forum on Racial Equality and Community Relations, I tell him.

There's a silence on the other end of the line. – Shit . . . listen . . . you'll have to go to that one. We'll need to make it Thursday afternoon. Three-thirty.

Niddrie puts the phone down on me. I keep the receiver to my ear and then I bell Toal, noting that Gus, busying himself with the coffee, hasn't seen me redial. He still thinks I'm talking to the Nid.

– It's Bruce Robertson, I whisper. – Niddrie's gied me a new time for the briefing. I have a forum meeting to go to. I'm informing you as my direct supervisor, I raise my voice for Gus to hear, – I'll come along, but I'll have a Fed rep with me. Drysdale from the south side.

Gus raises his eyebrows. He puts a cup of coffee in a Hearts mug in front of me. This isn't my Hearts mug, it's Inglis's. I'll fuckin catch something off that cunt.

– I think you've misunderstood the memo Robbo, Toal says.

– Aye?

– This is an exploratory debriefing session. There's no question of anyone being reprimanded or disciplined at this point.

– So what you're saying is that this may be a precursor to disciplinary action?

– No . . . not necessarily. It's an open-ended discussion.

– So it's a counselling session then?

– Well . . . yes . . . but not a counselling session in the sense of it being related, or even potentially related at this point in time, to the disciplinary systems of the Edinburgh and Lothians Constabulary.

– But my attendance is compulsory?

– Everyone must attend.

– You're asking me or telling me?

– Robbo, what I'm hoping from you and the rest of the team is your willing co-operation. If this isn't forthcoming then I'll be forced to introduce a disciplinary element.

– I see . . . I let the silence hang.

Eventually Toal says, – I don't have time for this bullshit. I'll see you in Jim Niddrie's office at the appropriate time. Cancel everything else.

The line clicks dead. Now Toal's hung up on me! Who the fuck does he think he is? Niddrie's fuckin office-boy, that's who. I shout into the mouthpiece, – I don't have time for your fuckin bullshit Niddrie! We've got a fuckin murder case tae solve! I slam the phone down.

Gus Bain raises an eyebrow, – Whoa, Robbo, ye gied Niddrie it tight there, did ye no?

– The only way wi these cunts Gus, I said. That's all they understand. I turn round and notice that Sonia, one of the civvy clerks, had come into the room. – Sorry aboot that Sonia hen, industrial language they call it.

– Sawright, she says. – It's Hazel.

– Of course . . . of course . . . Hazel. Bet she takes it aw weys. Bit young for me but. Mind you, if they're auld enough tae bleed . . .

– Ah'm sure Hazel's heard worse, Gus gives that wheezing, creepy laugh of his, and she grins nervously.

– What ye could do for me Hazel, is to gie they people at the Forum a phone. I had a meeting with them tomorrow at two. Tell them I have to cancel out, but I'll get back to them.

– Right. . .aw aye. . .there was a woman on the phone for you while you were out, she tells me.

– Whoah! Gus laughs, – Mister Popular.

– Aye? Whae?

– She wouldnae leave a name or number. She sais you'd know who it was.

– Right . . .

That's a bastard. Shit. Probably Carole crawling back. I'll leave a message on the answer machine tonight.

Those cunts Toal and Niddrie have upset me big-time. Making me miss important fucking calls with their shite. I should have fuckin well stayed in Australia. Then where would the fuckers be now? If I hadn't gone out there but stayed in

London wi the Met, I'd've probably been Chief Constable in a fair-to-middling size force by now. I feel a bad itch in my arse. These boxer shorts ride up and brush against the scar tissue. My arse shouldn't be fucking sweating as much. Stress, that's what it is, as Rossi said, and it's caused by these Personnel cunts who wouldnae ken what poliswork was if it was to suck their cocks or lick their fannies.

I decide to hit the canteen for lunch, well, pre-lunch, as it's a bit early for dinner. Too late for a break and too early for lunch. Bruce Robertson time, I call this. Ina sorts me out with some bacon rolls and I hear smarmy voices behind me which belong to some cunts in suits and one of them is that lippy fucker Conrad Donaldson Q.C. who spends his time coining it in from the tax-payer by defending the kind of fucking scum that we risk our lives to try and put away: rapists, murderers, child molesters and what have you.

— Practising cannibalism Bruce? he nods at the plate and smiles.

I'm looking coolly at the cunt. I'd love to have him. Just him and me, just twenty minutes in an interview room the gether.

— Hello Conrad, I force a smile back.

I want to punch his face and deck him and them stomp that smirking posh face into the ground under the heel of my boot and keep doing it until his skull explodes over the lino, sending its fucked criminal-loving contents squidging across that tiled canteen floor. I'd eat my dinner after and keep it down as well, I kid you not. — Remember what I told you that PIG stood for? Pride, Integrity and Guts.

He smiles and turns to his pals. — Detective Sergeant Bruce Robertson. One of the force's leading reactionaries. Comes from a mining family as well, I hear.

— You hear wrong, I say softly, looking him hard in the eye. — You must be getting me mixed up with someone else.

— Hmm, Donaldson mumbles, raising his eyebrows.

My knuckles are white on the tray as I depart. I hear Donaldson muttering a consensual goodbye, through a ringing in my ears. I feel sick and dizzy. I sit in a corner and devour the rolls, ripping and rending the stringy meat in my sharp teeth, wishing that it was Donaldson's scrawny neck. New Labour rising star Conrad Donaldson.

By the time I get back upstairs I've composed myself, but whenever I think of Donaldson and his ilk, a savage rage crashes inside my chest. At one point it gets so bad that I'm shaking and my teeth are hammering again. I need a drink so I knock off early and hit the bar at the social club downstairs. Just feeling the thick carpet under my feet composes me. It makes a change from the other rooms in the building with their thin, harsh, cheap Berber flooring. The bar itself is a lot more basic than it used to be. When it opened it was full of good bric-à-brac, antique vases and the like, but these kept going missing so they changed to a more functional decor. A couple of baby polis are playing pool, but I see Bob Hurley at the bar. – I arrived just in time I see, I smile at him.

– Alright Robbo, he turns to the barman, – Another pint of lager Les, and you'd better set up a wee Grouse as well.

– Make that a large Grouse Les, seein as this English cunt's on the bell. I wink at the barman. Hurley's face briefly whitens a wee bit. The race card is just one of the cards in the pack and if you're serious about this game you utilise that full pack as and when you need to. That wee aside is just to remind Hurley of his status as a barely tolerated guest, not just in this country, but in this life.

Hurley and I sit down in a corner and a few rounds later on we're still there. Toal, of all people, has just come in, but I'm ignoring that arsehole. He sits in the next booth to us, reading the *Evening News*. Fuck him, the sad, nae mates cunt. Only tries to socialise with the boys when he wants something. It's Hurley I'm more interested in.

He's still melancholy about the split with his wife. – What fucked it up with me and Chrissie was her family. You know what it's like being a polis, he sings in that Tony Newley voice that makes the word 'polis' sound so funny.

What's he on about: 'a' polis? Daft cunt.

—You tell them all, her friends, family, the neighbours what you do for a living and you get treated like a leper. They sit in the house, her pals and their spouses and they say nothing, it's like they're in an interrogation room. The conversation's full of awkward silences and they can't wait to make their excuses and go. Then they always put off coming round again. You get treated fucking . . . he gasps, seemingly in pain, his breath catching, — like a fucking leper, he repeats, — . . . that's what you feel like Bruce, a fucking leper.

—Yeah.

Hurley pulls a bit of wax from his ear and rubs it on the underside of the seat. — So I went through a phase of telling them that I was a plumber or that I sold insurance. Then they start telling you everything about themselves. It's like, 'I do this on the side' or 'I don't put that through the books'. They're all at it. Every one of them, he says, raising his voice in rage, — fucking Jackie Trent. The lot of them, they're all fucking Jackie Trent.

I clock Toal getting up and leaving, the nosey, eavesdropping cunt.

— Exactly. And you are a law enforcement officer, I tell him.

— Right, and that's what she can't bleedin well understand. When you do what you have to do as a law enforcement officer, when you blow the whistle on these bastards, she turns round and says, 'It's my family. I'm leaving.'

— That's women for you, I tell him, swigging back my whisky. If you drink whisky you'll never get worms.

She isn't much of a fuck that Chrissie. Quite into the video camera but went a bit funny on me when I brought out the vibrator. Had tae go aw lovey-dovey oan the daft cow to stop her becoming hysterical.

— I just find it hard to switch off sometimes. The thing about being a polis is that you get used to seeing things in a certain way: looking for things that are going wrong. It's the way you are; how some people behave, it makes you so suspicious. I just can't stop running routine checks on them. That's what wound her up, the questions I would ask her family. I didn't even realise that I was probing. I couldn't switch out of role. You can't be any other way Robbo, that's what you do.

— Take it or leave it, eh mate, I smile. I'll be taking your missus again, that's for sure you stupid cunt.

— Aye, he says, Tony Newley style, — so she left it. It's over. For good this time.

— Force marriage though pal. May the force be with you, cause sure as fuck the fanny willnae stick aroond.

— You're lucky though Robbo, he says, almost accusingly.

— Aw aye, me and Carole. Well, she's a wee bit special. No doubt about that. Steak on the menu tonight!

— She can cook as well! Hurley says, — Is there no end to this woman's talents?

The fuckin lecherous cunt's wantin me tae tell him aboot Carole and I's sex life. Nae wonder his wife's gittin fucked by everybody in sight. Aw mooth n nae troosers that prick. — It's a question of values, I say, draining the whisky glass.

Gus Bain comes in and we have a scoop. I'm trying tae watch myself but Gus likes a good jag when he's clocked off. Hurley fucks off back to his miserable life. Hurley isn't liked much on the force. I don't know why; there's just something about the cunt that makes you fuckin detest him and savour everything bad that happens to him, of which there is lots, I kid you not. You learn to sniff out a loser in this game. The worst kind of losers are the ones who think that they are winners and have to be reminded of the facts. Like a certain young gentleman by the name of Raymond Lennox, for instance.

— Young Ray Lennox didnae have much tae say for himself oan the course, I tell Gus.

— Aye, still waters, Gus smiles with a bit of affection.

— Listen Gus, I say, dropping my voice, — dinnae take this the wrong way, but watch what ye say in front ay Ray. I'm no saying nowt against the guy. In fact I lap him up. But watch what ye say aroond him.

– What dae ye mean Robbo? Gus looks alarmed.

– What I mean is that he's typical ay they young cunts. He'd drop ye in it in a minute if it suited him. Ye ken the wey it is Gus, five minutes oan the force and they want tae be the Chief Fuckin Constable. Thinks eh kens it aw. The thing is, they young cunts are totally ruthless and they certainly arenae above a bit ay back-stabbin and character assassination tae git oan.

– Surely no Ray . . . seems such a nice young felly . . . Gus says bewildered. I sense doubt through his antagonism. Time to hit hard.

– Listen Gus, whaire's Ray Lennox the now? Ehs no in here drinkin wi us, is eh? Naw. I'll wager three tae one, naw, make that four tae one on, that he'll be drinkin wi they silly wee lassies in some fuckin wine bar up the toon, just like eh wis eftir that fuckin course . . .

– But that's up tae thaim . . . thir young and they dinnae want tae be doon here wi the likes ay us . . .

– . . . Yes Gus, fair do's and good luck tae the boy. I hope he rides them both, I hope they make a fuckin sandwich oot ay him, one slice white, one slice yellay n young Lennox in the fuckin middle.

–Yir an awfay man Bruce, Gus chuckles.

– But the thing is, who dae ye think'll be the main topic ay conversation during this touching little tête-a-tête? You and I. The silly cunts who make the snowballs and also fling them.

– Hmmm, Gus says thoughtfully, – ah ken what yir gittin at. Ye think our Young Mister Lennox is running with the hounds and hunting with the hares?

– He's hunting the fuckin hounds, as far as I can see, as long as he's no fuckin well running off at the mooth as he tends tae dae.

– I'll keep a beady on that wee cunt, Gus nods, touching his eyeball.

Thank fuck it's Lodge night the night. We down our drinks

and head out to Stockbridge. The roads are slippy as the surface has frozen over. We see a lumbering taxi trying to turn slowly down a sidestreet but sliding on the ice and scraping its body-work against a lamp post. As it comes to rest the irate spastic of a driver springs out and inspects the damage. – Jesus fuck . . . he snaps, then truculently yanks open the door of his taxi.

I nod to Gus. The cunts inside are getting out. This one'll do us up tae Shrubhill.

A lassie's getting out of the taxi. Quite a young lassie. Or she's *trying* to get out of the taxi. The torn-faced cunt of a taxi driver is not helping her, he's just holding the door and impatiently asking her if she's alright. The lassie has one of her legs in a plaster and she's attempting to get up and at the same time position the crutches on that treacherous icy surface.

It's just like . . . fuckin hell . . .

I move over swiftly and I've got a hold of her. – Can you manage? Here, let me . . .

– Thanks. . .

I'm helping her to her feet and Gus has got the crutches positioned and we get her on to the pavement. The scent of her perfume is filling my nostrils. I'm up against her and I can feel her soft warmth. I could just hold her like this, forever.

God, I remember . . . it was so long ago . . .

Then it happens; a stiffening inside my flannels and y's and I have to adopt the old bent-double last-dance-at-the-disco posture to conceal it.

– Are you going far . . . the pavement's very slippy.

– Naw, I'm just in that stair there, she points over to the stair door.

– I'll give you a hand over, I smile, taking her arm.

– Thanks very much . . . that's very kind of you, she says as we reach her door.

– No problem. Can you manage up the stairs? I want her to say no, come up with me, come up and have some coffee, leave auld muppet-faced Gus to his silly masonic shite, come up with me and hold me in your arms like you used to . . .

. . . but it's not. Those were different times.

— I'm fine now, honest. Thanks again, she smiles.

— Alright then . . .

It isn't her. It could never be. But I wished with all my heart that it was.

Ha!

Bullshit! I wished with all my heart I could get another pint!

— C'moan Gus, time for the lodge. I'm fed up wi helping spastics on duty withoot daein it in social hours n aw. I pile into the taxi.

— Ye awright Bruce? Ye seem upset, Gus says, looking straight at me, as he gets in.

— I will be awright once I get to where we're meant tae be going. I shout at the driver, — The Edinburgh Masonic Club, at Shrubhill, driver. Next to the bus depot.

We cruise through the frozen streets in silence.

Coarse Briefings

Up the club, the lads are all raring to go as it's a big induction night. The would-be new recruits look nervous, as they well might. There's a couple of baby polis to be done, as well as some other young cunts; I don't know where they come from.

I'm already feeling a wee bit pished as I've eaten nothing, so I decide to hold back a bit until all the boring stuff is over, then I'll get myself charged up for our little specialist club's activities.

I have to keep it *00000eat000000000000* tedious ritual of putting Alfie Orr's *000eat0000000000000eat00* it. Grandmaster Bill Crozier's still g *000000I eat.000000000000* handshake, the young boy looks li *000eat000Eat.00Eat.0000Eat.* m Auschwitz or something like th *I eat. I eat through my skin and* ot.

There's still *I hold on with my jaws.0000* shaking like an old Ted with Parki *00000 Slowly, so slowly, I'm* ongue extended as a hot flush com *consuming the matter that* d ever after.

Crozier's voi *surrounds me0000000ingesting* ne steadfast in this my Great a *and excreting through my body,* ed Apprentice Mason! *through my skin.0000000 I have*

The young *to eat to move on, to consume* and twitches as Crozier gives it *to live, to consume to grow. I can* roat cut across and tongue torn *feel myself growing. Eat. Eat. Eat.* sand of the sea at low water m *Eat.00000000000000000000000000* . .

A load of o *000000000eat000000eat0000000* n a state of fear

and that always／ 000eat000000 this consumption, ＼nly too well. So
after all the dr￭ all this chomping and chewing, it ￭ree sheets and
Bladesey's off, ＼ provides me with more evidence of ╱he heads of the
hydra. Jake Bu╱ my existence than thought does. ＼tube of KY jelly
as his exposed￭ This is the only real way I can inter- ￭ing to struggle,
and the scream￭ act with the environment I am in. ￭tection of some
of the boys, th￭ My problem is that I seem to have ￭sing shooters.

    There's an￭ quite a simple biological structure ￭s a real lull in
proceedings bu￭ with no mechanism for the trans- ╱Lennox grabs
the yard of ale a￭ ference of all my grand and noble ＼ss, then to Bill
Armitage, one o￭ thoughts into fine deeds. Oh yes, ＼nd old Labour
Party stalwarts ￭ I can conceive of my body as that ￭I'm away with
the goalie and ＼ simple structure: input, process, ￭ight away with
it as the whisk￭ output. Eat, digest and then shite to ＼beef vindaloo.
Then I stand u￭ your heart's content. Right through my ＼a cab hame.
 I argue with th￭ skin as well, yes, that's me! 000000 ￭xi cunts, and
when my heid ￭ This simple thing 00000 but I know
          for sure that the complexity of my
          soul doesn't even start to approximate
          the basic organism that is my body. I
          just know this because I feel it, feel it in
          my essence, which I must trust as much as
          any limited sense data I acquire from
          my environment. So what can I call myself
          then? Well, all I can call myself is the Self,
          to be quite strict about it. But there has got
          to be more to this whole puzzle than just
          my beautiful Self. I somehow conceive the
          wee fancy that I'm living inside another
          organism. The environment is another
          creature, a host, no less. We can refer to it
          as Host. So just entertaining that wee notion
          makes me wonder as to whether Mine Host
          can perceive me, and if so, how this big
          creature feels about me? Because here I am,
          thinking that this Host, due to his greater

complexity is probably an empiricist; believing that intelligence can only be inferred from behaviour, which I know to be false. I know this as what I feel in my soul does not correspond with the constraints my physical form puts on me. But then I think that if my Host knows of my presence and deems it to be unwelcome, what will he do about this. It's terribly worrying. As a simple organism, I believe I should not be burdened by such concerns. Yet, I suppose we must all be concerned with the question of survival.

I'm sweating wh.. ..dit's like pints of whisky are com.. ..ers and my head is fuckin throbbing. It was one fuckin mad session up the masonic last night, especially with Bladesey, the daft wee cunt. He'll be as embarrassed as fuck this morning. My guts are greasy and the spice content of my burps and my heartburn is telling me that a strong curry got into the mix some way along the line.

I shuffle some papers on my desk, examining the witness statements again. They all saw fuck all of course. Sylvia Freeman and Estelle Davidson. The two rides we've interviewed in connection with the topped nigger. They were in the club that night awright. Must be game if they were there on a midweek evening. It's fuckin annoying but I cannae think what they looked like in detail, other than that they were rides. That's the problem, when you think of a bird you fancy, it's the clothes that come first, usually a dress or a top or something like that, when what you want is erse, tits, eyes, mooth, hair, etcetera. I mean, you arenae gaunny go intae Chelsea Girl or Next or River Island and have a wank over a load ay tops or pairs ay troosers or skirts hingin oan a rack, are you? No unless you're some sad cunt like my wee mate Bladesey. Anyway, I'll pull in these wee slags for some of the special Bruce Robertson interrogation. If ayy nighteengaahhle could seeng like yooo

Bored shitless here.

I shuffle the papers for a bit longer but the images of Sylvia and Estelle don't form in my head so I bell Bladesey at his work.

— Extension four-zero-one-seven, Cliff Blades speaking. How can I help you?

— You can stop talking in that poofy English accent for a start.

— Oh, hello Bruce. How are you?

— Right as rain Bladesey boy, I reply, as a wave of nausea crashes through my body and my hand starts to shake uncontrollably on the receiver. I want to go home. I want my bed. — It takes a wee bitty mair than a few wee nippy sweeties tae knock old Bruce Robertson out of his stride. I kid you not, my sweet, sweet friend.

— I must confess, I'm actually feeling rather rough. Came within an ace of phoning in sick. Actually I would have done as well if Bunty hadn't been at home today. I think I'd rather be at work than face her in this condition.

— What about the night, you and me, straight back on the pish! No surrender to the IRA!

— Eh, I don't know about that Robbo . . . I've actually go . . .

— C'mon Blades-ay-ay! The Blazer. The night.

— Well . . . you see, it's Bunty. She's a little . . .

— Tell ye what Bladesey, she's walking aw ower ye. That's why she's treating ye like shite, cause she can. The Blazer then.

— Well, alright. But I can only come for a couple.

— That's my boy! You've got bottle Brother Blades. Nine bells at the Blazer!

— Right . . .

— You were in some state last night, I tell him.

— Yes, I'm afraid I can't really remember much about it . . .

— Very convenient Mister Blades, very convenient.

— Did I do anything . . . eh . . .

— Tell ye in Blazer Bladesey. Must nash.

— Yes . . .

— Tro Bladesey, I slam the phone down. Hurley's right. The big problem with being polis is that you can't help but see people as either potential criminals or potential victims. That way you feel either a loathing or a contempt for anyone who isn't like you, i.e.: polis. All my mates are polis, all except Bladesey and Tom Stronach, the fitba guy next door, who I suppose is a mate of sorts. But it's mainly Bladesey. And I have to work hard not to let my contempt for Bladesey show.

I look at page three. Cathleen Myers today. A ride and a half. Great tits and a fantastic erse, which the photographer spastic hasn't given us a sight of with that shot. Still, she's got those come-to-bed-Bruce-Robertson eyes on. I dial Bladesey's home number. Thank fuck that 1471 call-back facility hasn't been installed here yet. It'll soon mean that you'll *have* to be polis, just to be able to play simple games like this one.

– Hello, three-three-six-two-nine-four-six.

It's Bunty's voice. I've never met her. I let the silence hang a bit.

– Hello? Who's there?

I try to picture Bunty. I think of Bladesey. He reminds me of Frank Sidebottom, the comedian with the big false head. A Manchester accent: you can do it by holding your nose. – Hello.

– Who's this?

– I got your noom-bih from a friend.

– Who are you? What do you want?

– Let's joost say, I've erd all about yaw, and them services that yaw provide.

– Listen, I think you've got the wrong number . . .

– This is three-three-six-two-nine-four-six?

– Yes . . .

– Then I aven't got the wrong number then, ave I?

– Who gave you this number?

– Someone who spoke very highly of you. He told me all about you. Said you were a brilliant fook . . .

My cock stiffens at Cathleen's face and Bunty's silence as the line clicks dead.

The problem with my game is that we're not great thinkers. We do. You have to keep doing, to find things to do.

We're the law enforcers of this society. I think of what that

73

means. It means we are paid to do a job we can't fucking well do because of all these snidey little cunts: the politicians, lawyers, judges, journalists, social workers and their ilk. Take the City of Edinburgh. Arm me and I would delve into the little black address book I keep at hame in the top drawer of my bedside cabinet. I'd pay a few housecalls, leave a little lead and you just watch the crime figures drop over the following few months. The Robertson solution. *Real* Zero Tolerance.

It's an internal call and it's Toalie. – Come up here straight away Robbo, he says, not waiting for a reply before hanging up. Cunt. Does he think I'm just at his beck and call when I've got fuckin work tae dae? Real fuckin work, work of the kind that spazwit would never understand. He's taken root in that fuckin chair. He probably wants another muthafuckin progress report. I hope we don't go on for too long as I've arranged to do other things. You can kiss my bacon-flavoured po-leese ass, muthafuckah.

I head up the stairs, cruising past central admin to see if I can get a glimpse of the big cock-teasing blonde civvy piece, but no fuckin joy. Lennox was sniffing around it in the canteen earlier, the dirty cunt.

Toalie looks stressed as I sit down beside him. You can tell. He's never very animated but Brother Toal's give-away gesture is the bending of his lips over his teeth. You could put a headsquare on the cunt and he'd look like your auld mother.

– We need to get our heads together Robbo, he tells me with urgency charged through his squat frame. – The hammer's been found. It was buried under a hedge at the top end of Princes Street Gardens. Forensic's managed to trace micro-particles of blood and tissue in the grain of the metal which match the victim's. Just found it there, under the bushes.

Bushes. Thick black bushes. Chewed lips from Amsterdam. If I had a hammer. Hammer house of horror.

– I don't suppose there's any prints? I ask mechanically.

– Naw . . . it's been wiped clean, that's if the killer wisnae using gloves in the first place. As you know, this man's a diplomat's son, he says, dropping his voice and raising his eyes, as if I'm supposed to go: Wow! Barry!

I couldn't give an Aylesbury Duck.

– I see, I see. What kind of a hammer was it?

– Oh, it's a steel-headed claw hammer with tempered shaft and rubber handle. Standard issue, you can get them at any B&Q or Texas hardware store. The serial number of the hammer was filed off. This boy meant business.

– Right, I'll get some lucky bastard checking all the sales of hammers from hardware stores over the last few months.

It fuckin well wouldnae be ma joab anyway. Some uniformed spastics and a clerical can go through that one.

I'm thinking to myself that a couple of neds in this city have topped this coon who's no business, as far as I can see, being here in the first place, so, fuck it. Who gives a toss? The answer is me. This reorganisation post comes up soon. I want that job, so I'm going to ferret out that murdering schemie bastard who topped our innocent coloured cousin. It's called, in a word, professionalism, and I'm a total fucking pro, something that the spastics around here wouldn't understand. Same rules apply in each and every case.

But Toal though, he's slavering on at me. – This is a bloody strange one Robbo. Nothing's turning up. We've been through all the revellers.

That wee Sylvia and Estelle, I'd go through them in a minute.

– Probably some young racist thugs out on the town, I tell him. Fitba guys or BNP members or something. Might need to get in about them. I'd like to lean a bit heavier on some of these young lassies that were there. They shield these guys, it's their boyfriends and what have you.

– I'm not so sure Robbo. I'm a wee bit fed up of having some silly wee laddies used as a dustbin for every crime in this city. It's lazy poliswork, that's what it is.

Him accusing *me* of lazy poliswork. *Him*, that's never been oot fae behind that fuckin desk in yonks. – Aye, awright. But I know they guys. Some of them arnae that wee now, and they're moving intae other areas besides fighting at the fitba. When these guys start tae believe their ain propaganda, then you have tae watch out. It becomes a self-fulfilling prophecy. I'm not convinced that those spastics are blameless.

Toal raises his eyebrows. — Just keep me informed, he says.

Toal either kens fuck all aboot poliswork, or he's holding something back, something about this coon case. Which is it? Fuckin both, that's obvious. Whatever he says, these cunts are a good starting point. It's time some of these fuckers went down; whether or not they did this one is immaterial, they are bad bastards and banging some of them up will make the streets safer. It's time to lean on some cunt, I'm bored sitting here shuffling papers. It has tae be Ocky. The weakest of weak links in the chain. An E-riddled fanny merchant who hangs out with some of the top boys because they like the cunt's devastating wit. Ha. He's been feeding us stuff on them for years. Of course, we still let them go about their business. Their antics mean newspaper headlines, which means big-time OT and a cry out for extra polis resources. That's the way it works. Let them knock fuck out of each other, but always be ready to pounce when they threaten commerce.

I go back past the central admin unit, but there's still nae sign of thon blonde piece. At the downstairs bogs I weigh myself on the metric scales. My weight is still going down. I hope I've not got Aids or something, from some fucking hoor. I must eat more. I can't put on weight, I never could. Fast metabolism, not like some of the blobs in this place. If it was up tae me, I'd weigh every cunt on the force annually and whoever didn't make the required weight would be out on their fat arses. Weightist? You fuckin well bet your sweet ass!

I get a whiff from the canteen. I investigate and there's fish pie which looks interesting. — Awright Ina? I ask the auld girl behind the counter.

—You're early the day Bruce, she says.

— I was tempted by the fish pie.

— With chips?

— Magic Ina, and bung on some beans as well, I tell her, savouring that big, gorgeous congealed mass of sludge. The fish pie isnae too bad either.

I sit down and enjoy my meal. Ray Lennox comes over and joins me. — Awright Bruce? Seen the paper? He thrusts it in front of me. There's another headline about local coons criticising the police. One of them's that Forum cunt Marshall, speaking, of course, in another capacity. They get in far too many capacities, shit-bags like that.

— Shite. These silverys are about naught-point-one per cent of the population. They've got far too much to say for themself. They should call that paper the 'Coon, Poof, Silly Wee Lassie, Schemie and Communist News'. I only read it for the fitba and Andrew Wilson. He's the only one that talks any sense on that fuckin paper, even if he is a Hibby Leith bastard.

— It gets on my fuckin tits, Ray says, shaking his head. His eyes are staring, the cunt looks a bit manic.

— Listen Ray, I wanted to speak to you about something. I ken you're no officially on this investigation, but I think we should pay our pal Ocky a wee visit the morn. It being Friday, it would be nice to fuck up the cunt's weekend fine-style by getting him to keep his ears open on our behalf. You might get some info on the collies if we shake the fucker doon. Wi Christmas comin up they'll aw want sorted oot wi gear.

— The spunk-bag's been a bit remiss lately. Forgotten who his real mates are. His mates on this side of the divide, Ray smiles.

Say what you like aboot Ray Lennox, he's polis through and through. — Time we reminded him, I smile. — So what's been happening your end young Raymondo?

— The usual bollocks. I'm still stalking those cunts from that Sunrise Community. They're supposed to be cannabis suppliers. It's a fuckin waste of time, but what can you do?

Anything other than posh is a waste ay time for that cunt. But I can see his point. What's the point of being on D.S. duty if ye cannae get access tae any decent collies?

– Listen Robbo, he whispers, – I'm on these benzedrines. They'll do the biz in the meantime. They keep you going when you're a bit fucked. Want a couple?

– Aye, I tell him.

He slides me a plastic packet of pills. – I got them on a bust. The charlie situ should improve tonight.

– Good, I smile, pocketing the pills.

– What about this fuckin EO's briefing? Ray asks.

– Shouldnae take mair than an ooir, I say, shuddering as the big blonde hoor from central admin comes past. I give her the eye but she's not biting. Probably lesbo tendencies. – Ride thon, eh Ray?

– No half.

– Any luck? Ah saw you sniffin roond it doon the cannie this mornin.

– Nah, she shags on recommendation only. Ah heard that she's a size freak. She finds oot fae the other lassies likes ay Karen Fulton n that crowd, who the guys wi the really big packets are and she'll only fuck them.

– That's you oot the runnin then, eh? I laugh, thinking about the time we had a session with my sister-in-law Shirley.

– Cheeky cunt, Ray says, a slight beamer on his face. – Listen, we'd better nash to this briefing.

– Aye, right.

In the event, the EO briefing only takes half an hour. I even get on Niddrie's good side when I hit a note with the cunt on politics, much to Amanda Drummond's distaste.

– Equality is a lot of nonsense, I say, goading Drummond, who expects me to hang myself by saying something stupid like the black man isn't the equal of the white man. Think again, dafty.

– How can you say that?

– Easily. It's a philosophical point. I believe in justifiable inequality. Example: aw that lot we put away. Criminals. Child molesters. They're no equal with me. No way, I say, as coldly and

78

dispassionately as possible. That struck a chord with Niddrie. He's an impassive bastard, but I ken he thinks like me.

Anyway, the gig finishes early enough for Ray and I to hit the cannie so we can have an afternoon break and practise our routine before we go and sort out Ocky. We are intercepted by Amanda Drummond in the corridor and she tells us that she's going to talk to Sylvia and Estelle and would I come along. I'm annoyed that the cow has pulled them in without consulting me, but chuffed at the prospect of being able to put a face, erse and pair of tits on those two rides. – Sure . . . I turn to Ray and raise my eyebrows, – . . . give us half an hour will you Ray mate?

– That's cool, Ray nods, – see you up in D.S.

I'll have to pull up Lennox about all this 'that's cool' and 'this's cool' bullshit. We're no running a fuckin youth club here.

I get into the interview room and Drummond's got the two wee hoors in there together. This shows her total cluelessness as polis. You never put them together, you always split them up straight away. The first thing they teach ye. Not that I'm complaining, it's wall-to-wall fanny in here and it's fuckin marvellous. Those bennies are kicking in, so I'll have to watch my gob. And my fuckin erse! Shite coming oot every orifice! Settle Bruce, settle. Estelle. Sylvia. It's funny, but the last time I was talking to them, I was sure that Estelle was giving me a funny look. Now I'm positive.

– I'm sure I've seen you before, she says. She's a fuckin hard wee cow and nae mistake. But that fringe hanging just above those club-mascara eyes and that scarlet red lipstick . . . ya cunt that ye fuckin well are . . .

I realise that I'm staring at her and that Drummond might be clocking my leer, but no, that dyke's looking just as penetratingly at her, probably fancies her as well.

– Aye, I'm sure I've seen ye, she repeats.

– Well as you were in here the other day being questioned by me, that's highly likely, I sniff.

– Naw, before but, she says.

79

— I'm sure I'd've remembered, a lovely young lady like your-self.

I hear Drummond's front teeth smacking off her lips. Spotted! Imitation Toal gesture! Her fuckin mentor. No wonder she's such a fuck-up! She puts some pictures in front of the lassies, two puss-bags known as Setterington and Gorman amongst them. — Did you see any of those men at the club?

They look fazed, especially Sylvia. I'd gie her one in a minute as well. Looks a natural blonde. Talk to Brucie baby.

— Naw, she says, too quickly. Even Drummond notices this.

— Do you know these men? she asks.

They're too intelligent to lie. — Know of them, seen them aboot, Estelle replies.

— Who are they?

— Dunno, just guys that hing aboot the clubs n that, Estelle says. She's much tougher, that one. A seasoned casual moll if ever there wis one. Those lipstick marks aroond that fag . . .

— So you don't know their names? Drummond probes. Ah'll fuckin probe awright: probe wi some prime Scottish beef.

— Nuht.

— Is there anything else you'd like to tell us about that night? Drummond's asking.

Estelle looks at Sylvia, then at Drummond. I'm being ignored here, ignored by slags, and I do not like it one little bit. I drum at the desk, but I still might as well be invisible. Estelle starts mouthing: — There was a funny woman in the club. It's probably nowt, but she just looked a bit weird. She was talking to the coloured boy for a bit, but he pulled away fae her, like they were having an argument. I mind because I saw her earlier in the toilets, she was putting on her make-up next to me.

— What was strange about her, Drummond's asking. I don't fuckin well like those fluorescent lights. All that seventies shite. Can we no get a fuckin decent office . . .

. . . the Met . . .

. . . Sydney polis . . . a decent office . . .

But that wis New South Wales.

– I dunno . . .

No you fuckin well don't know, that's the fuckin problem you daft wee schemie trollope, you know fuckin nothing, nothing at all . . .

– Was she young, old, big, small, dark, fair . . .

Ma heid's fuckin well splitting and I'm gonnae start shaking here . . .

– She was a bit of a dog, Estelle says.

I'm wasting my fuckin time with those slags. They ken nowt. That silly wee Roger Moore Drummond should realise that. Same rules apply. Polis? Her? That will be the day. I rise and leave.

Drummond follows me out of the interview room. – Bruce, we need . . .

– Yes, I raise my voice to silence her, – we need to follow this up but I've something *I* need to follow up and I'm running late . . .

– Is there something I should know? Drummond's irritated look is chilling me out. She's as fucked off as I am. The only thing I can think of that *she* should know is the obvious one: she's never fuckin polis.

Moving backwards I point at her and smile, – We do need to talk Mandy my darling. Later though. I'll give you a thorough briefing. Ciao.

I leave the flustered dyke farting and shiting in the corridor and head up to Ray's office in the D.S.

When I get up to D.S., Clell's there with a bottle of champagne and he's pouring it into paper cups. He hands me one.

– What's the celebration?

– I got my best ever Christmas present Bruce, a transfer from Serious Crimes to Traffic.

Anticipating what I'm going to say he carries on, – Yes, I'll be a pen-pusher in a dull, no-risk, no-fun job . . . and I can't wait! I've had it Bruce. I'll leave the Sweeney-type stuff to you cowboys! I'm hanging up my baton and cuffs and getting to know the simple beauty of this little felly here, he smiles, holding up a pen.

— If that's what you want, nice one, I say, raising my cup and loathing the smugness of the spastic. I drain it, and turn to Lennox. — Ready Ray?

— Cool, Lennox says.

I get a raging anxiety attack. I've got to get out of this place now. I'm bounding downstairs and out towards the car park and Ray has to get a bend on to keep up.

I Get A Little
Sentimental Over You

I'm happier by the time we've started up the motor. Just getting
out of that shithoose restores your perspective. We take a slow
drive down Leith Walk. I've got the radio on, as I'm reluctant to
start an argument with Ray over rock. He's a pedantic fucker
when it comes to music and he kens nowt about it. Lyn Paul, for-
merly of the New Seekers is singing 'I Get A Little Sentimental
Over You'. Lyn's solo career never really took off. I think about
mentioning this to Ray but decide that it would be pointless. I
mean, why bother? I'm feeling better though, more focused. My
anxiety attack has abated, as it tends to do when the scent of the
hunt takes over.

We pull up outside Ocky's flat and I get out and ring the
bell. No reply. I hope we've no missed him with Drummond and
her dykey casual moll pals wasting our time. We go back into the
car and wait for a bit. There's a baker's on the corner, so Ray nips
over and comes back with some sausage rolls with vanilla slices
for dessert, washed down by strong coffee in a styrofoam cup. It
gets rid of the taste of Clell's cheap champers which merged
with the bi-carb of Lennox's pills to form a corrosive, acrid bilge
in my gut. I burp.

— Looks like we've got those jakeys in that new age crowd
bang to rights Robbo. That fuckin Sunrise Community, or whatever they call themselves, Ray's telling me.

– Fuckin well time n aw Ray. These things are springing up everywhere. It's a threat to the great British way of life and it has to be stopped before it gets a toehold. Cunts think they can live just by looking after each other and dancing to fuckin music. They just want to hypnotise the young cunts with these free parties and get them on drugs. They havenae even got a fuckin telly in that farmhoose. They can afford a huge fuckin sound system, but they cannae afford a telly!

– Scumbags, Lennox shakes his head.

– Mind you, I admit, – they made a good job of doing it up. It was derelict before they got it. I'll need tae git the cunts roond tae dae up ma hoose!

– It'll be fuckin well derelict again soon. One of the guys that lives there, that Colin Moss, white, male, six-one, thin, filthy brown-blonde dreads, bad skin, green combat jacket, ripped jeans and boots; he's been seen coming in and out the flats in Leith. Where Allan and Richards live. We'll do the cunts. Turn over the flat, then the farmhoose. If there isnae any collies there when we arrive, there will be when we turn the place over.

– Tip me off when the action takes place Ray, I tell him. – I'd like to be in on that one.

The job *can* be satisfying.

I've just downed the last of my coffee when I clock Ocky in the rear mirror, he's coming towards the flat with a wee bird. They're wrapped up in each other. Dirty wee cunt. Mister Ockenden is sporting a fur-lined, dark blue corduroy jacket and a pair of blue jeans. He's about five-ten, five-eleven with striking blond hair and slightly girlish features. His girlfriend is a cracker, slim, five-sixish and exactly the same sort of blonde as him. You could take them for brother and sister. In fact ah widnae put it past that dirty wee cunt tae be shagging his sister!

– Tidy wee piece, Ray says, noting the scene. All that posh he does still hasn't strung him out or blunted his edge. Yet.

– Wee being the operative word. This is a stoat-the-baw situ. Ye reckon?

Ray looks at her, narrowing his eyes and curling his lip out-

84

wards. — Always hard tae tell. Curvy wee erse . . . he observes as they pass us.

— Never mind the fuckin erse, did ye clock her coupon? A wee fuckin bairn!

— Possible, Ray agrees, — A borderline case. There or thereaboots.

— Nae question. Forty sheets at five tae one, I'd gie ye.

Lennox shrugs and starts tae crap his breeks.

— C'mon Ray, double score. Five tae one, I urge.

— Naw, mibbee yir right, he concedes.

Too right I am. When it comes tae money doon, he's no bottle. Doesn't trust his instincts, that's why, as smart as he may be, the Lennoxes of this world will never oust the Robertsons.

— What dae ye want tae dae? he asks.

— Steam in Ray, I tell him. — Just what these cunts dae. Only nae cunt steams in like the polis. We're the hardest firm in this toon, and it's time these scumbags realised it.

— We have to watch here Robbo . . . Ray's bricking it.

— Baws. Same rules apply. C'mon. We use The Beast routine, that'll spook the cunt.

I know The Beast routine off by heart. I should fuckin know it.

— Aye . . . Ray raises his eyebrows doubtfully but he's getting out of the car with me, and by the time he hits the stair, he's aw fired up, bouncing with adrenalin, taking these steps three at a time, almost squashing a stunned cat which jumps out from under his feet. It's knocking on this old cat, getting slow. The stair fairly reeks of its pish.

We halt outside the door to get our puff back. — Reckon he'll be giving it one by now? I ask.

— I would think so. They were practically gaun for it gaun intae the fuckin stair. Lennox looks at me and then hesitates: — . . . Want a line?

— Right, I nod, looking around as Ray puts some posh on the corner of his credit card and takes a rough hit up that hooter.

I look a bit doubtful, not wanting my nose cavities fucked by roughage. – It's okay, this is good. It's as fine as fuck, Ray says, his eyes watering as he sniffs and sniffs.

I take a whack, and it is good stuff; that sweet smell in my head, my face numbing, a surge of power flowing through me. Time for action.

I rap heavily on the door. Once, twice, three times. I hear a whingy voice, – Awright, awright! Ah'm comin.

Ocky, aka Brian Ockenden, aka soft little twat with a gob who got in too deep, opens the door in his t-shirt and boxer shorts. His mouth and eyes widen in shock.

– Mister Ockenden. Hello, I smile pushing past him into the hallway.

– You cannae come in . . .

– SHUT THE FUCK UP! Ray screams in his face, causing him to recoil. Lennox's puffed himself up and he's standing right over Ocky who's aw cowed and bent. – You fuckin well speak when you are spoken to or I'll fuckin well have you right now! Get it!

This wretched wee cunt looks at him, trying to summon up a bit of defiance.

. – I ASKED DO YOU FUCKIN GET IT! Ray roars, and Ocky buckles a little bit more.

– Aye . . . cool it man, ah've no done nowt . . . he whimpers.

– You're in serious bother mate, Ray says, closing the door and shaking his head in disgust.

– Cool it Ray, I say, putting a protective arm around Ocky's shoulder. – Stay here a minute. Where's the bedroom? I whisper.

– It's . . . he looks sideways, – . . . but thir's somebody in thair . . .

– It's awright, I tell him with a matey grin. I open the bedroom door, and the lassie's sitting up in the bed with her t-shirt on. I go in, shutting the door behind me.

– What's this? she asks. – Who are you?

– Police, I say, whipping out my ID – Do not attempt to leave this room. Do you understand? What is your name?

– I don't have to say anything to you . . .

She's a wee honey. Still got those fetching freckles. – Make it easy on yourself hen, I advise, then with urgency ask, – How old are you?

– Sixteen, she says, lying.

– Any ID? I look towards a shoulder bag on the bedside locker.

Her cool's blown. Her eyes are like the satellite dishes on Tom Stronach's ootside wall. – Fifteen . . . but I'll be sixteen in September, she says hastily. Too hastily. Too quick to admit it. I wonder why she doesnae want me in that bag.

– Your boyfriend's broken the law if he's had intercourse with you. Has he? I ask, moving closer to get a wee scan of those titties under that T. Not large, but certainly firm enough. Yo ho ho and a barrel full of fun.

She moves back against the headboard a little and pulls the duvet up over her chest. The colour fairly drains from her face though, as I reach over and grab the bag, pouring its contents out on to the bed. This unearths a small plastic bag with what is obviously Ecstasy tablets in them.

– I . . . I didn't . . . she's stammering. She's lost it now.

– D.S. Lennox! I shout, and Ray comes through. I hold the bag of pills up to him. – Looks like MDMA tablets to me. Note that they were found on this girl's person. At least six hundred milligrams. Please also note that this girl is under the legal age of consent.

– Check, Ray says, exiting.

–You stay here, I say pocketing the pills. – You're in very serious trouble. What did you say your name was?

– Stephanie . . . she says sheepishly, hugging her knees up into her chest and letting her chin rest on them. Her hair tumbles forward. She pulls one side back and secures it behind her ear.

– Stephanie what?

– Stephanie Donaldson . . .

– Well Stephanie Donaldson, I'll leave you to think about how silly you've been. You're going to have to give us a wee bit of co-operation here my girl.

A whole fuckin loat ay co-operation. Stephanie Donaldson. Hmmm.

She sits stiffly up in the bed and I go through to see how Ray's doing. He's got Ocky in the front room.

– Judges are coming doon hard as fuck on stoat-the-baw, Ray's telling him.

– I thoat she wis sixteen. She telt me she wis, Ocky protests, then smiles at me, an all-lads-together smile.

I give him a hangman's smile in return. I run my finger across my throat and make a crackling, slavering sound. – Sorry mate, but as Ray here says, this isnae the time tae be done for stoat; no now, no wi aw that paedophile stuff in the papers. It's fair goat the magistrates oan the warpath, aw that palaver. Stoat man, thir daein time for it right now. Only aboot a year or so, which means six months. Nae real bother tae you. Mind you, this is posh fanny, so add oan a year. Which makes it a whole year inside.

He's no looking too happy.

Ray chips in, – Aw aye, Ocky here could handle twelve months inside, eftir aw, every cunt loves a stoat-the-baw. A wee bit ay tackle pits oan some make-up, aw the red-blooded males in Saughton understand the score. A standing prick hath no conscience, Ray smiles, a cold, ghostly grin. – They always ask aboot the ride, the other boys inside. What was she like? Did she have big tits? Schoolie's uniform? Lennox laughs, a dry cackle. He pulls a bogey down from his beak and examines it to see if any posh has got caught up in the mucus. Satisfied that it's clean, he rolls it between the forefinger and the thumb, wringing out the moisture, and flicks it on to Ocky's carpet. He stares at Ocky for a bit and shakes his heid. – Six months for a ride though, doesnae really bear thinkin aboot, eh no? Hope it wis a good one mate. Be yir last for a while.

– No necessarily, I chip in. – Cause, aye, they aw love a stoat-the-baw. Problem is, that thir's a thin dividin line between a stoat-the-baw and a nonce. Ye tend tae get a loat ay fishermen's tales oan the inside, only wi stoat, the size goes doon the wey instead ay up the wey, I spraff, in a pally, trade-secret sharing way as I push my palms together.

—Thing is, Ray says, — see if somebody fae the polis was tae tell a screw like Ronnie McArthur, a strict freemason and staunch family man, that the lassie was eleven . . . or ten . . . or even eight . . .

— Ah know what you're gaunny say Ray: the poor cunt's life wouldnae be worth livin. He'd be taken to The Beast's wing in Saughton. But ah dunno any polisman, any professional in policework who would stoop that low, I tell him, widening my eyes and extending my palms and looking around.

— For the greater good though Bruce, Ray agrees, advancing his proposition, — suppose that this stoat-the-baw had access to certain information and had the potential to help the police with a major investigation but refused to do so . . . you and Ronnie McArthur are pretty tight, aren't ye Robbo?

— In the craft, aye, I nod, switching my glance to Ocky. This cunt is shiteing it. I let the fucker stew and have a wee scan for potential knock-off. This cunt though: fuck all worth chorrin.

— C'moan boys . . . he pleads.

— Ye see Ocky, thir's this guy inside, on The Beast's wing. Thir's loads ay beasts oan the wing, but only one in the whole ay the Scottish prison system that they call *The* Beast. Follow? Ray explains.

The cunt looks shat up. It's like he's watching an action replay of his life with only the shite bits left in. A bit like watching *The Tom Stronach Story* on video, should anyone be daft enough to commit the commercial and aesthetic suicide which producing such a film would involve.

— He's no the felly ye want tae share a cell wi man. But Ronnie would be forced tae make that happen if it wis put aroond that the lassie thair was eight years auld or something.

— For yir ain protection likes, Ray says.

— Some protection, I laugh, —The Beast is fuckin mental. No way should that cunt should be in the jail. But that's the fuckin prison system fir ye eh? They did have the cunt in Carstairs for a bit. He escaped though.

— That was a fuckin big joke that eh? Ray coughs out another dry, humourless cackle, then rubs that hooter again. He's been on the sniff awright, and no just that one wee hit outside there. Just as long as he's no haudin oot on auld Robbo here, his mentor.

— You're tellin me. The good thing though, thir wis a few fields between him n the toon. So the local livestock took the brunt ay The Beast's frustration. They had tae put four cows doon eftir he'd finished wi them. Big-time OT for the vets. Peter Savage fi Strathclyde telt ays that in aw his years oan the force he'd never seen anything like it. The thing is, they've goat The Beast back in the mainstream prison system. The only wey that they can keep the cunt quiet is by pittin a new model in his cell every few weeks.

I look doon at this silly wee fuck. There's a faint noise coming from his throat. He's trying tae say something. Ray coughs and makes a wee comment which ah dinnae catch.

— What was that Ray?

— Models, Ray goes, — what's aw this models shite?

— Aw, that's what the local screws call the laddies they send him. Usually young pretty boys, early twenties . . . like this one here. I swivel and point at Ocky, who's now just a quivering wreck. No such a smart cunt now. — Ah'd say that you were an identikit model, I tell him. — See, the boys that get pit oan The Beast's wing are usually rapists rather than stoat-the-baws. They git a wee bit too carried away and cannae hear the word 'No' fae a lassie. Well, they git plenty ay opportunity tae practise that word wi The Beast; they can try oot aw the permutations ay pitch, tone and volume, but see The Beast? Well, he's goat that selective deefness n aw. N fact he's goat it bad.

Ray smiles at the young tube. — Bet ye eh enjoys the resistance. Likes tae see the boys struggle.

— Six fit four ay solid muscle. Hung like a fuckin hoarse. Legendary. Always splits thum the first time; even they wee Calton Hill rent boys they feed him, and these boys are used tae takin loads ay hard meat.

— Phoa! Makes ma eyes water tae think aboot it! Ray gasps.

— But the wardens indulge The Beast tae fuck like. They've goat a selection ay wigs, dresses n make up so that he can dress the models up as he likes. He gies them their names: usually French sounding ones: Juliette, Justine, Celestine, Monique an aw ay that. They reckon eh gits them fi the go-go's at the Bermuda Triangle in Tollcross. This yin here though, ah pucker ma lips at Ocky, — he'd be a Christine.

— How's that? Ray goes, letting his mouth go moronically loose, and I realise that I am too, as we're enjoying the twisted but undeniable sexuality which is part and parcel of the complete dominance over another human being. This is one of the things which makes poliswork such a satisfying career.

— Blonde hair, I say, slowly and softly.

— Aw aye, Ray picks up, — ah heard aboot that. When he gits a blonde he always calls them Christine. They say it wis tae dae wi his wife. They tell ays that ehs much mair possessive towards blondes.

— It's fuckin oot ay order really, but that's the system, eh?

— This is the perennial problem wi the system Robbo. A dustbin for society, for everything it cannae or willnae deal wi. Thing is but, ye'd find oot a lot aboot yersel n that situ, like. Banged up wi The Beast. Phew!

— Ah cannae imagine a worse fate.

— Might find oot things aboot yirsel ye'd rather no find oot, Ray notes sombrely. Ocky's done, we've broken him. We just need to rub his face in it a little bit more before reassembling him with several modifications in the psychic specification, in order that he does our bidding.

— Well one thing's certain: ye dae a stint n thaire wi that monster, ye come oot a changed man, I smile.

— That's if ye come oot at aw. They tell ays ehs chalked up a couple ay suicides over the years.

— Aye, and another young laddie went and hung ehsel eftir a few months oan the ootside. That experience changes a cunt. Defo, I snap at the terrified tube, who springs back from future hell to present hell.

– Maybe the guy would've done it anyway; a spastic, a fuckin common criminal. Whaes tae say?

– The Beast though man, daein time wi that would tip the fuckin scales. No think so Ocky? Help! Help! they shout at the wardens, those poor models. No that it does any good.

– So ah've heard Robbo, Ray grins.

The wee cunt sits there shivering. He's ours. He always has been.

– They tell me that he's HIV now. Dae they isolate the cunt though? I ask rhetorically.

– Dae they fuck, Ray replies.

– Effectively then, it's a death sentence for any cunt in that cell wi him.

– Effectively, aye. That's what it boils doon tae, Ray shrugs.

– I know that it sounds grim, but that's only the one choice but, eh Ocky? Thir's ways and means, I kid you not, my sweet, sweet friend, I say softly, cupping the terrorised cunt's face in my hands. – I know your whole life's been flashing in front ay ye, but aw that's just the worst-case scenario. Anyway, I twist the spastic's heid so that he's facing Ray Lennox who's smiling like a department store Santa Claus. – Uncle Ray here'll tell ye what ye have tae dae tae stey oot ay The Beast's vile clutches. Think ay him as your knight in shining armour.

Ray winks at him, then snaps his fingers and starts singing, – I feel a song comin on . . .

Ah feel the horn comin on. Stephanie Donaldson. Steph-fanny Donaldson. – I, in the meantime, shall go and check oan that wee drug-dealing slut ay a girlfriend ay yours Ocky. Honestly, the company you keep. Mind you, it'll no be the first time that posh fanny's dragged a good man down. Huv tae watch whaire ye pit that dick. Thir's eywis strings, I wink, departing to the bedroom.

When I'm back through, she's up and dressed and sitting on the bed.

– Well, well little miss, have we had time to think about our position? I ask. Ah'll show the wee fuck a few positions awright. Startin oaf wi fuckin doggy-style.

— Please don't tell anyone . . . I don't want my father to know. He mustn't know, she's begging.

— I'll have to charge you with possession and intent to supply. Of course, as a minor, it's likely that you won't receive a custodial sentence, but you will have to appear in court. What school do you go to?

— John Gilzean's . . . she bleats piteously.

— Well, I'm sure that such a reputable school will take disciplinary action. I will, of course be forced to inform them, and also your parents. Ecstasy is a very dangerous drug.

— Please don't tell my father . . . please . . . he's a barrister. It would be terrible for us . . .

Donaldson. Of course! — Your father isn't Conrad Donaldson, is he? I can feel my spirits lifting and I'm sure that my cock has never been as big in my pants before.

— Yes, she says, her eyes lighting up hopefully.

Oh ya fucker! Mister Fuckin Smug Cunt himself! Bingo! His offspring right here on Bruce Robertson's plate! A small world, a small city. God bless Edina, Scotia's darling seat! I clear my throat; lust and the prospect of revenge had furred it over. — Listen doll, I'm going tell him. As of now, I'm going to tell him. Whether or not I actually end up doing so is entirely up to you, but as of now, I am.

— Please . . . I'll do anything . . . don't tell him! she squeaks.

— Well, I'll tell you how it's going to be. You listening to me? Because I'll say this once. Okay?

She looks up and nods slowly at me. I can't see much of Donaldson in her. I'm not sure whether that's good or bad.

— You suck my cock and we're square. And you suck it good. Okay?

She's looking at the floor. Her shoulders are shaking.

— Okay, nae deal. Stephanie Donaldson, you are charged with possession of a controlled substance, with intent to supply. You have the right to . . .

— No! No! Please!

I'm smiling down at the posh wee fucker. — Come on baby.

93

End this nightmare. End it all wi a wee suck, I say softly. — Your wee scumbag boyfriend, dinnae tell me you huvnae done the biz wi him. One cock's much the same as another. A few minutes ay your sweet wee heid and the nightmare is over. You walk oot ay here. We're square. See if you dinnae fuckin play ball? The school and Daddy hear all about it.

A mining family. Ha! I come from a lot dirtier, filthier places than doon a fuckin pit, as this wee tart's aboot tae find oot.

— Alright . . . she says, making the contract. A verbal agreement will do nicely. It might not be worth the paper it's written on but you cannae very well take a blow-job back once it's been given.

— Good girl. Fair exchange is no robbery. Why involve the state doll? Why cause all the nasty paperwork? I smile as I unzip. It flies oot like a fuckin jack-in-the-box. — Suck me baby . . . I whisper, — Suck Robbo here real good.

She's looking at it then looking at me with large pleading eyes, but I'm holding the bag of Es in my other hand. — I'll be roond that posh school. Suck. I'll be sure Daddy Conrad Q.C. gets to know the whole story. Suck.

My balls feel scaly and crusty. The skin is flaking off them. My eczema's getting fuckin bad alright. Too many dirty thoughts. Too many bad places. But not now. What a lovely wee gob on it.

She puts her mouth slowly around the tip of my cock and winces. — That's it baby, that's it. Suck me like you suck your boyfriend . . . get that tongue working . . . you're a beautiful wee lassie, ye ken that? Touch ma baws. Touch ma fuckin baws wi yir hands! I command.

Daddy's girl
— Grip ma baws . . . harder baby c'mon . . . grip ma fuckin baws harder . . .

She's gagging and wretching and greeting her eyes oot, but by now I've a hold of that golden hair and her head is mine. Daddy's fuckin girl. Cannibalism, eh ya cunt? Well your wee lassie likes the taste ay that bacon, she fuckin loves that meat awright, loves it right tae the back ay her fuckin throat . . .

— Suck ya wee fuckin hoor or yer auld man'll ken yir a fuckin drug-dealing wee hing-oot!

Yes yes yes yes

She's suckin, she's fuckin well suckin awright . . . the wee angel . . . ahhh . . . ahhhh . . . ahhhhh . . .

—Yeahsss . . . swallay! I'm farting oot loads ay gas, it's burning my eyes. The power of that Lauriston Place Curry Hoose's vindaloo!

She's swallayin rather than spitting. I feel like I'm going to pass out as I pump it into her. There's a tense pounding at the back of the neck like my head was being lifted off with a shovel, but it's ebbing, just like my spunk against the back of her throat and down her gullet. She's choking, but I haud her heid steady until I'm ready, then I withdraw my cock from her miserable torn face, stuff it in my troosers, zip up and leave her to her tears. — That's us square hen, till the next time. Keep away fae this stuff, I smile, waving the pills at her and pocketing them. — And tell your auld man that Bruce Robertson was asking for him, I wink, brushing a few flakes of dead skin from her shoulders.

I was asking for him, but I got you instead doll.

I go through to the lobby leaving the wee slut to soak up that distinctive curry, Guinness and spunk atmosphere. Ray Lennox is warning Ocky to keep us posted on the movements of yobs like Alex Setterington and Ghostie Gorman. Poor Ocky; it was a bit of large hammer for such a small nut, but it's the sport that counts and it passes the time of day.

As we prepare to leave, Ray turns back to Ocky, —Ye should leave they pills alaine. I never touch them. Tried them once, but they didnae go wi the job. Made me feel too good aboot everybody. Nae use in my game. The charlie but, that's another story, he laughs.

Ocky just nods fearfully.

—Ye want tae teach her how tae gie a fuckin decent blow job, I laugh, pointing through to the room and shaking my head in a mixture of laughter and disgust as we depart. Outside the door Ray and I give each other the high five.

Sound cunt Ray Lennox. If every fucker on the force was like him, the job would be so much easier.

It's the weekend! Early knock-off eftir that and no way am I going back to the HQ to hear Drummond bleating on about two silly wee cows who know that Setterington and Gorman's mob were there but are trying to divert things by flagging up red herrings. I'm hame and it's on with my *Frank Sidebottom Salutes the Magic of Freddy Mercury and Queen and Kylie Minogue*. Kylie Minogue: say what you like about her singing and her acting but she's a wee doll. Things would be easier if we had birds like that on the force instead of dogs like Drummond. Or even these wee birds that Stacey likes, them that go, Tell us what ye want what ye really really want. The wee yin goes, Which one's your favourite Dad? Carole just looked over sarcastically and said: Ask a silly question.

I practise Frank's Mancunian accent for another small while then I give Bladesey a bell to check that he's still at work, which he is, and he tells me that he's coming straight out to the pub at nine. Working very late is our Brother Blades. That's a sure sign that you're either shagging someone you shouldn't be, or in Bladesey's case, not shagging who you should be.

Then I place another call to Bunty. Cunty. Cunty Bunty, how does your minge grow?

– Hello Boontay. That's your name, int it?

–Yes. Who are you?

– Bet you've got hairs on your fanny like the branches of a tree. When was the last time you made loove Boontay?

– I don't see that's any of your business . . . you must lead a very pathetic life if you have to take such an interest in other people's. I feel sorry for you.

My oh my. I do feel patronised all to hell. How can I recover from this shattering blow to the very core of my self-image? Easy peasy pudding and pie. – Well, thenkyaw! But what about your life Boontay? *Is* it that boring?

— That's my business. Who are you? What do you want? . . . What's your name?

Questions and answers; honesty, lies . . . — My name's Frank, actually.

— Well Frank, I think you're a very sorry excuse for a human being.

Do you now darling? How fascinating that you noticed. It was Daddy. I blame him. He was a bad man. But what about you sweetheart; what about you, who married one Clifford Blades? — They told us you take it oop the boom Boontay. Is that right?

— God you're pathetic. Who told you then? Who told you that nonsense?

— It were . . . it were . . . little Frank.

— Who's he then?

— Ee's . . . ee's . . . I'm not talking to you anymore, I squeak. This hoor is an A1 baw-buster. Cool as ye like. No wonder poor auld Bladesey's on personal hand-jobs with the old newsprint. The bigger they are, the harder they come though. This is going to be a challenge. We decide to beat a temporary retreat.

— Tell me, who's this Little Frank? she insists.

— Oops . . . sorry Boontay, me mam's joost calling for me, I have to go. You'll get me into trooble you will. Coming Mam . . . no I'm not making dirty phonecalls to prostitutes . . .

I slam the phone down. That big hoor can take the stick. Good. She'll fuckin well need to. The funny feeling in my troosers tells me that a chugging session with Hector The Farmer's material is well due. A good wank to some big-titted hoor, then try to dispatch the remains of last night's Ruby Murray intae the next life. My bollocks are still a bit raw and flaky, and I get further aroused at the thought of wee Steph-fanny's lips roond my cock.

It gets too much after a bit so I head down to Maisie's sauna, also known as The Fish Factory. Maisie isn't in for a blether and some advice as to how my specialist needs can be met, but I find a young hoor and take her over to Links B&B run by a guy from craft who owes me one. I try to ride her but my cock and balls

are tender as fuck with that eczema, so I finger-fuck her rough-
ly and get her to suck me off. She's not into it at all, but I tell her
I'll shut their fuckin place down if I get any bullshit off her and
she complies. When the smell of her gets unbearable, I tell her
to fuck off before I'm tempted to break her jaw.

I fall asleep for about an hour and I wake up with a bad
anxiety attack, and don't know where I am. I have to open the
window and look out on to the darkened Links to get my
bearings. It's quarter-to-nine and I'm going to be late for
Bladesey. I fire up town in a taxi, which is driven by a guy I
know vaguely from the

My guts are rumbl... ...arving again and I've
just been to the fuckin ...ut I meet Bladesey
doon the pub and get a ...he Blazer, where
Bladesey is also a bit po... ...er a steak pie and
fairly tear into the bastar...

Bladesey's looking ..., reminding him
in full of his humiliatio...
— I don't believe it ...fear and tension.
— Believe it, I say curtly, ...n the fuckin bell
and mine's a pint and a ...

Brother Clifford Bl... ...s already got that
worried face on the nig... ...is but young. We
tear into the bevvy, Blad... ...k is giving him a
different perspective, m... ...ne big joke, but
terror will be restored i... ...ngence especially
with Bunty nipping his ...e daft wee cunt.

Bladesey's dressed... ...nelled troosers,
pink shirt and blue tie... ...n top. I've seen
some of his workmate... ...ry bit the spastic
misfit that he is.

I set up another r... ...t up a Silk Cut.
Bladesey takes one, w... ..., with his brow
knotted.

—Your face is a bit... ...tell the cunt. —
Everything alright?

00000000*eat*000
000000*eat*000000
0000000*eat*000000
00000000000000000
0C00*eat*00000000000
000*eat Mine Host*00
000 *eat for your friend*
the Me. Eat 00000000
000000000000*eat*000
000000 *eat* 0000000
000000 *yes* 000000
000000 *yes* 00000000
0000000000000000
0000000000000000
0000000000000000
0000*the question of*
*survival*00000000000
00000000000000000000
00000000000000000000
00000000000000000
00000000000000000
000000000000000000
00000000000*eat*0000000
000000000000000000
000000000000000000000
00000000000000000000

98

— Eh, no actually *00000000000eat000* ot sure I'll be able to make the Amsterda *Mine Host eat for the self* w that Bunty would have a heart attack. *000000000000000000,*

— C'mon mate *000000000000000000*

—You don't kn *000000000000000000* a sip from his beer. There's another p *000000000000000000* ert's been giving her filthy phone call *000000000000000000*

I feel like t *0000000000000000000* ngland where they have that 1471 t *000000000000000000* he perverts. It's got rid of a lot of th *e00000000000000000000* irty callers, aye, but the net effect ha *000000000000000000* hat stalking has gone through the ro *000000000000000000* e to outmanoeuvre technological *00000000000000000000* al developments.

Stalking. Sta *0000000000000000000*

— Listen B *000000000000000000000* wee word with the both of you. A *00000000000000000000* that to allay fears and what have y *0000000000000000000*

— Oh Bruce *000eat000000000000000*

— Anything *00000000000000000000000*

— I'd really *0000000000000000000000*

—Then consi *0000000000000000eat00* more scoops and a Ruby Murray! *00000000000000000000*

After a few more *0000000000000000000* f Ruby Murray and we stagger into the Pass *00000000000* wee guy knows us and doesn't mind, or mat *0000000000* doesnae mind. I'm spending a bomb on ta *00000000000* ch is a problem and although I've had a g *000000000eat00000* the resentment gnawing through the alc *00000000000000*

00000000000000

0000000000000

00000000000

000000000000

000000eat000

00thank you from the Self0000000

This morning I'm hav *00000eat0000* benzedrine tablets that Ray Lennox found on a b *0000000000* farting like a trooper cause I was three sheets last night and in such a condition you always go one strength up in the curry stakes just soas you can taste it. I think those benny tabs have a high bi-carb content, so that's not helping either. I'm not working this Saturday morning. No, I've promised to visit my friends the Blades.

At Home
With The Blades

Bunty might be a tough nut to crack on the blower, but Bladesey's told me that it's all been getting to her. This is as it should be. Right now there's a lump in my flannels and I feel charged up with a sense of my own power over her. It's time I met up with this big hoor, as I promised Bladesey.

The snow'll be starting up again soon. It's going to fall heavily. You can feel it in the air. The decorations are up in the city and the lights are on. They finally buried the Wurie guy in London. There was a piece about it on last night's television news; as expected, it was critical of the investigation. Fuck it, the coon's well out the way underneath the earth and frost. The most important thing is that the roads are clearer, and I get out to Carrick Knowe in no time.

Bladesey's shiteing his pants. Possibly with good reason. Bunty's looking pretty severe, and he got in three sheets last night. I saw to that. She's a big woman, a hefty woman, but press the right buttons and that big hoor would go off like an alarm clock for all her superior ways. I know the type. Same rules apply. She's as straight as they come though; no knock-off in this Habitat/John Lewis furnished gaff. No tick, and not a smidgen of dust. Make a good polisman's wife. Or fuck. About five-five, but eleven stone plus, on the voluptuous side of fat, black hair curled and twisted into ringlets a younger woman would wear

(Bunty must be mid-thirties) and quite a bit of flash jewellery; necklace, earrings, bracelets which giving a tarty hint which is out of synch with her haughty tones.

The sum total of the particular equation that is Bunty adds up to: far too much woman for Bro. Clifford Blades. He's nearly stammering: – This is Bruce, my friend I told you about. Eh actually, he's the one I'm going to Scarborough for the masons' beano with.

I try to stifle a laugh. Scarborough. Huh. Catch me in a pleb resort like that? I think not my sweet, sweet friend. – Pleased to meet you Bunty, I smile, extending my hand and letting a full, wholesome grip linger.

She returns my smile. – Bruce, isn't it?

Yes it is, you meaty-thighed, big-titted whore. –Yes . . . I begin.

– Cliff's told me all about you, she says, a fraction teasingly.

– Oh, nothing defamatory I hope . . . I turn to Bladesey, – for your solicitor's sake, that is, I quip.

– Not at all. On the contrary, says this big tart with the huge earrings. Grab a hud of these and yank and she'd have tae go doon oan ye, nae choice, although her fanny might be like Murrayfield Ice Rink the minute ye did. But perhaps not, because this cow respects power. I ken the type. I snap into professional mode. – I understand how unsettling this must be for you Bunty. However, try not to worry unduly. I've dealt with creeps like this one before. Most of them, if you'll pardon the expression, are all mouth and no trousers. Slamming the phone down only goes to show them that you're frightened. They feed off that fear. Stay as cool as you can, and talk to them. That's when they start tripping themselves up. Getting careless, running off at the mouth.

– Your officer said not to get into it with them, she says, slightly quizzically.

– Yeah, we generally tell our younger, less-experienced officers that. And yes, I find that works if you want them to stop. If you actually want to catch these bastards though, if you'll pardon my French, you have to use different tactics.

– Oh, I want him caught, don't you worry about that, Bunty says in an almost low growl, – I want him to suffer.

I feel my cock stiffen at the emphasis this big hoor puts on the word 'suffer'. Phoa! – Well Bunty, I say, it comes out in a soft wheeze, – Ehmm, excuse me, bit of a throat, I cough, – The best thing you can do is offer a bit of self-disclosure.

– What do you mean by self-disclosure? she asks challengingly, sitting forward in her seat, pushing her long dark fringe out of her eyes. Yes, this big hoor would take some satisfying right enough, and I'd fuckin relish the challenge. Fuckin relish it, I kid you not.

– Tell him something about yourself. Play along. Turn up the heat. Up the stakes. That's the way to do it. Don't make up any nonsense, he'd probably be able to work it out. Just draw him in. That way you have control. He becomes the victim. Force him to confront his own need. Let the hunter become the hunted, so to speak.

Bunty's nodding with grim enthusiasm and our gaze is locked upon each other. I can feel the electricity flashing between us. I hold it for a second, just until she starts to look slightly concerned, then I turn to Bladesey: – We'll nail this creepy bastard Cliff. No danger, then I swivel back to her: – We'll get him Bunty. Cliff, I say, not looking at him, – I want you to take special care of this lady, this very, very brave lady. Our eyes lock again and there's a connecting laser beam of sexual energy shooting out from both our pupils.

– Oh I will, he says dutifully, and as I turn to face him, I can sense Bunty's look of contempt at his assurance, but I don't want to collude with it. Not yet.

– I feel so much happier now. Thank you so much Bruce, she smiles. The big cow stands up to move to the kitchen, allowing me an inspection of the goods. There's plenty of buttock-meat in those black leggings and a pair of tits you could lose yourself in.

– Not at all, thank your good hubby here, my pal Cliff. Low friends in high places, what would we do without them, eh Bladesey boy?

– Very true Bruce, Bladesey tries to come over all sage, but only sounds insipid. I look out of the windae behind this wearying, unsubstantial figure and sure enough, the snow's starting to fall.

I make my excuses and leave. It's Saturday, but Hearts are away today, so I elect to go into the station and get some more OT on the board. Time and a half. Can't be sniffed at. In fact, looking at my diary I see that I told the investigating team to be there for a briefing. I don't know why. I think it was because I overheard Drummond saying to Karen Fulton that she planned to do her Christmas shopping today. Think again dykeface!

Turning Off The Gas

HQ is the usual fuckin waste of time. I head to my office and force down two cups of black coffee before my briefing. Toalie has started to really fuckin mess up my heid big-time with this inclusion of Amanda fuckin Drumstick in my investigating team. I'm trying to brief the cunts and all I can hear is that high whine in the background, she's obviously nipped at being dragged in here today.

– So the situation we have is that on the night of Efan Wurie's murder, we've established that Gorman and Setterington, two known thugs with a record for organised violence, and I stress the organised, were in the vicinity of Jammy Joe's disco. Nobody saw them in the disco of course, but then they wouldn't. You know the reign of terror these thugs have imposed on the social life of this city . . . the best approach is to keep them in our sights and see what they're getting up to. We know their MO. So: what are they doing differently? Who are they seeing? We should also be leaning on the witnesses more, the people who were in the club: Mark Wilson, the doorman, Phil Alexander, the owner, those two girls Sylvia and Estelle . . .

– I disagree, she's saying.

Who the fuck cares what you think, ya fuckin silly wee hoor. Just let me do my fuckin job please.

– Really? And why, might I ask? I smile.

— Well, I remember at Tayside . . . she says, and then starts rambling on about some unconnected, irrelevant shite which happened in her last job at fuckin Tayside. Tayside. What ever fuckin well happened there? A sheep got shagged or something. That's big-time crime up there. Besides, she wis only thaire for ten minutes as an apprentice tea-boy's part-time assistant or something like that. She's going on about how this investigation presents an ideal opportunity to build bridges with the wog community and all that shite. It's fuckin bananay boats we want tae be building for these cunts; tae send them back tae whair they fuckin well came fae. I'm no having any ay this shite.

— To reiterate, I think the correct approach in this investigation . . . I begin.

— With all due respect Bruce, that approach has hardly been fruitful so far, she challenges.

— Thank you for that helpful comment. I've been given the responsibility for heading up this investigation. Until this arrangement changes, this is the approach we'll be taking, I frostily inform her.

Cheeky wee hoor. Needs a good fuckin seein tae, that cow.

Anywey, she starts wittering on again, daft cunt that she is. So at the end of the briefing, we've agreed that *she'll* build the bridges with the wog groups, which is fine by me cause I've no intention of listening to some jungle-bunny giving it loads with their chip-on-the-shoulder shite. I head off downstairs thinking about calling Bunty, but Gus comes in.

— Bruce, I just had an anonymous call. Male, young. Tells me that Setterington, Gorman, Liddell and one other guy were in the club that evening.

I know that you fuckin muppet. That'll be Ocky, the cowardly wee rat-bag. Worse than useless unless he grasses up in court which he won't do as it would mean the end of the cunt's sorry life.

— Right Gus.

— What do you want tae dae?

— It's the auld story, eh Gus? Nae cunt saw them. Nae cunt

will stand up in coort and say that they were there. I think I'll check out that wee hoor that works in the flooir shoap, that Estelle Davidson. She's a tough wee cunt, but she's the yin tae lean oan. I don't get the impression that Sylvia knows much. Drummond gies them the soft soap though. It's no a wimmin's support group for silly wee lassies we're running, it's a fuckin murder investigation.

Yep, I'll do that, then Ray and I will check on Ocky. That's after I've been tae the bogs with my copy of the *Sun*.

It's a page three stunner the day, and she's no unlike that wee Stephanie Donaldson bird that gied ays the gam. April from Newcastle. I've heard about coals to Newcastle, but ye certainly dinnae have tae take any *hole* tae Newcastle if it's aw like that.

The graffiti today:

KAREN FULTON TAKES IT UP THE ARSE

Don't recognise the writing.

C'mon baby . . . Bruce is here.

It's your big night . . . that's it . . . come on . . . I pull out my stiff, flaky cock. There's a bit of a pong as the helmet pops up, throbbing red raw, pushing past that discoloured foreskin. My fuckin nuts are so itchy . . . phoa . . . come on baby . . . that wanker of a doctor and his fuckin creams . . .

Don't think about that

. . . phoa baby . . . this is so good . . . oohh ooohh oooohhh . . . April from Newcastle ooohhh you're a reet bonnie lassinaw . . . oh ya fucker that ye are . . . ooohhhh . . . here I come . . . phoahh . . .

FUGGHHHKIGHNNN BINGO!

Oohh ooohh . . . phoa ya cunt . . . I let the spunk drip on to my thighs. Its alkaline properties might do the rash good, it won't do it as bad as that cunt Rossi's stupid creams anyway. They should sack incompetent doctors. If we couldn't cut it on the force that would be us in deep shit but these cunts get away with murder cause they've never had to put themselves on the line. The same rules apply or fuckin well should at any rate.

I sniff the crotch and thighs of the black flannels. There is a low, thick hum of stale sweat punctuated by the occasional sharp whiff of pish. Oh for a decent laundry service. Right now I need a bird who can cook and clean more than I need one who can suck and fuck. Of course, the dream ticket would come with all those attributes. A Carole substitute, until she starts to see sense which won't be long. It never is.

Karen Fulton takes it up the arse. Hmm. I've never fucked her up the arse. Fucked her up the cunt right enough, but that's hardly an exclusive club. The last time I had her was after Princess Diana's funeral. I got her three sheets and did the business with her. Fults has been know tae put it aboot awright, at Christmas and leaving perties and that, but the graffiti seems like wishful thinking to me, probably written by some inadequate like Toal.

I cross out KAREN FULTON and write BOB TOAL in its place. I stare at my handiwork for a bit and get a breathless fit of the giggles which immobilises me as the tears stream down my face.

I go outside and wash my hands but I can't get my nails properly clean. I look at my jaw in the mirror and rub the bristle. I need a good shave

00000000000000000000000
00000000eat0000000000000
000000000000000000000000
000000eat Mine Host 0000
000eat0000000000eat0000
00000000000eat0000000
00000000eat000000000000
000eat00000000000000eat000
000000eat0000000000000
0000eat000000000000000
000000000000000000000
000000000000000000000
eat, the Self needs nourished
00000000000000eat000000
000eat0000000000yes000

108

Simple pleasures. The fan heater under my desk is blowing out hot air against my leg as I recover from that Sherman Tank with a strong cup of coffee and a Kit Kat and a doughnut from Crawford's. The phone interrupts me. It's an outside line as well. It's not her. Not Carole.

It's *her*.

I told her never to phone here. Never. – I told you *never* to phone here, I say to her. – I'm in the middle of a serious investigation.

– I'm sorry . . . I had to talk to you. About what you said a couple of weeks ago, did you really mean it?

What is this fuckin spastic on about? – What? What was that?

– The other week Bruce . . . you told me you loved me? Remember? Her voice drops an octave. – Or was that just something you made up because you thought I wanted to hear it?

It was made up because I had a stiffer and a standing prick hath no conscience. And if that standing prick is attached to Bruce Robertson then it hath less than no conscience. You can't afford a conscience in this life, that has become a luxury for the rich and a social ball and chain for the rest of us. Even if I wanted one, which I certainly do not, I wouldn't have the faintest idea as how to go about getting one. Can you buy one from the record bar at Woolie's?

This is a dodgy one though: this cow's showing dangerous signs of intelligence. The thing is, I could handle another shot at that stupid, spasticated hoor. – I don't think that was what I said. What I said, if you remember, was that I could fall in love with you easily. But I also said that if I gave you love, spiritual love, you would have to be strong enough to take it. Remember?

There's a long silence, then she finally squawks, – I remember . . .

She remembers fuck all. Full of fuckin vallies or Prozac or whatever some Rossi-style anything-for-a-quiet-life quack has given her for her nerves. – I told you to go away and come back when you're strong enough. Cause I'll give you love awright. Ah'll give you all the love in the world. More love than you can ever imagine . . .

What the fuck is her name again . . . Hurley's missus . . . Brigitte . . . Sarah . . . Chrissie! – Chrissie . . . oh Chrissie . . . look . . . you have to be strong enough to take it . . . I let my voice quaver a bit, – . . . because if I give it and don't get it back, it's going to tear me apart . . .

Gus comes in and moves to the end of my desk, picking up my almost empty Hearts mug and pointing over to the kettle. I give him the thumbs-up. At least he's picked up the right cup this time. There's a funny gasping sound down the receiver which ignites into Chrissie's bleat. – Bruce . . . I'm so sorry . . . I just need to know where I stand. It's just with Bob and you . . . and I mean, what about Carole?

– This is *not* about Carole. Fortunately, she's at her mother's at the moment. This is about *me*, *Bruce*, and *you*, *Chrissie*. If there is a you and me. If there is a you and me, *then* we talk about Carole. Until there is a you and me, in a real sense, then Carole is my business and my business alone.

There's a pause. That fluorescent strip light's flickering again. No wonder I feel fuckin sick in here. Can those penny-pinching cunts no spend fuck all but sweeties on simple fucking maintenance? Gus comes over and dumps a full mug of coffee on my desk.

– Bruce . . . I need to see you. I've just felt so alone since I walked out on Bob. I've even been thinking of going back to him . . . you said that Carole's away . . . can I come over and see you tonight? Please . . .

I reach into my drawer and pull out another Kit Kat from the cellophane pack of eight. The cunt who invented the Kit Kat ought to be fuckin well knighted. I get through loads of them. Fuck knows why I dinnae put on loads ay beef. Fast metabolism, I suppose. – Aye. Awright. But I'll tell you one thing Chrissie. I am not, repeat not, in the mood for mind games. I'm not going to be exploited by you because I've made my feelings for you

plain. I'll keep a tight rein on these feelings until I get some spiritual commitment back.

The spiritual caird. It had tae be played. They always fall for
that one, they just cannae help themselves. I hear her voice thin
down to a gasp. – I need to see you, to talk face to face. I'll be
round tonight. When's good for you?

– Make it eight, I tell her, before signing off and putting the
blower down. – Getting rode, getting rode, getting rode, I sing
softly to myself, to the tune of 'Here We Go'. I wave semi-
euphorically over at Gillman and Inglis who've just come into
the office. Gillman gives a curt nod, that cunt never displays
emotion, but Inglis gives me a big, flouncy wave which sets off a
feeling of nausea in my stomach.

Chrissie tonight. Oh well, at least I've sorted out a ride.
Hardly a hassle-free one though. I'm hoping it's going to be better than it was the last time. She was a funny cow, the camera
seemed to excite her, but when I got out the vibrator she started greeting and going on about Bob and how her life was in a
mess. You can never fathom some fanny.

I look at my Scottish Police Federation calendar. December
the fifth. Not that long to Christmas, but fuck that crap, the winter's brek in the Dam comes first. That fuckin dull calendar. I had
a top one last year but then that memo came round from
Personnel, doubtlessly initiated by arid-twatted dykes like
Drummond, stating that 'pin-ups' were to be banned. Some
fuckin twaddle about negative images of women. If a shaggable
bird in the buff is a negative image, then what the fuck counts as
a positive one? A fuckin boot like Drummond in a polis uniform?
I think not. Same rules apply.

The nausea won't go away and I have to get out of here early.
Ray Lennox is out stalking the hippy community Sunrise fuckers
at Penicuik so there's nobody I can skive off with. I don't trust
Gillman, and Clell's lost the plot with all this Traffic bollocks. I
decide to head up town, and go for a little stroll. The town is
mobbed out with Saturday shoppers looking for Christmas bargains. You can almost breathe in the raw greed which hangs in the

air like vapour. As the late afternoon darkness falls, the lights look tacky and sinister.

The scene of the crime. Here I am, walking up the Playfair Steps. A young jakey, in filthy, threadbare clathes, holey trainers and sucking on an old purple tin, hopefully holds a styrofoam cup out at me. — Job Centre's yon wey mate, I point towards the West End.

— Merry Christmas, he says.

— You n aw mate, I smile. — Could be a cauld yin but. I'd check in there for a few weeks if ah wis you, I point at smug grandeur of the Balmoral Hotel, — lit room service take the strain. You know it makes sense.

The jakey shoots me a look of anger which can't conceal an underlay of sheer terror as he contemplates a cold season on the streets, and quite possibly the end of his miserable life. Still, if he gets enough of the old purple tin in him, he won't feel the cold taking him slowly.

I head up to the South Side and think about calling in at Alan Anderson's old boozer in Infirmary Street. I wonder what Alan's doing now. One of our spectacularly average players of the seventies; there was a factory turning them out. It's really busy up the Bridges with schemies purchasing shoddy goods from the wog discount stores and students between classes sniffing around the second-hand record shops.

I try to get a look at the scores in the window of a TV shop. In England Man U., Arsenal, Newcastle, Chelsea and Liverpool all won, so it's as you were. I'm waiting on the Scottish results coming through when a raucous shriek fills the cold air, stripping the flesh from my back. I turn and see a crowd forming across the road. I go over to investigate, pushing past the stupefied ghouls and see a man, about mid-forties, well-dressed, twitching away on the ground in an ugly paroxysm, one arm stiff and clutching his side.

The boy is turning blue and a woman is screaming: — COLIN! COLIN! PLEASE HELP US! PLEASE!

I'm down on my knees at the prostrate figure's side. — What's wrong? I shout at her. He seems not to be breathing. He's pissed himself; a black, wet patch is forming on his groin.

— It's his heart . . . it must be his heart . . . he's got a bad heart . . . oh Colin no OH GOD COLIN NO!

I've got the boy's head back and I'm giving him mouth-to-mouth.

C'mon you bastard

I can feel the life draining from him, the heat leaving the body and I'm trying to force it back into him, but there's no response. His face is white now, he looks like a manikin. I turn to the woman. There's a wheezing birr coming from her own bleached-out face. — What is . . . what can . . .

— Do something . . . please . . . the words seem to aspirate from a hole in her throat.

I shout at the guy, — C'mon mate . . . you cannae just go . . . I turn to the gaping crowd, — Git an ambulance! JUST FUCK OFF OOT THE ROAD!

I'm trying external heart compression, applying the pressure, thudding at the guy's chest, respect and expectation giving way to malevolence as he refuses to respond. I feel his wrist.

There's no pulse.

LIVE

LIVE

LIVE

— You have to live, I say softly to him. His eyes have rolled into his head.

The woman is screaming in my ear, — COLIN . . . OH NO GOD NO . . .

I don't know how long passes as I sit alongside this formless thing lying in the stench of its secretions and I've got the woman's hand in mine. I can hear the sirens and I feel the hand on my shoulder. – It's alright mate. You did more than anybody could do. He's gone. I look up and see a guy with red hair coming out of his nostrils. He's wearing a luminous green waistcoat.

The ambulance guys are taking him away. In a sudden, strident motion, the woman grabs me round the waist, her sweet scent merging with his malodorous reek. – Why . . . he was a good man . . . he was a good man . . . why? At first it feels awkward and invasive, but our bodies settle into a natural convergence, we fit each other like a hand in a glove.

– Was he? Was he? I nod, feeling tears rolling down my cheek and I'm rubbing at my face. The woman is in my arms, her head in my chest. I want to hold her forever, to never let her go.

They take the dead man into the ambulance and we break our embrace and I feel the cold shallowness of isolation as she's led away. I stand up and turn to face the ghouls. It's the same faces all the time. Like that daft film where they all gather for a tragedy.

– What youse fuckin well looking at? What dae ye expect tae see! Go back tae yir shoppin! Gaun! I flash my badge at them, – Police! Disperse!

The dead man is on the trolley and the woman collapses across his chest. That's what the ghouls want a shufti at, like at that Princess Diana's funeral, they want to scrutinise those who really knew her, to drink the misery out of their faces.

Somebody's talking to me. – Who are you?

– Bruce Robertson, D.S. Bruce Robertson, I shout at him. – Lothian's Police.

– What happened?

I look at the guy, – I tried to save the boy . . . I tried, but he just went . . . he just went . . . I tried to save him.

– How did that make you feel?

– Eh? I ask the cunt. – What the fuck . . .

– Brian Scullion, the *Evening News*. I was watching you. You did really well D.S. Robertson. How did you feel when he didn't make it?

I turn away from this spastic and push through the crowd. I

slope down Infirmary Street and head mole-eyed into Alan Anderson's old boozer.

The boy should have stayed alive. That woman, she loved him.

I'm shivering. It was cold out there.

A double whisky keeps the chill at bay. I change to voddy after that though; cunts can't whiff it on your breath in the same way. I knock back of few of those. I'm thinking about the guy. Pushing the life into him, all the time pushing against a greater force. Trying to fill the plugless bath but it's no use, it all just goes.

I leave the bar and find the motor. I swirl some mouthwash around my gob and spit it out on to the frozen snow, watching the clean blue solution indent the white. I rev up the motor and the end slides all over the place as I turn the corner. One spastic beeps me but I'm too pished to bother.

Work however has lost its appeal, not that it ever had any in the first place. I leave the car in the car park for appearances' sake and I knock off early, trudging homewards through the snow before flagging a taxi. Back at the ranch, I watch the scores on the teletext, noting that Hearts have lost three–nil at Rugby Park. I make an effort to clean up, and I manage to throw out some old plates of food and tin foil cartons of curry and chinky. Chrissie arrives early, which annoys me, as the place is still a shit-house. I'm chuffed though, to see that cock-stirring mix of need and devotion in the hoor's eyes. Chrissie's about five-four. I doubt she's above the six-stone mark. She's not so much heroin chic as hospice chic, and looks somewhat less than resplendent in a gaudy yellow blouse and an above-the-knee black skirt which looks like it's made from the same material as my flannels.

She expects me to say something. Wrong! It doesnae work that wey. Silence is golden and sometimes you have to struggle to control it. Any schemie convict'll tell you the same.

– Bruce . . . did you really mean what you said to me earlier, about how you could fall in love with me? she asks.

I'm looking closely at her, at the burst blood vessels around her nose. Fuckin Wurzel Gummidge here. I'm thinking: No chance. — Of course I could, and you know it as well as I do. Don't play the innocent with me. Sit down.

She takes off her coat, sits down on the couch and lights up a cigarette. She's just like one of them, the ghouls that stood by and watched as I tried to bring that boy back. The sickening, passive, idle, grateful ghouls. How does it feel?

— I'm so confused Bruce. It's not been an easy time, she says. I move on to the couch beside her. She's going to see how it feels to have her breath taken away.

— Listen, there's something you should know about me, about how I am . . . I open a button on the hoor's blouse and stick my hand down it. She's like a Belsen horror, all skin and bone. Her eyes have huge, black shadows under them. I look into the pupils and watch them widen in concert with the twinge in my troosers. I take the cigarette from her hand and stub it out in the ashtray. She twitches nervously and looks at me with a strange smile.

— Bruce . . . she says, looking at the smouldering fag.

— Ye ken the thing aboot fags? I ask, pointing to the ashtray with my free hand, sliding my other mitt under her bra and harshly tweaking her nipple. I watch her shut her eyes and gasp a wee bit. — What ye get from fags is an asphyxiation hit. It shuts oaf the oxygen tae the brain. That's the high, I say, tapping her head. Pushing the life in, squeezing the life out. I take my hand out and start undoing her blouse, button by button, and then I take the top button from her skirt and unzip it and I stand up hauling her to her feet with me and the skirt slides off her to the floor, like a piece of doner kebab lamb from the greasy hunk of meat on the skewer. I pull her towards me and stick my hand inside her pants, cupping her arse cheeks, pulling her up against me. I push my mouth to her ear, getting a scent of cat's-pish perfume. — Tell ye something, it's as wild as fuck when ye make love, that oxygen starvation thing. You and Bob ever dae that?

— I don't know . . . we never . . .

— Yis ever turn oaf the gas for each other? Ssssssssss, I say softly, in her ear.

– We . . . no . . . we never . . .

– You want tae play at turning oaf the gas? You daein it for me and me daein it for you?

I'm looking at the black roots at the bottom of her sick yellow hair, which looks like greased straw, the condition totally fucked by cheap dyes. A coffee, fags and vallies tart. There's a factory somewhere that churns them out. Turn left on the outskirts of the Boulevard of Broken Dreams.

– I don't know what it involves . . . she whinges. She's looking at a precipice which she can't really see over, blinded as she is by her despair and her medication.

– It's a wee adventure. In all adventures to different places you need an experienced guide. Let me be yir guide. Put yirself in ma hands. I'd never hurt you, I tell her, and I'm taking down her pants, exposing that dirty big black bush which contrasts starkly with that sick blonde hair. My skin tingles wondrously and the colours of the walls and furnishings seem heightened as I ease her back on to the couch. I loosen my flannels, ignoring a fairly noxious waft and let them fall to my knees. I'm losing weight alright.

I've got the two belts ready, which I retrieve from under the settee. One goes round her neck, the other round mine. I'm idly finger-fucking her and she's getting juiced up. She's a randy hoor awright: her clit's soon as prominent as Ray Lennox's cock. I spread her thighs with my hands and push my cock into her. No sense in wearing a condom because she tells me that she's only been with Hurley for years which is as good as being a virgin. My knob's not feeling too raw. As it inches home I tighten the belt round her scrawny neck. I find my stroke and start giving her it good-style. She's bucking away, getting right into it.

– Ma fuckin belt, I shout, increasing my pace, – turn oaf ma fuckin gas!

She tightens it a bit but her face is going red and twisting into a strange pout as I throttle her and she starts trying to scream: –You're . . . cack . . . cack . . . cack choking . . . cack

. . . me . . . cack . . . cack . . . cack . . . It sounds like an old banger trying to start up, which, I suppose, is exactly what it is.

How far do you have to go to be like that guy at the South Side? Is there a time during the struggle, the struggle for life and breath, when you finally consciously realise that it's all fucked and that you're going for good? How does it feel?

—YOU FUCKIN CHOKE ME THEN! I scream, choking and poking at it, and in the end *I* have to grab my ain belt and turn off *my* ain gas soas that I get there, but she does too and I'm so close to just keeping going, increasing the pressure and she sees it in my eyes for a second and I see the panic in hers and I come hard with an accompanying series of muffled heaves.

I let go and she's pulling the belt from round her neck, I can see the mark it's left and the blood vessels on her eyelids have haemorrhaged. She's trying to fill her dry, stiff lungs with air, but she's crying and laughing and she loves every fuckin minute of it the cow. She was never that far out, not as far out as the boy. He was way out of range. I couldn't bring him back, I did all I could.

How did it make you feel?

We sleep for a bit, as our breathing comes back to normal in unison. When I wake up I'm consumed by an overwhelming urge to be cruel, which I know that if I don't satisfy verbally will end up with me brekking the sow's jaw and as she's polisman's meat, rather than a common-or-garden Roger Moore, that could get a little bit messy administratively and legally speaking. —You're a cow, I state coldly as I sit up on the couch and light up one of her fags, — because I've been fucking you, we've been turning oaf the fuckin gas fir each other and you're my mate's wife. Ken what that makes you in my book? A cow. C. O. W.

I spell it out for the slag.

She looks at me like a wounded deer pleading with me no tae let it have baith fuckin barrels. — Don't say that . . . why are you being like this . . . why . . .

Why? Cause it's games time. — Ken how you're a cow? Ken how? Cause you let ays in here, I point at her minge, — but you'll no let ays in here, I point to her head, — or in here, I point to her chest, – cause that's love. That the now, that was nothing. That was just sad case games, and tae me that is what I'd call a cow, I shake my head. – That was a wee test, and you failed miserably. Failed wi faded colours . . . I take a bunch of her greasy straw hair between my forefinger and thumb to illustrate my point.

Her face seems to bubble and swell as her mouth opens wide. – What are you saying, she cries, – where does that leave us?

– I'm saying that you have to go away and have a good think to yourself about what your feelings really are. Otherwise . . . I'll be quite frank, this is fuckin useless. The same rules apply. Will you do that Chrissie? Will you do that for me? Because I can't sort out your head. Only you getting in touch with your heart can do that. If you just want fucked, I explain, flipping up a palm, – no problem, come roond, ah'll do the business. But I find it all a wee bit sordid, especially as I feel we could have a lot more.

– I just feel so confused . . . you're confusing me . . . she bleats.

– I shake my head slowly and sadly, – We're aw fuckin confused. Right now, I think you'd better go.

– I want to stay with you Bruce. We need to talk!

I move my head in a dismissive manner. I had planned to go up the club at Shrubhill tonight. A couple of civilised beers to relax. Socialising within a perfectly legal framework and long may it so remain. – Chrissie, I'm working tonight. Backshift. I'm investigating a murder. That's as in M-U-R-D-E-R. In my line of work that spells: S-E-R-I-O-U-S. I watch her incomprehending look. I do not think that the penny has dropped yet. – Serious. Which means I have to get my A-R-S-E into G-E-A-R. That's the situ.

The hoor starts w
fish supper doon the
thank fuck. I pad to
cram a fistful of del
haddock in golden

{
0000000000000000
00eat00000eat0000000
0000000eat0000000eat00
00000000eat0000000eat000
00000yes00000000yes00000
000000000000000000000000
}

in mind to get a
while she's away,
at the Dell, and
d tender white
what the doctor, though not that quack Rossi with his aversion to deep fries, ordered. Time to wash it doon with a few bevvies. I go into the Royal Scot and order a pint then call a cab to take me down to the club. When there's a law against that, we'll know that civilisation is truly fucked.

Carole Again

I like to go out. I don't really mind being here at Mum's but she can be very demanding. Still, we all have our crosses to bear. The big problem is that Mum's never really accepted Bruce. She's a bit strange at times. It's a funny thing to say about your own mum but it's true. I hate being up here but it'll just make it all the more exciting when Bruce and I finally get back together.

Stacey's getting me down as well. She's at a funny age.

I remember when I first met Bruce. My sister Shirley was seeing this guy who was on the force. Don, I think he was called. We met him at a pub at the West End and he introduced Bruce as this guy who was up from London where he was in the Met. Bruce and I had both just come out of pretty bad relationships so the pair of us were a little guarded, even though when I first saw him I thought, mmm hmmm. Well, we had a few too many and we ended up back at Don's. It was strange the way Bruce was looking at me in the taxi, I could just feel something happening, I could feel that we would become lovers. When he spoke to me, his dark eyes blazing ... I could feel myself going ... god, I just want to touch myself all over when I think about it.

But no. I restrain myself and I decide to go out.

The street is cold and grey, like so many streets in so

many towns in this country. This wind surges through you, lowering your temperature until you're too numbed to realise how sick and uncomfortable it's made you. And the people: nosey, predatory, always ready to revel in the misfortune of others. One man is looking at me. I know the type. A sleazy middle-aged guy who doesn't do it with his wife any more.

Repressed people; you have to pity them more than anything else. I know, because I was like that before I met Bruce. I still am in lots of ways, although he's brought me out of myself. Bruce realised that I had to come out of myself, needed, even in spite of myself, to come out of myself. That was what our sex club was about.

Bruce knows that our wee games and flirtations only serve to strengthen a *true* love, by making it confront its true nature, making it feel the depths and heights of itself.

He did it for *me*, and it worked.

I'm a different person now.

A better person.

Infected Areas

A lazy weekend. I did get semi-drunk on Saturday night with Lennox who booted a jakey's styrofoam cup into the gutter, spilling his coins doon the Walk. It was such good sport watching the cunt groping around for them. After this I gave him a couple of quid, solely to try and make Lennox feel bad. It didn't work and I regretted the wasted outlay. I laid off the whisky though, which made me feel not too bad Sunday morning, and Sunday was a quiet day.

I thought of Carole a lot. I know what she's up to. She's playing a very, very dangerous game and she doesn't even know it.

Let's hope she comes to her senses soon.

For everyone's sake.

I'm scanning the *Sunday Mail* and I jump as I see a picture of somebody familiar. Black and whi

Fuckin

A panic attack grabs me and shakes me. I feel like a psychic band in my body has been knotted to its tensile limit and twanged and my life-force is shooting for the stars. It reaches a pitch and then stabilises as I gasp and look again, trying to find clarity in the greyness of the newsprint.

I calm down as it's no who I think it is.

It's me.

An old picture.

An old picture and a new caption:

HERO COP IN RESCUE BID
by BRIAN SCULLION

A Christmas shopper tragically died in the arms of his wife yesterday, despite valiant efforts to save him by a hero off-duty policeman who came to his aid.

STUNNED

Shoppers in Edinburgh's busy South Bridge were stunned when retail manager Colin Sim (41) – who has a history of heart trouble – collapsed on the city street. 'We were shocked. He just keeled over', said Mrs Jessie Newbigging (67). 'I was just looking for something for my granddaughter's Christmas. I couldn't believe it. He was just a young man as well.' Her daughter, June Paton (39) of Hawes Road, Armadale, added: 'It's terrible something like that has to happen, especially at Christmas. It makes you think.'

HERO

While Heather Sim comforted her dying husband, a man in the crowd mounted a dramatic rescue bid trying both mouth-to-mouth resuscitation and external heart compression in a vain effort to revive the stricken man, who is the father of an eight-year-old son. 'The boy was a real hero, he tried everything in the book to bring the guy back,' said Billy Gibson (21). He added: 'I was feeling a bit sorry for myself as I have just been made homeless and have been sleeping rough, but something like this makes you realise just how lucky you are. Now I'm determined to enjoy my Christmas.'

SHOCK

Mr Sim was dead on arrival at the Infirmary. The hospital spokesman said: 'It was a severe attack. There was nothing anybody could do.' The police hero, Detective Sergeant Bruce Robertson of Lothian's Constabulary said: 'I tried my best to save him, but he just went.' Student Janet Onslow (19) added: 'I think we're all a bit shocked. One minute you're here, the next you're gone. It just goes to show.'

How did that make me feel?

It made me feel like watching one of Hector The Farmer's videos, then going out for a pint and a bar lunch at the Royal Scot, and reading the rest of the papers.

In the Royal Scot they have a wonderful fire going, giving off a roasting heat. After a filling roast beef, mashed potato, carrots, sprouts and gravy, the oxygen leaves my brain and the heat and the flame and the clicking sounds of cutlery on crockery become mesmerising. I can see them in the fire, the demons; their flickering, mocking dances as I recline into the chair. I lift the pint glass of stout to my lips and break the spell. I down the pint.

When I get home I take some sleeping pills and within what seemed like half an hour of unconsciousness it was Monday morning again.

Monday again. The phone drags me out of a stupefying sleep. It's Gus. He wants to make an early start. Yes, he likes to keep the credits rolling during the winter so that he's flush when the weather breaks and the gowf becomes a possibility.

There's a few messages on the machine, from people who read the piece in the *Mail*. – It's Chrissie. Congratulations Bruce, if you know what I mean. Phone me. Chrissie. – Well done Bruce . . . it must have been harrowing. Bladesey. – Bruce. Bob Toal. I'm sorry, but well done anyway. Toal. – I'm proud of you. Call me. Shirley. – Whatever happened to, all of the heroes, all the Shakespearoes . . . a coked-up Lennox sings.

I go to the toilet and give my hands another good wash and scrub in the sink. It's hard to get all the shit off them. I give the black flannels a chance to air, and put on a fawn pair. There's an old curry stain on them, but I manage to get most of it off, using Stacey's facecloth.

Then I head outside, taking the ice-scraper to the Volvo's windscreen. Julie Stronach's visible in her front window, straining to put a bauble on the Christmas tree she's just erected. Just erected? She can come next door and see if she can get mines up!

I'm getting a good decko of those full tits in that tight, white t-shirt. She catches me staring so I give a neighbourly wave, and hold up the can of windscreen defroster in one hand and the scraper in the other and let my shoulders rise. Julie smiles with cautious empathy. I get in the motor, sticking on Led Zeppelin's *Houses of the Holy*, and head for HQ to rendezvous with Gus who's just getting out of his own motor in the car park. I wave and he gets into my passenger seat. His nose is red with the cauld. — Well done Bruce. That must have been pretty terrible, Saturday likes, he says.

— Worse for the boy, I say.

We're off down to Leith, sitting in the motor outside yon wee Estelle's flower shop and who should come in but Gorman. It gets us off the subject of the boy that died. — I spy strangers, I smile at Gus.

Gus decides to nick into Crawford's while I keep shoatie. — Two sausage rolls Gus, one buttered roll, a portion ay chips and a vanilla slice plus coffee.

I start thinking about that graffiti in the bogs last week.

He returns with the goodies and we sit waiting for Gorman to depart. — Thing is Gus, that Karen Fulton, she wis a game cow at the start. The force bike she wis called, doon at the South Side. These fuckin hoors are ey on aboot equality. How the fuck did she git oot ay uniform? Ah'll tell ye how: shaggin fuckin Toal. Now she's above aw that, in wi that lesbo crew in Personnel. Every time they drop thir drawers they git a promotion, every time we do, it's a disciplinary. What fuckin equality is thir in that?

Gus laughs and goes, — Right enough Bruce.

This cunt'll never get a promotion. You have to spell things oot tae him. — Ah'm no saying that ah'd like tae shag Toal mind you, some price tae pey for a promo that, I grin, — but the principle's the same. Fulton now though, just look at her: snooty fuckin cow, willnae mix it wi the likes ay us. Senior cock only. Thir wis a time when ye only hud tae paint three stripes oan yir willie and she wis desperate tae pack it between her thighs.

—Yir an awfay man Bruce, Gus coughs in laughter. A good old boy, even if a bit slow. I suddenly get an uneasy feeling. That was a mistake mentioning both Fulton and Toal to Gus. He's probably seen the graffiti in the bogs as well. I'll be fuckin prime suspect now. Luckily Gus's mind isnae sharp enough, even in the narrow, proscribed, polis wey.

I'll hand it tae that cunt Ghostie Gorman. The fuckin evil little albino twat has the good grace tae leave twenty minutes later, after we've had our scran, and without any flooirs. — Never reckoned that cunt tae be the romantic type, I smile at Gus.

— Bingo, Gus says softly, veteran polis instincts tuned tae alertness. Aye, the auld boy might be slow, but he can smell prey. You never lose that.

This is what makes the job worthwhile, the scent of spastic schemie blood, even better if it comes in the shape of quality fanny. It's like two comes with one stroke.

I wait for Gorman to get out of sight and then I go in and have a look at the flowers, the prettiest one of all the one behind the counter. — Hello Estelle, I smile at her. There's an auld wifie in the shop as well. She looks challengingly at Estelle who's lost some of her hard cow composure, the juice draining from the hoor's tank slightly. The auld wifie raises her eyebrows and goes into the backshop.

— How's business?

— Sawright, she says, brushing her hair back in a nervous gesture.

— Funny, jist saw a guy come oot the shoap empty-handed. Did ye no huv nowt in his line?

— Nuht . . . she says doubtfully, avoiding my eyes and making out that she's tidying up.

—Whae wis eh?

— Dinnae ken, eh wis jist eftir a bouquet . . . changed ehs mind bit . . .

At this point, right oan cue, the wifie comes out and says, — If you're gaunny spend ay day talkin tae yir boyfriends, dae it ootside the shop n ah'll take it oaf yir pey!

Estelle gets a beamer at this one. — Listen, I think we should have a wee blether. Crawford's? Either that or ah haul ye doon the station now. Whit's it tae be?

— Awright, she says, coming out with me and making a big thing of shivering in her overalls.

We head for Crawford's, and I wink at Gus who's still in the car. We sit down with coffee. I have another vanilla slice. — Can I treat you to one of these? I ask.

— Nuht, she says dismissively.

She sits down and lights a fag. — I've done nowt wrong, she tells me.

Aye, right.

— Wasting police time, withholding information, possibly harbouring a suspect. You fuckin well listen, I point at her, — It's tell ays what ye ken, or you're gaunny be up in court. It's up tae you. If ye dinnae want tae be making soft toys in Cornton Vale fir the next year ah'd find that tongue if ah wis you hen, and ah widnae be takin ma time aboot daein it.

She's bending a bit here. I can tell. She lowers her heid.

— You gaunny co-operate?

— Look, ah ken that guy, fae the clubs n that. They call um Ghostie. Eh wis one ay the guys youse showed ays the photae ay that time. Eh jist comes in sometimes, tae talk aboot the clubs n music n that.

— Jist a wee two-person musical appreciation society. That's nice.

She lifts her head up and focuses on me in a tough stare. — It's no like that. Thir's loads ay people ah ken and half-ken that come in tae blether aboot what they've been up tae, in the clubs n that.

— So how often does this boy come in and see ye?

— Maybe once a fortnight . . . depends.

She's a fuckin hard nut awright. — And he was at Jammy Joe's oan the night of Mr Wurie's murder?

— Ah dinnae ken . . . look, ah'm oot nearly every night. Ah dinnae mind who's oot everywhaire and who isnae.

— Busy social life. They must pey ye well in that flooir shoap.

— That's ma business, she says. This cow has recovered her composure quickly. A real hard case, but what a fuckin little doll n aw. She's looking at me intently. — Ah'm sure ah ken you fae somewhere . . . she says, almost accusingly.

— Ye soon will, ah'll tell ye that for nothing. We'll be watching you Estelle, you and your boyfriend.

— Ehs no ma boyfriend, she snaps.

— Hope no for your sake. Gaun, git back tae yir shop, ah nod to the door. She gets up and casts another glance at me before she leaves. This wide wee cow needs fuckin well sorted oot. Sorted oot good and proper. Nice erse on it, even through the overalls.

My genitals are hot and tingling, so I head to the café bog with my *Sun* and thrash off to Tara from Portsmouth, the image of Estelle's receding arse complementing Tara's smallish but solid tits. I spurt in double-quick time. I then give my sweaty hole a good rubbing with the bog paper and my arse a good clawing. I'm seeing Rossi in a bit, as no progress has been made with the fool's creams.

I get back out and drop Gus off at the station. I drive out tae Rossi's and I stick on a Michael Bolton compilation tape I made. 'How Am I Supposed to Live Without You' off of *Soul Provider* comes on, and I sing my heart out. Then Bolton's version of 'When A Man Loves A Woman', which is ten times better than any nigger shite, comes blasting out and by the time I get to Rossi's surgery and park the Volvo I'm in better spirits.

They think that they can drag Bruce Robertson down? All the schemies, coons and what have you? Get fuckin real you sad cunts!

— I've been applying that cream you gave me, Doctor Rossi, but it just makes me worse.

— Mmm, says Rossi, — If you just drop your trousers.

I comply, wondering whether this cunt's an arse bandit. It seems that the bastard can never wait to get my fuckin keks off. Rossi, of course. Italian. Pape. These cunts are all shirt-lifters.

That's why the population of Ireland's so fuckin low. Tattie famine my hole, it's cause all these fenian cunts are erse-shaggers. Same fuckin rules. Rossi, well, I ken it's his job, but what a perfect cover for brown-bombers.

— Yes, yes, the infected area is more widespread. It's now all over the thighs as well as the testicles. Yes. Are you avoiding foods with a high fat content?

— Aye . . . I tell him. The cunt expects me to fuckin starve.

— Well, I think we have to change creams, he says, writing out a new prescription. — I know it's difficult, but try not to scratch the infected area. These look . . . well, they look like nail marks. I can't stress enough the importance of washing and changing underwear on a regular basis. Cotton briefs preferably, or better still, boxer shorts for the circulation of air.

I need a fuckin washing done. That slag's abandoned me; trying to fuckin well kill me! She kens I cannae work that fuckin machine. Huvnae hud a proper cooked meal in ages, a roast or something. When a man loves a woman right enough. I fuckin well followed her oot tae Australia. I fuckin well came back here for her. When a man loves a fuckin woman.

Trouble is, *they* dinnae love men!

— The thing is, ah'm eatin like a horse Doc, but I'm still losing weight . . . I'm worried I might have picked up something . . .

— You mean like an STD?

— Nah . . . well, aye. . .

— Have you been having different sexual relationships?

I smile at him. — You know how it is Doctor . . . normal heterosexual red-blooded male . . .

He looks at me strangely and I wonder if this cunt *does* know how it is.

— I want a urine sample, but . . . Rossi produces a plastic carton with a lid, — what I'd also like from you is a stool sample.

This cunt must be a fuckin perve of the highest order. I'll have to give Inglis his number. — What for? I ask coldly.

— Concerning the issue of your weight, I think you may have worms. Tapeworms.

— What does that involve?

— They are harmless parasites, but they can be hard to get rid of.

— I'll go to the toilet now, I stand up.

— That won't be necessary . . . he says, — in your own time . . .

— I can do it now, I tell him, exiting. I head to his bog and fill the container with sludgy lager and curry shite. The cunt wants shite, ah'll fuckin well gie him shite!

I leave Rossi with my crap and pish and drive into town. Worms. It doesnae bear thinkin about. My thoughts are interrupted by a message from Ray, telling me that it's going off down the flats. Colin Moss went up there carrying a holdall, so the D.S. boys've got the sniffer dugs down there and are raring to do Moss, Richards and Allan.

The roads are pretty bad and I'm shaking at the wheel, worried that I'm going to miss all the fuckin action. Fuck looking for somebody who topped a coon, this is real poliswork. I stick my light on the top of the car and hit the siren as I tear doon Leith Walk.

OUT MA FUCKIN WEY YA CUNTS!

By the time I get down to the flats, a huge crowd has gathered outside. Some jakeys from the lodging house sit huddled on to a bench, drinking strong lagers and fortified wines and making insulting comments at two young uniformed spastics, one whose ears glow red with the cold and the humiliation. Some other polis are trying to cordon the area off and disperse the crowd. I see that something's on the ground. As I get closer it looks like the remains of an animal but it has been ripped open and crushed beyond recognition, strewn all over the slushy pavement. I look towards the heavens suspecting our old friend gravity and the flats. This was probably last year's model whose collar had grown a little tight and was jettisoned to make way for the incoming Christmas puppy dog.

Then I clock Ray, who looks a bit sheepish and tells me that the dug was one of ours, a sniffer in the advance party. I savour the prospect of an alliance with the RSPCA, destroying the peace-loving, caring credibility of these hippy, squatting cunts. They murdered that poor animal! Ha! Gotcha!

Ray nods towards George Mackie, the dug-handler, who's sitting on the pavement being comforted by a poliswoman. I ken George from the craft. Lodge St John, Corstorphine.

– Bruce . . . he wheezes . . . – eh's gone Bruce . . . Pedro's away . . . ma Pedro . . . the best sniffer oan the force . . . eh's gone . . .

– What happened George, I ask, bending over him.

– Eh found a sheet ay acid . . . but they'd hidden it in the kitchen . . . he slipped his leash . . . they hid the acid wi these dug biscuits . . . poor Pedro ate the lot, Mackie moaned, sounding himself like a dog in pain. – Perr Pedro . . . eh jist totally loast it . . . eh freaked and even turned on me! Me Bruce! I had him since he was a puppy . . . the runt ay the litter . . . I admit that I truncheoned him . . . it wis self-defence Bruce . . . eh just lept oot the windae . . . the best dug ah've ever hud . . . the best sniffer on the force . . . fourteen floors up, eh never stood a snowball's chance in hell . . .

I move back over to Ray. – Where's Moss? Ms Richards? Mr Allan?

Lennox points across to this trio of crusty bastards looking smug and getting into a BMW. The car's being driven by Conrad Donaldson, Q.C.

– Nowt we can do Bruce, Ray says. – Listen Bruce, c'mere the now . . . Lennox furtively gestures over to a tenement stair door, far from the crowd. – I fucked up. I had the sheet ay acid to plant and I was about tae dae it when the fuckin dug ripped it out my hand . . . he showed me a toothmark on one of his fingers. – George was in the living room and it came intae the kitchen . . . he should have been with it at all times . . . he didnae follow procedure.

– What was in Moss's holdall? Can we no do them for that?

– A fucking Christmas pudding. I didn't even bother confiscating it to take it doon the lab for analysis. The smart cunt was straight on to Donaldson, who was here within ten minutes. They were laughing their fuckin heads off, Lennox smirks slightly, seeing the funny side. I don't. I walk away in a raging fury and get back into the car.

That night I go out for a drink with Clell, who's going on about his new job in traffic.

– It's great tae be free fae Serious Crimes Bruce, he says, raising his glass. – It's given me time tae think about what I want tae do with my life. That's the problem wi Serious Crimes, you shut off too much. You just go through it . . . he makes his palms go parallel and forward like a train.

– Well, you'll have plenty of time to think sitting with those vegetables in traffic, I tell him.

Clell looks closely at me. There's a slight tick in his eye. It seems as if I've upset him.

– That's just the way I want it, he bleats.

Cunt thinks that his worries are over and that he can rub our faces in it because he's got a job as a vegetable. Wrong! We are not interested in the trivial concerns of one Mister Andrew Clelland.

I make my excuses after a bit and head hame.

The Lie Of The Land

Tom Stronach, or Tommy Stronach, as they first called him when he broke through from the Hearts youth set-up in 1984, is my friend of sorts by virtue of his being my next-door neighbour. Tom Stronach: two Scotland caps, the first in 1988 due to several call-offs, which resulted in the largely unheralded through-ball for Coisty or some other west-coast fucker to score the winner in a three-goal thriller in Belgrade, against a fancied Yugoslavian side; well, fancied to beat Scotland at any rate. Then a spell in the wilderness followed by a further cap against Northern Ireland during his swan-song season of 1990–91. That was his last chance to do something, with Everton and Sunderland reputedly making offers which were turned down by the 'ambitious' board who, like Tom, spent another few trophy-less years in limbo. The spastics ought to have taken the cash: it was to be Stronach's last season as even a minor force in the game.

Alimony cases and paternity suits have taken their toll on his greengages and Tom's had to make the socially humiliating climbdown from Colinton Village with wife number three, to this pokey Gumley's job. He's a thick cunt whose only attrib-utes is being able to kick a ball badly and he has the nerve to think that *he's* slumming it, living next door to a law enforce-ment professional.

I'd taken the morning off to watch the female gymnastics on telly. There was some pubescent ex-commie Tony Hatch worth forty wanks. I couldn't really get into it though; when I woke up I wanted to hear something by the Michael Schenker Group but I couldn't decide between *Assault Attack* and *Rock Will Never Die*. After making myself a large fry-up and lighting the fire, I decide to take neither option and go for *Built To Destroy*. I do a bit of air-guitar work and make a mental list of the women I'd like to reduce to a state of slavery and bondage, Drummond coming in at num-bihr one. I check the post and there's fuck all from Chelmsford. You're keeping me waiting Tony. I don't like waiting. Loneliness and melancholy settle in after this and the breathless strains of the stoat-the-baw gymnastics commentator irritates and I decide to seek company next door. The newspapers are still lying around from the weekend. I can see that face in the newspaper. I rip out the page and crumple it up before tossing it into the fire. I quickly re-read the *Sunday Mail*'s postscript of Saturday's nil–three débâcle at Rugby Park.

> A poor performance by the visitors and one which Tom Stronach, in particular, will want to forget. It was his loose pass-back which gifted Killie that decisive second goal, effectively ending the game as a contest.

I go next door and Tom's in, still scanning the video action from the weekend's matches. Not for nothing is he constantly referred to as 'a keen student of the game'. Tabloidspeak for a lazy twat who sits on his arse watching fitba videos aw day.

Tom's wearing his tracksuit. He looks worried. He always does, when he doesn't look stupid, that is. – Awright Bruce, he says. I breeze in, past the spastic.

– Not bad Tom, I say, scanning the house for knock-off. There's some dodgy cunts on her side of the family. I'd ride it mind you, some dirty wee scanties oan the washing line last summer. That's the mark of a real hoor, leaving them on the line like an invitation. Decent fanny use a tumble drier for that sort of thing. I clock a nice lamp, on the teak cabinets Tom had got built recently. Blue and white china porcelain. – Nice lamp.

– Aye . . . Julie bought it. John Lewis's.

Mmm. Seems plausible enough. – What's the game? I point to the screen. Philips' newest model, four speaker quadrophonic sound, thirty-inch screen. Not bad. Checked it out in Tandy the other day. The one next to Crawford's in the centre.

– Belgian League fitba on Eurosport. Taped it likes. Mechelen versus Molenbeck. The Mechelen boy scores a cracker. Watch this!

Tom rewinds the video and this Belgian spastic hits a screaming twenty-five yarder home. They might be boring cunts but they can play fitba.

– Could have done wi some ay that style doon in Ayrshire on Saturday, eh Tom, I gloat, trying, as his face contorts defensively, to force some concern and empathy into my voice, – What went wrong?

Tom shrugs, – Dinnae ask me Bruce, he mumbles, shaking his head.

I consider it prudent to change the subject. – All geared up for the Testimonial?

– Aye! Tom's face lights up enthusiastically, – It's difficult wi the festive period coming up, but the boys on the committee have done a cracking job and it looks like Kenny Dalglish is going to come up and play for at least part of the game.

– Sound, I say, – that should add a couple of thousand oantae the gate. I'm looking for any additions to the CD rack, and sure as fuck Stronach's got the new Phil Collins. I pick it up. – What's it like?

– Brilliant, he says, – the best yit.

– What? I ask incredulously, – Better than *Face Value* or *No Jacket Required*? This spastic doesnae have a clue aboot music.

– Well, concedes Tom, – maybe no *No Jacket Required*, but it's definitely at least as good as *Face Value* and way in front ay *Hello*

I Must Be Going! and *But Seriously* and that last yin, what was that called?

— *Both Sides*, I say.

That's his missus; baith sides . . . dodgy.

— But that widnae be hard, eh?

I suppose Stronach kens his music. I would n aw, if I hud nothing better tae dae than tae sit listening tae shite aw day.

— I see you were in the papers as well though Bruce, Tom grins, picking up the *Mail* and waving that horrible image at me.

I shudder. — Aye . . .

— Must have been awfay, Stronach shakes his head, — . . . here, watch this! he points at the screen, — comin up now, Bergkamp's goal for Arsenal . . .

Dennis Bergkamp controls a Ray Parlour cross with a lovely first touch which serves to deceive the first defender, then he skips past the second one before picking his spot, with the on-rushing goalie stranded. One-nil to thee Ar-si-nil . . .

I have a couple of cans with Stronach to take the edge off my hangover, then I go back next door. I am itching and I need to inspect my genitals. This fucking rash is getting worse. Rossi could be right, it might be something to do with the fried food. I scratch and dig at my thighs and scrotum. I'm thinking that some hoor might have infected me. I might have an allergy to fried food, but it's more likely to be cheese. But I never eat fuckin cheese. I eat all day, but I'm losing weight. Maybe I've got something. Aids of a hoor. Naw . . . it can't be. I'm careful. Only queers and schemies get Aids. Worms, Rossi reckons.

Fuckin worms.

I'm too tired to go in today. Tuesday is a shite day and I've been doing too much OT anyway. Never dae on a Monday or Tuesday what ye can dae on a Saturday or Sunday at double time. That's my philosophy. I take the duvet from the bed and put it over myself on the couch and drift off to sleep watching Stephen Hendry thrash somebody at the snooker. It's as well at least one jambo can get his hands on some silverware, even if it's only at a Mickey Mouse glorified pub game rather than a proper sport.

00000000000 0
0000000000000 0
0000 *eat* 00000
00 *eat for the self* 0
000000 *eat* 0000000
000 *thank you* 00000
0000000000000000

I wake up starvin[ ] 00 *eat for the self* 0 ith Pot Noodles with McCain's oven chips 000000 *eat* 0000000 ottles of cider from the fridge.

I call Bladesey b[ ] 0000000000000000 aying in, comforting Bunty. I bell Ray Lennox but he's out. I can't face the Lodge again the night, but I decide to go out for a drink myself. Might get lucky with some stray fanny in the witching hour. On my way up into town I stop off at the library. I get a hold of a medical book and read about worms. It's fuckin scary. They picked one that was forty fit long out of a boy's arse. I reckon I deserve a drink after reading that.

The pubs are dead as fuck. One Victoria Street bar is like a morgue. It was a popular shop, dead basic, so they spent a fortune modernising it. Then no cunt went, so they spent another wad restoring it, only they restored it to some grand design of what they thought a traditional pub looks like rather than what this one did look like. So still no cunt goes. I'm thinking about Amsterdam and I get a flash of inspiration and phone up Grand Master Frank Crozier at the Lodge and tell him to put the bite into that cunt Toal, explaining that I'm booked up to take my leave in Amsterdam. Frank and I have never really hit it off. He wants to see auld Willie McPhee continue to address the haggis at the Burns supper, and I feel that a change is needed. So there's a wee bit of frost in his voice. One thing about Crozier though: he hates to see wide cunts like Toal who put little in think that they can use the craft when it suits them.

— This brother 00000000000000000 ot a regular attender, I explain. I can hea 00000000000000000 ttitude softening and he vows to sort it 00000000000000000

0000000000000000
0000000000000000
0000000000000000
00000000000000000
00000000000000000

*OOOOOOOOOOOOOOOOOOOOOOOOOOOOOO
OOOOO all this thinking and all this explorative writhing around is starting to pay dividends. I'm learning a lot about myself. There's not that much to know. I live in the gut of my Host. I have an elongated tube-like body, eloquently adapted to the Host's gut. It's indeed ironic that I seem to have no alimentary canal myself, yet live in that of my most generous landlord's. It's my solex which forms the main point of contact between Self and the Host's tissue. Sometimes I feel as if I'm holding on for my grimmest of lives as I continue to eat, ingest and excrete through my skin.OOOOOOOOOOOOOOOO To be quite honest, there is not that much to do around here. So I am thinking that might it not be a more fruitful way to spend my time trying to learn something about the Host? Why not! Mine Host, you continue to fascinate me. You must be leading a far more interesting life than myself, a primitive organism confined to dull, unexciting ritual. Only speculative thought produces the intrigue which adds quality to my limited life. So I will sift through the food the Host ingests, probe the cells of the skin that I'm so attached to, assimilate all the bonnie data from the braw yin's consumption patterns and physical condition. To do this means I need to eat and eat and eat OOOOOOO*

The old stor   et Toal off my
back, but the   eremonial role,
and to get wit   h will spread to
my face before   y fanny will look
at me, destined   ne like Bladesey.

139

I'm fuckin starvin

to be bothered making anyth n rolls with that scrambled eg magic! The nosh sets up a en going into the office doesn't s ast bearable. Not that a great deal of progress has been made. That little fanny-rat Ocky has vanished off the face of the Earth, and Lennox is of zero fucking assistance. He started bleating to me this morning aboot being stretched on this hippy stalk. A fuckin waste of time. Big operators flooding the city with smack and three-quarters of the cunts we bang up are daft schemies or students with a wee bit of hash or a few pills for their pals. Still, it serves its purpose and keeps the cunts in a constant state of terror and alienation and reminds them that this world was not made for *them*, it was made for *us*. They'll have to do better next time, after the débâcle at the flats. But we'll get the cunts.

What this means is that only that Estelle cow and her mate Sylvia are my means of getting anything on Gorman. I know he was at the club that ni st need to prove it. I drive past the flow by two Crawford's danish pastries and t ee on the stakeout. Fuel for the arduou s due to that cunt.

I blast out Foreigner's *Agent Provocateur* and anyone who hasn't got this in their record collection is worthless scum, although *Inside Information* is actually a better album. It serves its purpose and it blows away some of the cobwebs. In particular the single 'I Want To Know What Love Is' is probably the greatest single ever, well, ballad like . . .

. . . you know I need a little time . . .

. . . a little time to think things ov-uh . . .

I head back to the office, or more specifically, to the cannie. Toal's there, and he looks in a good mood. He has the air of the washhoose bully who's heard a satisfying piece of malicious gossip, but when he sees me he suddenly goes all serious, coming over and giving me a squeeze on the shoulder. I'm hoping that nobody noticed this gesture and I quickly glance around and to my dismay see Gillman's face set in a pitiless mask of loathing.

— Bad luck on Saturday, Toal says in commiseration.

I didn't know that Toal followed the fitba and I'm just about to criticise Stronach's performance, when I realise that he's talking about the guy I tried to save.

How does it make you feel?

— Thanks Bob, I nod. I think it might be a good time to arrange to see him, so I set up a wee meet in his office after lunch. His easy compliance sets up an expectation that I'll get a result out of him regarding my holiday leave. Otherwise, going to the cannie was a mistake. The curry looked good, but turned out to be bland and tasteless. I ate it anyway, but then bought a sausage roll which I smothered in broon sauce and pepper.

Amanda Drummond and Karen Fulton spy me and come across with their salad on their trays. Fuckin salad at this time of year. I can see Fulton wanting to lose a few pounds, but Drummond for fuck sakes. That yin would have to move around in the shower tae get wet. Probably does a good gam though, that's what they say aboot skinny birds. — It must've been terrible Bruce, Drummond shakes her head. She looks earnestly at me and asks, — Are you okay?

I nod, and split the sausage roll with a fork. Fulton gives a tentative, sympathetic smile.

— If you need to talk about it, Drummond lisps.

Aye, right. Tae you? That will be shining bright hen. Dinnae even insult me by pretending you gie a Luke and Matt.

— Not a very pleasant experience, it has to be said, I state in clinical tones, — but the show must go on. I have to see our good friend Mister Robert Toal. If you fine ladies will excuse me, I nod, rising and leaving.

I must try to save people more often. It seems to be not a bad device for attracting the fanny.

But it *is* time to go up to see Toal. He looks furtive as I enter his office unannounced and quickly does a bit of jiggery-pokery on his computer. The cunt'll have his fuckin screenplay on there, and will have just switched it over on to some organisational chart or something. Chancing fucker. – Bruce, Bruce . . . how goes the case? he asks, regaining his composure.

– Bob, I think it's basically cut and dried. Gorman and Setterington were in the area. I know that they were in that club that night. I've seen Gorman acting very friendly with Estelle Davidson. Gus is on surveillance. It's really just a matter of hanging fire and hauling them in.

– Aye . . . the political nonsense has died a bit of a death now. The papers are bored and the top brass are a bit less jumpy. It's as well we didnae panic. A wog's a fuckin wog, eh, he snorts, shaking his head.

– Yeah, I say non-committally. This could be a test to draw me. I'm not getting into this with him. – Bob, I'll come to the point mate. I need a break. I know you wanted leave suspended but I'm going to crack up if I don't get away. The last thing I want to do is to go the way of Busby . . . and that thing at the weekend was the last straw, I almost plead. I hate that light blue paint on the walls in Toal's room. Always makes the place look cold. There's the smell as well, that terrible reek of stale tobacco which seems to have impregnated itself into Toal's skin cells. I mean, I like a fag, but that cunt . . .

– Okay Bruce, okay. I can sanction special leave. I'm prepared to do that in your case only. Considering the unique circumstances, Toal looks searchingly at me, as if he expects some kind of reaction. Of course, he gets none. – Just make sure that everyone on the team is briefed to clean up this case in your absence, he continues, now quite snooty and authoritative as if I don't know what's changed the fucker's mind. Eureka. That wee talk with Grand Master Frank Crozier has paid dividends. He must've put Toal in the picture. The bigger picture.

– Thanks Bob. Appreciated.

Toal kens the lie of the land alright. And Niddrie had better come through with that promotion. It's my job. Yo ho ya cunt that ye are: a holiday followed by a promotion. Most importantly, that daft cow Carole should get her act together and get hooked up to the Starship Bruce Robertson, because that vessel is going places. And there might be very few berths available on that particular craft soon, especially seeing as the wey the fanny's stacking up, I kid you not!

I bell Bladesey to tell him we're on, then drive to the Lothian Road travel agent's which specialise in late bookings to get sorted for the Dam, singing along to Curtis Stigers' self-named debut album which yielded the classic singles 'I Wonder Why' and 'You're All That Matters To Me'. A tidy bird with a crop of long black ringlets for hair does the business for me, the only cloud on the horizon being that the direct flights are full and we'll therefore need to change at Brussels. The lassie tells me that she's never been to Amsterdam before.

— Maybe I'll take you sometime, I smile, rubbing my five o'clock shadow.

She gives me a strained, cheerless grin back. By the time I've got it all booked and confirmed it's been snowing again. My brogues scrunch the styrofoam beads of snow as I get back into the car and head for the East End. I park in Gayfield Square, near the local nick, then I buy a chicken supper from the Deep Sea which I ferociously gorge in the doorway of Bandparts. After that I hit Mathers for a pint. When I get into my third I decide that there is no way I'm going back to that shitehouse today.

I give Bladesey another bell at his office and confirm that I've booked up. I think about calling Bunty from somewhere but I don't want the daft hoor giein Bladesey it tight because I want that wee cunt out on the pish the night to celebrate our trip to the Dam. He's reluctant, but I tell him, if he gets his hole from somebody else (some chance) it'll make him feel better about himself and he might be more attractive to Bunty. If this had any chance of happening and working, no way would I have told him. Actually. I'm starting tae sound like the cunt now. Actually.

So I meet Bladesey in the Guildford and we fling back a few pints followed by a trip to the Indian in Hangover Street. Bladesey has chicken korma, which is par for the course for a wee pansy like him, while I rip through that beef vindaloo like there's nae tomorrow.

We head up to the Ritz Ballroom, tonight being the night for the divorced and separated, i.e.: slags that are desperate for it. And there they are on the flair strutting together round their handbags as Billy Joel's 'Uptown Girl's belting out: all stretch marks and crow's-feet and ragged necks and flab, but fuck it, mutton or lamb, it's aw fuckin meat tae Bruce Robertson, rag week or no, the bloodier the better!

So we take some seats, Bladesey and I, next to these two boilers and they are up for it when we offer to buy them drinks. The dark short one has a nasty look, the look of a cow who's bitter about men; a pseudo lesbian. Probably been with some fucking criminal type who knocked the dopey slut around and it was her own fault because she had neither the brains nor personality to find somebody better. Slags like that can't accept home truths so they often turn dykey. This red-heided hoor though, she looks a game bitch.

— So what's your name then?
— Michelle, she says.
— Where do you hail from Michelle?
— Kirkcaldy.
— So it's Michelle the Fifer? I ask. The silly cow giggles, burps then puts her hand to her mouth. Fuckin sow's three sheets. Her mate still has a sour puss on her. Don't fancy Bladesey's much. — So you're Michelle Fifer? What about your pal? Is she Demi Moore?
— Naw, this hoor says, as the red-head still giggles. The women who come here are so close to hoordom, it's a mere point of detail. Demi Moore. Semi Hoor. I like that, Semi Hoor.
— Well you're like a semi hoor, I tell her.
— What? she says, struggling to hear over the nigger music that's replaced Joel.

—You're like Demi Moore, I shout.

My flattery fails to cut through her lesbian bitterness. Bladesey's trying to chat to her, but he's just making a cunt of himself with his actually this and actually that. I decide to steam the red-heid. — How would you like to go out some time, for a meal maybe?

— Sorry, no, she shakes her head.

— C'mon, we could have a good time, I tell her. — What's your number?

— Look, we're just out for a quiet drink, okay?

—Aw aye, I say, looking disdainfully around the meat market, — just the sort ay place that ye'd go for a quiet drink, eh.

She scowls at me, then turns back to Semi Hoor. That wee cunt Bladesey's talking to the both of them. All I can hear is actually this and actually that.

I go up to the bar to see if there's any stray minge about. I wink at a brown-haired lassie in a green dress but she just looks away in an expression encroaching on disgust. It makes me feel good, so I throw back a nip at the bar. I could handle a bit of charlie right now.

There's a guy who looks like Father Jack out of *Father Ted* and he's with a young, foreign-looking bird. I wonder how much she cost the dirty auld fucker. It makes me think that Carole had better watch. It's easy these days to upgrade old models with newer, Eastern ones. I was reading in the Sunday paper about some old cunt who used to work for the Electricity Board who traded in his old banger for some premium fresh minge. We're no necessarily talking big bucks either; a Ratners' ring and a plane ticket can do the job in some instances. Of course, she's off by the time the ring falls apart, but you've had your use of her by then. This bird with Father Jack kens the score; grinding up against him, fussing over him, selling illusion as well as sex. For that you pay a lot more. Virtual reality? The rich have had it for fucking years.

I see that Bladesey's still deep in conversation. I go back over and push in beside him.— Bladesey, wee word mate . . . I say. He shifts over.

— What's up Bruce? Nice girls eh, he smiles.

— Watch these cunts. I thought I knew them from some-where. I know their fellas. Scumbags. Bad bastards. They catch you chatting up those slags, they'll fuckin have you.

— Honestly? But they seem . . .

— Fuckin tellin ye man. Keep away fae that trash.

Bladesey loses a bit of interest after that. The slags go away up to dance together, ambling pedestrianly around their hand-bags. — Bruce, he slurs, a wee bit drunk, — mind if I ask you a question?

— Fire away, I snap harshly enough for him not to make it *too* personal.

— What made you join the force?

— Why did I join the force? I repeat, — Oh I'd have to say that it was due to police oppression. I'd witnessed it within my own community and decided that it was something I wanted to be part of, I smile.

I'm certain that Bladesey's wallet is in his jacket pocket. When he hits the bogs I slip it out, removing the best part of two hundred quid which I saw him take from the cashpoint earlier. I quickly replace the wallet.

Bladesey comes back and we leave to go into the now piss-ing wet streets. It's still so cold though. The winds stinging my chafed lips and I think one of my brogues is starting to let in. I nod ahead where a couple of spare fanny are making their way up the road. They look quite young but they might be impressed by the coin. Does nae harm tae fire in.

— Awright girls! I shout.

They turn round. One's no bad at all. Again, Bladesey's I don't fancy. — No bad, the good-looking one says with a cheerfully defiant wariness. I'm instantly well into her: about five-five, dark hair with a fringe, a small turned up nose and lips nicely glossed. It's always a good sign when the honey acknowl-edges first, because the dog'll generally fall into line, few hounds being that choosy about what goes up them.

— Where ye off tae?

– Dunno . . . we were gaunny try tae get intae Jammy's. She gives me a slow, lascivious scan. This lassie is out on the town with debauched intent and her pussy's too itchy for her to be cool about it.

– Sounds good tae me. Tell ye what but, ah'm starving. Anybody fancy a curry? You're welcome to join us, I nod at Bladesey, – On my friend and I.

– Eh Bruce . . . I'm not that hungry . . . we just had a cur . . .

– Dinnae be such a poof Bladesey. Ye kin manage another!

We go to the Balti House and do just that. This is one of the low-life curry gaffs. Everyone in the place is a munchied-up pissheid. The food would be barely edible if you were sober.

The tidy wee bird's well up for a shag. She laughs at everything I say, and the racier I get the more brazen her response. I could sit here aw night and watch her lift the forkfuls of curry to those red lips. Almost. She's going on about some catering course she's doing and how she wants to open a bar-restaurant one day. The hound's saying nothing although she seems keen enough, even with Bladesey making a cunt of himself with all his ums aahs and actuallys. My one though: she's getting rode the night. No danger. Same rules apply.

After the meal I signal for the bill. When it arrives Brother Blades gets a little shock.

– I . . . I . . . don't believe it . . . my wallet . . . it's empty . . . I . . . I . . .

– C'mon Cliff, you don't expect the ladies to pay!

– No . . . I . . .

The dog looks disapproving, but the other, the ride, Annalise her name is, says, – I've got money . . .

– I won't hear of it! I insist, pulling out Bladesey's wad and making a big show of paying.

– I'm ever so sorry . . . I . . . Bladesey stammers.

As the fanny are getting their coats I whisper to Bladesey, who's in some distress, – I telt you about these hoors at the Ritz. Criminals can have vaginas as well as penises Bladesey. Right

147

now they're probably in some shitehoose of a pad in Leith with a cairry-oot of Tennents Super, Babycham and fags, provided by the generosity of one Brother Clifford Blades. I point at him, then put my extended hands on the top of my head to simulate donkey's ears. – Hee-haw! Hee-haw! I bray at him.

I run the dog hame, then Bladesey, who is too distressed to realise that she was gantin on it. I'm on the bypass with Annalise. I come off a slip-road and turn on to a country lane. – Where are we going? she asks. She's a bit concerned but far more intrigued because she's still smiling. Having flirted all night she won't want to go home dickless.

– A short cut, I say, pulling up in a deserted lay-by. – Ken how they call them lay-bys? I ask her, – Cause ye git laid when ye pill up in one.

– What? she looks worried as the control has been wrested from her.

– Right doll, stop fuckin aboot, c'moan: cock it or walk it. That's the options, I wink.

– No here . . . she says morosely, – Have you no got a place?

– You're no listening Annalise, I tap my lugs. – The cock or the walk are the choices.

– You mairried? she asks, looking straight at me.

I ignore her. – What's it tae be? I insist. There's a lot of nutters prowling around at night.

She wisely chooses the first option, although with a bit of reluctance. – Awright then . . . she says, looking intently at me, as if she expects me to say anything else. I pull her to me and push my whisky-saturated tongue into her mouth. As soon as she starts to respond and I feel the lump in my trousers, I gesture at her to get into the back seat.

We get in and she takes off one of her boots and pulls both her thick tights and knickers down, pulling one leg out of them. I consider trying to get her tits out but she doesn't look as if she's got much up there so I decide to head straight for the main course. My finger goes to her fanny, and as I suspected she's so juiced up I could have gone up to the elbow.

My flannels and pants are sliding down my thighs, the trapped warm air from the car heater giving the sharp fumes coming from them an extra dig. My cock's sweaty and my thighs sting, and at one point I think I'm not going to get it in after the distraction of fitting that fuckin condom. I shouldnae have fuckin well bothered. After a couple of duff attempts caused by the lager and the constricted space, I eventually manage to get it up and blow my load after a few strokes. My thighs chaffed badly on her tights and the car upholstery. A long fuck was out of the question in such circumstances. I got a little alcohol-anxious and was just chuffed to get a result.

Annalise pulls a kleenex from her bag and tensely wipes herself, even though I was wearing a spunk-bag. Mind you, the juice she produced, she'd want to. As I pull off the bag and throw it out the window, I see her quickly pulling on her pants, tights and boots. I'm up with the keks and flannels and we silently move back into the front seats.

I scarcely look at her again, although I can sense her mood of bitter lamentation as I drive her hame. Bruce Robertson, a gentleman to the last.

– See you later doll, I wave a fond *adieu* at her long-coated back as her heels click over the Pilrig paving slabs. She doesn't look back though.

Our Cover Is Blown

The aircraft. Peters and Lee. Lenny Peters was a great aviation singer. Jet plane flying high above me. Rainbow in the sky. But fuck that. I hate planes. All you can sense around you is sterile plane. The food tastes of plane; bland, cold, plastic. The air hostesses smell and look of plane; cool, pristine, fridgid. You just want to fill this environment with as much bawdy flatulence as you can muster. As we've had a few jags before getting on the flight, that's quite a lot.

So Bladesey and I are pontificating on the nature of arse-fucking. That wee hairy last night, I should've fucked her up the arse. Mind you, it took me an age tae get it intae her fanny, Christ knows how I'd've got it up her chorus and verse! It was a bit of a waste though: tidy fanny ganting on it. I should've stayed cool and taken her hame and taken my time. Then I could have fired into her casually for a while. Still, there's other fish. There's a stewardess I'd gie one tae, but Bladesey's on the outside and instead of getting a decko at her bum he's thumbing through the in-flight journal like the specky wee cunt that he is.

Bladesey's problem is that he tries to intellectualise everything. Ye cannae dae that with shagging. It's either gaun in the hole or it's no. – Heterosexual anal sex need not actually imply an attitude of misogyny, he says in his whisper. – It's just a value-free activity between consenting parties. Yes, there is a cultural misogynistic baggage attached to it, as in the rap lyrics, but it's essentially neutral. What people attach to it is their concern. I read in one of Bunty's *Cosmos* that twenty per cent of heterosexual couples enjoy anal sex, while only fifty per cent of homosexual couples do . . .

— Eh? I asked, — You're telling me that half the poofs around dinnae fuck each other up the erse? That sounds shite to me!

Bladesey looks shifty and panicky. — Keep your voice down Robbo. I'm only telling you what the article says.

— Listen Bladesey, I don't believe that for a second. And I'll tell you something about all those niggers with their fucking rap lyrics, aw that guff about shagging birds and blowing away pigs, it's just wishful thinking, that's all.

— The empowering fantasies of the dispossessed? Bladesey smiles, lowering those specs to the bridge of his nose. He's a funny cunt alright, is Brother Blades.

Mind you, he fits in well here, because there's a right bunch a misfits on this plane. There's a pair of comedians in front of me, dressed identically in dark blue suits and ties, carrying briefcases. Fuck travelling trussed up like that; what a pair of fuckin dildos.

I turn to Bladesey. This is my mate for the trip, God help us. I'd better do the best with the shoddy material I've got and try and put the sorry fucker right. — Gangster rap is fuckin bollocks. Gangsters my hole, it's a fuckin con job. If yir a real gangster the last thing ye dae is hing oot in a recording studio. Did Al Capone spend time in a recording studio? Did he fuck! He spent time being a gangster. Just wait till they get rap in Scotland. Every daft wee cunt who attended two or three matches at Easter Road wi a couple ay casuals'll be making rap records then.

— But surely those chaps in America that got shot, they must have had mob connections?

— Maybe they did. But the truth is, it's we so-called pigs who offed the coons. When I was in the Met it was open season on the darkies. Same in New South Wales. Abos and Pakis were fair game to us. If you had a scoreboard with a tally of pigs versus

niggers offed, we'd be well ahead. As for shagging, I read somewhere that white birds are ten times more likely to give blow jobs
than black women. So all that rap shite is just nig-bo fantasy.

— Unless it's white women that are performing for them,
Bladesey laughs.

This gets my fuckin goat. — Only a slag that's not right in the
head, that's sick and diseased would look at a darkie, I tell him.

— But you've, eh, enjoyed liaisons with ladies from different
racial backgrounds, Bladesey whispers.

I clock the stewardess and gesture for another whisky. If you
drink whisky you'll never get worms. Burn out the enemy within. — I've fucked hoors of different colours. That's different
Bladesey; we're talking about the unalienable right of the
Scotsman abroad: to fuck hoors up the arsehole! We're a dis-
persed race. *Slàinte!* I raise my glass.

— Do you mind?

A voice coming from behind me. I turn to see a
Brylcreemed cunt with prominent teeth.

— What? I say, staring at him.

— If you must talk such filth, I'd appreciate it if you lowered
your voice. There's women and bairns can hear you . . . he nods
to a furtive looking wee lassie and an embarrassed wifie.

Filth? Ah'll gie the cunt fuckin filth. Cunt's never fuckin well
seen filth yit. — Are you asking me or telling me? I say to him.

— What? he says.

— Terry, the woman says, tugging at his sleeve.

— Eh Bruce . . . I think actually eh . . . Bladesey's shiting it.

— Are you asking me or telling me? I repeat slowly and
emphatically.

— I'm asking politely . . . but if you don't keep it down I'll
get the stewardess . . .

I smile and shrug. — Fine. Sorry if we gave any offence. Just
as long as you're asking me.

I turn round and grip the armrest until my knuckles go
white. — I'll show that cunt, I hiss at Bladesey. — Mark my words
Brother Blades.

— Leave it Bruce . . .

The remainder of the flight is uneventful and we touch down in Brussels. Bladesey and I have an hour to kill before the connecting flight to Schipol. I change some cash and hit the bar to get in a couple of pints of Stella. You feel like a millionaire with those Belgian francs but they're worth fuck all.

I see that those suit and tie spastics who were in front of us on the plane have sat down and are having a beer.

Then I clock that greasy lippy cunt, the arsehole that pulled me up on the plane, Mister Happy Families. He's on his own, heading for a pish. I get up.

— Where are you going? Bladesey asks, a little alarmed.

— Business, I tell him. He raises an eyebrow in exasperation.

I follow the wise cunt into the toilets. It's just me and him. I let him pish and shake it out before he turns to face me. He looks puzzled for a moment, then his face contorts in recognition. —You . . . he sneers, dropping his hands by his side. — If you want trouble . . .

A bit of a cowboy this cunt. Good.

— I can assure you sir, that the last thing I want is trouble. I want the opportunity to explain myself to you. I pull out my ID. — Detective Inspector Robertson, Edinburgh and Lothians Police, I say quickly. Well, I will be an inspector soon.

— What's this? he says with a slight panic in his voice.

— Sir, I'm torn between wringing your neck and shaking your hand. Shaking your hand because I'm a family man myself and you were right to object to my crude and disgusting talk. Wringing your neck because I was working undercover in conjunction with my Dutch colleagues. My foul conversation was an attempt to draw in the two men sitting in front of me. Do you know anything about child pornography sir?

He nods uncomprehendingly.

— Snuff videos? I enquire.

— No . . . I . . .

— When little children disappear off the streets in Britain, they spend the last few hours of their miserable lives being abused and tortured in deserted warehouses and barns. This is video'd for the porn trade on the continent; Amsterdam, Hamburg etcetera. That's where those beasts in front of me were heading with their wares.

—You mean . . . those gents in the suits were . . .

I nod sombrely. — We planned to try and engage with those monsters to uncover their operation. We had to resort to that filthy talk in order to try to get on to their wavelength, to make contact. I could see they were almost ready to communicate with us, when, all of a sudden, a well-meaning but misguided member of the public comes along . . .

The idiot stands and looks at me for a bit. — Oh my God . . . what have I done Inspector . . .

—You've not helped our cause, it has to be said.

— Is there anything I can do to help? Anything!

— Sir, I came here to apologise to you as a husband and a parent for my language on the plane. The language I was forced to use in this investigation. I'm not asking for any assistance in a police matter. I want you to know that I hated talking like that, especially in front of your wife and child, but if you'd seen those videos, seen how those children are debased, made to suffer . . . I've been on the force for a good many years. I just feel so strongly that these bastards should be nailed. I'll do anything to get them!

— I want to help. Please Inspector . . .

— There is one thing you can perhaps do . . . no, I can't ask you, it's outrageous.

— No, I insist! I should have thought!

—You weren't to know sir, I shake my head.

—Yes . . . but I caused your cover to be blown.

—The situation is not irretrievable. We can still get them.

—Yes, and I want to help!

I raise my eyebrows and exhale. Another guy comes into the toilet, so I pull my man over to the wash basins and lower my voice. — Listen, you're obviously a good citizen sir, but this is high risk. What happened on the plane made me the centre of their attention. What has to happen is another altercation of some sort. Sir, I'm asking you to go into that bar and noise the bastards up. Call them for everything, tell the whole world what they are. Then they'll be ruffled, furtive and looking for friends. I'll be on hand to befriend them. *Their* cover will be blown and they'll get careless, I smile grimly, looking at my friend in the eye. — Have you got the bottle for it sir?

— Oh, don't you worry about that Inspector. I've got the bottle alright. I'll show that inhuman scum what it's all about!

I go with the guy into the bar. I see the businessmen sitting having a drink. I stand back and saunter away over to the news-stand outside the bookstore and watch from behind it. The wee bastard goes right up to their table and leans over, resting his knuckles on it.

— How's business? he asks.

— What?

— I'm asking you how your sick business is, you filthy pair of animals! How is it then? The greasy wee cunt booms at the busi-nessmen, — Eh? The pair of youse! Oh aye, I know your game!

— What is this . . . what do you want . . . ? one of the guys asks. Everyone's looking round.

— I know what you dirty bastards are up to!

The guy's wife comes over, — Terry, she screams, — what's wrong?

— I do not know what this is. Who is this man? One of the suits looks petrified with shock.

— These people, he spits out, — are dirty sleazy bastards . . .

— I don't know what you are talking about . . . we are on business . . .

— Oh is that what you call it? Is that what you call making those fucking videos? Porn merchants! CHILD PORNOGRA-PHERS! He's looking around and pointing to the two business-men. Then he grabs one of the guys by the lapels and the other stands up and pushes him. Two security guys are over in a flash and they overpower the spazwit and lead him away, arm up the back, polis-style.

— Terry! his wife screams. He turns to her and briefly catches my eye and pleads, —That man will tell you, he's a police officer . . .

— I'm sorry, I say to one of the guards, — this guy's a bit of a nutter. He started on me on the plane. He seems a mite confused, I tap my head.

Airport security drag the protesting, bemused clown away, as his shocked wife follows with the child who is now screaming. Bladesey comes over trying to figure it out.

— No time to lose Brother Blades, it's time for our connecting flight to the Dam, I tell him. — You know Bladesey, there's some right fuckin nutters about.

Cok City

We've checked into the Cok City Hotel which is in Newzuids-
voorburgwal, Amsterdam's second red-light district, handy for
hoors if you're too lazy to cross the Damrak. I'm not though,
and I soon give Bladesey the slip and head out exploring. Serious
hooring is a solitary activity.

It's too cauld for shoes, especially slip-ons, but you have to
be dressed for hooring and you cannae be daein with the excruciating hassle of lace-up boots. In spite of the chill, just the sound
and feel of my soles on the cobblestones of the canal streets is
enough to give me a semi.

I've gone into a cinema and paid for a hi-tech booth. The
green light is off and the red light is on. I'm snug. It's not too
bad, the film, a sci-fi effort about two extraterrestrial spacedykes who kidnap nubile virgin schoolies from an American
town; from schools, discos, outside shopping centres etc, and
condition them into lesbianism through forcing them into
repeated sex acts. The long-term plan of the crafty alien dykes is
to make men superflous and Earth into a lesbian planet, ruled,
of course, by them. A stud detective and his crew of sexual
athletes have to save the young schoolies from carpet munching
and bring them back over to the right side, through the power of
their cocks. Eventually, after fucking the schoolies back into
heterosexuality the ace detective faces his greatest challenge in a

conflict with the superpowered cosmic lesbos. He has to bring them over to the other side. It turns out to be a happy ending for all. The dyke spacegirls find out that they love cock, but the cop admits that lesbianism is a turn-on for men, provided the women are good-looking and they can watch. So they decide to join forces and exterminate all homosexual men.

Quite a sound movie, and it's good to see a film so politically correct. I can relate. The schoolies are all hot and the spacedykes pretty fuckin superb. I'm tempted to have a wank, but I need to keep a full tank for the serious business of hooring.

So I'm window shopping for a suitable prossy in the red-light district. Round by the Old Kirk it's all fat black mamas and that's no good to me at the moment. Then I come across an alley full of Thai girls, some with long pinched faces who are obviously rebuilt boys. Right now though, it has to be premium-priced caucasian minge after that video. Blonde as well, like in the film.

There's a fat cunt stuffing his face with chips and mayo ahead of me and I'm thinking that I could go for some of that, carbo-hydrates for the shag NRG. My aftershave stings my face in the chill night air. I had a good raw shave in the hotel in Cok City, which is ideal with all amenities including Dutch cable TV complete with the erotic channel. In every other country you have tae pey for it. Fuck that! Those Dutch cunts have got it sussed: sex, drugs, get it out into the open and let people buy it. It would never work in Britain though, cause there are too many sad cunts who would spoil it for everyone. Like the holidaymakers here. I get into my favourite alley and there's a crowd of smutty lads in front of me, giving it big verbal. One loud-mouthed prick is negotiating with this little angel who'd be ideal for me and I want to stove the cunt's heid in and just dive into the room with her.

I walk on, and one girl smiles and winks at me, spacedyke-style, but I go past her as I need to check out the wares. Possibly a bit too old and fat to be a real space lesbian. It's getting too busy here. I might visit the Pijp tomorrow. A Dutch guy I met here last year put me on to it: a twenty-minute tram ride from the centre of the city, where the locals do their shopping, and the locals always know where to find the bargains.

I spy another wee shag but too dark-haired, nonetheless mentally stored in the fuck-file for tomorrow. A big slut is giving me the finger as she sits in horrible lingerie on her seat, but then suddenly, a few doors down, this fat, greasy shit is excreted into the street, and behind him is a vision. She'll do nicely. She goes back in and says to me, – One minute please.

She's obviously going to wash her cunt out and ·the like which is fine by me because I want all that fat greabo's traces obliterated. I think of Bladesey, sitting in the room or in an Italian restaurant on his tod, looking like the social inadequate that he is. Or perhaps the bastard will be bouncing on top of one of those fat black hoors right now, or getting his sweaty little arse whacked with some implement as he kisses the heel of a new mistress's black leather boot.

I wish I was a spaceman. She beckons me into her chamber: red light, red bedspread, and red chaise longue. There's a print of Van Gogh's *Sunflowers* on the wall, which adds a nice homely touch.

– I cannot kiss you, she smiles, – rules. She gives a fetching little shrug.

I'm getting my kit off and laying out my clothes; jacket, jumper, shirt, flannels, on the chaise longue, while she sits on the bed. She's smiling and reclining in quite a graceful way and her caresses are superfluous as I'm already hard. She slips on the condom and lies back as I get on to her and up her, and start to give her one.

Okay baby, let's take this rocket to Uranus.

This hoor is perfect, and she can act as well. No way is she into it, but you almost believe her. A drama school training should be compulsory for all hoors. As I empty the bag, she does a fantastic stage groan with an appreciative – ohhh it's so beautiful baby . . .

–You must come again, she tells me, as I get dressed. – How long are you here for?

– A few days, I tell her. She's a good hoor alright, a true professional. There's no need for her to keep up the façade of interest now that the contracts have been exchanged; even at this time of the year it's a seller's market, but this lassie has her professional pride.

– So come again! Come again here! she laughs.

– I'll do that, I smile, and exit into the busy, narrow passage, nippy at being surrounded by loud, sweaty men after having been with a cool, serene woman. It's like moving from heaven to hell just by opening a door. It's freezing cauld out here and the rain has pished down on the cobblestones. You'd never think that it was further south than where I've just come from. Fuckit: I'm no here for the weather, besides it's warm enough up a hoor's chuff.

I'm suddenly bunched together in the alley with the same group of insolent mongoloid lads I saw earlier, who are joking and shouting. I slyly connect with one in the ribs and he's winded and bent over double as I push through the crowd, sliding away. I hear his mate asking, – Wat's oop Mick? Wat's oop? But this fuckwitted spastic is too immobilised and confused to work that out and by then I'm well away, bristling with excitement and satisfaction. It's that front-line feeling; that rush when you're at a picket-line or at a big game and you've got your truncheon and shield and the whole force of the state is behind you and you're hyped up to beat insolent spastic scum who question things with their big mouths and nasty manners into the suffering pulp they so richly deserve to become. It's a great society we live in.

I hate them all, that section of the working class who won't do as they are told: criminals, spastics, niggers, strikers, thugs, I don't fucking well care, it all adds up to one thing: something to smash. Yes, I might be a wee bit past that squeaky bollocks front-line bullshit, but what I still love, and always fuckin well will, is that good old-fashioned two-on-one with a scumbag in the interview room. The psychological warfare, far more satisfying. The harder they are to break, the more rewarding it is. You're right back in the territory of the games.

Like the next hoor I find after I've had a recuperative beer and whisky in a brown bar. I'm pumping away at her and she's just taking the fuckin lot. Nice girl. The spacedyke imagery is still vivid in my head and I blow my muck quickly. As I'm getting my kit on I'm asking her if she wants to make serious money.

– I do already, she says arrogantly, but the hoor's light of calculating greed ignites her eyes and when I'm back in my room at my hotel, she's right along once she's finished her morning shift.

Yes, she's expensive, especially a day session, but that's what overtime's for, to cover such costs. Thank fuck for the form OTA 1–7!

This lassie's a student at Amsterdam University. Six years' higher education the state provides for these pampered cunts. She's on the game cause she's been changing from English to Sociology to Philosophy to Film Studies and wasted six years of a grant. That's what all these wee students at our unis should be made to do: hoor for their grant money. Come to think of it, that's what some of them *are* being made to do. Nice one the free market.

This wee yin here, she's agreed to a fuck up the erse, with great reluctance as she's going on aboot Aids and she's no got any extra-strength condoms. Just as well, I wouldnae have been able to feel a fuckin thing. She's very athletic though, the way she bends over the back of the chair. My lips dry as I watch the sinew tighten in the back of her legs in those high heels and I'm getting as hard as rock. I've given the pole a good greasing but she's pretty tight. Once I get in though, it starts to slide up. I can tell that she's in a bit of distress cause she's making hissing noises and her back muscles are tensing, but it's probably just cause the fuckin hoor's loving every minute of it.

– Stop, please stop for a minute, she says nippy-like, and starts shifting her weight, readjusting, trying to find more space inside her and I'm back down here on Planet Earth, sending up this probe, which I use to detect signs of alien life inside her, this spacedyke, yes this fucking super spacedyke, like the alien life inside of me no no no that this fuckin space lesbian who's fucked all over the universe but who has never been fucked like this before and she loves she . . . – Uugghhh . . .

I blurt out my fucking load into the condom up her arse. This cow's erse grips my cock and as I pull free she still won't surrender the condom. She pulls it out her own rectum. There's little flecks of shit on the end of it. My knob's as clean as a fuckin whistle though. Thank fuck, the dirty wee cloggie hing-oot.

I pay the hoor and tell her to fuck off and leave me alone. I fall into the bed and into a good sleep for about half an hour. When I wake up, I feel lonely and depressed and hit the mini-bar. After a couple of whiskies I go to knock up Bladesey but he's out. Docile wee cunt. I get a notion to give Bunty a call, which I do from the cardphone outside in the street.

– Awright Coontay!

– Go away!

– Ya'll miss me? I've been tellin Little Frank about yaw. E wants taw give your fanny a lickin, e does! I drop my voice and make it go breathless. – Ah do not . . . Then nasal again, – Yes yaw do!

– LEAVE ME ALONE! the hoor screams, then slams the phone down.

I head back into the hotel and upstairs to my room where I watch the Cartoon Channel and have a wee giggle to myself. I'm a wee bit disappointed that Bunty felt unable to take my advice and give me some sport. She's probably feeling vulnerable with he-man Bladesey off the scene. Ha! Anyway, it's soon time to hit the pish, as I hear the man himself returning to his room next door.

– Awright Clifford, me old son? I smile, – Get any hooring done?

He smiles bashfully, – Eh, actually no . . . I went to the Rijksmuseum and saw Rembrandt's *The Nichtwacht* . . . amazing picture.

– Any shagging in it?

– Eh no . . . it's not a film it's . . .

— Ah ken what it fuckin well is! Ah ken who fuckin Rembrandt is! I point to myself. Cheeky wee cunt thinks he's fuckin smart. He knows fuckin nothing. The big zero.

We get out on the pish and I make the mistake of letting Bladesey bell Bunty. I was intrigued as to how my heat from across the street had affected her. Bad move. Even from the barstool looking at the back of Bladesey's heid and his reddening neck I can tell that it's a sair yin.

He's shattered when he comes off the phone. The cunt's shaking. — Bruce, he gasps, — I think actually I'm going to have to head back . . . Bunty's upset, the caller was at it again. I should never have left her . . .

— No way! It's yir fuckin hoaliday!

— She wants the number of the hotel. She thinks I'm in Scarborough. I had to sort of agree to go back . . .

— No fuckin way!

— I don't know what to do . . . he puts his head in his hands.

I stiffly let my arm fall round his shoulder. — She's makin your life a misery, eh mate.

— I seem to be able to do nothing right, he whines, — I'm either in her way if I'm there, or I'm neglecting her if I'm away . . . all Craig does is scowl and play that fucking techno music . . . what does she want from me Bruce? What does she want me to be like?

— Bladesey, listen. Ah'm yir mate, and mates back each other up. Ah'll tell ye exactly what's gaunny happen . . .

— I've got to go back . . . he starts.

I look into his large, shocked eyes. — You and I, I smile, — are going oot hooring. You are gaunny git that fuckin pole workin again, I point at his groin. — We are gaunny git you feeling hunky-dory about one Brother Clifford Blades here. And when you swagger back intae that hoose in Corstorphine, the first thing you dae is git a hud ay her and gie her, I grin, protruding my middle finger, — the stinky pinky here. And ah'll tell ye mate, she'll be that fuckin well juiced up that the lips ay her fanny'll part for you like the Red Sea did for Moses. You'll be fightin her

163

oaf wi a fuckin stick soon, I say, then I point at his groin again, — That fuckin stick.

— You really think that's going to do me any good?

— Same fuckin rules mate, I nod knowingly, — same fuckin rules. I turn to the bartender, — Same again my friend.

I'll tolerate no more talk from that sad loser about going home.

Still Carole

When I make up my eyes, I always feel a stirring through my body. I think it's because it's true what they say about the eyes being the gateway to the soul. And my soul is a very sexual one. You cannot deny your nature. Bruce taught me that. At times like this I am moved to touch myself . . . I love the feel of this silk blouse against my skin.

I love

My head swoons. It's as if Bruce were here with me.

Soon.

It's time to go out. I'm just going out Mum.

Tell Stacey I won't be late.

Bye.

The bar is large, ideal for people-watching. There are lots of little nooks and crannies to hide in.

Sitting here, alone here, I'm remembering when I first met Bruce's parents. They were good people, from a mining village in Midlothian. This was before they were corrupted by that Scargill, who split up families and turned everyone against each other. Bruce doesn't bear any grudges though, even though they were cruel to him and rejected him, their own son. That's what these people want though: to split up the family. It's not important to them but the way I see it, if you haven't got family then you haven't got anything. Bruce does too. It's so unfortunate that Stacey's said those horrible things, but we don't blame our little girl, all children go through a phase when they tell silly wee lies. In Stacey's case I think it's been the wrong crowd she's been hanging around with at that school.

Anyway, I must say that I look a treat and I know by the way that the guy behind the bar's staring at me that he feels the same way too. Well, you can look but don't touch my friend! I've got on my heels, *that* silk blouse and my pleated skirt. I catch myself in the mirror. Not bad Carole. Not bad.

I know what they're thinking; a woman drinking on her own. They think I'm a prostitute or that I'm easy. All I'm doing is confronting them with their own desire. That's what they cannot take.

They want me.

All those men, they all want Carole Robertson.

But there is only one man who can have me, although if he wants me to give myself to another man, I will, but only for him. He won't want me to give myself to any man in this bar.

I have made my point lads, and now I depart, to see my daughter. I am a good mother and a good wife.

All eyes are on me as I leave the bar. I have made my point.

Outside my vision is blurred. All the shop signs and advertising seem as if they're written in a foreign language. I don't feel safe here. I must go to where I feel safe.

The Nightwatch

Morning has broken; not so much with a bang as with a whimper as Bladesey knocks timidly on my door and asks me if I want to come down for breakfast. Actually.

– Aye, but I'll tell ye one thing Bladesey, ah'm no gaun doon there fir that continental breakfast shite. Ham and cheese and rolls? Fuck yon. There's a British café in the Haarlemerweg. Let's go.

We stride up along the Singel, feeling the bracing air blow away the morning cobwebs, and get into Barney's Breakfast Bar. It's full of fuckin student and crusty trash on tight budgets so I delight in ostentatiously flashing my wad around while I order the works: bacon, egg, sausage, tomato, mushroom, black pudding, toast and tea.

– You were AWOL yesterday Bruce, Bladesey chides. – Meet any interesting ladies?

– Yes, as a matter of fact. I met this Scots lassie in a bar. She was really nice.

– Was she, eh . . . a you know . . . lady of the night?

I look, in great irritation, at this wretched mess that has somehow insinuated itself into my life. – No. She was not. Do you think I can't meet anybody other than a prossy? Is that what you think?

– No . . . not at all . . . he stammers apologetically.

I sit up in the chair. I'd better put this cunt right once and for all. — Well I'll tell you something mate: I've had mair fanny than you've had hot dinners. And I'm talking quality fanny as well. Premium minge. And I'm no going that far back. Dinnae think that because I fuck hoors for convenience sakes that I have tae pey for it. Dinnae think that, I tell him, the cheeky cunt.

— I'm most terribly sorry Bruce . . . I didn't mean to give offence. You got the wrong end of the stick. I just assumed, you know, it being Amsterdam . . .

— Well you assumed wrong, I curtly inform him, skinning up a large reefer of skunk and lighting it up as our breakfasts arrive.

We eat our meal in silence and I leave the little cunt to his museums and galleries. I'm off for porn and drugs.

I head over to the red-light district and a languid-looking bag of shit hisses at me, — Video show. It'll be an ed-dew-kay-shon.

I feel resentment rise in my chest. A semi-jakey standing ootside in the cauld working for sweeties, thinking that he could be part of a process of educating *me*, in any way shape or form. I stop and I give him a slow, evaluating look up and down which I can tell unnerves him.

— Video show . . . he repeats more warily.

— Any good? I snap in polis mode.

— It's the best.

I look at the f25 sign behind him. — At twenty-five guilders it had better be. Or else I'll be back mob-handed. Right?

He raises his hands in the air. — Hey, chill out man. This is Amsterdam. It's the best video show you're ever gonna see.

— Let's hope so.

I enter and pay twenty-five guilders to a distracted gum-chewing slut who obviously does tricks and is thinking about the bigger bucks to be made on her back later on. I go into what is an old-style film theatre rather than a series of coin-operated booths. It's half-full and the show starts promptly. There's no privacy for wanking, but it doesn't stop an old cunt next to me, who's got his cock out in a hanky and is chugging away by the time the first power-dressed actress who looks like Victoria

Principal from Dallas gets felt up and fucked in a lift by two guys who stop it between the floors. I try to focus on the video but the picture quality is poor and auld cunt's groans distract me.

However, it then goes into a mad sequence at an office party, where everybody is fucking themselves crazy. I think about the fanny I'll fire into at our office parties this Christmas: that new young clerical bird for a start, then there's Fulton, and of course, that big hoor the Size Queen, and even Drummond, for fucks' sakes, if I'm desperate enough. I feel my hand go towards the lump in my flannels but, after a few tweaks of the cherry, I show my willpower, gritting my teeth and leaving it. No sense in running down the generator at this stage.

After browsing in a few porn stores I try in vain to find a hoor who looks like her, like my girl. I have her pants with me, in my pockets from last night. I can't find anyone. I'm getting frustrated and it's only going to get worse. I decide to go for a drink and resolve to try and find one who looks absolutely *nothing* like her. This tactic works because instantly all the rooms off the grey cobblestoned streets seem to offer endless possibilities. I find a likely girl. She's got ginger hair and a badly pock-marked face. I get the old spiel, this time done without any charm, as she tells me that she doesnae kiss. I felt like saying to her that I had no desire whatsoever to kiss her pock-marked coupon, my lips are chapped ragged enough with the cold as it is. She undresses and wanks me for a bit, trying to tease some life into my cock, and I only get hard when I look at her pock-marked skin. Like the other hoors here, she seems not to mind my rash and eczema, though with her skin you'd expect some sympathy.

When I fuck her she's giving it all the Ooohh baby, I'm so wet . . . oooh this is so good . . . and all that shite, which I enjoy. Again, it's good that she takes a pride in her work and makes the effort. It's definitely the hooring capital of the world is old Amsterdam. With this one though, after I've blown my muck into the rubber, her dead hoor eyes chill over mechanistically as she's already preparing for the next customer and I head out to get a bite to eat.

I go to one of the nondescript pizza places on the Damrak which are largely unspectacular tourist rip-offs. After eating I head back to the room. I still have her panties in my pocket. From last night. I couldn't ask that hoor I was with to wear them. I pull them over my head and sniff, filling my nostrils with her scent. I'm aware of the thudding sound of sobbing and a high, ugly moaning in the room.

I pull off the pants but the room's empty except for me.

The Rash

The next morning I shit on the hotel's traylike bogs. A pile of chestnuts faces me, foul of Dame Judi, but yielding no signs of the alien monster. I know it's up there though, inside of me, twisting and growing, biding its time, like an Arthur Scargill in the healthy body politic of eighties Britain, the enemy within.

I get out and visit another couple of hoors, one Thai, one black. The black one looked at my balls as if she had never seen white meat before. Maybe it's the rash, it's definitely getting worse.

Worse.

I put in another shift of afternoon drinking, Heineken and geneva, before I scored some good, gum-numbing cocaine fae a guy in a brown bar. Then I was back out on the piss. That's the thing aboot charlie: gies ye superhuman drinking powers. No that I need them.

In one bar I have a bottle of Grolsch and I see that they are daein that space cake. I take one piece, then another. A wide cunt behind the bar tells me that I should watch that stuff and I just laugh and have another piece. I'm getting a good buzz in my head.

When I leave the bar it hits me and I feel really sick and nauseous.

The hippy cunts've tried to poison me, me a fuckin polisman. I'll get ontae the Dutch polis and close the cunts down. I'm staggering around, too scared to cross the road cause these trams are coming from aw directions and the cunts on the bikes as well, and I'm too close tae the edge of the canal in this condition . . . these Dutch cunts . . .

. . . the EC should shut this fuckin place doon . . .

I get off the Damrak but I'm staggering down a narrow street and I bang into someone who shouts at me but I keep moving, it's like a fucking nightmare where ye darenae look back. I'm hyperventilating when I get back to the hotel. Bladesey's lying on the bed in his room, watching the telly. I head to the bog and shit again and I see that there's something in my stools. I can't look at it. I sit there for a while and calm down before I go back and face Bladesey.

His face seems to reverberate against the wall and all I can hear is that fucking actually voice. I don't know how it happens but Bladesey's giving me gyp. He seems to be three sheets and tells me that he met some Londoners and they got wrecked. The conversation seems to drift to music. I mention I like Motown; Marvin, Smokey and the like, or I did before I destroyed my albums realising that it was a sign of weakness to have coon music in the hoose.

Bladesey's voice is a high, incessant squeal through drink. — How can you be a racist and like Motown? he's whining, — I mean, how can you be a racist and like Marvin Gaye?

— Marvin Gaye was not a black man.

— How can you say that?

— He wasn't a black man to me. The cunt that shot him, that was a black man. That was a fuckin nigger.

— But that was his father!

—Yes. A black man.

I can't feel anything, there's no sense of me standing up and moving over to him, but I have some sense of grabbing Bladesey round the neck and him shouting: — What are you doing Bruce? It's me! It's me!

But I *know* it's him and I want to choke the living shite out of the cunt, just turn off his gas for good cause I detest the bastard and he's just one of the cunts who's got it in for me.

Can't fuckin save them

The boy up the Bridges

You can kill them casually

why can't you fuckin well save them so casually

stop them

stop him

The walls are reverberating and it's out of my hands . . . his neck . . .

How did it make you feel?

He's still on the bed as I leave, rubbing his scrawny pigeon-neck, gasping for air.

I don't believe I attacked Bladesey. My mate. My travelling companion. Brother Blades. A stalwart in the craft. A brother.

I'm down the narrow stairs, staggering past the pouting blond guy on the reception. In the street, a ragged junkie hoor smiles at me from under a streetlamp, a remnant of a t-shirt Amsterdam which seldom resembles the more sanitised and regulated real life. I get into a bar and order a Heineken. I'm thinking of Bladesey, that sad little cunt who needs very little and who can't understand what a grievous rage his attitude and manner induces in the rest of us for whom everything in the world could never, ever, be anything like enough.

My chest throbs as I sit on the barstool. My hands are tingling and voices are ringing in my ear, speaking a language I can't understand, but there's no mistaking their murderous intent.

Bladesey. I've got to get back to Bladesey.

Bladesey.

The longer our friendship has developed, the more the destruction and humiliation of this sad little creature has grown to obsess me. He needs to be confronted with what he really is, he has to feel, see and acknowledge his inadequacy as a member of the human species, then he has to do the honourable thing and renounce that membership. And I will help him.

First I have to drink off those fuckin hippy drugs.

Goals

— You were in some fuckin state last night Brother Blades, I tell a furtive, shaking Bladesey at breakfast. He looks terrible, there are bruises on the side of his face and on his neck.

— I . . . I . . . can't remember . . . I woke up feeling . . . he hesitates.

— I remember alright, I say wryly. — I came back to the hotel blissed out on this hippy dope and you came back three sheets after spending the day on the piss with these London guys. Anyway, you insisted on going out . . .

I look at his bemused face.

— . . . Do you remember Hunter's Bar? I ask.

— No . . . I don't actually . . .

— We got into a ruck with these German cunts. Then when we got back to the hotel you fuckin well went for me!

— God . . . I don't remember . . . I'm terribly sorry Bruce . . . I was so drunk I . . .

I raise my brows and lower my eyes disapprovingly. — Fuckin well should be, I tell him.

I look at his wretched, uncomprehending expression and leave the cunt in his misery. I play at being in the huff and swan off to get a paper.

One of the brilliant things about Amsterdam is that you can get the *Sun* at the same time as you would in Britain, if you go up to Centraal Station. I bought a copy of the *Sun* for the football pull-out 'Goals'. It's a habit. Football is a habit. I think it's a sex substitute for most men, admittedly not as blatant as rugby, because the guys actually fuck each other up their holes in rugby clubs. But that's more to do with social class, because they're rich pricks who went to all-boys schools. But football's like that as well. When you think about it, most guys get into football when they're too young to get their hole. When you go to the fitba you can always tell which of your mates has a bad or non-existent sex life. They always seem just that bit *too* much into the game. I'm sounding like fuckin Bladesey actually, with all this actual psychological analysis, actually. That wee cunt has to wait for his poxy *Independent* or *Guardian* or whatever commie shite he reads. I always buy the *Sun* on Monday back at the work to have a wank to page three and read 'Goals'. Simple pleasures. Not that I really give that much of an Aylesbury right now. Out here I've been far too preoccupied with the Roger Mooring to be bothered aboot the fitba.

Anyway, I hit a bar to mull over the results and tables and I'm astonished to note that Tom Stronach's got on the scoresheet in a two–one win at East End Park, which lifts us into third spot in the table, ahead of the fenian scum. Kiss Europe goodbye Leith motherfuckers. It's there in black and white, Stronach (74). At the next table, these scousers have got the *Mirror* out. I've never been partial to scousers; those cunts ooze criminality. The Irish influence, no doubt. Same rules.

— Don't know how you can read that shite, one of them says to me.

— Easy, I smile at him.

— Nobody who's alright on Merseyside reads the *Sun*, the nosey scouse git continues in his preachy manner, — Not after Hillsborough, not after Souness, not after Bulger . . .

I feel an uncontrollable urge to laugh in his face. — You know something about scousers? I'll tell you something about scousers, I snort.

— You don't have to tell us anything about scousers mate, we're from Liverpool, he pulls himself up to his full height.

— I noticed that alright, I bellow in a jocular way, pointing straight at him. — Scousers are a bunch of fucking sad drama queens. It's like the whole fucking cess-pit of a city is auditioning for *Brookside*. Cannae be denied.

— You're fucking out of order there mate, the big guy says, looking harshly at me.

— C'mon lads, says his mate, trying to calm him down.

— Cannot be denied. Same rules, I shrug cheerfully.

— C'mon Derm, don't get involved, his pal's saying. — C'mon mate, you're a Jock, we're from Liverpool, we're just the friggin same for fuck sake. He tugs at his t-shirt, a red one, which has a quote from Bill Shankly on the front of it.

— No, we're not the same. I'm not the same as you, I shake my head.

— We're having a crack here, a drink . . . fuckin hell . . . the guy says. — You can read which paper you want mate, we're only pulling your fucking leg, he tells me. He's very upset which is good, because he should be upset coming from a shithouse like that. But he shouldnae be upset at me. The wanker should learn not to shoot the messenger, he who reminds one of bad tidings.

— Listen, you've obviously been thieving or fiddling the dole to be able to afford to come across here. That's the way it is with you people. Same rules apply. I'm telling you what I think, I say. — I bring bad tidings.

— We don't wanna know what you think!

Nearly Christmas. Santa Robertson. Yo ho ho ho ho! Bad tidings!

— Lerim speak.

— All I was saying is that when something bad happens in Liverpool, youse cunts go fucking do-lally. You take it as an excuse to parade banners at the football . . . illsburgh . . . i-sell . . . I put on an imitation gasping scouse nasal bleat. — Why can't you just sit in the fuckin hoose and mourn quietly, why do you have to turn everything into a tasteless audition for *Brookside*, to show who can be the most fucked up by tragedy?

— Because we care, that's why. Because we stick together!
The t-shirt spits out.

— Stick together! Ha! Youse cunts are in and out of each others' hooses with each others' property all day long. Show the
fucking professional ghouls in that city something to mourn and
they'll be out in force. That *Boys From The Blackstuff* shite. . . you
bastards are glad that there's nae jobs, n that, cause it gives you
something to act so fuckin tragic and hard-done-by! The biggest
tragedy though for you cunts was that the Lockerbie disaster
happened somewhere else. Imagine the fun youse cunts would
have had if that plane came down on some shitey Liverpool slum
estate! It would've kept youse greeting and snarling in front of
the camera for years!

— You're a fuckin sad case . . . I'm out of here right now. If
we weren't on friggin oliday I'd have you outside you fucking
toss, he snaps, throwing back his drink.

— Oooohhh, I'm scared shitless.

Bad tidings

Santa Robbo

Yo ho ho ho ho

— Leave im Derm, he ain't friggin worth it. Leave im to his
fun-packed life, the sad, lonely cunt. I knew what you were like
straight away. I thought, naw, we're on oliday, chat to the poor
sad case on his own, this wide cunt smiles sarcastically. — We'll
just leave you here then, with all your mates. C'mon lads.

I'm not taking this from a piece of shite, this piece of fucking red scum. — Go back to your hotel room and fuck each other
ya fucking scouse queers!

One guy comes at me, but his mates pull him away and they
go, uttering curses.

— Inadequates, I shout to the barman. — Ah ken their type.
They get their kicks noising up hoors and banging on windaes in

the red-light district. Then they go back and screw each other. That's scousers, big fuckin drama queens! I blame the Beatles, they've got a lot to answer for! We're still putting up wi that auld troll that does the bag-off programme on telly cause ay them! Ever since these cunts and Liverpool FC's success in Europe – a success built by Scotsmen: Liddell, Shankly, Dalglish, Souness, Hansen, etc. – scousers all think that they've got talent. They're nothing! Nothing!

He turns away aw frosty as if it was *me* that was the fuckin freak. Cheeky bastard. I down my drink and head outside. Ambling down the narrow street in the cold I'm aware of someone alongside me and as I turn I feel a crack in my face and my head snaps to the side. I try to react, but another guy advances and boots me in the balls and I feel the sickness rise up inside me. I fall down on to one knee and throw up over the cobblestones.

—You fughin twat! the guy shouts.

Where's the fuckin back-up here . . . I'm fuckin polis! Where's the fuckin cloggie polis! Fuck sakes!

— C'mon Dermot, let's get friggin movin! I hear one of the scousers say, and they're off down the road.

I sit for a bit, my head pounding and my eyes watering. The sickness has abated slightly, remaining just under the level where you want to vomit. Eventually I'm helped to my feet by a smelly fuckin hippy. – You English, always you are causing the trouble man. Mellow out man, this is Amsterdam, he says.

— I'm no fuckin English, I tell him, and move off down the road. I want to get out of here. – Cowardly scouse bastards, if I see those cunts again . . .

I cross over the road and a tram just misses me. My nerves are shot to pieces. I'll get these cunts back

I'll

I go into a bar and smoke hashish and drink some beer. It's a dimly lit touristy place. After a few drinks and smokes I feel better. The side of my face is swollen.

— I got mugged by some fuckin scousers, I tell an Irish guy. – They took eight hundred guilders off me. Three of them.

He just nods in a neutral way. I didn't expect anything more from a criminal. All the Irish are like that, except the Protestant Northern Irish, our brethren.

I buy a phonecard and call Bunty.

– Awright Boontay loove? Ow are yaw?

– Leave me alone! she shouts, slamming the phone down. I've got a stiffer, so it's over to the red-light district.

I try to get it on with a black hoor, but my nuts are so sore after that kicking that I can't get it up. The scouse cunts have spoiled my day's hooring; a few hours OT wasted. I go and do some more hash, but I hate this stuff. It's powders I need. I get in tow with these Dutch guys who are going to a party in a houseboat. When we get there the place is full of scum, just like these Sunrise fuckers at Penicuik, but the cocaine I get is the best I've ever had. I tell this to one of the cloggites with skin so clear, so like a doll's you just want to taste it and she just says, – But of course. This is Amsterdam.

Anyway, I get fucking wrecked. I remember getting asked to leave. When I get home Bladesey's still up. He's been out and he's bought a bottle of malt whisky by way of an apology for his shocking behaviour the previous night. We arse the lot and then clean out the mini-bar in his room. I stagger back through to mine and crash out into a pulverising sleep.

' . . . the essentially depraved nature of the creature that she married . . . '

I wake up in the night with a shuddering spasm; it's as if I'm falling through my own body. I'm sweating and trembling. There's no hoor by my side but my baws are red-raw. Objects start to come into focus through the dark. It's the hotel room in Amsterdam. I think of Carole and a crushing pain almost rips me apart. It's only a reaction to my loss. My mouth feels like it's been blowtorched and had the skin from my scrotum grafted onto it, but when I go to the mini-bar and down a soda water it only succeeds in turning my guts over. I lurch back to bed as the light comes up. The light. I'm safe again. I get a good bit of kip in.

I wake about lunchtime. My calendar on my watch tells me that it's the fifteenth of December. Christmas is coming. I get showered, the side of my face still swollen and tender, and I dress and head next door. Bladesey's still asleep. The cunt sleeps deeply. He's half-blind withoot his specs. There they are on the bedside table.

I pick them up.

Leaving the hotel I take a stroll over by the canal streets and I spot a likely corner café for a late breakfast. En route, I pull the specs out of my pocket. These lenses are so thick. I put them on and lean over the green balustrade and watch a distorted tug go down the canal. How could any cunt wear those?

Thick though they may be, in a contest with the grinding,

seg-ridden heel of Bruce Robertson's shoes, there was only going to be one winner. I twist, grinning at the satisfying crack they make on the cobblestones. Then, with a piece of footwork so deft that it would have Tom Stronach hitting the rewind button on the VCR in appreciation, I flick the broken specs into the Herengracht and watch as its still waters claim them.

When I get back to the hotel Bladesey's in a hell of a state, sitting on his bed. – Bruce . . . is that you . . . I can't find my glasses . . . I don't know what I've done with them . . . I had them last night . . .

– You were three sheets last night, I tell him.

– Yes, but I had my glasses . . .

– Listen Bladesey, come to think of it I dinnae mind ay ye having glasses oan last night . . .

– Oh my God . . . I can't see Bruce . . .

– Never mind Brother Blades. Bruce Robertson will be your eyes. Ah'll pick the hoors for ye son, dinnae you worry. Premium minge.

– But . . .

– The only butts that come intae it are the ones we'll be fuckin doon that red-light district. Now fling that coat oan and let's paint the toon red. It's oor last day!

I'm leading Bladesey over to the red-light district. The hurdy-gurdy wheezes out some atmospheric Dutch music. The guy that winds it up has his hat out for change but he's wasting his time with me. Every red cent is designated hooring and drugs money. Even grub is a luxury at the moment. I turn away from the outstretched cap and scramble to avoid an approaching bike as we're standing in the cycle lane, but Bladesey's too slow. It rams him, though not at force. The Cloggie cunt starts shouting at him: – Klootzak! Asshole!

I keep a tighter grip on him. The wee cunt's shaking through pish withdrawal and fear. After a bit I steer him into a fat hoor's den and leave him.

– Bruce, I . . . I . . . he stammers.

– Look after my mate doll, I wink at her, – he's lost his specs and his mince pies arenae too good.

— I look after him good, she says in a Caribbean accent.

— . . . I . . . I . . . I . . . Bladesey moans.

— I take special care of you big boy, the hoor says, leading him into her den.

I then set out on *my* day's hooring, leaving the wee cunt to find his ain wey back. I go back to my wee student girl. I got so carried away, I just clean forgot about my mucker Brother Blades. An oversight on my part.

When I return back to Cok City a few hours later, Bladesey's home and he's pissed off. He looks terrible.

— I told you to stay there Bladesey, where did you get to? I was worried sick!

— I . . . eh, actually eh, took a taxi . . . you were gone so long . . . she wouldn't let me stay until you came back . . . the girl in the room . . .

— Well, you missed a good time, I tell him.

I was sorely tempted to leave the half-blind cunt in the Dam, but I decide that he has his uses. In the airport lounge bar at Schipol I wait until Bladesey's gone to the lavvy then I put a porn movie and some of the charlie I scored earlier into his bag.

It's a no-lose situation for me as we go through the Customs back in Edinburgh. I either have the pleasure of seeing Bladesey's coupon as he gets huckled, leaving me to explain to Bunty that I wasn't into Amsterdam, I was convinced that we were going to Scarborough, but Cliff insisted; or, alternatively, he gets off scot-free and I've got the some quality sniff and wallpaper-paste mix. It's the later scenario as Bladesey strolls through the Customs with ease.

I'm more relieved that they didn't open my bag; the flannels, shirts, socks and keks were kicking up a real eye-watering furore in there. While I'm obviously happy to have some quality gear as I retrieve the goods while Brother Blades takes another piss at Edinburgh Airport, I'm a little disappointed that Bunty hasn't had the opportunity of seeing the essentially depraved nature of the creature she married.

But there's time enough for that.

Post-Holiday Blues

My first day back after a holiday and that cunt Toal calls me into his office. There's something different about that spastic, and it takes me a second to realise what it is. Then I see it: he's dispensed with the Brylcreem and blow-dried his hair, back-combing it. A new Toal! A media-friendly, softer, slicker, more youthful trendy image for the modern law enforcement officer in a democracy. He looks like a fucking simpering poof, self-conscious and effete. That barnet will take some getting used to. Oh no you don't Sister Toal. Same fuckin rules!

— In your absence Amanda Drummond's been taking the leading role in the investigation. I've decided, after a great deal of deliberation, that I want this state of affairs to continue.

I feel my holiday euphoria evaporate in the face of the heat from Toal's bombshell. My response is unformed and undignified. — A silly wee . . . I stammer.

— I expect you to give her full co-operation. Bruce, since you've been away the media have got interested again. The Forum's been making a lot of noises. It seems that you've been a bit lax on the community relations side. It's exactly that area that Amanda's strong in. It's horses for courses Bruce, Toal nods semi-apologetically. —You'll have to go with me on this just now, he snaps truculently, as I feel the words Listen Brother Toal dry in my throat.

I can only stand there like a fag-hag outside the bogs of some nancy-boy meatpacking disco just before last orders as Toal picks up the phone. — Amanda, Bruce's back. Can you come up here and brief him on what's been happening?

He puts the phone down.

— Look, eh, Gus Bain has filled me in . . . I start. I just want to go. I need to take stock before I can face that gloating dyke Drummond.

— Gus isn't on the ball Bruce, he's going nowhere, Toal says impatiently.

That makes me feel good as I had Gus marked down as almost a serious rival in the promo stakes. It's out of order though, Toal badmouthing the auld cunt like that.

Good news for me but. I'm feeling a bit more up as Drumsticks comes in and gives me a look of distaste and it makes me feel even more comfortable that she evidently hates doing this as much as I do. — Hi Mandy, I smile.

— Did you have a good holiday Bruce? she asks with a forced civility for Toal's sake.

— Not bad at all.

— Holland, wasn't it?

— Yes. It's a regular jaunt. A very civilised country.

— The landscape's a bit flat though, isn't it? Toal interjects.

— I like it, I shrug, — it provides an interesting contrast with Scotland's more rugged terrain.

— What is there to do there? Drummond probes. She wants me to say 'hoors and drugs' in front of Toal.

— It's a very relaxing place. You can sit in a café and just watch the world go by with a nice coffee, I shudder slightly as the hangover kicks in. Fuckin cunts are trying to wind me up. But what do they know? Nothing, zilch, sweet fuck all. Sum total: the big fuckin zero.

— I've heard that Amsterdam has a lot of drug problems, Toal says, looking at me challengingly.

— Yes, that's the downside of the city. It's far too liberal and as a result it does attract scum. Anyway, enough idle banter about holidays, what about the case? I say coldly and briskly, making Toal and Drummond look like the frivolous lightweights they are. Toal looks a bit narked that I've stolen a mark on him. He'd better get used to it because once I'm promoted, that's the way it'll be. Fucked if I'm taking any of his bullshit then.

Drummond starts rabbiting on a load of shite which, however you dress it up, amounts to fuck all has happened since I've been away, just as I guessed. How the fuck did they ever expect to make progress with a case like this in the absence of the main player? That's the problem with this wee team of ours: too many Stronachs, no enough Dalglishs.

— . . . and Valerie Johnston, the girl on the cloakroom, has stated that Alex Setterington and David Gorman were definitely in the club that night.

Drummond's wearing a white blouse and has a darker coloured bra on which is visible through it. I'd gie they tits a wee squeeze, only as a personal favour to her, mind you. That would gie her something to frig aboot! She catches where my eyes are and ostentatiously does up her jacket. Aye, *you wish* ya fuckin daft cow.

— So what we have to do is to pull in Setterington and Gorman for questioning, she continues.

— I don't think that would be the way to play it Mandy, my sweet, I pleasantly interject, and she goes to pull me up but I talk over her, raising my voice, — Setterington and Gorman are hardened criminals. They're veterans of questioning. They'll give away Scottish Football Association, and they'll have a smart-arsed lawyer like Conrad Donaldson doon here straight away. I note Toal's mouth puckering in resigned distaste at the acknowledgement of my point. — If they know we're on to them, they'll just close ranks. I know these bastards. I think we should keep them under observation, see what they're getting up to. One of their mates is a grass and I can lean on him.

Drummond has lost the moment and Toal's nodding vigorously. — I agree Bruce, he says, — these are crafty bastards. We need to have hard evidence before we make any move on them.

This informer you know, do you reckon he'll come up with something?

— A racing certainty, I smile.

— Good, says Toal. — Right Amanda, keep on with the surveillance. Bruce, could you hold on for a minute?

Drummond coughs a nervy: — Certainly Bob, and departs, kip as rid as my cherry eftir a night's hooring, and Toal's probably ready to tell me that the inspectorship is as good as mine.

— Do you have a problem with Amanda? he asks.

— Not at all, I tell him.

— She's complained to me about your manner. Do you have to refer to her in that condescending way? Her name's Amanda, it might be better if you called her that, rather than Mandy my sweet.

Fuckin stroppy dyke.

— C'mon gaffer, I smile, using the casual but respectful tone to soften Toal up, which it does, — she's being far too uptight. I'm just being friendly and informal, that's all.

— Bruce, you're a good and experienced officer, but you're going to have to relate better to all other officers, particularly if you become an inspector. These things are important in the modern police force, mark my words, Toal reprimands, sweeping a hand through his bouffant hair, but it's a gentle reprimand and he can't keep the underlay of complicity out of his voice.

— I hear what you're saying Brother Toal, but it takes two to tango. I suggest you have a similar word with our Msss Drummond.

I'd like to turn of the gasssss for Mssss Drummond, fuckin well turn it off for good.

Toal sits up in his seat somewhat pompously, as he tends to do when I play the craft card, — I have spoken to Amanda and made her aware of her responsibilities.

I'll fuckin well bet. That wee slag thinks that crawling up Toal's erse is the way on to the fast track. Wrong!

Later on I'm in the cannie, catching up on some of the gossip and the wee cow comes over to me. – Bruce, can I have a word? She nods to the corridor. A uniformed spastic from the craft raises his eyes. This wee cunt's goin tae rub ma face in it already about her new role. No way am I taking any bullshit fae the likes of Drummond.

– I don't know if you've heard Bruce, but it's Gus's birthday tomorrow, and we're planning a wee surprise party for him. In Serious Crimes.

So that's all it is. Nae cunt telt ays, Lennox or any of them. Bastards. – I was aware of that, I say haughtily.

– Just making sure, she smiles, and turns to leave. – See you later.

She thinks that she can get roond me wi the softly-softly approach. Wrong. Same rules apply. I head back downstairs but it's typical post-holiday blues and I'm hating it at this shitehoose.

I'm sifting through the papers on my desk for the case file and I see out of the corner of my eye that a woman has come into the office with Drummond and Hazel the clerical. She looks vaguely familiar. Drummond's pointing over at me.

The woman has a wee laddie with her and they tentatively approach my desk, following Drummond.

– Bruce, my colleague informs me, – somebody to see you. It's Mrs Sim.

Who the fuck's this

– I came last week, the woman says meekly, – but they told me you were on holiday. I wanted to thank you personally for everything that you did for Colin. She turns to the wee boy. – This is a good man Euan, this is the man that tried to help your daddy . . . she stifles a sob.

The wee boy keeps his head bowed, but raises his eyes up at me and pushes out a smile. He'll be about ages with Stacey.

– His heart was bad . . . it was a family thing . . . hereditary. I'm watching her lips moving. – He never let it bother him. He was a good man, she whimpers and sobs and Drummond's got her hand, and she looks back at the wee laddie and then at me,

— . . . and this is a good man. This man tried to help your dad son, tried to help him when the rest just stood by and gawped . . . he tried so hard for your daddy . . .

How did you feel

— . . . I just wanted to say thank you Sergeant Robertson . . . Bruce . . . I just wanted to say thank you for trying to help him . . .

— I'm sorry I couldn't save your husband, I tell her.

— Thank you . . . you did all anybody could. Thank you. This is a good man Euan, she sniffs, as Amanda leads her away, looking back at me in a deep, soulful and human way.

Gus comes over and grabs my shoulder tightly. — Perr lassie. An awfay Christmas for her and the wee felly.

She doesn't know, the woman: she just doesn't know.

I have a bash at the crossword. I can't concentrate, and I decide to take an early finish. It's Stronach's testimonial match at Tynecastle the night, but no way will I go there and line that spastic's pockets. It would be too much to see him poncing around full of himself. I can't see there being much of a crowd. It'll be Gary MacKay or Craig Levine size I should imagine.

So the evening finds me down at the Lodge listening to some referee twat who's a building inspector with the district council. He's holding court and it's not a bad crack. Bladesey's lost. He comes over to join us sporting his new glesses, but like most English cunts, he kens nowt about fitba. Ray Lennox appears with a couple of uniformed spastics, who aren't wearing their uniforms but are still uniformed spastics and always will be. I nod to him to come over and he's squeezing in beside me. I've tipped him off before about hanging around with these nonentities. Associate too much with losers and that's exactly what you'll become.

This referee's some cunt. — So there I was at Ibrox and they need the three points to clinch the title. I mean, they're about thirty points ahead so it's a foregone conclusion, it's mathematically impossible for them to be caught. It's a gala day, and the families are all out, the bairns with their faces painted up, the lads looking forward to celebrating. Coisty's put them one–nil up with a close-range tap-in at the back post. Ha ha ha. He's some character. Suspicion of offside but Oswald Beckton's flag stayed down. Oswald, Lodge 364. You'll ken his face, the ref prompts.

There's a few nods and knowing smiles around the table. – So anyway, the whole place goes up and it's party-time. Everybody's singing 'we're up to our knees in fenian blood' and it's a gala atmosphere. But then, with a couple of minutes left, a long ball gets punted through the middle towards the Rangers goal. This young lad nips inbetween Goughy and McLaren and they bring him down heavily inside the box. Now, it's a blatant penalty, but of course there's no way I'm going to give that and spoil the party. I mean, they'd've had to have gone to Firhill the next week to win it, stuck with a fifteen thousand capacity. How could I spoil it for them to lift the flag at home? They were going to win it anyway! By the length of Argyll Street! No way was yours truly going to be a killjoy. Imagine what the boys in the Lodge at Whitburn would have said! My life wouldnae have been worth living. Spoiling a gala day out! So I waved play on.

– As ye do mate, eh, Councillor Bill Armitage said.

– I had to send off this tube for arguing. The ref's decision is final. This arsehole wouldnae let it go, even after I'd booked him. There's always one, eh!

– Fenian bastard, Bill Armitage scoffed.

– I don't mind telling ye, the ref continues, – that it was a bit embarrassing watching it on Scotball the next day. The boys were great though, they kept the replays to a minimum and avoided any reverse-angle showings. Anyway, I spoke to the SFA observer at the match in the Blue Room afterwards and he understood the situation fully. Turns out that he's in the same Lodge as wee Sammy Kirkwood. You mind of wee Sammy! He says to me.

I nod. Wee Sammy used to get me magazines. Good stuff n

all, though not quite as good as Hector The Farmer's. I'll have to bell that auld fucker and see if he's got any new gear.

— Anyway, thank God for the presenter. He said there was no way I could have seen the incident as I wasn't up with play. The guys at the press were great as well, played the whole thing down, didn't let on that the switchboards were jammed with callers. Passed off the odd one or two as token Tim bigots who would say that anyway.

— These cunts are paranoid, Armitage laughs.

— A chief sports writer for one of the dailies told me at the Lodge, he says: normally we'd have made a bit more of a song and dance about it but it does nobody any good to keep running Scottish football down.

We then listen to Armitage going on a bit about the new Scottish Parliament. — It'll be a good thing; mair opportunities for our people. Of course we'll have tae deal with the Papes, but there's nothing new there. The party in Scotland's always had that horse-trading between the Catholic mafia and the craft. Ah wouldnae mind gieing them anti-abortion legislation in exchange for some plum chairmanships of working parties or committees . . . particularly licensing, he grins. — It just means that some daft wee hairy that gets knocked up the duff has tae get oan the bus tae Carlisle tae get cleaned oot. Hardly a staggering blow, I would have thought.

— Right enough, Ray nods, then turning to me whispers, — Fancy some coke the night?

I fancied some fucking coke awright, in fact I had some on me. Especially after Toal's news, Drummond heading up the team. Toal. The cunt'll not be happy until he turns me into a fuckin junky.

Me answering to a silly wee lassie?

Aye, right. I d 〔*00000000000000eating, on*〕 There's a failure on Toal's part to reali 〔*and on. 00000000 eating.*〕 lly blank and can't see the possibiliti 〔*Perhaps there are others like*〕 if it bit his fucking useless erse. 〔*me. I can certainly conceive*〕

I'm up to the 〔*of this, the notion that I*〕 dge business is the

only thing that k[...] am not the only one of my kind. d the rest of the
polis boys again[...] *Why should I be? Perhaps there* guys. They tend
tae be a sorry bu[...] *are others in here, sharing the* [...]eve situation. So
it's me, Lennox, [...] *parasite role with me. I even* [...]rian Main, Steve
Underwood, Ke[...] *fancy that I can feel them in* [...]from Aberdeen.

Masonic ritu[...] *here, twisting and writhing in* [...]ressed sexuality
in that keeps th[...] *the Host's gut with me, but this* [...]the likes of Ray
Lennox and tha[...] *may be just a response to my* [...]e business with
any of them. An[...] *melancholic state of mind.* [...]lture within the
masons, but wan[...] *I've my Host, my friend who* [...]uch further than
any of those cunt[...] *gives me everything I need to*

In the back r[...] *survive. But to live, I need much* patterns, and a
strobe light which[...] *more. I need to feel part of* ng and shaking
as Coulson cuts [...] *something bigger perhaps* hed whine, and
Underwood's on[...] *something that is a part of me.* the tube into the
incision and suck[...] *0000000000000000000000000* g the bottle and
it gets auld Gus s[...] *00000000it has to be said that* out women in a
lusty way, which[...] *this laddie's diet is not that* honour, and the
withering looks [...] *nutritious. This points to my faux pas* has been
made. Still, we a[...] *Host coming from, perhaps, a* auld spastic.

poor disadvantageous starting-out
point in this great journey of life.
He's eating all sorts of cheap and
useless garbage. But on the other
hand, the sheer volume consumed goes
against this; so maybe we can postulate
that the laddie has grown up in a world
of privation and although he has been
able to accumulate more resources he
has not quite been able to shed himself

We get [...] *of all those proletarian habits.0000000* Phillip, as the
dark beers ha[...] *The Host's philosophy of life seems then;* ng just about
every cunt's [...] *more rather than better. 00000000000* ty. Ray and I
shake off Bladesey after I've pumped the sorry cunt for more
information about Bunty's mental state. Then we absond back
to his flat. Ray's place is furnished post-Thatcherite nouveau

schemie single-shagger style. That is to say, no real style at all. It's dominated by a red suite, a two-seater velvety love-couch and matching chair. It's like a hoor's room back in the Dam! I'm no sitting in that couch, Lennox should be so lucky. If it was fuckin Inglis, he'd be oan it like a shot! No that he would feel anything if it was Lennox that was up him!

Ray's looking for the mirror, spoon and razor-blade kit I brought him back from the Dam. He reckons that it gives extra quality tae the chop and never uses credit cards indoors now. I realise that the set cost me the equivalent of twenty quid in UK cash and feel a resentment rise up in my chest. It was a moment of weakness giving Lennox a present, even if I only gave him it in order to encourage him to sort me out with posh. I idly press the tip of my fag against his velvet cushion, feeling a satisfying rush of adrenalin and a lump rise in my chest as it browns and parts on the first, second, third and fourth contact. Then I admire my handiwork, before quickly flipping the cushion over to conceal the four new holes.

Lennox returns and chops out some lines. He's been on D.S. duty and has nabbed quite a bit of high grade, the lucky bastard. I've divided up the stuff I brought back from Amsterdam, and though it pains me to admit it, Lennox gear's even better. The perks of the job. Okay for some. What about me? What perks do you get on topped coons? Going round community groups talking to chip-on-the-shoulder darkies who hate your guts. And that daft wee lassie Drummond sticking her oar in. Fuck that for a game of soldiers. Big-time OT on this one mind you, especially with that docile mutation Toal's breeks full of sludgy, soft shite. Same rules applying in that case, I kid you not.

— The last sniff I got off these morons I busted, I'm telling you Robbo, what a total waste ay time. There was so little coke in it, I should've just left the spastics to it and saved myself the fucking paperwork. They'd have felt a hell of a lot worse if they had done that rubbish than they did getting a poxy two hundred quid first offence fine.

Lennox is letting his mouser grow a bit. — That's fucking

disgusting. Two hundred poxy quid! Who was the magistrate?

— Urquhart. Surprise surprise, Lennox says, not looking up, firmly engrossed in the chopping up of the lines. He's got patience Lennox, he knows that I want that line, but the cunt'll play around until he's got it as fine as fuck.

— Mr fuckin pat-oan-the-heid-and-penny-oot-the-poor-boax, my head's shaking in disgust.

— Conrad fuckin Donaldson defending the cunts as well, Ray scoffs.

I smile at that name. I wonder how his wee lassie's doing. We could handle another gam fae that little sweetheart. I kid you not.

Ray nods at me to come ahead. I'm on the first line, my twenty's already rolled. I close one nostril and snort for Caledonia. It hits me hard. Good gear. Phoah, ya fuckin cunt that ye are. My mouth is instantly numbed and I start gabbing. — Listen Ray you should've heard that cunt Toal on aboot you the other day. It was Ray Lennox this, Ray Lennox that. I said to the cunt, there's an awfay lot ay things getting attributed tae Ray Lennox here. I think Ray Lennox would be baulking at some of the stuff his name's being mentioned in connection with.

— Eh? What's this, Ray asks, looking at me tentatively.

— Between you and me Ray, I wouldnae be surprised if you get drafted into the team on this coon case.

— Like fuck! Ah've been stalking these fucking Sunrise Community hippies on this cannabis bust for months!

— I'm just saying Ray. You know these cunts, same rules apply. One other thing as well . . . this is between you and me likes, I drop my voice canteen-style, even though we're in the privacy of Lennox's gaff.

— What? says Ray, trying to be cool but obviously alarmed.

— Watch Gus.

— Gus Bain?

— Precisely.

— Gus is awright . . . he's been good tae me . . .

— Of course he's awright. He'll have been awright tae you as long as he sees ye as a young laddie, as second fiddle. The thing is Ray, you've earned a lot ay respect in this department, and it's starting tae get tae the auld boy. Ye ken what ah'm saying? I look Lennox in the eye. He's getting the drift I want him to get. – It's the young stag syndrome. Gus is set in his ways. One of the auld school. But he fears the new breed and he can be quite a vindictive old cunt and he's been taking an unhealthy interest in the career progress and extracurricular activities to date of a certain Mister Raymond Lennox.

– You saying that Gus is a squealer?

– Known for it. Watch what you say about cousin charlie when he's around.

– But I never say anything about charlie.

– Aye, well mind and keep it that way.

– Right . . . Lennox nods thoughfully. – I appreciate this Robbo.

This is all bullshit, but life is one big competition. Ray is a pal, but he's also a potential or actual competitor and the only way to handle competitors is to control their level of uncertainty. That's what life is all about: the management of your opponents' uncertainty levels. We don't want this cunt getting too big for his boots, thinking that he somehow counts.

It's a troubled-looking Ray Lennox who snorts his line. The drug instantly restores that veneer of arrogance, but the seeds of doubt have been planted and the comedown will see the harvest of confusion just ripe for us to reap.

A Testimonial

I got in early last night but I couldn't sleep. I'm back in the office early this morning but I'm totally fucked with that cocaine. I was wired. My sinuses are shrivelled and my nose is running constantly. My nerves are jangling. We'll have to be stronger. That's what makes me better than the scum, than the weak Ray Lennoxes of this world. I can laugh at all that shite. But I have to get it together. The phone goes and I jump and shake before lifting the receiver and predictably it's that spastic Toal. This is all part of his psychological warfare but that imbecile has been desk bound far too long to be able to outmanoeuvre Bruce Robertson. Well, spazwit, we have news for you: the same fucking rules apply.

He tells me that he wants to see me in his office straight away. Never mind our routine, the selfish cunt. Thinks of nothing but his ain fat erse and how to keep it covered. Does fuck all but write that film script. Ah ken what the cunt's up tae. I put the paper down and head upstairs. I feel nauseous by the time I get up to Toal's office. The lifts are out of order and I'm out of breath after these two flights. Those fuckin maintenance cunts, they dae fuck all.

— Bruce, we need to have a wee blether. Niddrie's called a team meeting up at his office this afternoon, this sweetie wife tells me. He's using a distasteful 'Niddrie' rather than a pally

'Jim' or a respectful 'the Super'. He's obviously had his gangrenous nuts chewed and is looking for pals. Or perhaps not. The cunt could just be fucking me around. Drummond still hasnae been in touch. Playing silly fannies again.

— What time? I ask. I need to spend some time with the paper. That Claudia Schiffer's in it. A fuckin ride, nae two weys. It says she's opening a restaurant or something like that. Who gives a fuck about that? Show us your erse and tits doll, that's what we want!

— Three.

Page Three.

— Could be t-toiling. I said I'd be at a Forum meeting then.

— Oh God . . . Amanda should be handling that side.

— Well, she ain't been in touch with me to tell me not to go. Are you saying I shouldn't go?

— God . . . no . . . that's what Niddrie's been doing his nut about. The Forum people have been talking to Malcolm St John of STV and Andy Craig of the *News*. Seems they've been very critical of the investigation again, he puffs sourly, as if it's a personal criticism of Toal himself. Mind you, it fuckin well should be, he's the cunt in charge of this investigation, or meant to be.

I've got a copy of last night's late final downstairs. The clerical brought one in. I never saw anything about the case. I remember glancing through it, the back page and the leader column, but all I mind of was the piece on Tom Stronach's testimonial:

> The Edinburgh footballing public can hang its head in shame at the derisory attendance of under two thousand at the testimonial of one of its favoured sons, Tom Stronach. Granted, the recession has meant that for many fans extra games are now a luxury, particularly just one week before Christmas, and the Edinburgh weather had a lot to answer for. However, this level of support for a such a loyal servant to the capital sporting scene is nothing short of an undeserved snub.

I also read that Tom's idol Kenny Dalglish had been unable to attend due to other commitments, but he did send his congratulations to Tom on his gala night. Dalglish was probably washing his hair or something. He had the right idea, keep away from all that shite.

I wished I could keep away from all Toal's shite.

— Nothing's happening Robbo. This investigation just won't move forward. We've been checking all the stores, but we can't trace that bloody hammer, he whinges.

As if I give a Luke and Matt Goss aboot that.

— I see. So Niddrie expects Scottish Television and the *Evening News* to solve the case do they? What spastic journalist has ever solved a fucking crime in his puff? Answer me that?

— I'm as upset as you are Robbo, Toal's old woman's mouth twists. That mooth: the gob of a thief who cannae help but gossip about what he's knocked off, and then is stupid enough to be surprised as the cell door slams behind him. — Anyway, have you got any other news? he asks.

— No, I'd liaise with Amanda as you said.

That will be shinin bright.

— Mmm. Right . . . says Toal. I can already feel his disenchantment with this silly wee tart setting in.

— I'll rearrange the Forum meeting and come to Niddrie's at three.

— No . . . I'll go to Niddrie's. You go to the Forum meeting.

— Right, I tell him, then as I exit I think: what the fuck is that wee Amanda Drummond daein? I should go back in and tell Toal this, but I can't be bothered. My arse is itching like fuck. Why is it always me that has to dae this fuckin shite? If I just jacked it in the morn, that would show the cunts. See how they got on then. This whole fuckin place would grind to a halt, simply because it's stuffed full of the most clueless cunts that ever hid behind a polisman's uniform. They cunts wouldn't last ten minutes over in New South Wales or even doon in the Met. Don't know what real fuckin poliswork is, any of the cunts.

Fuck'em. I head downstairs, stopping off at the bogs where

I give my hole a good clawing. The flannels are damp with my sweat and I have to take some toilet paper and place it between my skin and the saturated material in order to try and dry the fuckers out. Then it's back to the grind.

I study the papers on my desk, then look around at my clueless colleagues. I've never, ever seen such a motley crew of useless spastics gathered under one roof.

— Aye, it's a strange one awright Peter, I say to Peter Inglis.

— What dae ye mean?

I feel like saying, You, ya poofy cunt, you're the fuckin strange one, but instead I scrutinise the documentation on my desk. — Sometimes I look at this and think, the clues are staring us straight in the face but we just can't fucking crack it.

— Just one breakthrough and it would all fall into place, Gus shrugs.

— That's it though Robbo, Peter says, — always the same story. Ninety per cent perspiration and ten per cent inspiration. We'll just have to keep at it.

— Too true Peter, I nod, lifting up the paper.

ACROSS

1   Speed (8)

7   Lowest of the low (4)

8   Twenties short hairstyle (4,4)

9   From France (6)

10   Sheen, lustre (6)

11   Sight organ (3)

12   Telling fibs (5)

14   Dark beer (5)

16   Grieve loudly (3)

18   Bespatter (6)

20   Divisions of foot or yard (6)

22   Day after today (8)

23   Orange-skin (4)

24   Buyers' snips (8)

DOWN

1   Stand-in for monarch (7)

2   Sharp citrus fruit (5)

3   Work playspace (6)

4   Group of players (6)

5   Falls, plummets (5)

6   Spotted jungle cat (6)

13   Strait (6)

15   Incompetent (7)

16   Himalayan guide (6)

17   Nob, dignitary (6)

19   Flat-antlered deer (5)

21   Bay of Naples isle (5)

– C'mon guys, let's see some fuckin action. Gus, I shout over at him, – Twenty-one doon. Bay of Naples isle, five letters. C'mon! Crime: together we'll crack it.

Gus screws his face up. – We wir in that part ay the world, Edith n me. Sorrento. We took the hovercraft over tae Naples for the day. Ah didnae see any islands Bruce, n we were right acroas Naples bay, comin fae Sorrento likes.

– Well, they've obviously got them Gus, according tae the fuckin paper anyway. Mind you, it's a plebs' paper, I only buy it for the tits, the telly and the fitba . . . what about one doon: Stand-in for monarch? Seven letters.

– Regent.

– That's one . . . two . . . six. Naw.

– Jeanette Charles.

– Eh?

– That Jeanette Charles. The Queen's double. Stands in for the Queen.

– I'm just no gettin this at all the day. Here's one though: Lowest of the low. Four letters. Toal. No, we should get this one awright: SCUM. We deal with them every day. Mind you, Toal: the same fuckin thing, eh.

Later on I see Lennox in the cannie. He's still on the trail of those hippies. The cunt's been avoiding us a wee bit. We run him into town. We pass one of those posh girls' schools. – Mary Erskine's . . . James Gillespie's . . . the sound ay they posh schooly citadels, Ray. It sets up the horn in ye. Erse. Skin. Lesbians. It was some dirty cunt that named they schools. Some fuckin pervert.

Lennox laughs and shakes his head. – You're some man Robbo.

– Tell ye Ray, I say, – they wee lassies: like wee angels. Then they grow up, that's the problem. They grow up intae cows and fuckin hoors. And a cow's worse than a hoor. A least you ken where you stand with a hoor. A cow? You never fucking well ken.

Lennox is looking uncomfortable. – Well, aye . . .

Doesnae understand a thing, that's his problem. Thinks he kens the fuckin lot. But what does he know?

He knows nothing.

Absolutely sweet fuck all. Too fuckin big for his boots, that cunt.

We stop in for a bite to eat at the pie shop on the South Bridge. Eddie Moncur from the South Side office is there with a uniformed spastic. I nod at them. There's a slow, lazy, overweight cunt serving us, or who should be serving us, but he's taking his time. — Who ate all the pies . . . I start up a slow chant, but Mister Cool Wanker Lennox refuses to join in. Above and beyond it all is he? I think not.

— A couple ay pints later but, eh Ray? No way am I gaun back intae that place this affie, that's for sure.

Ray looks at me as if I'm mental. — You're forgetting something. Gus's surprise do.

Of course. How could I forget that. I get to thinking that there might be a surpise for Mister Ray Cunty-Baws Lennox as well.

Surprise Party

It was a good idea to throw a wee surprise party for Gus, as it's the auld cunt's fifty-fifth. Christmas is all but with us, so any excuse for a piss-up. Gus but: he should be thinking of early retirement, no fuckin promoted posts. What an auld spastic, spoiling things for every other bugger. Or *trying* tae spoil things. Think again, old man.

However, we've got a few cans and bottles in, and there's a fair crowd here. Yes, even Drummond's here: one gless ay wine, then making a big point tae every cunt about needing to get back tae work. Nae cunt takes a blind bit ay notice ay her though, even if the atmosphere lightens up as she leaves. Needs cocked badly that yin, for every other cunt's piece ay mind as well as her ain. Anywey, I'm mair interested in *real* fanny. That big civvy piece, the Size Queen, she's around. Lennox is smarming and getting nowhere. He's smarming, but he's no thinking. I am. We made a fifty-quid bet on who'd be the first yin to get into the Size Queen's knickers, and that dosh is going in the Robertson coffers. I kid you not. I watch what I'm drinking and bide my time until every cunt's three sheets. Then I start shifting the conversation round to the topic of a gentleman's size, watching Lennox go all nervy and trying to change the subject.

— Mind back in Oz, at the New South Wales Police Department, I carry on, we used to play this party game . . . in our station at College Street. The Aussies . . . well, they can be a bit *risqué*.

— Aw aye, what was that? asks Karen Fulton. She's a game cow. Known for it. Gone a bit snooty these days, but the alcohol and the festive atmosphere of the holiday period are just the ticket to pull a slag back into the fold. They just can't help themselves.

— Perhaps I'd better not say, Karen my darling. Our colonial cousins . . . can be rather coorse.

— C'mon! Spill the beans, Fulton urges.

— This sounds intriguing, the Size Queen purrs.

— C'mon Bruce, don't start something you can't finish, says big-mooth Lennox, raising an eyebrow, blissfully unaware that he's signing his ain death warrant.

— Well . . . okay . . . what it was, right, was that the guys would take it in turns tae go into the photocopier room and photocopy their wedding tackle on to a sheet of paper. Then they'd write their names on the back, and put them into an envelope. Once everybody's been done somebody then tacks the prints on to the board.

— Get away Bruce! Lennox scoffs, but to the cunt's embarrassment, everyone else seems captivated. I look at the big hoor, the Size Queen, whose eyes are like saucers.

— Naw, bit listen, I continue, — The lassies would then try to match the cock to the guy.

— Lit's dae it! roars the Size Queen. I clock Lennox looking stricken, but there's nothing he can do. Even auld Gus is up for it. Peter Inglis goes first, the fuckin animal. Fags are the biggest size queens of the lot and a repressed, inadequate closet case like him must be drooling at the prospect of checking out all that meat. Aye Inglis, ah'll have you outed ya cunt. Promotion? That? Aye, sure. It might be some equal opportunities cunt's idea tae turn the force intae a bastion of buggery but old values die hard here, especially in the craft. He'll ken awright.

Inglis emerges with a sheet of paper in an envelope. He hands the envelope to Ralph Considine, who's only a uniformed spastic and thus shouldnae even be here in the first place, and he goes in and does the business, handing the envelope to Gus. There's whooping and cheering from everybody, except a tentative Lennox, when auld Gus goes in. Then Lennox reluctantly disappears, trying to brass it out. I'm next, but when I put my gear oan the gless plate, wiping it first after the rest of these cunts have been against it, I turn up the enlarger switch to full and take the copy, before sliding it back to its normal setting. I stick the name on the back of my enlarged dick. Thankfully the rash doesn't look too noticeable with the black and white image and paper quality.

I emerge with the envelope. Clell and some spastic who worked with Gus do their bit, then we're away.

The game is interesting. One cheeky cow marks me down for what's obviously Lennox's tackle. That will be fuckin right. Eventually they are all turned over and put in descending order:

BRUCE
    GUS
        ALAN
            ANDY
                PETER
                    RALPH
                        STEVE
                            RAY
                                PHILLIP

It turns out that auld Gus's is almost as big as my enlarged one. Nae wonder the sly auld fuck was rarin tae gie it a go! The biggest shock though was that someone was smaller than Lennox, a uniformed spastic called Phillip Watson. I'd've thought that impossible without him having a fanny!

After the disclosure, everybody's giving me loads of attention. I catch the Size Queen's flirtatious eye. As time and drink pass she's embarrassing herself over me, and Lennox has taken the hump big-time, the moosey-faced rat-bag. I'm playing it cool: just flirty enough to keep the cow on the boil, making her suffer, always the best way. I'm doing a James Bond here, firing out the suave *double entendres* left, right and centre, one or two of them across the bows of a certain Mister Raymond Lennox. The same rules apply.

I'm going to say fuck all to this big blonde hoor. I want the Size Queen off her high horse, I want *her* to proposition *me*. Which, after a while and more drink, she does. She sidles up to me and vampishly announces, – The winner deserves a prize. Let's go back in there . . . and she takes off and I follow her at a discreet distance into the copy room, clocking Lennox with a wink as I depart. She leans back across the desk and I don't even kiss her. I lift up her skirt and pull down her knickers. – Give it to me, she's saying, just give it to me now, her eyes shut.

I push in and watch the Size Queen thrust and buck with an increasingly puzzled look on her face. She's daein aw the work and that suits me fine. After a while I shoot my load and leave her wondering what's been happening.

I collect my fifty quid from Lennox then I'm off hame, as high as a fuckin kite. Even the short drive gets me horned up again. It's the rhythm of the traffic and the heat in the car, as well as the lyrical content of the Motley Crüe album *Girls Girls Girls* on the stereo, which has mair references tae hot pussy than a Dutch newspaper would if someone had torched the floating cat home in Amsterdam.

When I get hame there's a couple of letters. One's a gas bill, the other has a Chelmsford postmark and it's from Tony and Diana. I feel my cock stir and think about the four-hundred-mile drive to Chelmsford. I could do it through the night on charlie, fuck myself blind for a couple of hours, then head straight back. Yes. I ignore the gas bill, I ignore all of these. Carole takes care of that shite, and I've enough fuckin paperwork in my job, for fuck sakes. I eagerly tear the Chelmsford letter open.

Dear Bruce,

   I hope all is well with you. We are writing to
tell you that we all feel that it's not a good
idea that you join ourselves and Laurence and
Yvonne next month. I am sorry that you and Carole
are having difficulties, but I don't think it
would be appropriate for you to join us without
her.

   We've had some great times together, but I
think that any period of experimentation needs a
little bit of time for reflection. This is what
Diana and I are currently undertaking.

   I hope you and Carole resolve your difficulties
satisfactorily.

   Best wishes,

   Tony

   Tony Crosby

Tony, the fucking twat. I feel a spasm of hatred twist through
me as the power simultaneously leaves my cock. Fuckin soft
Tony: lecturer in fine art at the Chelmer Institute or whatever
you call it. All our frenetic fucking going on and him mincing
around like a vegetarian in an abattoir. Carole fuckin well shiting
it as well, giving him a nervous hand-job. They don't have the
big-match temperament. That Diana does though. Fuckin hell, I
could have done with going another fuckin few rounds wi yon
big hoor.

   I think about phoning Geoff Nicholson of the Essex police,
and telling him about this sordid little club. Solid in the craft, is
Geoff. I'm just about to pick up the blower when there's a knock
on the door and it's Tom Stronach, his wavy fair hair sticking up
in tufts. He's dressed in a grey Russell Athletic sweatshirt and
grey tracksuit bottoms. He looks quite downcast.

   — Tom . . . how goes it? I ask in phoney concern.

– I'm fuckin Zorba'd Bruce. One thousand, two hundred and thirteen paying customers. I gave that fuckin club twelve years of loyal service.

– I see. I thought the gate was nearer two thousand.

– Naw, the *Evening News* bumped it up a wee bit.

– Well, I was there, I lied. Some fuckin chance. Versus a Derby County reserve side on a pissing wet Tuesday with only eight shopping days left until the gig?

Tom shakes his head, then brightens up a little bit, – I did get a nice note from Kenny Dalglish.

– I'm sure he'd have been there if he could, I shrug. – Guys like that, they must get loads of requests. It's a bad time of the year.

– Aye, right enough, Tom concedes. – Anyway Bruce, I've a couple of tickets for you for the Sportsman's Dinner, for my testimonial likes. We're gonny huv it in that lull between Christmas and New Year. Any excuse to keep the perty going!

– Nice one Tom, I say, grasping the embossed tickets he hands over with the leaflet. Instantly I see that it was a mistake, the bastard has stung me. The ticket reads:

YOU ARE INVITED AS A V.I.P. GUEST TO
THE TOM STRONACH TESTIMONIAL SPORTSMAN'S DINNER
at the Sheraton Hotel, Lothian Road, Edinburgh
on Monday, December 28th, 1997
Dress is informal (lounge suits)

Donation of £60 for all ticket holders to the Tom Stronach Testimonial Fund.

Donation. Sixty bar. Stung by that bastard Stronach! I'm saying nothing, but the cunt's straight in. I might have guessed. He's known for it. There's always a bit of jiggery-pokery, high drama and stand-offs reported in the *Evening News* when his contract comes up for renewal. The bastard isnae slow when it comes to dosh. – Sorry I cannae let ye have them buckshee Bruce, but it defeats the whole purpose, if ye ken what ah mean.

– Mmm, right Tom, I cough, – I'll just get my cheque-book. Cunt.

I'm scribbling out a cheque and he's rabbiting away in my ear, – Graeme Souness might be one of the after-dinner speakers. I'm hoping that Kenny'll make it this time as well. And Rodney Dolacre's definitely coming up. He's a great speaker.

– Mmm. Rodney Dolacre, ex-England. I hear that he makes a bit of money on the circuit. He's done some stuff with Besty, Marshy and Greavesy.

– Aye, it was good of him to express interest.

No way will Dalglish, Souness or Dolacre come to that tube's testimonial dinner.

Stronach wastes little time in donning that mantle of arrogance which characterises most fitba guys on a roll. – If ye want any mair tickets Bruce, just gies a shout. Ah'm no sayin ah'll be able tae get them mind, but ye ken, seein as it's you n that.

– I'll bear that in mind, I snap, handing over the cheque which is equivalent to twelve blow-jobs from a Leith hoor. Bastard.

The cunt leaves with a smile on his face. He's aw fuckin pleased wi himself cause he thinks that he's got one over on Bruce Robertson. Well you are in for a shock, my dim-witted spastic footballing friend, because the news for you is that the same rules apply.

Later that night Chrissie comes over. Stronach's net curtains twitch, but he's playing tonight, so it'll be that nosey golddigging hoor he married. I pull Chrissie in and we start to turn the gas off for each other. The hoor is getting good at this, her that wisnae intae it at all in the first place.

–Tighter Bruce . . . tighter . . . she groans, and I feel my own windpipe constrict a few centimetres as she twists her belt.

I'm finding it difficult to keep enthusiastic. I keep thinking about the rivals in the promotion stakes:

GUS BAIN
PETER INGLIS
JOHN ARNOTT

Fuck every one of youse plebs . . .

— Fuck me harder Bruce! Fuck me harder! Chrissie's imploring.

Fuck every one of youse . . .

There's Stacey's school picture on the sideboard. I can't look at it, I wish I'd turned it away, or put it in the drawer. She's watching us . . .

Stacey's watching me and this cow . . .

. . . this isnae . . .

I'm a good man . . . she said it . . . the woman, his wife . . . I tried to pump the life back into the boy . . .

Pump

Like I'm pumping this bitch . . .

Pump

— Oh Bruce . . . c'mon . . . oh . . . oh . . . oh God . . . oh . . . oh . . . oh . . . ooohhhhh . . .

And I'm still pumping, but the mair ye gie this hoor, the mair she takes. I'm really fucking well trying and it's a relief when that horrendous shriek fills the air to signal that she's getting there and I feel the belt slacken from my neck and I twist my hips deftly and start to fire my own spunk home.

— Fuck sakes Chrissie . . . I gasp as my ejaculations fade like the pulse of a dying man and my gyrations settle to motionlessness.

I collapse on to her, roll off and we doze for a while. I wake up first and inspect the damage.

The blood vessels in my eyelids have ruptured and there's a thick mark on my neck. I'm a professional law enforcement

officer. I have to deal with the public. I can't go around looking
like this because of that selfish bitch. No with a promotion board
coming up.

— That was great, she says, stretching languidly before getting up and getting dressed. — Listen Bruce . . . she says as she
moves fluently into her underwear then her skirt and blouse, — I
know we need to talk about what kind of commitment we want
to make to each other, but I don't see that there's a need to rush
things.

— I think that's quite sensible, I say. She's looking smart. Put
on a bit of weight, had her hair tinted. There's more confidence
and grace in her movements.

— I mean, I don't think that coming out of a relationship
straight into another is something that's very sensible, she
smiles, tossing her blonde hair back and tugging a brush through
it. Let's just keep it on this basis until we find out what our real
feelings are.

— I couldn't agree more. We should look before we leap, I
tell her. She's worth a poke alright. — Why don't you stick about
for a bit, have some nosh and we'll maybe have a bit more fun
later on? I move across to the sideboard and put Stacey's picture
in the top drawer.

— I'd love to Brucey, but I've got somebody to see.

— Oh, I say.

— See you later Brucey baby, she swings her bag over her
shoulder. She turns back to me and kisses my forehead and winks
and then says in an American accent, — Glad we're parking in the
same lot honey, then she's oot the fuckin door.

— Right . . .

Gone.

Fuckin

Thinks that she can just go like that after trying to fuck up
my promotion. Who the suffering fuck does *she* think she is?
She'd never replace Carole! She's never the one!

A ten-a-penny polisman's fuck, that's aw she is!

She's left her lipstick. Her red, red lipstick.

More Carole

I have to admit it, leaving Australia was a mistake. Bruce and I were at our happiest there. It was just that we went out to be with my mum and when my dad died she wanted to come back. There seemed no point in staying over there because Stacey was just a baby and she hadn't started school. I know that I was selfish and that I didn't really think of Bruce's career. He was doing so well in the Sydney police. I think it's diabolical that he had to return to Scotland on a lower grade than the one he was on in Australia.

I'm looking forward to seeing Bruce again, so we'll be back together as a family; me, Bruce and our little girl Stacey. She has to accept the wrong she's done and the hurt she's caused everyone with her silly little lies. I often feel guilty, I feel that I should have taught her better, taught her the difference between right and wrong. She's a good girl really though and it's important for her to know that Bruce and I forgive her.

All families go through these kind of traumas and it's important not to make more of these things than is necessary. It's a complicated world enough to grow up in these days.

I am back in the bar again. Two men are looking at me.

One says something that I don't catch, but the hostility is unmistakable.

Why is it that a woman cannot drink alone?

You want me but you can't have me.

Robertson's my name.

I took the name of my man.

I am his.

If he was here now, he'd silence you, your leering, sneering faces. You would never be able to stand up to my Bruce. You're not men.

Private Lessons

Worms. I'm not happy. I've been reading more about them at the library. There's a tidy bird works there as well. When I get bored looking at the books, I look at her. I've been here most of the morning, after another sleepless night. But it's soon time to relocate to the office, as Saturday means big-time OT. Predictably, it's mobbed out. Lennox is in as well. We agree to shuffle some papers for an hour, then head out.

It's great to be cruising around in the motor. I'm well wrapped up and the roads are clearer. Lennox is obviously uncomfortable, shivering away in an inappropriate suede jacket.

— Dressed for the weather, eh Ray, I snigger.

— Fuckin plain-clothes allowance is rank, he grumbles.

Moaning cunt. If he didnae spend aw his money oan design-er labels, he might make the allowance run tae some practical gear. Thinks that the taxpayer's nowt better tae dae than tae fund that fucker tae prance about on an imaginary catwalk while he pretends that he's polis.

As our trip progresses, it becomes abundantly clear that Lennox is keeping his cards close to his chest. The thing is, we are aware of that. Lennox is second division. He is not aware of that. There is a set of rules which apply and those are rules that the likes of Ray Lennox could only ever have a rudimentary knowledge of, whereas the Bruce Robertsons of this world, we are moving off on a different tangent.

We kid you not.

— Maybe call in at the Fish Factory, eh Ray?

— Okay, Lennox says.

I turn off Junction Street into Ferry Road. — Shirley, we muse, — ma sister-in-law. Mind the time we both rode her?

— Aye, says Lennox uneasily.

Mr Top Shagger Lennox, huh! Thon daft wee laddie couldnae satisfy that piece. Exposed as an inadequate. She's sucking me off and Lennox puts it in her from behind and she's backing intae him and after a bit she's gaun, — Change ends . . . Bruce . . . fuck me . . . fuck m *000000000000eat Bruce* d Lennox removes the toothpick he e *eat, eat it all up000000they* 's her away, as her lips try to tease *told you it was good for0000* nox's limp piece.

— The hoor' *000000000they were right000* bad's ay thum oan the go. *00000you didn't believe them*

Lennox smile *then0000but they were right,* bugh, Robbo.

You are *not* som *so eat 0000eat everything0* mond.

The Fish Factory is our name for a Leith brothel which operates as a sauna, or is it a Leith sauna which operates as a brothel? No matter. Auld Maisie, the most experienced madam in the city is in, and the kettle's oan.

We pit the squeeze oan Maisie that often the ex-hoor can hardly be chuffed tae see us, but a good hoor (and Maisie was one of the best) is always a superb actress so we get the red carpet treatment. That's the beauty aboot being polis: it doesnae really matter whether or not everybody hates you, as long as they're civil tae your face and can put up a good front. You can only live in the world you ken. The rest is just wishful thinking or paranoia. — Bruce darlin, Maisie states (correctly), wi a wee peck on the cheek for yours truly.

— So Maisie. How goes it? I enquire, flopping back on to the couch and putting my arms around the back of my head. I get a whiff from my armpits and almost lower them in panic. Fuck it. Let the cunts smell Bruce Robertson. Maisie doesnae register. A hoor must learn to live with unpleasant smells. She's kicking oan now Maisie, but she's still a looker; in a heavy, print-dress matronly sort ay wey.

— No bad Bruce, no bad. We've a new lassie sterted; a wee lassie fae Aberdeen. Ye want tae check her oot?

— Later maybe Maisie, I smile, with a broad wink.

She looks up at Lennox, — Mibbee yir young pal here might?

Lennox gets a flush roond his eyes. He smiles stoically.

I catch this and turn to him. — Tell ye what Ray, Maisie here, she'd teach ye things thit yir ma couldnae. Forgotten mair thin you're ever likely tae learn. Ah keep tryin tae entice her back oot ay retirement, but she's havin nane ay it.

Maisie's laughing and shaking her heid as Ray continues to look uncomfortable. I lean forward and pull out a pen from my top pocket and start tapping with it on the glass-topped table. — Even for a fresh young piece ay meat like Detective Sergeant Raymond Lennox here Maisie?

She gives Ray, who now seems in excruciating pain, a quick once over. — Sorry sweethert, ah jist dae it fir love now, no fir money. Ah leave that tae the youngsters. Ah'm a one-man wimmin these days.

— Ray here's gittin himself a bit ay a reputation oan the force as a stud, I smile, puckering my lips and poking the pen languidly in and out of the ball I've made of my fist.

— Aw aye? Maisie leers.

That puts our Mister Lennox in his place. And I'm not finished yet. — Aw aye, so if yir ever coaxed oot ay retirement, this is your man: definitely. They tell me he's the best.

Maisie kens that she might have to do business with the up and coming boys on the force like Ray Lennox, so it serves no purpose to humiliate him. She moves from the particular to the general, in an obvious attempt to spare Lennox's blushes. — Tell ye what Bruce, Maisie says with an air of confidentiality, — if ye could measure aw the inches ay cock ah've hud in the line ay business, n pit thum aw the gither, ye'd be reaching tae the moon n back!

Of course I'm well wide for this game and I'm fucked if that spastic Lennox is squirming off the hook until I'm ready for him to do so. – Well Maisie, if ye wanted tae get yir lips around the sweetest piece ay prime Scotch beef, I kiss my fingertips and shut my eyes in an exquisite gesture, then thumb over at Ray, – D.S. Lennox here is yir man.

– As ah say Bruce, those days are over for me, but if they wernae, wi this fine lookin laddie here, well, it'd be mixin business wi pleasure, ah kin tell ye. She licks her lips at Lennox, who's looking like his fuckin soul has just imploded.

Aye Lennox, you'll ken. To save his further embarrassment Maisie goes off on a story concerning one of our city fathers. – Thir wis one Lord Provost, this wis wey before your time son, Maisie nods at Ray, then turns tae me. – You'll mind ay him Bruce?

– Oh yes . . . by reputation alone though Maisie. Ah'm no that auld!

– Ah didnae mean it like that, yir jist a laddie bichrist, she smiles with those cat's-erse lips, the moisture having been sucked from those just as sure as they've sucked out the semen of millions of punters from here and overseas. – Naw I'm talking aboot Provost . . . well, it wid be improper tae mention names. Bit this Provost was well known amongst the local girls for wanting tae conduct his liaisons wearing the ceremonial robes and chains of the City of Edinburgh.

– Rumour had it, I interject, – that he couldnae get it up otherwise.

– That's true Bruce son, and take that as comin fae the horse's mooth. Eh telt ays himself, he said: Maisie, ma wife disnae understand me. She disnae like me wearing the robes around the house. The thing is Bruce, Raymond, she wouldnae let him dae it with her wearin these robes. But you know how the Provost looked: an awfay indistinguished wee man. Naebody recognised him oot ay the gowns, the man's whole identity and sense ay power came fae they robes. One day the administration at the Provost's office sent the gowns away tae be cleaned. The

Provost had tae conduct his duties in his suit and tie. The thing was, that every Thursday night the perr wee man had booked in doon here fir a wee session wi a couple ay the lassies. The Provost was nervous aboot having tae perform withoot his ceremonial robes, so he had a few nippy sweeties fir Dutch courage.

— As one does, I smirk.

— Well, Maisie continues, taking my hint and refilling my glass, — the Provost got really drunk. When he came doon here he took oaf aw his clathes and refused tae leave or pit them back oan until he had his robes. He was screaming: I am the Lord Provost of the City of Edinburgh and I will shut down this foul house of debauchery! Ye could hear him right acroas Leith! The only thing that would satisfy the Provost was the return of his robes. Now they were in Pullars of Perth, the South Side branch, who at the time were drycleaners to the Provost's office. We had the number of the Provost's chief political ally, the chairman of the housing department. He got oantae the Chief Coonstable who did a deal wi Alec Connolly whae wis in police custody at the time, oan a drunk n disorderly charge.

— Post Alec, I smile. — He's still kicking aboot. A top house-breaker before the bevvy claimed him and he lost the plot. Spent a good number ay years working for the GPO eftir that, before he got even too pished up to haud doon these duties!

— Aye, ehs an awfay man is Alec, Maisie says with some affection. — Well, she continues, — they said that they would drop the charges against Alec if he broke intae Pullars of Perth and recovered the robes. So Alec said, Aye, nae bother. The thing was, and you ken Alec, Bruce, I nod with a smile, — he wis fleein, that was the reason eh wis in your custody in the first place. So Alec's brekin intae the shoap, while the Provost's still doon here, and he's screaming: I want my robes! If you don't get my robes I'll close this place down! And mind, what he said went. Then he went tae the kitchen and got a knife. The girls were terrified, but he got his own clothes and started ripping and tearing them to shreds. I am the Lord Provost! I wear the robes of my office! I do not wear this fucking shite! He was shouting. Well, Alec had broken in awright but something went wrong. He either lifted the wrong packet or it was unclearly labelled and he picked up this bag he thought was marked Lord Provost's Office. In the meantime we had got the Provost so drunk that he'd passed oot. When Alec got doon here wi the package, we found out there was just a lady's fur coat inside. It seems that they'd taken the Provost's robes up tae the head office in Perth for specialist treatment. So we dressed the Provost in this coat and stuck him in a taxi hame, Maisie smirked.

I nudge Lennox, – Wait till ye hear this bit Ray.

– Well, the taxi driver, unknown tae us, had just been bumped for his fare by a squad of laddies gaun oot tae Niddrie. He wis in nae mood tae find that when he got tae the Provost's address, that there wis only an unconscious, naked man in a fur coat wi nae money in the back ay his car.

– What did he dae? Ray asks.

Maisie takes a bracing sip of whisky. – The driver thinks, I'll show this cheeky swine. He drives back into town and up the Calton Hill. He drags the unconscious Provost oot the car and lays him out on the monument, the big half-finished yin wi the pillars, the one they call the disgrace ay Edinburgh. A patrol car came along a bit later and found a group of the young funny fellies that used tae hing aboot up there having a line up wi the Provost.

Ray's eyes widen.

– Provost . . . well, let's just call him Provost X, was well known for his hostility tae the gay community, I explain. – He'd knocked back permission for them to open a drop-in centre. Said it would be a hot-bed of sodomy. Anyway, the Provost was found by that patrol car a little later on. The young queens scattered. It was kept out the papers, but it was all around the grapevine. As you say Maisie, that monument had long been known as Edinburgh's disgrace, but the name had dropped out of common usage. That incident certainly popularised it again!

– Rumour had it that the Provost gave up the whisky after that, Maisie cackles, – reckoned it gave him a sair erse!

We laughed for a bit until I grew fed up and stopped abruptly and looked coldly at Maisie. – The new lassie Maisie. I think
I'm ready to check her out now. Meet her, and perhaps arrange
a wee date for the night.

– Surely Bruce, surely, Maisie says, rising from her chair and
departing.

– She's some woman Maisie, eh, Ray smiles, – a real character.

– Aye, sure. That's no the wey it works wi women Ray, I lecture sagely, – Women are like tetrapaks: it isnae what's inside
that's important, the crucial thing is tae git these flaps open.
Never forget that, I tell him.

The visit has a spin-off. – This is Claire, Maisie introduces us
tae this wee doll.

Maisie's new hoor is a class act who has split from her
murderous bastard of a pimp in Aberdeen and she's into doing
good turns for the polis in order to get some level of protection.
I take one look at this wee waif and volunteer myself for the
job. Of course she's anything but, merely employing the hoor's
acting skill to the full. I crack this code straight away and
arrange for her to call at mines tonight. This is a risky approach
for all sorts of reasons but if we wait for Carole to get sensible
we'll be waiting *00000000eat000000000000* problem with some
women: they all *000000eat for the Self0000* thing.

I hear a little *000eat00consume for freedom* ad saying it's time
to go to Crawfo *000eat000000eat000000000* uring some scotch
pies with chips, the wey only Crawford's can do them, stacked
high and smothered in grease. Just fuckin flour really, but they
do the job.

I'm looking forward to checking out Claire from Aberdeen
the night, but it's time Ray and I were back at the office. It's
expedient to hit the canteen first, as it always is. It's busy but
there's an eerie atmosphere and I look over and see Drummond
holding a huge card. I know something's wrong straight away by
the quiet vibe. She looks devastated, as if somebody's told her
some horrific news. I feel a sense of elation. I head over to

Dougie Gillman. – Dunno if you've heard, he tells me, – but Clell tried tae top himself this morning. Jumped off the Dean Bridge.

This news sends me into an excited rapture. Even more thrilling than Clell attempting suicide is the thought that he must have been so miserable to try, and that by failing he's merely succeeded in humiliating himself and the pain will still be there.

How did it make you feel?

I try to compose myself, to convert my feelings into a horrified shock, but I can't hide the glee and don't really have to try too hard as Gillman is more than complicit. – What happened? I cough.

– The trees broke his fall, but he smashed his hip tae pieces. He's in the Princess Margaret Rose hospital. They're operating on him the morn. A hip replacement.

– Is that all? I ask.

Amanda Drummond has moved alongside me with the huge card which has been signed by everyone. – I'd 've thought that was enough, she says coldly.

– Of course . . . I didn't mean it that way, I protest convincingly, making her look a bit petty for suggesting that I did. – Let me sign that card . . . it's all a bit of a shock . . . it's just that he got the dream move to Traffic . . . I can't take it in . . .

– Of course it is . . . I'm sorry, Drummond says, – I wasn't implying . . .

– Is there a collection?

– Karen and I are collecting, she says.

I thought as much. Nursemaid a mental cripple while neglecting your duties. Carry on featherbedding vegetables, it's only a murder we're trying to solve here.

A rummage through my pocket produces a crumpled tenner which I hand over to Drummond. I know a lassie who'd suck every drop ay spunk oot ay yir baws for that note.

– Bruce . . . have you spoken to Bob yet?

– Toal, I correct her. – Not today. Why?

– He said to get in touch with him as soon as you came in. There's a note on your desk about it.

– I'll go straight up, I tell her, exiting.

Toal's hammering away on his fuckin film script as I go in, because he sneakily saves what he's got and switches the programme over to something else. He's trying to be cool, but he looks as guilty as a Begbie in a jeweller's stockroom. He asks me to excuse him for a minute, nature calls, he says. As he exits, I move behind his desk. There's nothing on the screen, the crafty cunt. There are a set of keys in the lock of the top drawer of his desk. They are obviously house keys and car keys, so the one that sticks in the lock must be valuable to Toal for him to keep it with those. I pull my jersey cuff over my hand and turn the lock.

Inside is what looks like a thick report, only it isn't a report, it's a draft screenplay. The title page:

CITY OF DARKNESS: A MURDER MYSTERY
Screenplay by Robert S. Toal

Who the fuck does he think he is? Does he think he's going to get out of this place, that Hollywood's going to come along and say: Aye, you're a thick Scottish cop who couldnae catch a cauld and cannae write his name, here's a million quid for a fuckin screenplay? We'll get fuckin Tom Fuckin Cruise and Nicholas Fuckin Cage tae star and Martin Fuckin Scorsese tae direct . . . aye, sure. I want to just rip up that cunt's shite, fuckin well burn it in the fire, keep me warm this Christmas, the only fuckin use fir it . . .

Alongside it is a key. It looks identical to the one in the lock. I take it and close the drawer. I'm going to get Toal's script, and his disks. I should just do the lot of them now, and there's fuck all the cunt can say about it either. That would be excellent! But the promotion board . . . no, I'll have to keep him sweet. He mustn't suspect that it's me who's fucking him over. Stick to the guiding principle of destroying without overtly making enemies. The corporate way.

I sit back in my seat as Toal returns. He tells me curtly that Mssss Drummond is no longer lead officer on the case. Muggins here is back in the front line. I have mixed feelings about this. She's obviously been exposed as the dippit cunt that she is, but it means more fuckin work for me and I'm too fuckin busy to chase around looking for some fuckin criminal spastics. He tells me that he wants a progress report on his desk, by the end of the day, letting him know who is working on what.

He can stick it up his bouffant erse. I go downstairs and brief Drummond and Gillman. It's pleasurable telling Drummond that she is to oversee the clerical procedure of tracing the hammer. – I want the net cast wider on this hammer search, every B&Q and Texas in Scotland, I smile.

She goes to say something but composes herself, while I drink in her discomfort before asking, – Is that all? I give Dougie Gillman a wink as Ms Drummond scuttles off in a most unprofessional manner!

We once read some cunt saying that it was better to travel hopefully than to arrive and just thinking this makes us want tae smack the bastard ower the heid with a truncheon because if this is as good as it gets then we are well and truly fucked. I sit down trying to fill up three sides of A4 with Toal's fuckin report.

After two sides and a paragraph, I go hame to tidy up. This means I pull out a black bin-liner from under the sink and lob all the shite that's accumulated into it. I need a second one before I leave the front room. I would normally never go to such lengths for a hoor, it's just that I need the place looking right for that sense of theatre. I get the desk and chair in from the garage and I bring doon Stacey's toy blackboard and chalk from her bedroom. That's me ready. I stick one of Hector The Farmer's videos in to get me in the mood before the Roger Moore shows up.

That wee Claire's a good one alright. Nice one Maisie. It's taken me ages to find a lassie that would be ideal for all this. The thing is I know most of the girls through working on vice. Down Dock Street. I looked after them and they looked after me. The best pimp those hoors had ever fuckin well had. This one's special awright. She's done the biz as I specified: short permed wig, tweed skirt, green jersey with brooch on it. The brooch is fuckin essential. Perfect. Just like Miss Hunter.

— Bruce Robertson, come out here, she commands us.

This hoor has the correct expression, pitch and tone. Maisie has briefed her excellently. We are compelled to obey. We? Me. I. — Yes Miss, I say softly.

— You are a disgrace, Robertson, she says to us. — The sneakiest, most evil and vile little human piece of excrement who ever walked this Earth . . .

— I suppose so, we agree. We are disgraceful. All of us.

I start to pish myself. The hot urine trickles down my thigh, burning the eczema.

. . . but at the same time I have paradoxically never known a boy who places me in such an intense state of sexual arousal . . . the lips of my vagina quiver and widen when you walk into a room Robertson . . . she gasps. Fuckin hell. — Are you aware of that Robertson? Are you?

— Suppose, we tell her. I'm getting stiff. Very stiff.

— I want you Bruce Robertson. You make my cunt wet. I am going to have you Bruce Robertson . . . she's over to me and she's on me, pushing me back across the desk I bought recently, undoing my snake belt and pulling my soaking flannels down. She hitches up her skirt and she's got no knickers on, she's impaling herself on me and fucking me slowly telling me what a bad boy I've been to have caused her to do this and I've got my hands clutching her buttocks and I'm calling the frigid auld hoor for everything under the sun and this is therapy in its purest and simplest form and a mist rises and spots appear before my eyes and my head spins and the lesson today is: BRUCE ROBERTSON.

I sit down and compose myself, lighting a cigarette. — You're fucking excellent Miss Hu . . . eh Claire.

— Anything else ye need? she smiles sweetly, tidying her gear away.

— Naw, not just now thank you, I consider, thinking if she'll be game for a little scheme that Hector The Farmer and I talked about sometime ago. Worth thinking about.

She departs and I shower and get changed. The dirty clothes are piling up. I've not much clean stuff left. I'll have to do a laundry soon.

Refreshed, I decide to head out for a late-night drink doon the Lodge. George Mackie, the dug-handler's there, looking lost and lonely in the company of a uniformed spastic whose name escapes me. Poor auld Dode looks three sheets. I order a triple whisky and a pint of Guinness and join him and the non-person.

Dode's still greeting his eyes oot over that fuckin mutt that got topped through Lennox's incompetence. As the night wears on he becomes increasingly tedious. Even the uniformed spastic fucks off. At one point, the tears well up in Gorgeous George's eyes.

— It's no something that ye git ower Robbo . . .

— Man's best friend right enough George, I nod, slinging back another double Grouse.

— . . . that dug wis ma partner. That dug . . . he looks lairily around the bar, — . . . that dug hud hert. That dug wis mair polis than any man in this bar!

— Sure George, I say.

Get them in you daft auld cunt.

— He wis polis awright. Polis through and through. Ah loved that dug, n that dug loved me.

— It wis a relationship, I tell him considerately. — A full and loving relationship between man and beast.

George focuses on me in bemused shock. — It wisnae like . . . we wirnae like . . .

— No no no . . . I didn't mean . . . I tell him, — I mean . . . suppose that aliens landed. Aliens fae outer space, I endeavour to explain. — They would only see two species of Earthling . . . I mean they wouldnae see like . . . *Homo sapiens* and canine. Aw they would see was two Earthlings . . . it's the relationship . . . I raise my near-empty glass in the hope that this sad cunt will see through his selfish grief and hit the bar, – To Earthlings! I toast.

He raises his glass slightly and mumbles some distracted rubbish which I don't catch.

I stand up and think about getting them in. I decide against it and leave the wretched old fool. I flag down a taxi and I'm just about to say Colinton, but I feel Toal's drawer key with the change in my pocket and I get a surge of excitement and decide to take it to Stockbridge. It's a short hop, so I get out and walk through the dark streets up towards our headquarters.

There are still a few lights on, but the place is almost deserted. The cleaners are in, but they're on our floor. They have keys which fit all the office doors, which I obtained copies of some years ago. I used to fuck a clerical bird across the desk after hours. Maureen. She got married and left. No a bad ride, pretty game.

I take the back staircase, emerging on the records floor corridor. I go inside, open the drawer and take Toal's hard copy manuscript and stick it in my document wallet. Then I go into the hard disk and erase the file: 'DARK/wks' from the C-drive, making sure it's the correct one. I find the A-drive disks and have to search through them in order to make sure I'm erasing the right ones. He's done two and called them different names from the C-drive ones, 'BOB/wks' and 'CITY/wks'. They get the same treatment.

I leave the spare key inside the drawer and head off. I hear the hoovers of the cleaner and as I pass downstairs I look through the glass of the office door, shuddering to see Inglis and Drummond. Those cunts, putting in a nightshift. They're obviously going through the clerical procedures involved in tracing the hammer. They'll never find where it came from, the sad bastards. I think I can hear Gillman's voice as well.

Then my heart skips a beat. I hear somebody coming up the back staircase.

I get down on my hands and knees and start to crawl under

the glass section of the partition. I'd love to eavesdrop on what this motley crew are talking about and as I creep along under the windowspace I'm sure I hear someone say 'Robertson' but if I don't move whoever's coming up the back stair will find me squatting here in the corridor. I'm trembling with excitement and I'm almost three sheets and the thing is to get out undetected.

The windowspace becomes the wall, and I stand up and strut down the corridor.

Fuck!

I can hear voices coming towards me, and a cleaner with a mop and pail comes on to the first floor behind me. I jump into the shadows and turn towards the front staircase. I descend stealthily, then I duck into one of the toilets on the landing at the bend of the stairs to compose myself. After trembling in the cubicle for a few minutes, I venture outside. The coast is clear. I'm out the door. Thank God we've no security here.

I can't believe my luck as the building recedes and I skip down to Stockbridge and up into the city, my feet light over the hard, compacted snow. I fall once and laugh, lying on my arse as it starts coming down again, the beautiful, perfect white flakes. I get up and walk for a while, singing in the snow.

. . . though we sometimes go down we kin ey go back up . . .

The numbing wind is kicking up and after a while I can't compete so I flag down a taxi back to Colinton. I can't stop laughing in the cab. The driver turns around and says, – You've had a good night mate!

– Certainly have, I agree.

We blether away about fitba and Hearts and how Stronach should hang up his boots. I'm almost tempted to give him a tip, but think better of it, drinking in the stoical disappointment on his face as I count out the exact fare.

Ladies Night

Sunday morning and I get the *News Of The Screws* and have a quick scan at the Saturday night telly I video'd, after I get the fire lit. At least I managed to keep the coal deliveries going. This is one thing I ken how tae dae in my hoose: tae make a real fire. Carole could never dae that, she always left it tae me. I've tried to hand-wash one pair of flannels in the sink using washing-up liquid and I've hanged them on a collapsible clothes-horse in front of the fire to dry.

The telly is fuckin pish as usual, but I've always preferred working at night. That dog's on the box with three rides who need fucked. One of them bears such a strong resemblance to that wee Annalise bird I fucked at the lay-by before we went on holiday that I almost expect her to have a Scottish accent. Turns out she's Lesley from London. The fuckin questions get on my tits. I know what I would use for the *Blind Date* questions:

No. 1: If I were to ask you for a gam, would you gie it to me?

No. 2: Do you take it up the arsehole?

No. 3: Have you ever eaten the worm-ridden faeces of a non-uniformed police officer while he's working you with a vibrator?

That's the real questions the nation wants to fuckin well hear.

It's so tedious that I take a look at Toal's script.

EXT. STREET. NEW YORK CITY. THURSDAY NIGHT, 3AM.

A solitary man is nervously walking down
a darkened, cold, deserted street. He gives
the odd furtive glance backwards as if he
is concerned that he is being followed. He
heads down towards the waterfront with the
lights of Brooklyn Bridge visible ahead of
him. Someone shouts and he turns around.
As this happens, we see, in slow-motion,
a youth with a crowbar running towards the

Fuck off Toal! What a load of shite! The cunt's just ripping off whatever current bastard case we're supposed to be solving and setting it in New York. That's no fuckin screenwritin!

I rip off the title page and the first two and stick them in the fire I've built. The last copy of Toal's masterwork and here it fuckin well goes! I decide to get down to some real writing and try the *News Of The Screws* crossword.

This crossword's getting harder every fuckin day. The rings of Saturn . . . the rings of Uranus . . .

The ring of that fuckin phone.

And I left the machine off.

It's always a mistake to answer the phone at hame. It's a weakness, a polisman's weakness: nosiness. I needed to find out who it is and it's fuckin Toal. This means that I'll have to watch what I put on the OTA 1–7. He's giving us grief. He's not impressed with two and a half pages of a progress report, I mean, how could a prodigious writer like Toal be? So he's blabbering on about the topped coon, this Efan Wurie (he's a Effen Worry tae me awright), how the Sambo-boy's auld man's sent a letter to the Home Secretary who's nipped the Chief Constable's heid who's nipped Niddrie's heid, who's nipped Toal's and now he's nipping mine. This is why he's taken Drummond off the case as lead officer: too many big guns firing off in all directions for a lightweight. I feel like asking him, But what about D.S. Amanda Drummond, what about her pivotal role in this investigation? Surely she proved a capable enough team leader for the Home Secretary to directly address such concerns to her? Ha!

But I can't speak up. Toal. He's giving me grief, but only because he has grief . . .

All I can think about is that boy's skull, bashed in, the way his head was caved in and how it wasn't like a heid at all, just like a broken silly puppet face, about how when you destroy something, when you brutalise it, it always looks warped and disfigured and slightly unreal and unhuman and that's what makes it easier for you to go on brutalising it, go on fucking it and hurting it and mashing until you've destroyed it completely, proving that destruction is natural in the human spirit, that nature has devices to enable us to destroy, to make it easier for us; a way of making righteous people who want to act do things without the fear of consequence, a way of making us less than human, as we break the laws . . .

. . . but she was wrong. Wrong to do that; to try and prove something to me. Or try to get me to prove something to her about how I feel for her. I'll never turn her in though. Never. But she was wrong, she shouldn't have fuckin done it.

Toal's stopped rabbiting. He's looking for us to respond. We tell him what we have said in the report, that we have sent Dougie Gillman on liaison duty with the Forum on Community Relations and sweet darling Mandy Drummond has been given the task of overseeing the clerical procedures of tracing the hammer.

We, I, on the other hand, am engaged in active surveillance of the enemy. The ned enemy.

— Lean on these fuckers, these silly wee fascist cunts, Toal's telling us. I wonder if he's sussed out the missing manuscript yet. Poor Toalie boy.

Toal of course is the enemy. This is stark crystal clear. We were compelled to engage with this man, as outright opposition would have aroused his suspicion, but our strategy of quietly finding his weaknesses, then undermining him has paid dividends. We must continue to put our distaste for him to the side in order to keep achieving this.

We have been negligent in our duties. Other matters have dealt with too much of our time. Possession by hoors. Running after witches. Containment. Control. We have to break free. *We have to contain. We hav[...]*

There's no respite [...] lebs only. Gus has put the file on my [...] trying to show some interest, basically [...] what day of the week it is. The fuckin [...] t fuckin nerve. At least Toal has some [...] e doorman was seen with Estelle, the [...] g that wee ride in a fuckin minute. On [...] making a deal with the wee hoor that [...] ae my best to keep her arse at liberty [...]

I should go out and [...] have a dug and bark yourself? I bell G [...] alivating at the mouth, stoking his hati [...] Lennox kens, and Gillman, that cunt [...] next time. The computer is only as goo [...] on it, or as the information on it, and t [...] cunts have the clerical staff to input [...] o just bung in anything, but that's wl [...] cumentation.

I'm just another fu [...] wheel . . .

0000000000000000000000
000Eat eat eat.0000000000
It's hostile outside. There is no food. In here, it's all around me. Eat eat eat. Grow bigger, grow stronger, grow thicker, grow longer. 0000000 The Host is now aware of my presence. Eat eat eat. But in here there is another presence. If there is me, there must be more. More like me. This awareness has been growing for some time. Now, I can feel something other than the intestinal matter of the Host around me. I can feel the one I must now refer to as The Other. I am not alone. My soulmate is here.0000000000 We engage with one another in that most delicious and intimate of congresses, that exchange of the chemicals through our bodies as our means to the joining of the souls . . . to merge . . . to become

one with our universal identity . . .
so much better than the bitter and
lonely destiny I thought mine, this
merger, here, in the vast
tunnelling that's the gut of mine Host,
our two organisms are too far apart
in scale for him to regard the sorry wee
Selfs that we are with any equality. No, what
this fine laddie feels towards us is that we
are nothing but an infestation: parasites
feeding off the bilious contents of his gut.
We are under attack. As well as foodstuffs
we are bombarded with corrosive chemicals.
But we love our Host. Yes we do.
For love him we must. How can we help
but love him, more than our own
wretched Selfs? For I bear the laddie no
harm with my trifling wee life, and God
knows, I would not wish any living
creature ill to save that life. The Other is
different though, the other understands.
We feed each other through our
breathing, eating, excreting bodies,
intwined infinitesimally through the
intestines of our most glorious Mine
Host0000000000000000000000000
00000000000000000000000

The truth o[...] [...] them see me this way, in [...] darkness and step into th[...] he previously handled it o[...] sonable man, but when th[...] death must follow. Ever[y...] king off time, thank fuck.

I go into Toal's office and he's looking destroyed. The thing is I can't seem to derive any pleasure from it. Something is wrong. With me. I'm feeling out of sorts. I must cut back on the drink. It's fuckin well killing me.

I'd been thinking that I'd perhaps be in a strong position to blackmail Toal into supporting my promotion application as I have the only copy of his draft screenplay, albeit minus the first few pages. After shop-talk on the fruitless Wurie case, he says, – It's not been a good time for me Brother Robertson.

231

Does Toal suspect that I've half-inched his screenplay or is he just playing the craft card to cast the net? — How so Brother Toal? I ask haughtily.

— I've lost some files, he points at the machine on his desk.

— Computer files?

— Yes.

— I'm not a great fan of new technology. That's computer files for ye. They're a bit like brother freemasons in the craft: it doesn't matter how full of shit they are, you have to remember to back them up.

Toal smiles painfully, then looks thoughtful for a bit. Then he says something which confuses but encourages me. — Often brothers are being supported in ways which they cannot imagine. Then he says, wearily, — If you hear anything Bruce, let me know. I'd appreciate it.

— You mean with files and things . . . I ask, playing the daft laddie to give myself a bit of space.

— Anything, he says sniffily.

The conversation with Toal has made me feel uneasy. What should have been a fucking triumph has a bitter and hollow aftertaste. I can't think why. Anyway, the day seems to be drifting away from my control. I keep thinking about . . . stupid things.

Stacey. Christmas. Carole.

Fuck all that shite. She's fuckin poisonous. A danger to herself and to other people. Well, I have news for her, and for Mister Toal, and for Mister Niddrie: you don't fuck about with Bruce Robertson. Same rules apply. My methods are my methods are my methods.

You think the day cannae get any worse. Wrong! Things can always get worse, it seems as if they now can't fucking improve. A social ratchet, that's my life. What's a ratchet? A wee bit bigger than a moose's shit.

But it is getting worse Bruce, my sweet, sweet friend, because she's here, waiting for us, *here*, outside the fucking station. — Bruce, she says, as we pretend not to see her and go to the car. That snakelike hiss of a voice. Broossssss . . .

Brooosssss

Let's turn off the gassss Brooosssss . . . no, that's Chrissss-ie. Thissssss isss Shhhir-ley. Mind Ssstacey's *Jungle Book* video. That sssnake that used tae sing, Trusssst in me . . . what wis that cunt's name again? Sheer Khan? Naw, that wissss the fuckin tiger. That's right, that's right, that's right, that's right . . . Tiger Feet. Mud. Or Les Gray and Mud as they became.

– Hello Shirley. We cannot talk here. I shall see you in the pub on the corner in ten minutes.

– But Bruce . . . she says, her face twisting in that plea for clemency, but there can be no clemency, there is only the law which must be obeyed. The same goes for social laws, the ones we make in our daily interactions. She is trying to renegotiate the contract between us. The contract stipulates that there will be no fucking about with us in our private and personal life and this fuckin contract is being broken. No, no and no again!

Brooosssss

– I repeat, we can-*not* talk here. Listen, because I'm not going to say this again, I kid you not. I'll see you in the pub in ten minutes. My eyes glint in the sunlight which insipidly tries to negate the chill of a Scottish winter, blocking the hoor from my vision. I turn sharply away and out of the car park, stealing off down the road.

Ten minutes my arse, I can hear her following me, her creepy footsteps. I'm hoping nobody sees us. She doesn't realise that she's giving those cunts weapons to destroy me; cunts like Toal, Lennox, Gillman, Drummond and the like. Her presence in my company could, in the wrong hands, be a lethal weapon.

Tough Scottish cop Bruce Rabertson could hear the foot-steps of the broad behind him as her heels clicked the tarmac. He thought of the legs attached to those heels and that Mecca they led to. No matter how many times he made that particular pilgrimage, Rabertson always reckoned that another visit was in order. He could hear her breathing heavily, her pursuit of him causing her heavy breasts to rise and fall, those warm and inviting mammaries that Rabertson knew so well . . . there ye go Toal, ya cunt that ye are! That's fuckin screenwritin! Any cunt can fuckin well dae that shite!

That's the right idea though that Toal's got. Get as many voices in your head as you can and hide in the crowd. We've got loads of them. Probably as many as there are worms eating away inside us. There's some billboards telling us to drink Tennents Lager: we can do that! None for the purple tin but: they know it's not a recreational drug, any more than smack or crack is. There's another one telling us to test drive a new Fiat Uno. We can do that; at the same time as the Tennents if ye want!

Ha!

Gotcha!

Wrong!

Come taste the bacon baby, come taste that muthafuckin bacon!

We go into the bar of the Rag Doll and get up some drinks. We are thinking that we should perhaps be more annoyed at this stupid cow than we actually are. Actually.

Actually!

Shirley is a funny bitch; fucking desperate for it. Everything's fake about her, but with her skill at applying the make-up she can approximate how she used to look, or at any rate her make-up colludes with our hormones into making us believe she approximates it. After we've blown our muck, all we can see is her as a caricature of a former self.

Muthafuckin ho, that's all she is. Dat ho is desprit to taste di bay-con.

This gets us thinking of all the times we've, I've fucked her over the years. Loads n loads n loads n loads n loads. —We should be able to do things for each other, we, I once told her. —The laddies are at school, so's wee Stacey. You're fed up, ah'm fed up. We should be able to have a wee bit of harmless fun. Only get one life, eh.

All those years of deceit. We turn round and see her. She reminds us more of Carole now that she's getting older. She was always heavier built than Carole.

Come taste that bacon baby . . .

She opens her mouth and there is a noise in our head, and we, I, we see her mouth going oval-shaped and pleading and in our head we hear the message: Brooooosssss

She's getting it. They're all fucking well getting it.

She is telling us something as we sit at the table in the pub. The bar is almost empty. The sun streams in across the lino. We see a report of a game on the back page of the *Evening News*. I wonder if Stronach was playing. We nod over to a uniformed spastic who comes in and says something to the publican. A uniformed spastic with a loose mouth in the canteen and the malevolent ears of the vicious gossiping faggot Inglis tuned in to every salacious tit-bit spewed from those embittered lips. Time to go.

– We can't talk here, I say, and we call for a taxi. Thankfully it takes no time to arrive and we get in it with her. The engine and the heat and her perfume make my flannels start to rise and my mouth is on hers silencing that whingeing racket as I force my tongue as far into her gob as I can, poking it into every crevice. The taxi shudders to a halt and we are back at our place.

Gotcha!

I, we . . . I take her to our unmade and smelly bed, full of stale spunk and crumbs. I'm straight down on her cunt with my mouth, slurping, devouring. It tastes of strawberries. The soap. She's loving it but will not take my stiff cock in her mouth, my scaly, flaking, stinking cock, and she's pushing it away from her face and pulling at it and we are about to come so I pull away and go round and stick our cock up her, and she is disappointed as she doesn't want the rancid prick that Rossi has been unable to cure inside her but she wants to come and we're fucking hard and we come and she does too, and it's the same rules.

The same rules. She's lying chuffed and dreamy, she's had her dose of cock. Her sister's man. She's fucking well won; she's debased us again. We are empty.

Brooossss

We're in bed, sitting up in bed, and I'm lighting a fag and saying: – Mind the first time ah rode you?

235

· – That's a horrible way of putting it! she pouts obstinately.

– What the fuck dae ye want us tae say? Remember the first time we made love darling? Ha ha ha. Eighty-five? Eighty-six? Over ten years ago now anyway. Carole . . . we were no long married. You were at ours and the pair of you were quite pished. Drove you hame. Mind that?

– I remember, her face twists in recall at this shared but unacknowledged history.

– Rode you in the back of the car. Portobello, we smile. – Mind what you said then? Naw? Never tell Carole. That was what you said. Ten years on and off and you've been getting rode by your sister's man. Mind the time you came ower tae Australia? You n me n that Abo bird I used tae shag. Madeline. We had that threesome. She licked you oot. You couldnae wait for it. As soon as Carole's back was turned. Mind?

– You can be so cruel, she's shaking her head. – What do you get out of being like that? Eh?

– Just stating a fact. Ten years it's been gaun oan. Kicked off again as soon as I got back fae Oz. Hudnae even unpacked the suitcase before ah wis pokin you, fir fuck sakes! That's a cow in any book, I shake my head, watching her simmer in rage. – Once, even twice maybe, an indiscretion, but ten years? That spells cow. C. O. W. Cow. I tell her.

– Yeah? Well have you ever thought what that makes you son? She coughs out.

We, I, we, ignore her. – Mind when you got thegither wi Danny. The first time you brought us round tae yours was when he was on the rigs. Funny, mind a while back, ah brought Ray roond, you mind ay ma mate Ray? He was a D.C. at the time. D.S. now. The pair ay us rode ye. A right motley *ménage à trois* that yin. That's you goat the set now, a threesome wi an extra bird and an extra guy.

– That was . . . we were all drunk . . . you . . .

– Perr Danny. Two weeks on, two weeks oaf. Know just how the cunt feels!

She looks at us, in a bitter, focused way. – I don't know why

I waste my fuckin time oan you! You're not that fucking good, she sneers.

— There's three reasons: one, Danny's in the UAE, two, I have a cock and three, I am discreet, we smile at her.

— Nae wonder Carole's away! She did right tae get shot ay you! She's up, getting dressed in haste. There's nothing that excites the morbid fascination more than watching an old boiler you've just fucked struggling into her clothes without dignity.

But we are injured by what she has said and want to shout, She'll be back, but we say nothing on the subject. — Just go, I command.

— Don't you fuckin well worry, she spits back, and departs.

After a while we, I, we find that we have become aroused again. We, I, we could have done with another go at it. Still, she'll be back. Nothing surer than that. We put on our Frank Sidebottom *Timperley* EP. Then we, I, we put on a video in which this big blonde hoor takes on a couple of lumberjacks in an Alaskan forest. Now we are most definitely aroused and decide to call Bunty.

— Hello Boontay!

— Frank. If that's your real name . . .

— Course it's me real name! You don't know what you're talking about you fooking stupid big-titted whore.

There's a bit of silence. No so sharp now Bunty. I have got this fuckin cow on the run. My breathing is getting out of control.

— How do you know what size my breasts are? She eventually says, tentatively.

She is now following the advice given to her by Detective Sergeant Brooossss Robertson. Detective Inspector Elect Brooosss Robertson. We find that our cock is really stiffening now and we are required to unbutton our trousers.

— I know everything. Now tell me your sexual fantasies Boontay.

– Shut up! You disgusting little creep! Leave me alone will you? She slams the phone down. This cunt's riled.

We wind on the video to the place where a tired-looking, greasy continental stud is fucking a stretch-marked boiler up the arse. Worn goods, but some excellent close-up shots. The pole must be well-greased to get that kind of motion. We discharge over the axminster.

Later on we decide to telephone Bro. Clifford Blades.

He's a bit upset. – Sorry Bruce, can't make the club tonight. Actually, Bunty's in a state. The pervert called again.

– Oh God, Bladesey. It never rains, eh. Look, you console her, and I'll be right over.

– Thanks Bruce, I really appreciate it. She's beside herself.

We go to the bog and give our arse, thighs and genitals a good clawing, then we cut up a line of coke. This is washed down with a Glenmorangie to get the taste of diseased druggy scum out of our tonsils.

Then we realise that our car has been left in the works car park, due to the self-centredness of the hoor Shirley. We get a taxi out to Corstorphine, the meter running to the price of a gam from a half-decent hoor, just to be with our friends Cliff and Bunty Blades.

Carole Remembers Australia

The things my Bruce has seen, the things that have hurt him. They don't know. They would never know. But he shared them with me. Always.

He explained to me why he went with that prostitute back in Australia. He needed to be with someone. It meant nothing. I failed Bruce by not being there for him. I was with my mum.

Bruce had been working all the hours God sends. He had been operating undercover in the Kings Cross district, on the trail of these gangsters.

He told me about that terrible day. There he was, trying to open the huge, swinging doors of the garage. He couldn't get them open properly, only just enough for him to squeeze through. He looked into the darkness, venturing right into its black heart. Looking back, behind him, he could see a ray of sunlight across the garage forecourt. The odd car drove by, perhaps the odd working girl swinging along in her short skirt and high heels.

Inside, at the dark end of the garage, Bruce heard the low groans. He told me that it was the worst sound that he had ever heard in his life. They were scarcely human groans. Something was in the office at the back of the garage. He moved towards it.

Bruce opened the door and switched on the lights. There he was. Costas. Or what was left of him.

His torture had been systematic. He was lying across the table, face down on his belly. His chin is on the table, his head tilted up, facing Bruce. His jaw has been broken and his teeth have been pulled out. They lie next to his amputated fingers. His eyes witness this. The eyelids have been cut away and the eyeballs have been carefully removed from the head without severing the optic nerves. These had somehow been stretched like a cartoon character's and the eyes lie, each one on a pile of books, each one facing some of the fingers and teeth and eyelids and ears, which have also been removed and cut off with surgical scissors. The scissors lie with the pliers, and the nail gun which has secured Costas to the bench by his hands and clothing. The genitals have not been severed, possibly to avoid him bleeding to death. His tongue has been cut out.

They wanted to keep him alive as a message to his associates.

Bruce stood there, facing him, thinking how could anybody do this to another human being. But all he said to Costas was, You've been keeping bad company mate.

He puts the gun in the man's mouth and fires. He cannot look but the groans are no more. Bruce shakes and moves out of the office across the forecourt. The door is stiff, and it is a tight squeeze to get into the Sydney sunshine. He panics, trembling with anxiety. He tries to phone me but I'm at my mum's. If only I'd been home for him.

Bruce walks for a little bit, then runs into a prostitute, a half-Aboriginal girl called Madeline. He takes her to a hotel and pays her five hundred dollars, just to talk to her.

Just to talk. She sits warily as he speaks in measured tones, telling her about Costas and about the war he is having with the others and the consequences for him.

It should have been me that was there, not that whore.

I think that for Bruce that image of Costas became a symbol for extreme possibilities of evil. That's why Bruce is how he is.

Worms
And Promotions

I'm driving out to see Rossi, but Carole's on my mind. I used to tell her a pile of shite when I was knocking off Madeline, this half-Abo bird I used to leg out there. I made up a lot of bullshit about working undercover down Kings Cross to put away a villain called Co *OOOOOOOOOOOOOOOOOOOO* he other boys got to Costas I had to *OOOOOOOOOOOOOOeat Bruce* undercover as they were becomin *eat! I wish I could make you* r and Stacey involved. In fact, I h *eat more. You're a terrible man.* ut moved in with Madeline. *There was somebody who could always make you eat. I sense this. Just moving around inside you I can feel all your ghosts. You've internalised*

Then I to *them Bruce.OOOOOOOOOOOOOOOOOOO* fety couldn't be guarantee *OOOOOOOOOOOOOOOOOO I can sense* she had to go cause there w *one that looms large in your life.* on in the NSW police and I w *OOOOOOOOOOOOOOOOOOOOOOOO* Costas, yes the cunt existed, h *OOIan Robertson was his name.OO* t half-Abo cow Madeline was putting pressure on me to leave Carole. She was very headstrong and less easily controlled than Carole. The old country called.

Carole always believed every word I told her. She was happy in her own world with the kid. Always a domestic type, old Carole. Dirty cow in bed mind you. Give her the meat and the dosh, and she'd accept anything. It was all the dyke politics that fucked up her heid, when I slapped her after she'd overstepped the mark and she freaked and went to that refuge. I apologised for that, but she overreacted. She'll come to her senses soon though, nothing surer.

I'm so lost in my thoughts that I miss the turning for Rossi's. I stop off at a newsagent for *Playboy*, *Penthouse* and *Mayfair*, before pulling up outside his surgery.

This Dr Rossi cunt fancies himself. Swarthy eyetie bastard. Dresses well does Rossi. Nice suit, shirt, shoes. Bet he makes a bundle on private consultations.

– Yes, we've got the test results. As I suspected, you've definitely got worms. We'll have to carry on with this treatment.

– Eh!

I can't believe it. This is another price I have to pay for hanging around with schemies and criminals.

– It's only tapeworms, nothing for you to worry about. They're very common, but not at all dangerous.

– Something's growing inside me and you say it isnae dangerous!

– It's not. What you have to do is take this solution and it'll help you move your bowels more frequently.

– This isnae anythi *00000 more chemicals00000000* i ma rash, is it? *00 more sophisticated warfare 00*

– No, that seems to be a persistent nervous condition. You don't have anything on your mind, anything you haven't told me about?

Rossi's just an exploitative quack, but that's GPs for you. Fancy themselves as something else. Some want to be surgeons, Rossi evidently wants to be a psychologist. We ken you Rossi.

– Nothing on my mind at all, I say stiffly.

Dae yir fuckin job ya cunt.

I'm glad to get away from Rossi and back to the station.

I'm back just in time for lunch so I hit the cannie. Ina's

haggis is on the day. Lennox and the closet-faggot Peter Inglis are sitting together. I join them. Drummond and Fulton were behind me in the queue and they come and sit with us.

Karen Fulton, Drummond's new best pal. Was not always thus. I'm sitting opposite them looking at the haggis and I feel like shouting at Fulton: Mind the time I fucked you Karen? After Princess Di's funeral? I've never seen such a big, thick, black minge in my puff. C'mon everybody, let's take a look at former W.P.C. Fulton's hairy pie! It's a fuckin jungle: curly hairs right up to and around the arsehole.

Drummond's going on about her favourite shite: politics and changes in legislation and how it affects policing. She's looking a bit tired. Too many long nights at the office, trying to trace where a hammer comes from. That'll never be detected. I heard that cunt talking about me as well, her and the fag Inglis.

— Poor old Clell. He's defo lost the plot since that move to Traffic, Ray says. — Went to see him the other day. He looks at me and Drummond. — He was saying that we were working for the alcohol marketing board. He's obsessed with this Drugs Führer the Government's appointed.

— No, we are working as enforcers of the law. The democratically elected government of the day makes the laws in Parliament. We enforce that law, Drummond squeaks, in polis rhetoric.

— Hmm, I say teasingly. Clell may have a point. This new Drugs Führer wants to attack demand rather than supply. That means sending more kids to jail. If that works and kids are scared to take illegal drugs, then they'll turn on to legal ones like alcohol as a substitute.

— Which means more violence! Ray gives us the thumbs up.

— Tougher sentences! I say.

— Mair polis! Ray laughs.

— And, mair promoted posts, I rub my hands. — It also means mair prisoners, mair prisons, mair wardens, mair security guards. Pump-priming, basic Keynesian economics! Then we'll get Maggie back in ten years' time telling us we've been spending too much!

— But we can cut back on education, social work and health and aw that shit, Lennox nods.

Drummond's looking horrified. — We're only the enforcers of the law of the land. I mean, if a left-wing government was elected to power and had a radical agenda which became law and that law was ignored or opposed by vested interests then that law would be enforced by us just as rigorously. That's how it is in a democracy, she says smugly.

— Bollocks, I tell her. — If you believe that then you're even thicker than I thought.

Ray raises an eyebrow as Drummond pouts sourly.

— I mean . . . go back to the miners' strike. Our job then was to crush socialism on the s *00000000000000* were rewarded for what we did. We destr *Ian Robertson. He made* n power. Our power lies in our mono *you eat, Bruce.0000 His*

— Too much like t *methods were his methods.* of trying to call me a fuckin red? *Did you learn those methods* gs he comes oot wi is too fuckin *from him? He made you eat coal.* o much like communism. *Black, shiny, filthy coal.0000000*

I don't know who asked that queer to open his flaccid mouth. That cunt should stick to thinking about young laddies' cocks or whatever pervy shite goes on in his sick head and leave the politics to the experts.

— No, we upheld the law, Drummond's screeching. Fulton nods supportively.

— If unions had never broken the laws, we wouldnae have any democracy . . . in the first place, I say, wondering why the fuck I'm coming out with all this wank.

— But that's history. It isn't like that now, Drummond says.

—Yes, you're right Amanda, I correct myself, — But there are people within the unions now who don't give a fuck about democracy. Maggie sorted them out, but they're still there, just waiting for that Tony Blair spastic to show signs of weakness and let them back in. That was why things got so messed up with the last Labour government. These bastards held sway. Scargill and the likes. That's why we had to sort them out.

—That Scargill was a trouble-maker, Inglis snorts, — but Tony Blair though, gie him his due, he's got rid of that unions and socialism nonsense in the Labour Party now.

As usual Lennox says fuck all. The best way I suppose. — Right enough, same rules apply. Anyway, I say, — enough boring politics! It's Christmas! What's the story with the Christmas do? You were organising that Amanda.

With great restraint I stop myself from adding, That's aw yir fuckin well good for.

— Yes, well, we've booked The Burning Ruby Tandoori House in Cockburn Street for the meal, she says with distaste. Her and Fulton wanted to go to Pierre Victoire's, but no way would the lads have that. I wasn't into any sick frog poofs lisping around me while I was trying tae eat. I'm surprised Inglis didn't want that, mind you.

— There is just one problem though Bruce, Ray says.

— Aye?

— Well, Ralphy Considine's been on the team, and I suppose he counts as one of us. We've yet to decide whether or not he should be invited for the curry.

No way is a uniformed spastic one of us, but then again, I know that Drummond's against Considine coming on the Christmas session.

— Of course Ralphy Considine has to be asked, I tell them. — I'm getting a little bit sick of this division between uniformed and non-uniformed officers. We're all on the same team and should reap the same benefits.

I'm thinking about these scouse spaswits that did me over in Amsterdam. One of them had that t-shirt on. A red one. Commemorating Shankly, I think.

— Very laudable sentiments Bruce, Drummond says, — and I think everyone sitting here would endorse them. But surely there are other issues to consider.

I raise my eyebrows noncommittally and let Drummond launch into one about however we may personally feel about it, we have to acknowledge that the force is a hierarchical organisation and if we try to fly in the face of the organisation's culture we will set up opposition, division and disillusionment in what are, after all, sensitive times with the reorganisation pending.

– That's an interesting point Amanda. I think I'm reluctantly coming round to your view. Maybe it does seem a wee bit self-indulgent to make personal statements of our liberalism at a time when the organisation needs continuity of practice.

There's a few nods around the table, all except Inglis who doesnae look happy. He's an irrelevance. No votes for queers in this section. So Drummond has her way and we decide that it's expedient not to invite a uniformed spastic to our Christmas do.

Result!

Of course, if I had said, No way a uniformed spastic gets invited to a plain-clothes do, then Drummond would have been the first to shoot me down in flames. But the last thing I want is to be sitting in my brown (the new black) leather jacket, checked shirt and fawn flannels in the curry hoose beside Considine decked out in a white shirt, black polis troos and shoes.

After this little meeting I get restless, and I feel a chug coming on. I head downstairs with the paper.

I do a bit of graffiti in the bogs:

PETER INGUS IS A FUCKIN HIV SPREADER

and:

INGUS = SICK, DISEASED QUEER

I'm sitting there looking at it for a while. I start chuckling and my sides ache. Then a depressed feeling digs in, followed by a steady outrage. It was wrong to do this to a brother officer. The force can't have this going on. I'm the fuckin Fed rep here. To describe a brother officer in this manner . . . I'm psyching myself up, getting into role.

I pull the chain and flush away my shit. There's some traces of worm, but no sign of the head. I'll get the bastard though, sure as fuck I'll get him.

I'll get him alright.

I go upstairs and stride purposefully over to Peter, tapping his wrist and steering him over into a corner.

— Peter, have you seen the graffiti in the toilet? I ask, in a low concerned voice.

— Ach, thir's always something thair. Ah nivir take any notice, he shrugs.

— Maybe ye should, I tell him, letting my anger rise. — I'm getting a bit fuckin well fed up of this shite. As fuckin Fed rep ah'm no having people's character defamed in this way. I'm gaun up tae see Toal now. I raise my voice and look over the room, — Some cunt's playin silly fuckers here. Just hope ah dinnae find oot whae it is!

I storm out of the room, leaving them looking bemused. I'm charging up the stairs to Toal's office and I'm in without knocking. — Gaffer, a wee word.

— Bruce, I'm a bit busy right now, Toal says, shuffling through some papers. He looks so fucking low.

— I want you to come and see something, some graffiti in the toilet.

— I don't have time for . . .

— As Fed rep, I don't have time to see brother officers being slandered by other members of the service!

— What's this?

I explain the graffiti to Toal and he's following me down to the bogs. The others have come along, their faces like the ghouls when that Colin Sim guy died. They are looking at Inglis for a reaction and he looks crestfallen. — It's jist a load ay bloody nonsense, he's saying over and over again, torn between trying to make light of it, and being genuinely staggered.

How did it make you feel?

I head back up the stairs with Toal, who beckons me into his office and closes the door. — Listen Robbo, he says, — Inglis isn't, well, you know, is he?

— What? I ask. I'm starting to enjoy this.

— Like the graffiti says, Brother Robertson, Toal snaps.

Toal must be upset to resort to playing the craft card so nakedly. — Whether he is or isn't is irrelevant surely, I say, planting the seed, — Peter's sexuality is his business. He's being harassed and we operate a non-discrimination policy on the grounds of sexual orientation.

— But he can't be being sexually harassed if he's not a . . . well, gay, I think the fashionable term is these days.

— Well, you can call it sexual harassment or just plain harassment Bob, but the way I see it, is that this is the unacceptable face of canteen culture . . .

— Whoa Bruce, whoa, I'm on your side . . . this has to be stamped out. It just came as a bit of shock to me . . . I mean, Peter's a craft stalwart . . .

— Peter's a lonely guy Bob. What he gets up to is his own business, and I don't profess to know much about him, but I'm not having a brother officer harassed in this way.

— Exactly. I'll make sure this is dealt with.

I walk out as high as a kite. The concepts 'Inglis' and 'poofery' are now indelibly associated. The concepts 'Inglis' and 'promotion' not so. Ah, the games, the games.

You should keep moving when you're on a roll and I decide to call on Estelle at the flower shop. I'd like tae fuckin gie that wee shag one. She's probably feart of Gorman and Setterington. What she needs is protection from those monsters. Someone she can trust in her life. An older, more mature man who can respond to her needs. If there are damsels in distress need saving, then I can think of no better knight in shining armour than Detective Inspector Elect Bruce Robertson.

That old familiar lump in the flannels starts rising as I think about Estelle and a combination of positions and girlie sex noises. A threesome with her and wee Claire, the hoor fae Maisie's. Just what the doctor ordered. That'll sort ma fuckin rash oot Rossi!

When I get to the shop, the only person there is the disapproving auld boot, who tells me that Estelle is off sick with the cold.

— A lot of it going about, I cheerfully say.

— Aye, sure, the auld cow mumbles. She doesnae like Estelle at all, that's as sure as another trophyless season in Gorgie.

— Does she get many callers?

— Too bloody many, the wifie says, then crinkles her nose and commences hostilities, — What's it tae you?

Looks like the auld cunt just woke up and smelt the bacon. The Scottish working class and respect for the polis go together like Mother Theresa and *Playboy* centrefolds.

I decide not to probe. — Just trying to make sure I've no rivals, I smile, heading for the exit.

— I never thought she wis that desperate, the cheeky old boot says.

I stop abruptly and look around at the stock and give some of the plants a sniff. — Bad time ay the year for flooirs, I say, then: — You got a staff toilet back there?

— Aye, she says. — Anything else?

— Not for now.

That cheeky auld boot is getting a visit from the environmental health; we're fuckin sure the auld cunt is. Anyway, it seems a good idea to take the rest of the afternoon off and let the form OTA 1–7 take the strain. Call it stress management Mr Toal. Call it stress management Mr Niddrie. Bruce Robertson stress management.

It's time though *000000 eat that's it 00* the lavvy. I take the worm laxative and *00 eat 00 eat for the Self* h immediate effect and I go to the si *and the 00 what is this 000* brown water from my arsehole fe *hold on tight 0000 hold on 00* there's no head in evidence. *000hold on hold on 00chemical attack0must weather the storm0*

I leave the Hunter's Square bogs, then stop into the pie shop for a chilli pie. I almost got the bastard worms right out there. There can't be much of them left. I get in the Volvo and head out to Colinton. The worms are on the run. The worm called Inglis is being flushed out the system; outed and routed, before further infestation can take hold.

At home I cut myself out a big, celebratory line of posh. I'm soon dying on a shag. The only person I can think of belling is Shirley. It's either that or hooring and she's cheaper.

Shirl girl.

I succumb to the force of libido and make the call, but as soon as she arrives I can see that I've made a mistake and that I'd have been better off with a wank. She's like a block of ice; she's staring at me, leaning back on the chair, smoking a fag, looking really nasty.

— I don't know why I'm here, she says bitterly, and I'm about to retort along the lines of 'because you're a slag who wants fucked' but I bite my tongue. — Carole phoned, she says suddenly in a gleeful inspiration, hoping to get to me. — She told me that she doesn't want anything to do with you. If you try to see the bairn . . .

— Huh! What does she know? She knows nothing! That's what she fuckin well kens. The sum total, I snap, feeling my anger rising. I try to control myself. — I mean, she's deluding herself Shirley . . . it's sad. I'm more sad than angry about it. She's unstable: I personally think that she's had some sort of breakdown. I worry about her.

— She seems alright to me . . . Shirley says doubtfully, folding her arms, fixing her eyes on me. Her dark eyes. She's a sexy cow from a certain angle.

— Believe you me Shirley, the game I'm in, you become something of an expert on human nature. She's obviously had some kind of breakdown that's gone undetected. She's telling lies; lies to poison you against me.

— Poison me against you! Huh! You've been quite capable of that yourself, she scoffs, her face contorted in petulance, almost cracking that foundation mask which she wears to cover the acne scars she has. I like the way she does her eyes but, always have.

Time to move. I get ready to make my pitch. — Look . . . I

know I've been cruel to you in the past. But you know why, surely to God you know why, I plead.

— I wish I did Bruce, I really wish I did, she says, shaking her head.

— Don't wind me up Shirley, please, and don't insult the both of us . . . I stand up and walk to the door. Surely the whore can't be stupid enough to fall for it.

— I'm sorry Bruce, I don't follow you . . . she says. Her pupils are widening. The fuckin spastic. I don't believe it. She's doubting herself. That's step one: establish doubt. Step two: drive the bus right through her fucking doubt.

— Shirley, you surely to God know only full well that I've been trying to drive you away . . . cause I . . . fuck . . . I'm saying too much . . . I shake my heid.

— What! What are you saying?

— I tried to drive you away cause I couldn't fuckin stand it!

— What! What couldn't you stand?

— Danny! Carole! Him being with you! Me being with her! Making love to her and pretending it was you! Putting up with sneaky shags in backs of cars when I wanted to take you to my bed and hold you in my arms and make love to you all night and shout to the whole fuckin world: This is her! This is the lassie I love!

She holds my gaze and her eyes start to water and I think of all the injustices that have been perpetrated against me recently and I hope that I feel sorry enough for myself to make my eyes moisten as well and I hope that she mistakes this for some of my soul sliding into them and the spasticated cow does and I can't hold this gaze for long without bursting out laughing so I pull her towards me in a tight embrace and listen to her sob, — Broosss Broooosss can we no work something out Brooosss, I love you . . . and I see my eyes in the mirror behind her, like the eyes on that Tory Party election poster about that Tony Blair spastic.

I fuck her, and I'm regretting it and regretting my stupid spiel even before I've blown my muck inside her. After I have to listen to her rabbiting on about her plans and ambitions for us.

The sex with her is nothing like I imagine it to be prior to commencing it. I feel entrapped by my lust, but when I actually get round to doing it, it just seems so pointless and tedious. She's jabbering away and I'm telling her about Inglis and his misfortunes.

— Bruce, she laughs, — why is it you have to savour everything bad that happens to others?

I think about this for a second or two. — It stems from a belief that there's only a finite number of bad things that can happen in the world at any given time. So if they're happening to someone else they ain't happening to me. In a way, it's a celebration of *joie de vivre*.

She wants to stay the night but I tell her I'm on backshift. She reluctantly leaves and I do some more lines before tanning a bottle of Grouse. This gives me the shits and I stagger through to the bogs.

I whip down my keks *0000000000000* and it's popping and farting like I'm pissin lik *00 no no no no 00* his shit comes flying out. It's there! I can se *oh no you bastard* astard. The head and everything, in a pile of *000000000000000* runny brown water.

Result!

Masonic Outings

It's there! Waking up from a maddening half-pished sleep and seeing the fuckin thing! It's slithering out of my arsehole, lying across my hips. I touched it. Its black eyes. Its hooked, sucker mouth. Like a stick of tagliatelle with a head. I went to grab it only for it to be sucked up my arsehole like you eat a piece of spaghetti . . .

. . . and we are awake. I am awake. On the couch. The video's on: the ones that Hector The Farmer got for me. *Vibrator Massacre*: the dykes who do the young lassies in the woods.

I can't fuckin well breathe . . . I'm falling apart at the fuckin seams . . . we're falling apart . . .

These cunts are trying tae kill us with this OT cutback because they know we cannae kip during the fuckin night, never could. They know we need very little sleep and that all we do in darkness is think and think and think. In order to stop thinking we have to fuck and then you get the complications; financial in the case of hoors, social in the case of slags.

I'm sitting up and waiting, praying for the light. I get through by reading 'Tam o' Shanter'. It's an apt that I'll be asked to toast the haggis at the Lodge Burns supper this year, especially after the mess auld Willie McPhee made of it the last time. I know he's done it for over fifty years, and it's the only thing he lives for, but it's getting beyond a joke and it's time the auld cunt left the crease and embarked on that long walk to tae the pavil-ion. Eventually the light comes and I sleep for a few hours.

Then I'm up and into work. It's the Christmas Party the night. I take some more of Rossi's laxatives. We'll flush this fuckin thing right out of Bruce Robertson, every last trace, sure we fuckin well will. It'll be an early start the day alright; I want the first bevvy sank before midday and nae fuckin nonsense aboot deid coons or any ay that shite.

At the station everyone's in a party mood. Inglis has already had a few, probably been drinking alone in the sad way of the closet homosexual. That, an inspector? I don't fuckin well think so. A bum inspector, maybe. He's fuckin well gettin it, I kid you not. The graffiti was only a start. Soon everybody's gaunny ken what kind of a nancy-boy's been sharing their cutlery in the cannie.

Karen Fulton and Amanda Drummond are the only fanny around so the prospects aren't looking good. That big hoor the Size Queen has apparently been transferred up to the South Side. Karen says something about Clell's hip, and Lennox asks: — What albums does he have? What clubs does he go tae? It's above every spastic's heid though.

Drummond coldly says that Clelland has been taken into the Royal Edinburgh Hospital, the Arthur Dow clinic. Apparently he tried to top himself again, while in the hospital! Pills and voddy job!

This puts me in high spirits.

We leave the office and we go to the restaurant for the Christmas curry. — This is the only kind ay networkin wi the wog community that ah'm interested in! Gillman says, raising his pint of lager. Cheers!

— Merry Christmas everybody! I toast loudly, raising my glass and cutting off Drummond as she's about to pull Dougie up about his comment.

After the meal, we head up the street on a pub crawl. A loud party of pricks in suits and similarly power-dressed fanny stag-ger out of a Cockburn Street pub, struggling to keep their footing on the slope and the ice. One fat-chopped wanker with an Arthur Scargill hairstyle throws up in the gutter, sending kidney beans everywhere. A horse-faced bird looks at us in embarrassment and another rotund figure chides the puker in a high, squeaky voice, – C'mon Hank! Too much Christmas spirit!

This is a right spastics' convention. I thought that I was with a sad bunch, but there's always somebody worse than you. I spot Drummond giving a disapproving Toalesque gesture and this immediately instils a surge of goodwill in me for those part-time seasonal drinkers whom I had instinctively hated. I pull some Kleenex out from my jacket pocket. I always keep them handy for wanking purposes as you never know when the tight-arsed cunts at HQ supplies will run short. I hand the boaking mess a couple. – There you go mate.

– Thanks, the squeakoid says on his behalf.

– Office do? I ask.

– Aye, Standard Life.

Ah, Standard Life. The citadel of spare fanny in Edinburgh. You dinnae qualify as a fully-fledged male native of that city unless you've fucked at least a couple of birds from Standard Life by the time you've hit your quarter century. Mind you, the fanny on display here looks far from impressive, probably senior minge. Forget the models-in-suits bullshit in they women's magazines. Generally speaking, the further up an organisation's hierarchy you go, the uglier the birds get. This isnae because tidy fanny have less brains than dogs, it's just that tidy fanny wi real brains always take the short-cut by marrying wedge and getting sorted out with some plastic before heading off with a tidy settlement. I look around and decide that we must be near boardroom level here.

We head into the pub vacated by the Standard Life crew. I get them in, ordering myself a vodka and tonic water. I've got the horn set up and I fancy firing into somebody later on. Fulton's the obvious candidate, but she's taking things quite easy. No like last Christmas or Princess Diana's funeral when I got her three sheets and rode her back at her flat in Newington.

— Not firing on all cylinders yet Karen? I ask, noting her nursing her drink.

— I've gone off the drink a bit, she says. Drummond looks approvingly.

— Mind after Princess Di's funeral? We were three sheets then!

I couldn't resist that one, and I drink in Fulton's visible cringing.

— We ended up back at yours . . .

— Oh aye, Inglis laughs, — tell me more . . .

Fulton winces again, but Drummond interjects, — That was a very sad and emotional day.

— Aye, Gus says. — I watched that Mother Theresa's funeral again the other night. Ah wis checking tae see what old tapes ah could record ower. Ah watched it aw the wey through again, but it wisnae as good as Princess Di's.

— Papes though, what dae ye expect, Gillman says.

— Mind you, the papes usually ken how tae pit oan a good funeral, ah'll say that for them, Gus comments.

— Calcutta but, fuckin wogs eh, Gillman rasps, — what dae ye expect. They cannae fuckin well run the country withoot us, ye dinnae expect them tae be able tae dae a funeral withoot fuckin things up.

— I don't think . . . Drummond begins.

Gillman dismisses her with a contemptuous scowl. — Fifty fuckin years they've hud tae git it right. If they'd goat it right they widnae need any Mother Theresas cause they widnae huv any slums and poverty in the first place.

— Well, Inglis says cheerily, — we've goat our ain parliament now. Lit's hope we make a better job of it!

— That'll be a load ay fuckin nonsense n aw, I snort. — Whose fuckin shout is it? If we cannae git organised tae get tae the bar wir no gaunny be able tae run oor ain affairs!

Inglis takes the hint and gets them in.

We lose the disapproving Drummond after a few drinks, but Fulton goes as well, which fucks up the prospects of a gang-bang later. Still, that's force fanny: no worth the cock that's pokin it.

The crawl progresses down through town, to the St James Oyster Bar. I end up necking with some tart who's groping my arse, and I only decide not to take her back for a shagging when Lennox points out to me that she's a total fuckin hound. I sneak out the door and we head down the road.

Inglis makes some comment about dubious ladies, and I decide that that poof is too lippy and he's fuckin well getting it. I arrange for us all to have a late night drink up at the casino, which I know is closed for refurbishment. It's now freezing and we're walking through driving snow.

— Shite, I moan, on seeing the boarded-up doors, — it'll have tae be one ay they arse-bandit places, I tell them, pointing to the Top of the Walk.

— Ah'm no gaun thair, Inglis scoffs. — Doon tae Shrubhill tae the masonic . . .

— What have ye goat tae hide? Ray laughs. He's taken his pint out with him and is drinking it.

Inglis looks at Lennox as if it's him that's the graffiti artist. — You sayin ah have got anything tae hide likes?

— Naw, Ray shrugs and takes a sip from his pint, — ah'm sayin nothing.

I smile at that.

— Look, c'moan, it's jist for a fuckin drink, Dougie Gillman snaps.

Ray drains his pint and hurls his glass at a council gritting lorry. It smashes against its hull. — Spastics! he shouts.

We head into the club. The bouncer looks piercingly at us, but we get in as soon as he tipples we're polis. It's a drinking club full of all sorts of sad poofs. There's the camp type, the seasoned scene-queens and the hard ex-cons who've got a taste for it in Saughton. There's also a smattering of tourist puffs, wondering what the fuck they're doing here. I go downstairs and spot the man of my dreams, Sinky, a mercenary wee Calton Hill rent-boy. I brief him on what to do before returning upstairs to the boys.

We're having a good crack. Gillman's already burst one

queer's mouth in the lavvy for looking at him funnily. After a couple of drinks, Sinky appears and heads down the floor towards Inglis. — PEA-TIHR! OH PEA-TIHR! he shouts camply, — LONG TIME NO SEE! Brought some friends along I notice!

— Ah dinnae ken you! Inglis shouts.

— Oh sorry . . . didn't realise it was that kind of a scene . . . so exclusive . . . Sinky retreats, raising his eyebrows. — He can be sooo immature, he adds as an aside to several shocked parties around him. Gillman is looking at Inglis with sheer loathing and Lennox has moved slightly apart from him.

— AH FUCKIN DINNAE KEN HIM! Inglis squeals and makes to go for Sinky. I grab his shoulders. — Fir fuck sakes Peter, we're polis! Dinnae cause a fuckin scene in here!

— Bit ah dinnae ken him! Inglis pleads.

— Well he seems tae ken you, Dougie Gillman says, eyes narrowing into slits of hatred.

— You wrote that shite . . . Inglis accuses, his voice in exasperation going all high and fey like a pansy's.

— Ah didnae write anything aboot ye, it wis probably one ay yir fuckin boyfriends . . . Gillman sneers, his chin jutting out.

— Ya cunt . . . Inglis swings at Gillman who steps back and bangs him on the side of the face. I grab Inglis and I'm hoping that Gillman will let fly again and smash that queer coupon, but Ray and Gus have got a grip on him and are restraining him. Gillman's tidy and Inglis knows this, his struggle becoming more pathetic and those startled eyes making him seem more wretched than ever.

— Look, lit's git oot ay here. Wir aw a bit pished. Lit's jist git doon tae the masonic, I urge.

We stagger outside into the blizzard and Inglis is already away, a lonely figure trudging through the snow up Leith Walk. — C'moan Peter! Gus shouts.

— Leave the fuckin poof, Gillman says.

— Fuckin arse-bandit! Ray shouts after him.

— BIG FUCKIN NANCY BOY! Gillman roars, cupping his hands round his mouth. The rest of the boys might pass this off as just a load of drunken nonsense tomorrow, but Gillman's tasted fag blood and he won't let go of this now. We bay mocking lynch-mob laughter at the broken figure of the sodomite Inglis as his hunched back recedes up the Walk.

Ray has another glass in his hand. He chucks it in Inglis's direction, but it falls a good few yards short and breaks with a muffled thud in the road, its impact cushioned by the thick snow. *(0000000000000)*

— Who'd've belie *000000000000* it, eh? In the craft n aw, I muse, as we he *000000000000000* down to the club. A great fuckin w *00000000000000000000* Christmas night with more dri *000000000000000000000000* nd the crew.

0000000You need to be at work. You need the job; hating, yet at the same time thriving on, its petty concerns. These concerns are enough to distract you from the Self you must only face up to at night between the extinguishing of the television set and the onset of a jittery and fitful descent into a physically bruising sleep. How can I forgive you Bruce, after the ruthless shedding of my most significant Other? That creature of sublime beauty, that purest of souls who trusted you, our Host, who didn't want to hold on grimly for life, here in those exploding gaseous bowels. That soul who believed that you had the purest of intentions towards the Other, just as the Other did to all the others in this world of ours.

My pain.

My pain.

A curse upon any god who visits his most evil tax on that goodness of spirit. Let us curse any unfair and unjust society of souls that chooses to punish that goodness as a weakness and that fills that great essence with cynicism and vileness in preference to knowledge and even greater goodness.

How can I forgive you?

But forgive you I must. I know your story.

How can I forgive you but forgive you I must.

Must I? How can I forgive you?
Forgive you I must. Must I?
Your story.
It started for you in a little mining village
called Nittin, just outside of the fair city of
Edina. You were the first son, born in troubled
circumstances to an Ian Robertson and a Molly Hanlon.
They were mining folk. You were their first son, but
something wasn't right. They were people who were used
to a life of struggle. Nothing, however, could prepare them
for the personal trauma they would face.
The people in the pit communities always knew where
they stood. They knew that throughout their history the
governing classes had always looked after their own; the
aristocrats who owned the land the miners dug the coal on
and the capitalists who owned the factories which were
supplied by that commodity. Very seldom, if ever, did
government take the side of the people who worked in
these factories or dug that coal. They did win battles
though, the miners, as they stuck together and were strong
and solid. But on the one occasion they weren't they lost
it all. But your family Bruce, they lost it all the moment
they first had it. So you came from a mining town and
a mining family. You even went down the pit when you left
school. Yet when the police lined up against them to enforce
the new anti-union laws on behalf of the state, and break
the resistance of the mine workers picketing against the
closures, you were not on the side of the mineworkers.
You were on the other side. Power was everything.
You understood that. It wasn't for an end, to achieve
anything, to better one's fellow man, it was there to have
and to keep and to enjoy. The important thing was to be
on the winning side; if you can't beat them join them.
Only the winners or those sponsored by them write the
history of the times. That history decrees that only the
winners have a story worth telling.

The worst ever thing to be is on the losing side.
You must accept the language of power as your
currency, but you must also pay a price. Your
desperate sneering and mocking only illustrates
how high the price has been and how fully it has
been paid. The price is your soul. You came to lose
this soul. You came not to feel. Your life, your
circumstances and your job demanded that price.
Frightened that you wouldn't cast a shadow when
you faced the sun, you stopped looking up at it.
Your head stayed bowed, except in the service of
your new masters. But this didn't happen with
a strike. This happened way way back. I would

like fuck th *have said that you had a journey into the* dn't said a
word about t *darkness, but in truth you never made* lling in sick.
As Gillman sa *it out of it*00000000000000000000 dnae have tae
phone in sick, because we knew the cunt was sick anyway.

So Gillman was the perfect man to send to the Forum. That latent Nazi was the man tae gie it tight tae aw they fuckin smart bastards. Toal's doing his nut at me. The spirit of Christmas my arse. I look out the window at the snow falling. Christmas Eve and I haven't even had time to go Christmas shopping thanks to this dead wog case. The snow's really falling though, and Toal has a tree in the corner of his office. It's nice and warm, and his voice is oddly lulling. It raises up a level of sharpness though. – Why Dougie Gillman? Why did you send him?

I look intently at Toal, his ridiculous bouffant hair. Toal. Thinks he's an intellectual. His first fantasy was that he was a manager, after they sent him on that MBA course. That was bad enough. His second, that he's a screenwriter, is just fuckin stupid. These, however, pale into insignificance beside his greatest and most damaging conceit, namely that he's fuckin polis. I feel like laughing in his face. Instead, I fire out the spiel. – As the responsible officer, I have to consider the development of all the officers in my charge. Dougie Gillman was weak in the community relations area. I made a supervisory decision that he could improve in this area by guided exposure to community relations activity, so I got him to liaise with the Forum.

– Well, I don't know what guidance he got, because they've only gone and filed a complaint against him. A serious complaint. Even worse, it was initiated by the San Yung woman, the one who ran the EO's course with Amanda Drummond. Niddrie's insisting on a disciplinary. I've had to inform Gillman.

I'm not in the mood for this. It's almost tempting to tell Toal that I knew those dykes would be trouble, but I bite my tongue. – Well, we have a conflict of interest here. As Fed rep . . .

– Don't even think about representing Gillman! Toal shouts.

– We'll see, I tell him, standing my ground.

Toal rolls his eyes. – Look Bruce, things are bloody difficult here. We've got Arnott on long-term sick, OT cut-backs, and this racism thing. On top of that there's a bloody jessie-boy in the hat for the inspector's post!

– Are you referring to Brother Peter Inglis?

– Yes I am Brother Robertson, Toal squeals, unawares that he's falling into my trap. – Look Bruce, I'm as liberal as the next man on the force, but I understand how cops think. I understand canteen culture. How can we have someone of his disposition, policy or no policy, leading brother officers?

– What do you mean? I ask.

– How many officers could take orders from someone like that? It would be a recipe for disaster. No way. I'm going to have a chat with Inglis, talk him out of applying. And I don't want any Fed rep or craft-led objections.

I say nothing.

– This is professional concern not personal prejudice, Toal spits as if through an ulcerated mouth, every utterance causing distress, – . . . I won't pretend that I don't find the idea of men doing that to each other absolutely disgusting . . . but that's by the way.

I give Toal a look which I hope says that should be taken as given by all right-minded people and the fact you felt the need to state it indicates to me that you might be a latent puff as well.

He seems to get the drift and coughs nervously, — But I'm far more concerned about the professional implications . . .

— I still don't see what you're on about, I tell him.

— Come on Bruce! If he was to get the promo, what would that do for morale? How can you have respect for a . . . I mean, how can you have confidence in a man who's going to be constantly undressing you with his eyes, masturbating over images of you! It's going to compromise everyone!

— This is a bit caveman Bob. The force in some parts of the country advertise in the gay press. We're meant to be hot on non-discrimination with regards to sexual orientation.

— This isnae some parts ay the country! This is Scotland! Toal bangs his fist off the desk, and then looks mildly embarrassed.

I shrug, — He's a brother officer in the force and the craft.

He shakes his head and composes himself. — Look Bruce, I know that you feel that because he's up for the same job as you, you don't want to be seen to be gaining advantage by undermining him. I appreciate your integrity on this issue. But I'm telling you straight: Inglis is last Tuesday's *Daily Record* as far as promotion is concerned.

Toal has swallowed the bait, but I still nod sternly. Best let him think I'm far from amused at this. Inglis may be a sad pansy, but I still object to the general principle that Toal tells me anything. Anyway, I take my leave.

I meet up with Gillman in the office and we go to the Rag Doll and shoot some pool. He needs friends in the Fed and the craft. Or to *think* that he has friends in the Fed and the craft. — Dinnae worry about an internal polis disciplinary. Nae cunt's gaunny dae nowt. Guaranteed, we tell him.

— Hope no, eh, he shrugs. This cunt acts like he really doesn't give a fuck. — For a few coons? Problem is ye canny call a fuckin spade a spade, or in ma case a fuckin wog, he says humourlessly.

— No way. Ah cannae mind ay the last fucker that got disciplined seriously on the force as a result of a complaint by a member of the public.

Gillman is a good old boy. I suspect that he knows that the best place for an instinctive man of violence is on the force, with total state back-up for when things get nasty. Most polis are just ordinary guys doing an extraordinary job, which makes it such a pleasure to come across a genuine psychopath like Dougie. I was impressed by the way he took out Inglis. Not the sort of man to let the belligerence of others deter him from his chosen course of action. All it means, of course, is that I have to do him. Gillman will be a worthy scalp. He's in my sights. And maybe he's just a wee bit more worried than I thought. – Ah do, he says, – Artie Hutton, for smashin that boy's heid in in the cells. The boy nearly died. Emergency op saved him.

– But that was drugs, Artie had nae choice, I tell him.

– What, you mean the boy was under narcotic influence and was potentially dangerous? Gillman asks.

– Naw . . . I mean Artie. He had just come oot ay detox the week before for his coke problem. He had the heebeegeebees big-time and this spastic with a shrill voice started giein it loads aboot getting a fucking lawyer and making a fucking phone call when Artie was just trying to ask a few simple questions.

Gillman smiles, in the cold manner of an assassin. It's like looking in the mirror. But he's never a Bruce Robertson and he never will be. He thinks I'm his only friend on the force; me, who wound him up like a clockwork toy and sent him into the coons' den. Think again my simple friend. – Dinnae worry Dougie, I tell him, – we'll get this nonsense sorted oot.

When I return, I find Toal back on the blower. He's on about the lack of progress again, which means that Niddrie's been on to him and somebody's kicked Niddrie's erse. Nowt surer. Not my problem sonny boy! Busy busy busy!

I head for the bogs with the paper to have a wank to Jilly from Bath. Somebody has written in magic marker over the graffitti in our favourite trap, new graffiti. My blood runs cold for a moment:

265

HALF-MAN
HALF-SPASTIC
ZERO COP
ROBBO COP
THE FUTURE OF LAW ENFORCEMENT MY ARSE

I can't concentrate on Jilly from Bath now. All I see in my
hand is a flaccid, flaky, itchy cock. I scratch and claw at my bollocks. Funny fuckin joke. Ha ha you cunts. I force myself not to
think about who could have written this . . . Toal, Lennox, Inglis
. . . but he's no been in the day . . . Gillman . . . Bain . . . they
lack the imagination . . . or perhaps a uniformed spastic who
knows the contempt I hold those losers in . . . no . . . I force
myself not to think of who it could be cause it means that they've
won if you do that. Sorry, my sweet, sweet friend, Bruce
Robertson is made of sterner stuff.

Nice try spasticworks!

Ha. No way, Jilly's here . . . Jilly from Bath, you fuckin little
hoor . . . Lennox spreading rumours . . . no, c'mon Jilly . . . your
fuckin paps are gorgeous . . . would you like me to suck and
lick them . . . Toal . . . claims to be above all that *canteen culture*
as he calls it. . . . fuck them, c'mon Jilly, Robbo's the boy to
do it for you baby . . . I bet you shave your little cunt . . . if only
you'd just slip off these little panties for Robbo . . . the future of
law enforcement CHEEKY CUNT GILLMAN, represent him,
me?! but naw, Jilly n me, Jilly n me, nae cunt else just that flesh;
flesh she's put intae newsprint all for Robbo, fuck aw the other
spastics who read the *Sun*, they dinnae understand, this is our
wee secret Jilly, our little love letter. . . . likes riding horses . . .
I'll fuckin bet . . . take it baby . . . take all of Bruce . . .

. . . I'm coming . . . I'm spurting mair muck than a Weedgie
on amphetamine sulphate and Toal and Lennox and Clelland and
Inglis and Lennox won't stop me now, fucked youse ya bastards,

fucked youse . . . Bruce Robertson, INSPECTOR BRUCE
ROBERTSON YA JEALOUS INADEQUATE CUNTS!

That was a good one.

After a Christmas canteen dinner which isnae too bad (Ina's
pulled oot the stops, turkey and trimmings), Lennox and I
decide to go out and get hammered. We enjoy a few civilised
beers at the Lodge, then we're back at Ray's, and there's a blizzard, but it's inside his flat. The blizzard is one of cocaine. We are
feeling weak and the drug is giving us the illusion of strength. We
are telling Lennox of the conversation we have had with Toal and
know that we are talking too much, yet to stop will leave gaps
and into such gaps unwelcome thoughts will intrude. We have no
alternative but to keep on. Lennox though, did not do the graffiti. We know that he would not be able to look us in the eye had
he been the culprit.

— Ken what he says tae me, we ask Ray Lennox.

— Naw, Ray replies, chopping out another quality line.

— He goes: The craft's changed. Ah goes: What dae ye mean?

— Fuckin spastic.

— And he turns roond and ye ken what he says tae ays then?
Ray shakes his head.

He goes: If ye dig yerself intae a hole, dinnae rely oan your
connections in the craft tae pull ye oot ay it.

— What's that cunt on aboot? Lennox asks, exhaling in slow
exasperation, his eyes wide and wired. That moustache is coming along. Bandito Lennox.

— Ah goes: What dae ye mean by that? He says: Just what I
said. Dinnae rely on the craft tae dig ye oot ay a hole.

— Cheeky cunt, scoffs Lennox.

— See, he's feart Ray. He's feart ay our craft connections.
Our influence in the craft. Hunts wi the hounds and runs wi the
hares that cunt. Ken what eh sais as ah walked oot the door?

— Naw.

— Eh goes: Craft connections can only get ye so far.

— Eh! What a fuckin . . .

— But wait till ye hear this, then eh sais, wait till ye hear this yin, eh goes: Besides, you're no the only one wi craft connections!

— Hah hah ha! What a fuckin wanker! That's . . . that's . . . ah mean, ye cannae take the cunt seriously.

— Exactly Ray. That's what we felt like saying: You cannot be serious. Ah could hardly keep a straight face, ah kin tell ye. Ah just goes: Thank you, Brother Toal.

Ray smiles and then lets a silence hang for a bit. I can feel the cunt has been working up to something. — Listen Robbo, I've got something to tell you, he says, lowering his voice, — I don't want you getting the wrong end of the stick, that's why I'm telling you first. I want to get on in the department, but I've no real chance of a promotion over the next few years. Not enough experience.

You've just got your D.S. you cheeky wee cunt. Of course you huvnae goat enough experience. — I dunno though Ray. It's how good you are that counts.

— I was even thinking of applying for the D.I. vacancy in the reorganisation myself. I ken I've nae chance, but it would be a good idea to give myself the experience of applying for some of those jobs, of going through a couple of promotion board selection procedures, just soas I know what tae expect when I am experienced enough. I'd hate to think that a couple of years or so down the line, when I was ready, that I'd fuck up, simply because I'd no experience of a panel interview. What do you think?

I think you're a smarmy wee cunt. — Don't see why not Ray, can't do any harm, I nod.

Ray Lennox now, after our job. Ray Cuntybaws Lennox. Big Dick Lennox in the canteen and the club. Arselick Lennox in Toalie's office. Shitey-drawers Shrivelled-knob Lennox when it come doon tae the action wi ma hoor ay a sister-in-law.

Treacherous Ray Lennox.

— Not a bad idea Ray, we wheezingly repeat, — can't do any harm . . . puts a marker for the future.

— That's it Robbo, just fly up a wee kite to let them know who Ray Lennox is, the cunt smiles and chops up more cocaine.

Criminal Lennox.

When he goes to the toilet I watch the hoor-house red cushion covers on his settee retreat under the implacable heat from the end of my cigarette. I do a few more of these, then turn it over.

Merry Christmas Mister Lennox.

Christmas Shopping

Cuntybaws Lennox, having dropped the bombshell that he's trying to take my fuckin job, then has the audacity to all but chuck me out into the snow as he's off to the paternal home for Christmas. Fuck'um: I need to Christmas shop anyway. They're open late tonight. I have a pint in Alan Anderson's old boozer, then repair to the bogs where I chop up a huge line on the cistern and snort it back. I need it to brave this shopping hell. I get down to the St James's Centre. I have to use the coke energy to shop. Christmas fuckin Eve. Need tae get something for the bairn . . .

C&A's catches my eye, as I need to get some new flannels. All my others are getting a bit smelly and I refuse to wear jeans as it's the mark of a schemie. I grab a pair of fawn ones which look like my size, twenty-eight waist, medium leg, and I shakily hand over my credit card. The Visa credit limit is fucked, and I face up to the humiliation of the rejection. I pay it by Switch, and get the fuck out of here, loudly announcing as I go, – Cash flow, that's all. Professional. Not a schemie. Man of wealth! Man of wealth!

But the vultures are circling. I can't face that fucking Toys Я Us place. Where now . . . where now . . .

Fuckin John Lewis.

JOHN LEWIS STORE GUIDE: LADIES' FASHIONS

I'll maybe get something for Carole. Something nice. A Christmas Carole.

I can't hack this though, the crowds and all that shite. I do another big line in the store bogs.

I'm still losing it outside because I'm standing alone (can we stand any other way) and they're flying past in all directions those shoppers in John Lewis's those eyes everyplace but mine just please look at me and one bitch in leather troosers does then averts her gaze to the OTHER GOODS heading for HABERDASHERY KNITTING WOOLS CUSTOMERS COLLECTIONS DRESS FABRICS DRESS PATTERNS . . . I say madam, go one floor up just past CARDS and LOST SOULS

Then I see it: £2.35 for a black, paper gift bag to put small gifts into . . . gifts . . . gifts for gifts . . . better to give than to receive . . . still to come . . . the fat, sweating midget spitting tersely into his mobby . . . the vacant procession of sheep up the escalator . . . the big cow you want to just scream GIES A FUCKIN SHAG at or even just look at me please police please please look at me

And I feel the hand on my arm and somebody's asking if I am alright sir and I pull away and whip out my ID and snarl: – Police! please me like I please you . . . and then I move away through the house of the lord this great temple of worship to our God of Christian givingness spendingness consumer expenditureness business competitiveness shop and cheat deathness and into the street where the excluded jakeys beg for pennies . . .

> last night I said those words to poor Ray
> Our Shirl she reckons you're a crap lay
> fuck off, fuck off, fuck off, fuck off please police me oh yeah
> like I police you

I'm fucked and I'm away hame wi nae fuckin presents expect my Man At C&A's flannels.

Nae presents.

Naebody tae gie them tae anyway.

No way will I sleep. No way. I chop out a line and watch some porn. I'm unable to raise a wank though and it depresses me. I put my decomposing prick away and watch some of the Saturday night programmes I've taped. *Jim Davidson's Generation Game*. Davidson's a good comic. He keeps the trash in their place but the ponces at the BBC don't let him show his full range. It passes the time until the twilight comes and it's safe for me to crash.

Not Crashing

But I couldn't crash.

So here it is, Merry Christmas, everybody's having fun . . .

Some might be, but others, we have work to do. These OTA 1–7 forms won't complete themselves, worse luck. So I'm out, bright and early, with Gus Bain and we're cruising deserted streets, looking for a bit of action. The wide cunts will never ease up for something as trivial as Christmas, so neither do we.

It's no difficult to find your fuckin fly-boys in this city. You've got the Leith ones, the Gorgie ones, the South Side ones and the Tollcross ones, although the latter two are fewer now thanks to the redevelopment of the city centre. Theatre and student types have colonised the South Side, with business sorts doing the same to Tollcross.

Ignore the schemies: these cunts are a law unto themselves. As long as they stey oot ay the city centre, they can kill each other as much as they like on cheap bevvy, fags, drugs and high-cholesterol food. Zero tolerance of crime in the city centre; total laissez-faire in the schemie hinterlands. That's the way forward for policing in the twenty-first century. Tony Blair's got the right idea: get those jakey beggars out of the city centres. Dispossessed, keep away . . . we don't want you at our par-tay . . .

Gus and I are both early birds. I couldn't kip so that was me.

If only I could sleep, but I get the voices in my heid at night and then I start thinking of that thing inside me, eating my guts out. Too many anxiety attacks at night. I wish it was daylight for twenty-four hours. Gus seldom sleeps as well, less so now that the promotion is on the line. We both want to be seen in early. I sometimes leave my car in the car park just to give that illusion. You don't need to do fuck all, as long as you're seen to be in early and to leave late. This tactic paid handsome dividends for Toal who was known as an incompetent officer. Look at that cunt now though. But he'll fuckin well ken.

The first thing Gus said to me on this dull, cold morning was: – Merry Christmas Bruce.

– You n aw Gus.

Christmas Day. Gus wants to start early and finish early for the family dinner. I want to start early and never fucking finish.

– What's yir plans fir the day then Bruce? he asks.

– The usual family stuff Gus. Yirsel?

– Aye, me too. Edith's cooking a huge turkey. She's got Malcom's wife, Sarah, helping her oot. They've got the two wee ones. Then Angus and Fiona are coming over. They've just got the one wee lassie. Edith'll be makin that mulled wine ay hers. We'll aw be a wee bit tipsy this afternoon. I thought, best just get oot fae under everybody's feet until it's aw ready.

I nod knowingly.

I mind of Edith, Gus's wife. I've met her a few times. A cheery soul. Her and mister big-cock Gus wi their family Christmas. Nae wonder the auld hag's always got a dopey smile on her face. Any hoor gitting that length ay Gus's fuckin well would. See her mind you: stinking carrion dressed as mutton. I almost feel sorry for auld Gus. It's nae good huvin the biggest widdin spoon in the kitchen if you're only using it tae stir the same auld fusty pot ay broth that has long since gone off the boil. So sayeth Bruce Robertson.

Anyway, we're checking on a morning opening bar doon Leith. One part of the bar is full of polis from the Leith cop shop. Same rules apply in the early opening salons, Christmas fuckin Day or no. They're mostly uniformed spastics who've just knocked off, therefore not worth talking to, but it's fun to dish out the odd terse, serious nod which makes them para that there's some internal investigation going on and some of the more corrupt cunts finish their drinks quickly and move on. We dismisseth them. I recognise a couple of faces from the craft; one cunt who I never even knew was polis.

We're looking over at the other side of the bar which is populated by the criminal classes. I recognise one face at the pool table straight away. A Begbie, definitely. I'm not sure which one, Joseph or Francis or Sean or some other filthy pape name. They all look the same. I think it's Francis, the worst one. A nasty piece of work. The bastard looks up, then turns away back to the table. That bastard's so paranoid that if you were to casually ask him in a boozer if he remembers where he was when John Lennon was shot, he'd say that he was playing pool up The Volley and he had loads of witnesses.

But there's no sign of my pal Ocky. Tisk, tisk, tisk, as they say in the comics. – Maybe get a bit of brekker in, Gus, then hit the spastic's gaff. See if he's still stoatin-the-baw.

– Right Bruce, Gus smiles.

Yep, auld Gus is a good old boy. A grandfaither who dotes on his grandchildren, but still one of the most feared interrogators in Christendom. That's the great thing aboot cunts like Gus, it's no just a job tae them. He's a churchy guy and genuinely hates crime and law-breaking. His problem though is he can demonstrate a bit too much Christian compassion at times.

We hit a greasy spoon, a place we know down by the docks. Again, it's always open, Christmas Day or no. Thank fuck for those places. – What do you think of Ray Lennox putting his name forward for the job? I ask.

– Well, I can see young Ray's point: it marks his card for the future.

– To me it shows lack of respect for the likes of us Gus. It's his way of saying he doesnae rate us.

– You reckon?

— I thought that you'd be mair fucked off than anyone: a classic recruitment tactic to narrow the field. If you've a choice of three it's harder than a choice of two. So it was me, you or Arnott. Forget Inglis. No way they'd take a pansy on.

Gus nods intently, concern starting to show in his eyes.

— Now Lennox goes and throws his hat intae the ring. What do the cunts on the board say? They go: It was bad enough with a choice of three, but now it's four. So the standard tactic is to take the youngest and the oldest and knock them out, just don't consider them, soas you only have to choose between two. I should be thanking the wee cunt, he's just eliminated the favourite, that's you, I point at him, raising my eyebrows in a baleful expression.

Gus looks flabbergasted. — What the fuck . . .

— It's an auld ploy Gus; as I said, standard Personnel practices. Same rules apply. Probably been advised by that silly wee lassie Drummond. That's how she goat her stripes, overhauling the Personnel procedures. C'moan Gus, you saw how tight her and Lennox were oan that daft race course. Pillay talk. That's the new freemasonry for ye Gus, the wine-bar freemasonry. New Labour, New Freemasonry. That sort ay thing. They're setting it aw up tae feather their ain nests.

Gus looks in shock as my spiel starts tae sink in. He's just shaking his heid slowly, watching thirty-odd years' service bubbling down the plug-hole.

— Five minutes they've been in here Gus, I remind him, shaking my head in disgust, — five fuckin minutes.

The eggs, beans, bacon, sausage, tomato, black pudding and tattie scones arrive. Gus though, seems to have lost his appetite.

—Ye really reckon that's his game? The words rip from his throat like an Elastoplast torn from a wound.

— Guaranteed, I nod. — Pass the ketchup Gus.

Gus is beelin on our way up the Walk. Yes, it's a shame for the poor auld cunt, but he still needs to be kept in his place. Keep him on edge, keep him nippy and his confidence low and the daft auld cunt will strop oot and shoot himself in the fit long before this promotion interview ever comes to pass. Sure as night follows day.

We pull up outside a second-hand furniture shop in the Walk. Used to be auld Rab Vance's place until Franco Begbie and Alex Setterington strolled in one day and retired the cunt. They just told him they were taking over the lease and that was that. Rab was a semi-jakey anyway (he went fully-fledged shortly eftir that) but essentially harmless even if as Clark Kent as fuck. It's obvious that those cunts are selling drugs from there, just look at the fuckin dregs who come in and out: Keasbo Halcrow, Nelly McIntosh, Spud Murphy, Johnny Swan, Simon Williamson, Raymie Airlie, Juice Terry and every casual and clubby wee cunt under the sun. I don't think those fuckers are in the market for old suites or used fridges. Begbie and Setterington think that they're being subtle if they meet somebody in the pub on the corner or the caff over the road. Wrong! Their fetid erses are mine. But we're not going to bust cunts like that oan something trivial, we're going tae pit them away for good.

Especially Setterington. What him and his mates did to that wee lassie that time was out of order. Conrad Donaldson was defending him. Well, I got that cunt back, and I'll do the same to old Lexo Setterington. No fuckin worries.

We get up to Ocky's but he's not at home. This is far from surprising, with the filthy wee stoat probably enjoying a family Christmas.

– Listen Gus, I'd like to keep tabs on Lexo. Don't worry so much about Franco; that cunt's so predictable. Thinks you need a passport to go past Pilrig. But watch Lexo. And keep a look-out for Ocky showing up.

– Will do Bruce. If that Setterington goes ehs Ma's messages ah'll ken aboot it.

Hardly anybody'll be in the office today, and the phones'll ring through to me. No way am I going to do a uniformed spastic's job by going out to prevent a bloodbath at some dysfunctional schemie family Christmas or other. Toal should have sorted oot a rota for Serious Crimes staff. Toal. That cunt leads a charmed

life. The screenwriter. It's funny, but as much as I want to see the
~~likes of Gorman, Setterington and Begbie banged up for life,~~ I'd
swap it all to see Toal and Niddrie reduced to jakey status.

Gus and I depart, having completed our overtime sheets.
Christmas Day counts as double-time. Public holidays.

At home I have beans on toast for Christmas dinner. There is a
message on the answer machine. A wee lassie's voice, tired,
strained. – Happy Christmas Dad.

I hope Santa was good to the wee shite, because I sure as
fuck huvnae been.

I'm sitting in front of the fire with the telly on. It's a James
Bond film I've seen about a million times. Connery's the Bond in
it. He did the right thing: get tae fuck oot ay Scotland, and stey
oot. Come back for ten minutes tae tell the daft cunts that they
need a parliament, but dinnae stick aroond long enough tae vote
in it! The daft cunts lap that up as well!

I heat up some beans and toss another couple of pages of
Toal's manuscript into the fire. It's so satisfying watching them
burn. My attention is caught by the next page though:

INT. BILL TEALE'S OFFICE. DAY
A stark, functional police office. There are
family photographs on the desk. BILL TEALE is
a handsome, refined middle-aged man who has
worn well. TEALE is unlike a stereotypical
cop: he has an urbane, intellectual air
about him. A slim, attractive woman,
ANNABEL DRAPER, enters his office carrying a
report.

[BILL]
Annabel . . .

[ANNABEL]
Bill, about last night . . .

278

[BILL]

Annabel . . . last night was . . . I mean,
this whole thing is getting out of hand.
I never meant for us to . . .

[ANNABEL]

Say it Bill. Just say it. You said enough
last night. But that was before you got
what you wanted!

[BILL]

Jeez Anna, I . . .

[ANNABEL]

You never meant for us to fall in love Bill.

[BILL]

Goddamnit Anna, we have to be mature about
this. I'm a married man. I'm old enough to be
your father. And we're professional police
officers. Last night was . . .

A dull, flat, monotone voice from BILL's
intercom cuts in. It belongs to Sergeant
BRETT DAVIDSON.

BRETT (V.O.)

Chief, it's Brett. We got a positive I.D. on the stiff.
I think you oughta come and see this.

[BILL]

Okay Brett, I'll be right out.

He switches off the intercom.

This is gonna have to wait young lady.

[ANNABEL]
Oh, very convenient. I suppose you . . .

[BILL]
I said that's all Sergeant Draper!

ANNABEL turns and exits furiously.

What the fuckin hell are we gittin here! Does this shite mean that Toal's fuckin legged Drummond, or is it just wishful thinking on the dirty cunt's part? All of a sudden I've become interested in Mister Toal's budding screenwriting career!

I let the manuscript fall on to the floor, but decide against chucking it in the fire. Brett fuckin Davidson . . . dull, flat, monotone voice. . . . cheeky fucker! I pick it up and start to thumb through it for more Brett Davidson references but then I decide that if I do that, if I give in to my curiosity, then I'm letting Toal win. The purpose of knocking off the manuscript was to fuck Toal's head, not to let him fuck mine.

I have to be strong. The weak person would look at the script. I have to be strong.

I put the manuscript into the fire, watching with rising panic as its bulk starts to blacken and shrivel from the edges. My hands grip the handles on the rocking chair. At one point the urge to wrench it out of the fl *0000 put more fuel on* e towards it, but thankfully the whole *the flame Bruce00000000* ast of heat and I feel simultaneously *more coal 0000 more black,* d sickened by the experience. *filthy coal. That was the fuel. Eat.*

No way can I stay in on my own. I drive into the deserted city, at a loss as to what to do. Then I get a flash of inspiration and head back out to the southern suburbs. Half way there, I realise that Clell's no longer in the PMR, so I change course for

Morningside and the Royal Edinburgh Hospital and its rather colourful annexe, the Arthur Dow clinic.

There's some right fucking comedians in this place. Poor old Clell is one of them. It's funny, but I thought that Clell would be sorted after leaving Serious Crimes for Traffic, but it seems he's been a bag of nerves. As if I care. The only reason I'm here is out of morbid curiosity and because I've fuck all else to do.

— Good of ye to give up your Christmas Bruce, he says flatly. — Much appreciated like. I'm wondering whether or no he's saying it cause he's doped up or whether he understands exactly why I'm here. As if I give a fuck either way.

He breaks into a wheezing rant, expecting me to just sit and listen, as if I'm a fuckin priest. — Serious Crimes . . . seeing aw that shite, dealing wi it day eftir day . . . it's bound tae fuck ye up . . . I thought it had made me a bit harder and mair cynical . . . I thought I'd weathered it . . . come through it all . . .

I clock a sexy looking bird in a nurse's uniform. Phoa. — Tidy wee bird Clell! You've got it made in here!

— . . . ah didnae cotton on tae the extent ay the damage . . . ah mean, two marriages doon the tubes in seven years . . . drinkin like a fish . . . ah should've seen it . . .

— A wee darling like thon lookin eftir ye. Nae wonder ye want tae spend Christmas in here!

— . . . it wis only when ah got the dream move tae Traffic . . . the third day at the desk I was scraping my pen intae the report sheets. . . . normality was so hard tae handle Bruce. . . .

— Reckon she's got a boyfriend? Mind you, tidy fanny like thon, bound tae.

— . . . ah wis peyin the price Bruce . . . ah wis peyin the price.

She's a lovely, awright. Whoah-ho-ho! — Sorry Clell, what wis that? Aw aye, somebody has tae pit in the pest control shift. For aw the bollocks, I'd rather do that than be a deskbound spastic. Same rules.

— Naw Bruce . . . it wisnae Traffic that wis the problem . . . it wis Serious Crimes. It wis huvin the space tae think again. Tae open up. They aw came back Bruce. Aw the corpses, aw the abused bairns . . . aw the twisted and broken people . . . and ah kept thinkin why? It shouldnae be like that . . . it shouldnae . . . why?

He grabs my wrist and glowers at me, but I'm looking right past him at the nurse. She's wearing these stockings which are probably tights but I choose to think of them as stockings and they have the seams which run right up the back of her legs defining those excellent calves and thighs and phoa . . . but I can't say anything to Clelland, who's still whispering 'Why?' intently at me. I feel like just telling him why. In two simple words: natural selection mate, natural selection. The twisted, broken people go to the wall and you are one of them my friend. Same rules. Clell was always a weak, sensitive, commie poof under that jokey exterior. Lacked the big-match temperament. Didn't have the bottle. The Inglis factor is well at play here. Personally, I'd rather wade through a stack of bodies than a stack of forms any day of the week.

It dawns on me that I don't know what I'm doing here. I feel like that Rolf Harris fucker, or whoever it is, that goes to visit the bairns in hospital on Christmas Day. Only it's the big bairns who are unfit to do a man's job that I'm visiting.

– Must go Clell, I say, forcibly freeing my wrist, – Carole's pulled out aw the stops wi the turkey dinner this time roond. Call ays a traditionalist if ye like, but there's something aboot that faimly Christmas dinner.

– Jackie never came in . . . she phoned but . . . he says.

– They tell ays that they fair dae the business on Christmas Day in these places. Yir in the right hands Clell, I tell him. I clock that wee nurse again. – Especially wi her there! Ah'd git a bedbath fae her . . . never mind a bedbath, ah'd git a fuckin enema off her! And return the fuckin compliment! Phoa! Anyhow, see ye Clell! Merry Christmas! Keep the pecker up, I wink departing, – Mine would be up anywey, in a place like this! Too right!

As I leave the gibbering oaf I see the nurses start to serve up the Christmas nosh for some other enfeebled lunatics on the ward. They're mostly stupid young cunts; anorexic, junkies and what have you, inadequates who can't cope with life. They should sling the fuckin load of them oot intae the snaw instead of wasting the taxpayer's dough pampering them wi turkey and trimmings served up by rides in seamed stockings. It's a fuckin disgrace. We'd aw like that!

I consider trying to take one of the dishes, but there's too many staff around.

Instead I go back hame and re-stoke the fire, Toal's manuscript now reduced to a pile of ashes. I heat up some more beans which I spice up with curry powder and do some toast. I listen to that daft, smelly, rich auld cunt talk her usual shite at three o'clock. I'm a mason awright, and I swear allegiance to the crown as an institution, but as people the Royal Family are the saddest shower of spastics that ever walked the third planet of the solar system.

Thankfully, for Christmas night there's a do up in the club at Shrubhill. No many people in though, it being Christmas and that. Brother Blades is present though, and we both get three sheets. He has to hold me up for 'God Save the Queen'. He's droning on about Bunty, something about an argument and his mother but I can't make out a word of it. I lose him and stagger out into the cold. The chill revives me a bit and I get a taxi from a guy in the Lodge and head back home. I get in and I snort back some more charlie and I'm tanning another bottle of Grouse. I stick on Van Halen's *Women and Children First* as loud as it will go and play air guitar, specialising in the Jimmy Page chicken dance. Inbetween tracks I hear a loud knock at the door.

Stronach and his wife are on my doorstep. He's playing tomorrow, against Motherwell, I think. Boxing Day fixture. I can't hear anything, because the next track's started up and it's really loud. I can just see the two mouths opening like fish. They're both in their tracksuits. I raise my hand to silence them then I go through and turn the music down before coming back out.

— Merry Christmas Tom! Julie! I shout.

— God Bruce! Cool yir jets man! We're tryin tae git some
sleep! Stronach whines, his stupid belligerent face scanning for
signs of me registering his plight.

— Don't fuckin trespass on my property Stronach! If you've
a complaint to make about the noise level, call the fuckin polis!
It's Christmas fuckin Day!

I push him in the chest and he jerks backwards off the
doorstep. I slam the door shut in his daft face.

That cunt's got all fuckin year tae sleep. I work aw fuckin
year.

I try to watch some telly through one eye. There's a Channel
Four film on, where you get a brief flash of some wee French
slag's fanny, arse and tits. I think about that wee nurse again and
I resolve to keep up these visits to my mate Clell, on a regular
basis. It's impossible to read the Teletext to see what's due on,
and just as hard to read the fuckin *Radio Times*.

I'm cunted.

Car Stereo Chews Up
Michael Bolton Tape

Big Ben chimes, *Radio Times*. Meant to be fucking Christmas and the telly is shite, all repeats. Stronach's got the right idea with that dish of his. I bitterly resent paying a licence fee to those BBC wankers for absolutely fuck all. I'm feeling rough this morning, channel-hopping rough, my heid nipping. I try to light the fire and get a reasonable blaze going. I'm almost tempted to shelve my plan to get Bladesey. The fool seals his ain fate though, by phoning me up, reminding me of the Boxing Day game of ten-pin bowling we'd arranged when we were three sheets the other night at the Lodge. Iain McLeod from the craft has gied me the keys for the alley, he reminds me. I was wondering what these things jangling in my pocket were.

Ten-pin bowling on Boxing Day. With Bladesey. How sad and nae-mates can you get? Decline and despondency in all I see. The house is like a toilet, there's rubbish and smelly auld clathes piling up everywhere. Even I'm beginning to notice the Judi Dench when I come into the hoose. Those irresponsible weak suicide cases, those druggy kids and those fuckin jakeys have got a better deal than me at this time of the year. Carole wants to get it sorted. If she could only see the inconvenience she's fuckin well caused me . . .

I'm shaking, sick and jumpy. I won't drive today. The car stereo chewed up the Michael Bolton tape. I must get a fuckin

CD fitted in the car. The thing is, you get fucked as the issue of storage always raises its ugly head. That smart wee cunt Bladesey's gone and got one, the wee bastard. He's roond for me early doors for the ten-pin, as planned.

I look witheringly at his CD. – I considered switching to compact disc but then I thought: storage of discs. The same rules apply, I tell him.

– Well, I um actually find that they don't really take up that much more room than cassettes.

– No go. Storage, I snap at the wee cunt.

Then this spastic's smiling like the retard he is and pulling out this drawer below the stereo unit that's crammed with fucking discs. – They fit this storage unit underneath. Takes up to fifty discs, he smiles. Cock-eyed wee cunt.

– Right, I say, my voice coming out gruff and duty-polis like. We go indoors and I've accidentally on purpose got the box on. The little creep's looking around disdainfully at the mess, but he kens better than to say anything.

I fling out a pre-emptive strike, in case he asks about Carole and the bairn. – So how do things stand with Bunty . . . you were trying to tell me the other night, but I was cabbaged.

– Not so well Bruce, Bladesey looks mournful. – Actually, I'm driving down to my mother's this evening, down in Newmarket. Just for a few days. See the family and all of that. Bunty's decided she's staying up here. She's making such a song and dance. I mean, I only see them once in a blue moon for goodness sake.

– Hmm, right enough, I nod. – It does seem a wee bit much.

So old Cunty Bunty's going to be on her own for a few days. Well, we can't have that!

– Yes . . . it's a real problem . . .

– A tough one Brother Blades. So, this creep that's hassling her, what does he sound like? I ask.

– Actually I believe it's sort of a nasal accent, um North of England, Manchester actually . . . Bladesey says.

– Man-chesh-tehr, I say crappily, – I'm shite at accents, I'm

afraid, except for the Cockney cause I used to live down there.
– Orlroight moite? Dahn the old frog n toad . . .

Just then, as I had planned, Frank Sidebottom's large head appears on the screen as the announcer of the next dire pop act on. The *Radio Times* does have its uses.

– My God . . . that chap on the box . . . that's exactly the way Bunty does his voice. That puppet on the television.

– Eh? I say, turning up the volume. Frank's going on about how this act's usually on very late at night on Jools Holland and his mum won't let him stay up to see them . . .

– The chap in the mask . . .

– Right. Somebody's obviously impersonating that television personality.

We wait for the credits to come up. – Gosh, says Bladesey, – his name's Frank. Frank Sidebottom.

– Right, I say, standing up and moving to the phone. I pretend to dial the operator, then I pretend to ask for a number for Granada studios, – Just getting their PR people on the line . . . Right, hello . . . I'm wanting to enquire about Frank Sidebottom who was on your show . . . I stand talking for a while to a dead line going, Mmmhhmm yes and doodling on the notepad, occasionally winking at Bladesey's huge startled eyes. Magnified under that glass, they look bigger than Frank Sidebottom's. Meet Bladesey's new specs. Same as the old specs.

We slam down the phone and give Brother Clifford Blades the thumbs up. – Right, we have to take off to the record shop and find some of Frank Sidebottom's albums and tapes. This is where this cook conducts his fantasy world from. The lassie on the phone was saying that it's easy to do his voice. You just put your fingers over your nose. Mahn-chestehr, I go, again sounding crap deliberately.

Bladesey's away though, – No, listen, I've got it. Muhn-chiz-tih! He's chuffed.

– That's more like it Brother Blades! Nice one! I start to choke as the hangover from last night is really coming on. Now that my kidneys are so inefficient with pish over the years it takes later and later to kick in, and you sometimes feel that you're going to escape, but when it comes it comes harder and longer than ever and I'm as jittery as fuck as we drive into town. Fuck the ten-pin, Rose Street here we come. Hair of the dug that mauled you. Bladesey's on orange juice, as he's driving south later on. I don't try to discourage this as I want the wee cunt to leave Bunty on her lonesome.

Although it's Boxing Day, there's loads open in toon. Some of the shops have decided to start the first day of the January sales today. Bladesey gets a couple of tapes from Virgin and HMV and listens to *Frank Sidebottom Salutes the Magic of Freddy Mercury and Queen and Kylie* and the *Timperley* EP. We hit a few more Rose Street pubs with me getting semi-pished and I give a couple of criminal cunts the eye, particularly that fucker from Oxgangs, Fingers Billy, who's dressed in his regulation white coat and carrying the clipboard he always uses when he rips oaf shoaps.

Fingers Billy's usual M.O. is to just stride into a shop and order the backroom staff to load up his white van. Then he gets them to sign and he's away. – Billy, I nod.

– Mister Robertson. How's business? the shifty cunt asks.

– Oh very good. Yourself?

– Fine Mister Robertson. You, eh, working the day?

– Would ah tell you if I was? And you? Dressed for it I see.

– Mister Robertson . . . Fingers Billy smiles and turns up the palms of his hands. Then he smiles and departs.

– A friend of yours? Bladesey asks.

– Of sorts, we smile.

We get back to mines with the tapes and a carry out and spend the entire afternoon doing the impressions of the recorded material. I deliberately screw up, but Bladesey gets it off-pat. The wee cunt really seems to be having genuine fun. I'd say it was sad, but in reality it's way, way beyond that. – Yeah, you've got it Bladesey. I think it must be because you're English.

– Would that mean that the pervert's English too? Bladesey asks eagerly.

We choose to humour the doss wee cunt. – Sharp Brother

Blades, sharp. But we don't know that. He might just be better at impressions than the likes of me. But on the balance of probability it might be a good starting assumption to at least entertain the possibility. We have to start from the principle of the application of the same rules.

Bladesey gives a pathetic knowing nod and grin. — Well, I must set off. South of the border down Newmarket way.

My friend Brother Clifford Blades departs for the bosom of his spastic family in England while I give Hector a bell, to make sure that we're still on for Monday morning. Then I check with Claire at the Fish Factory. It's all systems go.

Just the thought of Monday's frolics sets up the horn in me. I consider calling in at Bunty's, seeing as she's on her tod, but I decide to leave it till the morn, let Bladesey get further out of sight and mind first.

I just realise that he's left the tapes he bought from the record store on the coffee table. I chuck them out with the rubbish, embarrassed at being party to something which gave that simpleton his petty pleasure, no matter how fleeting. I throw some McCain's oven chips into the tray and heat up some beans, adding curry powder.

To my great elation, my friend Brother Blades realises that he's left the tapes too. I thought that this would take a while to happen, but no, the stupid little twat is cutting his own throat for me. He phones up later that night and I don't lift the receiver, letting him babble into the answer machine. Fate can be a cruel bastard, especially to the likes of Bladesey.

— Hello, is that Bruce Robertson. This is Frank ere. I should be sal looky, looky, looky, looky, I should be sal looky in loove . . . I'm on my way to my mam's . . . but I left me bloody tapes. Look after em for me, will ya!

And he does it all in a beautiful, impeccable Frank Sidebottom voice. I rub my hands together and press the 'Save' button on the answerphone.

Gotcha!

To Lodge A Complaint

Sunday. For some a depressing day, for me the happiest day of the week: it means big-time OT. I can't find my slippers. I go through to the front room and my heart skips a beat. Her picture's gone from the sideboard. Of course. The top drawer.

I open the top drawer and put it back.

It was Christmas and I never got her anything.

That was

I look at the picture for a while then push it back into the drawer and slam it shut. That poor wee lassie, what a fuckin legacy. I'm better away from her. I'm better away from them all. It's a dormant virus and it's becoming more manifest.

But it was Christmas and I never got her anything.

It was cause of Carole that I . . . she usually gets her . . . she would have, surely, she would have bought her something from the both of us.

Surely.

Maybe though, that's the way her mind's working: trying to turn us, me against the bairn. She's living in a fool's paradise. Same rules. I do not give a Matt and Luke Goss about her. Not an Aylesbury Duck.

I pull on my stinky old clothes and defrost the Volvo. Getting the motor charged up and storming round the city bypass to Meat Loaf's *Bat Out Of Hell* album restores some cheer. Jim

Steinman, probably the greatest rock composer of all time. That cunt is operatic.

When I get to HQ, I find that most of the crew are in; they've had their fill of that Christmas shite. For all the bullshit talk of the family, close friends and the festivities, I've always found that most people can't wait to call a halt to all that garbage and get back to the two-slice. I find that polis can't function for very long in the company of non-polis.

— Who's in the *Screws* the day? I ask Peter Inglis who's got his paper open.

— Nikki from Somerset. Good tits like. Fill paps. Dirty cow's been tweaking her nipples fir the photae. Like fighter pilot's thumbs, he says in the fake-coarse way of the closet homosexual in desperate fear of being outed. Mister Inglis has recently dropped his application for the promotion. On the advice of a certain Mr Toal, no doubt. He holds the page up for my inspection. Thinks that keeping a low profile and talking dirty aboot birds will set up a smoke-screen. Such an obvious attempt to be one of the boys just grates and only serves to isolate him further.

— A pump and a piece thon, I nod appprovingly.

You fool nobody, Mr Inglis.

I open my file wallet and pull out my own *Screws* for closer study. No bad, worth forty wanks later on. I'm as itchy as fuck in the genital region. I go downstairs to the bog and wipe the sweat from my arse-crack. Then I line my buttocks and thighs with toilet paper, putting my y's over them. That should absorb the moisture generated. I put the flannels I washed back on, and catch a whiff of detergent from them. They seem discoloured as well.

I'm not in the r[...]ven a wank, so I head back up th[...] fantasy fitba league tables. Not th[...] out that crap. Thankfully there'[...] dress it up amounts to zer[...] my filthy Hearts mug, al[...] disease that comes out[...] he can

> *0000000000eat eat eat, that's the way.00000000000000I can feel how it was for you. When he came into the house, covered in black coal. You, picking nervously at the food he'd put on your table with his sweat and labour. Trying not to meet his eye. Then he'd see that*

291

wash the fucker all b— *you were not eating. –* Like Macbeth trying
tae wash the blo— *Eat! he'd roar. Your mother* in Inglis's case,
the blood from— *would look away as Ian Robertson*
pulled you up to the fireplace and
pointed at the coal in the bucket. –
Ah've been fuckin diggin this shite aw
day for you! Eat! But you still
couldn't eat the food. Then he'd
The horri— *pick up a lump of coal and make* —ing no headway at all today, *you eat it. – Eat, he'd say.*000 —e whole sordid
business remains as unsolved as ever. Yes, there are clues, but it's
working out what they mean . . .

ACROSS		DOWN	
1	Urban dweller (8)	1	Outer garment (7)
5	Stinging insect (4)	2	Narrow part (5)
8	Gave money (4)	3	Pondered (5)
9	Joined using a hot iron (8)	4	African river (4)
10	External (7)	6	Fruit (7)
12	Bumptious (5)	7	Short form of Patrick (5)
13	Holy place (6)	11	Eyot (5)
15	Hand gun (6)	12	Dry, brittle (5)
17	Trainee (5)	14	Wine or cake (7)
18	Pain-killer (7)	16	Archer's weapon (7)
22	Friendly (8)	17	Category (5)
23	Dingy (4)	19	Water vapour (5)
24	Lodge (4)	20	Scarcer (5)
25	After today! (8)	21	Aid in crime (4)

— Gus, I shout, — Urban dweller, eight letters . . . N dinnae
say citizen cause that's only seven.

—Aw . . . that's what ah would have said. Citizen. Here, what
did you get for that nine across?

— Soldered. Join using a hot iron, I tell him. There's a fuckin
good one here for ye. Twelve across. Bumptious. TOAL! Pity it's
five letters but.

Gus's laugh ricochets around the open-plan like a workie's drill in a built-up area.

I turn to the football pages. BOXING DAY DISASTER is the headline.

> an anonymous, lacklustre performance by Tom Stronach, normally so full of endeavour in the visitors' engine room, led to his substitution in the second half.

Dougie Gillman looks over my shoulder. I shake the paper at him. – Did ye go Dougie?

– A bloody nightmare. That Stronach, he's a fuckin imposter, Gillman scoffs.

– Ah ken why he was so crap yesterday, I tell him knowingly, – the cunt was up till the wee small hours on Christmas Day, off his fuckin tits . . . no just on bevvy either by the look ay things.

– Aye, thir aw it that fuckin cocaine . . . they fitba players, Gillman shakes his heid.

– Thing is, thir short-changin the fans Dougie. We pey they cunts' wages.

Gillman nods in bitter agreement as Lennox comes in. He has a copy of the *Screws* as well. He sees Gus at the crossword. – Seven doon, he says, – Short for Patrick. That's easy: Dirty fuckin thick fenian terrorist bog-wog cunt.

Lennox is now sporting a huge, Zapata-style moustache: it seems to grow along with his charlie intake. I keep thinking that I can see bits of coke stuck in it.

– No bad Ray, mair than five letters in that though, eh, I smile.

What made Ray Lennox want to be all palsy-walsy and one-of-the-boys all of a sudden?

– What about twenty-four across: 'Lodge?' Gus asks with an edge in his voice, turning away from Lennox.

– File, Ray says.

– Eh? Gus snaps challengingly.

– Tae file a complaint. Tae lodge a complaint, says Lennox, all superior-like. – I'll bet the first thing you thought of was masonic or orange! he laughs.

— And ah bet it was the last bloody thing you thought of! Gus almost takes his heid off.

— Eh? Ray asks, bemused, almost rocking back on his heels.

I'm shaking with laughter behind my paper. Growl! Growl! Go for him old boy, go on and teach that smart young pup a thing or two! Go on old boy! You can dae it! Ruff ruff!

— Dinnae think yir behaviour's no gaun noticed in the craft, son, Gus says, pointing the finger.

— What ye on aboot Gus? Lennox turns to me and then Peter, —What is this? We don't respond, so he looks back at Gus.

— Jist what ah said. No wise, son, Gus hisses, tapping his muppet heid, — no wise at aw. Then he turns away and leaves. Inglis follows him like he was his boyfriend. Yes, buftie boys are the biggest size queens.

—What the fuck was that about? Ray asks.

— Listen Ray, it's what I've been telling ye aboot, I whisper confidentially as I see Gillman going into the photocopying room. —The young stag syndrome.

Ray looks flushed. — He doesnae ken anything aboot the charlie, does he? he whispers eagerly.

— I doubt it, I smile.

I'm looking at my stars while, yes, I can almost hear it, the slow delicious sound of that wanker, Ray Lennox, stewing in his own fucking juices. My sign is Taurus, the bull. Fuckin appropriate cause that's all I get aroond here, usually from that sad spastic Toal. Nope. Wrong! He is not a sad spastic, he ain't that fuckin interesting!

> TAURUS (April 21 – May 21): The combined influence of
> Mars and Pluto, two rather volatile planets, together with
> your ruler Venus, indicates a time of smouldering passion.
> But seriously, don't get too carried away as it could all end in
> tears. As for someone who is coming on strong today,
> you need to question their motives.

The *News of The Screws* disgusts me after a while. It's all shagging, drugs and crime triangles featuring fat schemies. I'll have to get back to buying the *Mail On Sunday*. I used to get it for the politics, but I packed it in after Princess Diana's funeral. Every person that was interviewed outside the Palace all seemed to be sad, nae-mates spastics, sort of Bladesey types. Then I read that the majority of people who attended were *Mail* readers. That terrified me into dropping the paper.

I decide to go and see Bunty. — Ray, I'm going walkabout. If that docile mutation Toal is looking for me, tell him that I'm away to the Forum.

— Will do Bruce. When will you be back?

— A couple of hours or so. How, ye wantin ays tae bring back something fae Crawford's?

— Aye . . . I suppose a Cornish pasty wi chips, Ray says hesitantly, as if he is thinking of something more tasty.

Peter comes back in. — Peter? Scran?

It'll be sun-dried tomatays, olives and feta cheese fir that big nancy-boy.

— You gaun past Brattisani's?

— Could do.

— White puddin supper then, he says. Probably sees the white puddin as a guy's cock. Ah'll fuckin well bet ye the cunt wants one awright!

— Well, if you're gaun by Brattisani's, ah'll take a fish supper, Ray decides.

— Roger. Lis[t] in provisions for the microwa[ve] [n]g. These wee pizzas are jus[t] [fe]ways in packs ay te[n]

— Aye, [I]

— Too [are we] trying tae

Here's [Bunty's] gittin shag [?]ed the fuckin en[d] [s]atisfy yon big h[o]

000000eat000eat00000can you taste it Bruce? Can you taste the filth, the dirt, the oily blackness of that fossil fuel in your mouth as you choke and gag and spit it out? Do you still hear his voice in your head urging you to eat? Eat, eat eat. Your mother's cries. Do you hear them? You should be Bruce. Because I know that it's never ever left you alone. Now you can eat what you want to eat. For me, for you, for all the others. Now you can consume to your heart's content or your soul's destruction, whichever comes first. So eat. 00000000000000000000

A Society Of Secrets

Bladesey's hedge is cut more precisely than any of the others in the street. He's neat, that's what he is, is Brother Blades. Probably from a posh family but thick and thus only suited to prole white-collar work. Then again, could have come from an upwardly mobile, but not too upwardly mobile, working-class home where neatness and obedience is stressed as a virtue. And it is. Serve them all my days. This means that the same rules apply.

I drop in accidentally on purpose, seeing as I'm in the neighbourhood and all that shite. It's a cheerless morning. There's a pinch in the air but it doesnae look like snow. My lips are chapping a bit, but I've applied the greasy stick.

Bunty seems pleased to see me. She bades me enter and she's got the kettle on. She's wearing a thick angora sweater but these tits won't be beaten, they still cry out for attention underneath it. She looks sour when I start to tell her what a great guy I think Bladesey is.

—Yeah, sure, she says with contempt in her voice. This is too much of a woman for you Brother Blades. I'm sorry, but yes, the same rules do apply. She puts a pot of tea on a green plastic tray with two cups and a jug of milk and bowl of sugar. It's been a long time since I had tea served this way, outside of the office. Every time I go to make a pot at home, there's always used teabags lying in it and in the sink, and it just got too much hassle cleaning it all up. Besides, I never mind to get milk, though there's generally beer in the fridge.

I take a sip and raise my eyebrows.

– He's weak. That's what he is. No backbone, she spits a bitter elaboration.

Well, Brother Blades is in shit street alright. But I have to support the Brother here because to slag him off would show lack of character in her eyes, although I must do it as though I'm being loyal to him, rather than sincere, as that would show lack of judgement. – Cliff's one of the best in my book, I tell her, forcing a look which I hope is pained and embarrassed.

– He's your friend and you're faithful to him and that's good, she says, swallowing the bait. – I sometimes wish I had a friend who was as loyal to me. Is that this masonic brotherhood I hear so much about? She drops her voice a little and stares flirtatiously.

– Well, I hope you don't hear too much about it, I smile back.

– Oh not a great deal of interest. It sounds intriguing though, a secret society.

– Not a secret society, a society of secrets, I wave my finger gently at her.

– Oh I see. And there's a difference is there?

– Well, I don't really know. But I do know one thing about the craft: it's basically now a glorified drinking club for silly wee laddies if the truth be told.

– You don't seem like the silly wee laddie type, she smiles obsequiously.

I'm getting the come-on here big-time. – It's really just something that you get into on the force. It's a way of meeting people who aren't on the force, well, not necessarily on the force. You need that break from other policemen sometimes. We tend to be quite an incestuous mob, the shifts, you know. And the job can get quite demanding.

– Yes . . . I imagine you see some pretty distressing things.

—Yes, but you deal with it. It's your lot and you have to show them all that you're stronger than they are and you show that by not letting it get you down. Like you. You're a very brave lady. You're facing down this creep. Showing him that you're better than him.

— Sometimes I don't feel so strong . . . I just wish that Cliff could be more help. He's not exactly a tower of strength, she says, giving a little bubble, breaking down slowly. For all her tough talk this hoor cannae stand the heat. The Bruce Robertson heat.

I'm over in one elongated stride and I've got her hands in mine. —You deserve somebody who could really look after you, a woman like you.

—Thank you for being so kind . . . it's hard not to feel isolated . . . Craig's at a difficult age . . . I just don't seem to have much of a life I'm afraid . . . God, I'm feeling sorry for myself and I hate that . . .

I look deep into her eyes. — You'll come shining through. You've got what it takes.

—You really think so? she says balefully. I love doubt in a woman. It's nearly as sexy as determination.

— Listen. I'm going to say something here. Something I shouldnae say. No. I'm not, I tell her, shaking my head slowly.

—What? she says, sitting bolt upright.

— No. It'll only cause bad feeling and complicate matters . . . neither of us need that at the moment . . .

— Please. Say what you have to. I want you to. Please. Her fingers ravel round mine and tighten.

Please. Police. Me.

I inhale sharply, then let it out with a long, slow pant. — Right. I will. It's breaking me up what this freak's doing to you because I've got strong feelings for you. There, I said it, I'm sorry, I shrug. I pull our hands apart. Then I stand up and raise my palms in a surrender gesture. I turn away and let a long silence hang. I go to the window and pull back the net curtains. There's a white Nissan Micra on a double fucking yellow line. M reg. Where are the traffic spazmos?

– Bruce . . . it's okay . . . I hear a thin voice from behind me.

I go and sit on the couch. I put my head in my hands and let my elbows rest on my knees. I put on a low, pained voice and say, – There's nothing I can do or say . . . I've messed things up.

– No . . .

I hear her getting up and coming towards me. I feel her light touch on my neck. She's massaging me, her thumbs kneading at the red liver-spotted back of my neck, and she's crying in heavy, halting sobs. – I don't know what to say . . . she bleats.

I look up at her and let a tremble come into my voice. – Just tell me that you don't feel anything for me, just call me a creep, no better than the scumbag who phones you up . . .

– . . . No . . . No . . .

– . . . because that's what I am, a dirty, filthy, sick creep, talking like that to the wife of a friend, when she's emotionally distressed, when she doesn't know her own mind . . .

– No! No! I do! I do know my own mind Bruce! I want to be with you!

I pull her on to my knee, fuckin hell, there's some weight on this hoor, and move her red, swollen face to me. Holding it a few inches from mine, I slide at her tears with the edge of my finger, like the windscreen-wipers on the Volvo. – Ah'm gonny brush these tears away hen, believe you me, ah'm gonny brush them away. Same rules apply, I whisper softly.

At that point I hear a crackling from inside my pocket. I give her a disappointed look.

– Foxtrot calling Z Victor BR, come in BR, over.

– Roger Foxtrot, over, I groan wearily.

– Specify location, over.

– Twelve Carrick Glen Gardens, Corstorphine, over.

– Please proceed to HQ, over.

– Roger Foxtrot, I'm on my way, over and out.

And I was, after I fucked Bunty in the bedroom. I took my time though, you always do with new fanny. What I usually do with a new bird is hole up with them for a weekend and spoil them with loads of foreplay, champagne, takeaways and undivided attention to all the preposterous shite they drivel. That usually does the trick for getting into them on a casual basis for months. The best thing to do is to give a new bird the very best possible time, and then she knows you have the capacity to do that again and she's always looking inwards blaming herself for not being able to reactivate that passion in you. The best lovers ken that you only need tae be a good lover once with one bird. Get it right the first time and then ye can basically dae what ye like. Eventually they tipple that you're just a selfish cunt, usually eftir a few years ay fruitless self-analysis, but by that time you've generally had your fill and are firing into somebody else.

Bunty is a powerful woman, but Bladesey obviously hasn't been doing his homework satisfactorily. I thought she'd take some satisfying but the dirty cow went off like an incendiary device. I suppose after Bladesey *any* performance would be more than suitable. As I get dressed after, I'm conscious of the smell coming from my flannels. I hope Bunty didn't notice. I should have fucking well minded to put on the fresh ones I got from C&A's . . . fuckin stupid bastard . . . what's the point of getting them if you don't wear them . . .

Fortunately, she doesn't appear to notice, and we say our lovers' goodbyes and I head off.

When I got back to the station it was only Gus wanting to know about the sweep for the fitba and the fantasy fitba league.

Shearer's goals last week at Tottenham put me in a nice position, just behind Peter Inglis and some uniformed spastic. I'm ready to pounce. Behind Peter Inglis. Mind you, ye dinnae want that cunt behind you!

I'm thinking that I could handle another shot at that Bunty and I call her to arrange to come round to mines tomorrow, which I instantly regret, a real sign of weakness that was. The problem with hoors is not so much the getting into their keks, but the keeping them at arm's length afterwards. Life can become complicated, which is fine; only simpletons live simple lives. Trouble is, mine's is complicated enough right now.

When I finish (*00000000000 I miss the Other.*)ome wanking
material. It's a c *I miss that soul so much. How can* etting it up
the Gary Glitt *you live like this Bruce, like the way you've* eed is the
remote contr *made us live, alone in this world? We need* plenty of
McCain's ov *to be together Bruce, together in our own* ce, and
of course, t *societies and communities. How can you do this* aterials
which Hect *to us? 000000000000000000000000000000*
00000000000000000000000000000000000
00000000000000000000000000000000

A Sportsman's Dinner

Karen Fulton is looking sexy today. She's put on a bit of weight which doesn't suit most women but she carries it well. Festive overindulgence perhaps, or maybe the classic sex substitute. That's the best dieting plan, fuck 'em regularly! Nae time for munchin on fuckin biscuits then! Too much munchin oan carpets wi Drummond, that's the problem there. Same rules apply. – Looking drop-dead gorgeous Karen, I tell her.

She smiles at me, but there's a touch of frosty lesbo coating which I expect is Drummond's doing. All it takes is the probing tongue of one spacedyke for the impressionable to stray from the path of righteousness. But all it takes is some prime Scotch beef to get them back on the fast track, I kid you not. She's long overdue a length.

Anyway, Bulldyke Drummond comes in with Inglis and Gus Bain. She seems to have warmed to Inglis since he's been all but proven to be a sad buftie-boy. If being befriended by a fucking fag-hag doesnae establish the bastard as a rubberwrist, goodness knows what will. Inglis knows this and obviously hates her following him around.

I've summoned the team in early doors today, and I can tell that some of them arenae too chuffed. As if I care: I've a very busy day. I'm seeing Bunty later, but first I've got an urgent appointment at Hector The Farmer's oot at Penicuik, the old stomping ground, in a couple of hours' time. We need all the light we can get.

I give a brief lack-of-progress report on the Wurie case. Then I open up the discussion. – Okay folks, any news from your ends? Gus? I ask.

– I've been keeping tabs on Setterington and Gorman. They're still hanging around that bloody second-hand furniture shop all the time, Gus tells us. The old boy's looking bitter; lost a bit of pep that yin! Could dae wi some fuckin charlie in him! Chop yirsell oot a line ay posh ya muppet-faced auld cunt!

– Aye, Ray Lennox and some of the boys in D.S. are convinced that Setterington and Francis Begbie are dealing hard drugs from there. I'm chuffed at Gus's expression of scorn at my mention of Ray Lennox's name. – Just keep those beady eyes open Gus. Peter?

– This mystery woman's still no checking out. I've shown pictures to just about everybody from Jammy Joe's, all the stewards and most of the party crowd, but it's still no checking out.

You are *checking out* as a sick perverted arse-buggerer of other men. – We still have this mystery woman in our lives . . . how exciting . . . I turn to Drummond: – Mandy my sweet, what news from our friends in the ethnic community?

– I don't think it's appropriate for you to refer to female officers in that way, she challenges.

– Absolutely right! I sing. – Apologies for any offence caused my darling, force of habit. Bad habit yes, but habit nonetheless. That's why I rely on people like your good self who are so much more aware of those issues than I am to keep me informed of my transgressions in this important area . . .

– I'm not your darling either, she says. Karen Fulton nods supportively. Drummond stares at me for a second, then she says, – Look Bruce, you may think that I'm being pedantic, but it's hard enough getting all the abuse under the sun out there from the public, without being patronised and sneered at by your own colleagues. All I want is equal treatment, that's all.

Do fuckin equal work then ya wee cunt and stop poncing around with wog groups.

– Point taken. Now, what news from the Forum?

She bleats on for ages about the hopes and fears for wogs in Lothian around this case. After we finish, Peter Inglis sidles up to me. – Needs a good seeing tae, that yin, he says bitterly, trying in vain to establish heterosexual credibility.

Aye Inglis, right ye are. What are you gaunny dae? Strap a fuckin dildo on her and shag her up the arse? – Too right, I tell him. – She wants equal rights, get her tae dae equal work. I'd like tae see her go doon tae Leith and haul in Lexo Setterington or Ghostie Gorman or Franco Begbie. Whae'll have tae dae it? You or me Peter. She'll be shuffling papers or counselling some daft slag whose scumbag ay a felly's tanned her jaw.

It's expedient to leave Inglis believing I'm his only pal on the force. He stands fomenting his rage as he looks across at Drummond who's giving it loads with Fulton. Inglis *is* basically homosexual. I'm no saying that he's the sort ay guy who would feel your bum in the lavvy or anything like that, but his *psychology* is homosexual. It makes sense to expose him. The same rules apply.

– Who's for Crawford's? Gus asks.

– Sorry Gus, I have tae nash, I announce, slinging on my overcoat. It gives off a stale, rancid smell, but at least I minded to change into the new C&A's slacks. The material seems to irritate the rash on my inner thighs though. – Got a wee lead with a mate of Ocky's. Might be something, might be nothing. Have to check it out but. See youse later.

I hurry upstairs to the audio-visual section to pick up the tripod and video camera that Pete Loburn, the technician, is letting me take out for a few days. A good boy, in the craft. I hurry downstairs and load the gear onto the back seat of the Volvo. I have to pick up Claire at the Fish Factory before heading out to Penicuik for the shoot. Then I have to bomb hame and do some tidying up as I'm fucking Bunty over there this affie. I'm also, in a sense, fucking Bladesey. Fucking the poor wee bastard for good. It's all go!

Thankfully the roads are still not very busy. I tear down the Walk in the motor and park indiscreetly outside the Fish Factory. Normally I'd keep the Volvo a few streets away, but the clock is ticking. Maisie's there with Claire, and fortunately she's all ready.

— Cup ay tea or something stronger Bruce darlin? Maisie asks.

— I'd love to Maisie, but I can't. Time is of the essence. Claire, my sweet, are you ready?

— Aye, she says. She's got her knee-length fur coat on, and I hope she's wearing what I specified underneath it. It looks like it as she's on heels.

— Gie's a flash then, I instruct.

She opens her coat, exposing the black bra, split-crotch panties, stockings and sussies. Phoah!

— Magic.

Claire goes to put a tracksuit top, bottom and trainers on, but I tell her to take them with her and come as she is. — The car's warm, the engine's running, I urge.

— Look eftir her now Bruce, Maisie half-warns as we depart, — she's a good yin.

She fuckin well isnae half. I could gie the hoor one now.

— You know me Maisie, I smile. — Call me old-fashioned, but I believe that ladies should be treated with the utmost respect.

It doesnae take long tae hit the bypass. Deep Purple's 'Highway Star', the orignial version off *Machine Head*, is blaring out the stereo. Ah've got the wheels, the hot chick, now aw ah need is a line ay posh! It's as well that the road isnae too busy as I can hardly keep my eyes on it, with her sitting next to me and her coat sliding over those thighs, exposing the sussies. At one stage I thought, fuck it, I'm going to have to pull on to a slip-road and a country lane and blow some more OT dosh.

Funny, what stops me is having to listen to her whinging. She's started to have second thoughts about the project. – Ah'm no sae sure aboot this, she says, lighting a cigarette.

– C'mon Claire, yir gittin good dosh for this. Besides, look on it as an education, a new experience beneficial tae yir career development, I reason. I'm sounding like Toal talking to a jug-eared raw recruit of a uniformed spastic before sending him down to Drylaw. – It's a good dug. A sheepdug. A collie, for fuck sakes. They're gentle, obedient dugs, known for it. And I guar-antee that the video is only going to be for private use. Hector and myself. Two grand Claire. It's good dosh.

– Aye . . . awright.

It's just as well that Hector's wedged up. Farmers always complain about their lot, but you never see a skint one. They tend to be the one profession that gets on well with the polis. They have the property, and we're in the property protection business. So they have a tendency to be more instinctively well-disposed towards us than most. Like us, they tend to have a high depression and suicide rate. It's that seasonally adjusted depres-sion wi them. Look at that Ted Moult guy that did the Everest Double Glazing.

We pull off the road and up the gravel track towards the farmhouse. Hector has heard the Volvo tearing up and comes out to greet us in his usual hale and hearty manner. He's a real fer-min vermin archetype awright: stocky, ruddy, white hair and beard, tweed jacket, cords and boots.

– Hello Bruce.

– Hector.

His eyes open like saucers. – And what am I to call this love-ly young lady?

– Claire, she says.

His face ignites further. – It's an absolute pleasure and an honour my darling, he says, taking her arm in his and leading her to the Range Rover. I follow with the camera and tripod. It's muddy, very fucking muddy and I'm trying to watch those new fawn flannels.

– Is this your farm? Claire asks Hector.

– All mine, my darling, all mine.

Hector's House.

– From the road into town back there, he stops and sweeps his free arm around to the ugly, desolate brown mounds which tower over us, – right up to the base of them there hills.

Claire gives an impressed, evaluating smile. That lassie will go all the way to the top in her profession. She has that premium-range hoor's instinctive understanding of value.

Hector gives a whistle, and from out of nowhere a collie shoots towards us like a missile. Just as you think it's going to collide into us, it slows down and circles us a few times, yelping with excitement.

– This is Angus, Hector says proudly, petting the panting, enthusiastic beast.

We get into the Range Rover.

– It's freezing, Claire says, lighting another fag.

– Angus here'll warm ye up, I say, getting into the back after her, letting the dog sit on the front passenger seat.

Claire looks dubiously at her leading man.

– Silver medal at the Royal Highland Show in ninety-five, eh boy, Hector says fondly to the dog, starting up the car.

The mutt leans over and starts licking my hand with its sand-paper tongue. – He likes you Bruce, Hector observes, starting up the motor.

The track follows a serpentine route over frozen ground, cutting through a range of ice-encrusted trees into a clearing and down the hill towards the barn. As it dips, the path deteriorates into a patch of muddy swamp which has failed to freeze over.

I turn to Claire. – You should be used tae this sort of gig Claire, coming fae Aberdeen. Ewe'd have tae be good at your trade tae compete wi aw the sheep up thaire. *Ewe'd* have tae be good! Get it?

Nobody does, and the fucking Range Rover grinds to a halt,

sticking in the mud. I look at my watch as the car snarls ineffec-
tively, the wheels spinning, failing to grip.

Hector turns round in the seat. — Sorry Bruce, but we need
a bit of your muscle. I've got tae dae this, he protests, shaking
the wheel in response to my cold stare.

I get out of the vehicle, my feet sinking into the mud which
covers my brogues. The bottom of my new slacks are fuckin . . .
that useless auld cunt Hector . . .

I push in exasperation as I look at my watch and the motor
springs free, sending a shower of mud on to my shins.

When I get back in Hector and Claire are grinning at me. —
Sorry Bruce, but you're no exactly dressed fir the ferm! Mind
and no get a mess on Claire now!

I seeth silently as we get to the barn. It's a huge, ugly, cold
place, but it's pretty isolated. I quickly set up the camera, though
not fast enough for Claire.

— It's freezing Bruce, hurry up!

The light's still good, but it is cold. The frosted wind whistles around the barn with a clinical, cutting ozone smell of Arctic
origins.

— Right Claire, I direct, — off wi the coat and oot ay they
panties . . . if ye could jist lean ower that bar and spread those
legs . . .

— How's it lookin Bruce . . .? Hector says through pursed
lips.

— Pit that fag oot Claire! A wee bit tae the left. . . . that's it.
Hector, it's all yours.

Hector pulls the dug ower tae Claire and lets him have a
good sniff of her. Then he starts pulling on the dog's cock; at the
same time he's massaging his own through his troosers while
staring at Claire. The dug's tongue is hanging oot and his pink
cock shoots oot like a plastic attachment on a toy, that Darth
Vader's lance in Toys Я Us.

Hector starts the ghetto-blaster which plays *The Archers'*
theme tune. That was his idea. He points the yelping dug at
Claire, restraining it by the collar. Then he lets it go.

The animal ignores her completely, springing at me and attaching itself to my leg, thrusting ferociously. – Get that fuckin thing off me, I shout, trying to push it away, but the bastard's nostrils flare and a low growl comes from its throat. I stagger backwards, knocking over the tripod and camera. Hector grabs the dug and pulls him off me, by which time my C&A's troosers are covered in canine spunk.

– Her, no me! I shout at the stupid, panting beast.

We set it up again for another try. Once more, this daft fucking thing flies at me and attaches itself to me. – Jesus Fuck Almighty!

That thin pink cock rips and spurts against my flannels. – Fuckin new troosers!

– Sorry Bruce, Hector shrugs and grabs the yelping, demented beast by the collar. Claire starts laughing, a loud, horsey hee-haw.

– That dug's a fuckin queer, I curse, pointing at the fucker.

Hector's got the fucking audacity to look affronted. – That dug's sired mair championship pups than you've had hot dinners son, he grumbles. – He just likes you.

– I like you Hector, but I don't fuckin well want to shag you. The dug's a fuckin poof and that's aw there is tae it!

Hector goes to console the animal, as if its feelings are hurt. – He's just new tae this, that's aw.

– It's nae good him liking me, he's meant tae like her! I point at Claire, who's back in her fur coat. – There must be something we can dae . . . put something on her . . . like dog food or that.

– No fuckin way, Claire snarls, – Ah'm no gittin eaten alive by that thing!

– It was just a thought, I say. I try to give my flannels a wipe with my hanky, but I'm messing them up more with the snot and the charlie. This is a fuckin mess of a day.

We try the same thing, one more time, and again the dug goes for me. My new fuckin troosers are ruined. It's totally useless, a complete waste of time. Darkness is creeping in and we've lost our chance. I accidentally-on-purpose stand on the collie's tail and the cunt lets out a loud yelp followed by a series of accusatory gasping whines.

— Mind the dug! Are you okay boy? Hector coos. Claire looks disapprovingly at me.

She's getting rode and no mistake. I've just about time for a quick one in the back of the Volvo. I proposition her but she's informing me that she's staying on at Hector's to earn some more cash from her new sugar daddy. They link arms and smile smugly at each other. Cunts. I head back to mine in the Volvo, stopping at Crawford's for some takeaway food.

I wanted those new strides for Bunty coming. Now I have to stick the cunts on the laundry mountain and dig out some soiled, but not quite so soiled ones from the stinking pile. The place is a real shithouse. The Dame Judi in here is worse than back at Hector's barn. I pile everything I can into bin-liners, attack the surfaces with a damp cloth followed by some polish, and drag the hoover across the floor. I'm sweating when the doorbell goes. I switch off the hoover and breathe deeply.

Bunty comes in and I'm leading her straight up to the bedroom, where I've changed the sheet and the duvet cover and I get her on top of it. She's well on, her twat dripping like Niagara Falls and as wide as the city bypass. I've banged on my tape deck and Bachman Turner Overdrive's 'You Ain't Seen Nothing Yet' is blaring out. There are noises coming from next door, shagging noises. Stronach is fucking someone, probably that wee tart who works behind the bar at the hotel; I think that was her Mini parked outside. Of course, Julie's away on some fucking daft course, he did mention it. I waste no time getting into Bunty. She's game for it as well, the strong silent type. So Stronach's headboard's banging off the wall and so is ours, and there's quite a competition going on. We'll show that cunt. Thankfully Bunty's taking a while to get there. But after a bit it starts to become too long, and I can't hear Stronach next door. It's taking her ages and in truth, it gets a drag, uncomfortable even, but I stick it out, even though I'm gritting my teeth at the end. When she does come I think we're going to go crashing through the wall into Tom Stronach's bedroom. That would show the cunt alright! Same rules!

As we settle into a post-coital snooze, I'm satisfied to note the silence coming from Stronach's next door. No fucking staying power, either on the field or in the scratcher.

When we get up, I prepare a light lunch with the stuff I'd got from Crawford's on the way hame, then absent-mindedly check the messages, playing the one Bladesey had stupidly left.

I casually observe as Bunty's blood runs cold with Bladesey going into his spiel just after my daughter wishes me a Happy Christmas. Then I witness her going off again. It's like a second orgasm, but this time the hoor freaks on outrage rather than sex.

— It's him! On your machine! she raves.

— Bunty, that's Cliff, I tell her. He's just mucking about.

— But it's him! It's exactly like him!

— Anybody can do that! Manchistih! I say badly.

— It's him! It's him! I'm calling the police! That sad little bastard! I should have known! Living with a pervert! The things he wanted to do! I should have known! I've been such a fool!

She bursts into tears, her mascara running. — I'm going to make him suffer!

That word again.

— Bunty . . . we don't want to be jumping to conclusions . . . there may be a perfectly good reason as to why Cliff . . .

— No! Don't defend him! she shrieks.

— I'm not defending him, I'm just saying that we cool our jets, I snap. — If Cliff is guilty of humiliating the both of us then believe me, no power, no fucking power on Earth will stop me from tearing him apart with my bare hands. Believe that, I say, staring at her with resolve and almost feeling sorry for Bladesey as the hatred glazes over in her eyes. — But we need to be sure.

— I'm sure! I'm fucking well sure . . . Oh Bruce . . . she moans softly, her face twisted and traumatised. She focuses on

me suddenly. – What did he mean about tapes? He said something about tapes! What was it!

I make a show of swallowing some air. – Look Bunty . . . it's
. . . God, this is so difficult.

– Tell me!

– Cliff was . . . Cliff and a few of the lads at the Lodge . . .
they . . .

She's looking manically at me.

– They used to get video tapes from some guy at the Lodge.
A farmer guy. It's not really my scene. I obviously knew what
they were but I just thought, well, that's up to them. Cliff wanted to watch them here, he didn't want you to know anything
about them. He obviously thought you'd object.

– What sort of tapes . . .

I go to the cupboard behind the telly, and pull out a couple
of Hector's choicest. – They're pornographic. I've never looked
at them myself, but I can imagine what's in them.

– I knew it! I want to see them. Put one in!

– Bunty, I don't think it would be wise.

– Oh yes, I want to know everything! I want to know all
about him. The real him! she sobs.

I acted reluctant, but Bunty was insistent. We watch a bit of
Vibrator Massacre, and she runs to the toilet puking, just as I was
getting into it. She's seen enough.

I calm her down a little and eventually call her a taxi home.
I was certain she'd phone the police and make a formal complaint against Bladesey. I kept half-heartedly trying to talk her
out of it, gently urging her to call Cliff at his mum's, give him a
chance to put his side of things and all the insincere bullshit
under the sun, but I knew that her mind was made up. I get a bell
from Gus at the Lodge after tea, telling me that they are planning to haul Bladesey in for questioning. Good news travels fast.
Later on Bunty leaves a message telling me that she's gone to *her*
mother's with Craig. She didn't want to be there when he got
back from Newmarket.

This sets me up in fine fettle for the do tonight, with the

earlier débâcle with that stupid dug now last Tuesday's *Daily Record*. I've given Ray Lennox my spare ticket and after meeting for a pint in the Antiquary, we head to the Sheraton for Stronach's Sportsman's Dinner. I'm a wee bit concerned as I haven't spoken to Stronach since our little neighbourly tiff over noise levels on Christmas Day.

I'll be three sheets but I take the motor; I'll pick it up later if I'm too wasted. I switch on the car radio. It's that Celine Dion bird singing that horrible song, the one she was just made to sing. Lennox is blabbing on about some departmental shite and Dion goes off, only to be replaced by the Eurythmics. Lennox is going on about how Gus has got it in for him.

I've got Annie Lennox on the radio whinging in one ear and Fanny Lennox next tae me daein the same in the other yin.

To my surprise, Stronach greets me heartily. It seems as if he wants to let bygones be bygones, or perhaps it's because he senses my potential to wreck his big night if fucked with. I brazenly install myself and Lennox at his table which he's not too pleased about as he's in the company of the former England forward Rodney Dolacre. Wonder of wonders: Dolacre has actually come up for the do. Dalglish and Souness couldn't make it; both rise further in my estimation. I'm astonished that Dolacre has, until I learn that the real reason he's in Scotland, with his agent by his side, is to arrange his own testimonial match with Celtic.

It's a good crack with the usual loads of jokes about how fitba guys are the salt of the earth and women are only good for cleaning, cooking and shagging. I'm enjoying the fact that Stronach is ill-at-ease because Dolacre's upstaging him, though Lennox fucks up by saying something sycophantic to our testimonial sportsman. When was the last time Lennox was in Gorgie in a non-working capacity?

The meal is pretty good. I start off with the prawn cocktail, then go for steak, chips, mushrooms and onion rings, followed by Black Forest Gateau. Stronach and Dolacre have some pasta dish while Lennox has Chicken Kiev. There are quite a few hingers-oan at this table, loads of minor football celebs trying to catch Dolacre's attention as he's still a pretty big name. Stronach, now bolstered by Lennox's arse-licking, has stopped trying to compete with Dolacre and is basking in the reflected glory.

I have to give it to that English cunt Dolacre, he's got us daft Jocks well sussed out. — These arseholes'll always bring between five and ten thousand down, which at our prices could mean an extra quarter of a million quid in the kitty. All I have to do is play up this old Irish granny routine. Suppose I'd better dig one up from somewhere, he winks at his agent, before elaborating. — See, a couple of the lads, English boys, used to play for the Republic. They've been teaching me all those daft Mick songs.

Someone produces an *Evening Times*. It contains an interview with Rodney:

> I grew up in a large Irish family in North London and all the folks back home in the old country were mad keen Celts. I would have dearly loved to have been able to pull the hooped jersey over my head.

— I said striped jersey at first, he laughs. — I couldn't remember that they played in hoops! Thank God the journalist was sympathetic! Bleedin Nora, he snorts, — I mean, one Jock team's much the same as any other to me. All shit, ain't they? Still, I'll take their giros! Another ten thousand on the gate: can't be sneezed at, can it?

I saw Stronach go red at that point.

Dolacre gives a witty speech, as does a Scottish First Division manager, but the rest are just fucking windbags who like to hear the sound of their own voices. Dolacre leaves early, before the auction takes place. The strip he wore in the England B international versus the Czech Republic a couple of years ago in his last representative game is auctioned and fetches a hundred and fifty quid for Tom's testimonial fund. It was bought by Alan Beach, the plumber's merchant, who's on the testimonial committee.

At the end of the night Lennox departs and I decide I'm too fucked up to drive the Volvo so I share Stronach's taxi home. — That Rodney Dolacre is a laugh, eh, I smile, — It was great hearing his fitba tales.

— Arrogant English cunt, Stronach spits.

I go into my home and Shirley calls. I let the machine get it. — Broosss . . . I need to talk to you Brooooss, her distressed mechanised tone whines. — It's very important . . . phone me Brooossss . . . please . . .

I put on a Private video, one of Hector's, which features some good arse-fucking shots. It never fails to amaze me, the purchase those male actors get on the old arse-fucking. Poles must be well-greased. Mind you, these birds but, their arseholes must be stretched like a mother-of-ten's fanny.

Shirley. Don't mistake me for somebody who cares my love.

I go to do a shite. I've taken some of Rossi's laxatives but I can't see any of the worm. It's no good just getting its body out anyway, you need to get the whole head, otherwise it just keeps growing. I try to turn in, but I feel uneasy and sleep with the light on. These cunts with their OT cutbacks'll kill me.

I need

00You were always aware of your mother, but your father was a shadow when you were a child. There was no warmth or tenderness coming from him. When you did try to go to him, he brushed you away. Sometimes you would see him looking at you, when you were playing with your toys on the carpet. Looking into you, beyond you. You would turn and smile because you were a good wee boy and you wanted to please your father, really wanted him to love you, but he would wince and look away. You stopped trying to go to him. The look was enough. Then he started doing the things to you. With the coal. Making you taste the coal, taste the filth. You could understand none of it. What had you done? Why was he doing this? What had you done to deserve this?

*Your mother would come when you cried in the night. You're a
good wee boy Bruce, you're mummy's wee boy, she would tell you.
Yet you could sense the pity in her love. You knew right from
the start that there was something wrong with you.
Then there was a baby. A baby brother. You were only marginally
interested, but everyone loved the baby, your wee brother Steven.
Your dad, your uncles and aunties, they all loved that child.
You thought that if you loved him too, they would see that you
were a good boy and they might love you. You looked into
the cot and touched the baby's small hand. Your father pulled you
away with a violent jerk. Your arm wrenched in its socket
as he tugged it. Don't you go near him! Don't you ever lay a
finger on him! he snapped. You didn't cry. You just bowed*

W *your head. Your mum came and led you away. Her look,* b, but
char *that pitying look, which you now were beginning to* ush my
tee *resent almost as much as your father's sneers*00000000 cups of
bla *00000000000000000000000000000000000000000000* axatives
follo *0000000000000000000000000000000000000000000* h out this
fuckin *00000no0000no00000000000000000do not do* ckin thing
inside *this000000000hold000000000000hold00* wipe at my
arse as I s *000hold0000000000the pain000000* it hanging like
tagliatelle *000000000000000000000000000000* u need tae get
the fucking head of those things and I can't get the bastard out.

I decide that there's going to be no work done today, so I fill out
an OTA 1–7 for the overtime, and sit back watching videos until
I drowse. When I wake up, I note that it's the evening. This is
when I come to life. That was a great kip. It's got me going.

I've snorted my last half G and I'm on the mooch for mair
posh. I call cold round at Ray Lennox's gaff. Always the best way
tae call anyone. The polis way. One heavy-knuckled rap on the
door and I hear that characteristic sound of the occupants scut-
tling like disturbed rats, their pathetic lives swamped in criminality. Lennox is daein something eh shouldnae be. Then the door
opens. He has a bird round, she's just on her way out.

— Eh, Bruce, Lennox says, — this is Trudi.

— Pleased to meet you my darling, I lift her hand to my mouth and kiss it, an extravagant gesture. Worth forty wanks as well. Mmm hmm. — Pleased to meet you Trudi. Ray's not mentioned you to me. That's remiss of him, I smile. I turn to Lennox, who now looks a bit off-white, — I can see why you'd like to keep a treasure like her well away from an old prospector like Bruce Robertson!

She smiles and departs, Ray instantly recovering his cool.

— Tidy piece Mister Lennox, I say approvingly.

— A lovely girl, Lennox replies in fake pomposity. He's already gone to his stash and started cutting oot the lines. I'll say one thing for Ray Lennox, he doesnae let the grass grow under his feet as far as the posh goes. Fuck work today, even the backshift.

I snort back one of the lines, — I believe in law and I believe in order. This is a treat, a perk for enforcing . . . Jesus fuck . . . good shit . . . where was I, aye, a perk for enforcing law and order. I mean, we know that there are shite laws, so there's no point in obeying them ourselves, even if it's our job to enforce them for others. The problem is, most people are weak, so if you don't have laws, even shite ones, then you certainly don't have any order matey. Same rules.

— Agreed, Ray points at me, then bends down to the mirror to fill his hooter full of gear, — Phoah . . . Aye, sometimes I think that the best solution to the whole fuckin mess would be if we could just go around and shoot any cunt we felt like at any time. Most of the time, simply through experience and professionalism, you'd get it right. Then wide bastards wouldnae go around with such an attitude. Imagine, all the fuckin scumbags with big, apologetic stares on their faces . . .

— Niggers doon in London and Abos over in Sydney aw smiling and going 'Yez baz' like they did in the fuckin fields . . .

— . . . Birds comin up n giein ye a blow-job in the street for the privilege ay no gittin thir fuckin heids blown oaf . . .

— . . . but maist of all, just fucking well shooting spastics stone dead, I smile, forming a gun out of my hand, putting it to my head and making a loud exploding noise as I violently jerk the hand and head away from each other.

— Good coke, eh Bruce?

— Too good for spastics Ray. Too good for spastics. I kid you not, my sweet, sweet friend.

Ray Lennox. A sound guy and a fuckin good polisman. I don't care what anybody says.

After another blitz on the posh we hit a few bars, then it's back to his with a cairry-oot and mair posh. The cunt makes me listen to his shite records aw night. Starts trying tae tell me that The Verve or whatever they're called are better than U2 and Simply Red! Get a life Lennox! It gets too much and I leave and head downtown. Fucked if I'm paying for a taxi. I think I might have missed the last corpie bus. It'll have to be a night bus. It's fucking freezing out there. I head into St Andrew's Square station to see if there's a bus for any of the outlying scum towns that can drop me off in Colinton.

My luck might be in as there's still one or two people hanging around. I see a jakey out of the corner of my eye. He scrapes along the wall, coming to rest against a bus shelter. The jakey seems to have a kind of fear in his eyes, as if it's just dawned on him that whatever he's drank it's just not been quite enough to blank out the hideous reality of his miserable life.

And I know him.

Alan. Alan Loughton. Used to be a member of the strike committee, back in the day. How's it goin Al buddy? How's it going now that the pits been shut down for over ten years? How is it going now that you're no longer seen as a socialist hero back in the village, but as a boring auld pissheid and that things are *00the strike00000000000* d down the country and posh unde *000you had two strikes Bruce* long-gone? How's it going? We tak *0000000 when the filth first* how it's going. *came 000000000000Three strikes and you're out 00 00 at the old law game 00*

But let's no wor 00 at the old law game 00

— Awright! Alan isn't it! What's this? I nod at his gold tin of

Carlsberg Special. — Nae old purple tin? Going bourgeois on us? Cleaning up our act are we?

He's looking at me now, trying to get me into focus.

— Bruce! Bruce Robertson, I tell him. — Mind ay me? I joined the polis just before the strike! If you cannae beat them, join them, I always did say. What aboot yourself? What are you up to these days? Politics no doubt. Always did have a way with public speaking!

Loughton groans an incomprehensible recognition.

— Seem tae have lost it but mate, eh? That silver-tongued oratory. Anyway, I must fly, see you, I turn and stroll across the concourse. Behind me I can hear a pained growl of sheer anguish.

There's two words though, that I, we, I, we can make out.

Filth.

The other one is bea

No fuckin way a jakey, a purple-tinned cunt is fucking with my head. It's me, Bruce. There are no others. I'm not the one he's on about. Loughton. A nothing. A nobody. A set of fucking dormant social problems waiting to be cleaned up. That's the real filth, that's the real garbage.

At the other end of the bus park, two uniformed spastics are talking to an Eastern Scottish Transport inspector. I approach them.

— Alright officers, I flash my ID.

— Aye, one says nervously.

— How auld's yir granny? I ask.

— Three hundred and sixty-two, he replies.

— Good lodge. Dougie Millar still grand-master?

— Aye . . .

— Well, officer . . .?

— Cameron sir.

— Well P.C. Cameron, I suggest you and your colleague here get your fingers out of your arseholes. Are you aware of the policy of zero tolerance of crimes and misdemeanours in public areas?

—Yes . . . we . . . he stutters. A fledgling spazwit.

— I'm assuming that you are beat officers here?

—Yes sir.

— Glad to hear it. There's a fuckin jakey over the concourse, I point in Loughton's direction. — He's been abusing passengers, including me. You get that cunt or you're getting it baith weys, through the service and through the craft. Savvy?

— Right, one says nervously, turning to the other one, — Let's go.

The two uniformed spastics race across the tarmac and grab a hold of the bemused Loughton.

I always liked Loughton but it seems to me that he's been going nowhere since his salad days of the miners' strike. The best I could do is to help the cunt relive old memories and it was almost like auld times watching the poor fucker get huckled away into the back of a police vehicle by the boys in blue.

Come In Charlie

The new area office in the South Side looks tatty already: those sticky-fingerprinted glass doors and that fag-burned public desk with the badly printed and faded posters on the noticeboard above it. There's a smell of disinfectant, that strong institutional kind that looks like it's been put down to conceal the smell of pish, even when it husnae. An old cow is giving the desk sergeant a hard time. It's Sammy Bryce though, and Sammy's too professional to let her faze him. — . . . I understand that, he's saying, — but if it doesn't have a crime number then there's nothing we can do.

— How dae ah get a crime number? she asks.

— You have to report to the nearest local station to where the offence took place.

— But they said any police office . . . she's almost in tears with frustration.

— Any police office if you have a crime number.

I wink at Sammy, not a bad guy for a uniformed spastic, and then I head upstairs to meet Davie McLaughlin.

D.S. McLaughlin from the South Side is heading up the investigation of Bladesey, who has returned from the bosom of his spastic family in Newmarket to find himself minus a wife and in our custody helping us with our enquiries. McLaughlin is a good choice on this one: a dirty carrot-topped bastard with a filthy fuckin pape name, not in the craft, an odious piece of racial vomit. It's quite fortuitous as it's an excuse for not pulling strings for Brother Blades. The pervert Brother Blades.

– So you know Cliff and Bunty Blades well? he asks.

Of course, we find it distasteful talking to a freckle-faced left-footer, but it's serving our purposes. I slip on my concerned face. – Aye Davie, we're friends of the both of them. I've kent Bladesey, eh Cliff Blades, for a couple of years, but I've only got to know Bunty recently. She was going through a pretty hard time with this sicko hassling her, so Bladesey wanted me to come around and give them a bit of support.

– Did you ever get the idea that he was the one making all those calls?

I give a slow, deliberate swallow. – Davie, I've been polis longer than I care to remember, and I've investigated loads of cases like this. At the time, I have to admit it, it was the last fucking thing on my mind, I shake my head. – Now I can see that this was how he was getting his kicks, enjoying the element of risk. He was wanking all over me! I smash my fist on to the table.

– Don't give yourself a hard time mate, honestly, says the concerned Romanist. Seems not a bad guy, for a pape. – We all have to switch off and have our own lives. Sometimes we get blind spots about people.

– But I feel like a fuckin monkey Davie . . .

– Bruce, ye cannae go around in your private life thinking that every single pal you've got can or cannae be Jackie Trent in some way or another. If the truth be told, when we walk out that door, we all put the job on hold to an extent.

Maybe you do, but you're a pape. As your family are probably all criminals, you *have* tae pit the job oan hold.

– I want to see him . . .

– I don't think that's a good idea Bruce . . . , the bead-twirler tells me.

– Just give me two minutes with him, I won't fucking touch him, I swear.

– Okay, he says, raising those ginger brows. McLaughlin may

be a Romanistic, anti-abortionist cunt, but he's polis through and through.

I head down to the detention room where Bladesey is being held. A uniformed spastic stands over him, but departs as I come in.

Bladesey says nothing, but his eyes are burning and eager. He's pleased to see me. This pathetic little bastard's genuinely pleased to see me!

He really thinks that I'd be friends with a sad pervert. Best put him right. – You fuckin little cunt! I snap. – Fuckin piss-taking little fart . . . you fuckin strung me along from the start! All that fuckin shit about Frank Sidebottom! You were wanking off in my face ya fuckin cunt!

Bladesey's now a picture of wretchedness. – No . . . he protests. He looks so bad, that it's hard for me to keep looking at his eyes. I turn away briefly, but then the need for sport takes over, as it always does, and I glare at him.

– Bruce, you have to believe me, it wasn't me!

– Don't make me fuckin punch your heid doon through your fuckin shoodirs – right oot yir fuckin erse ya wee cunt! I move towards him, and he cowers away. I stop and turn, then do a full circle back towards him. I think of all the injustices I've suffered, more injustices than that wee cunt could ever know. Spreading my palms I plead, – Why mate? Why the fuck did you do this Cliff? Why did you drag me intae it? I thought we were mates!

– I didn't, I didn't, we are! Bladesey begs, and then breaks down. – I digh-hi-dent . . . I digh-hi-dent . . . he chokes, biting into the sleeve of that checked jacket to stifle his sobs.

It's pathetic watching a grown man cry in that manner. No fuckin pride. Do you see me break down like a fuckin wee tart, and all the shite I've had to contend with as well? Do you fuck! We cope. He deserves to die, to be forced into committing suicide and dying. Like Clell. Aye, if I had my way that would happen with the fucked up: a sort of psychic natural selection. I'd take over the fuckin do-gooding helplines and if one of those sad cases phoned up I'd say: I think you're absolutely correct to feel such despair. Gie the world a brek and take your own miserable life. If you need any help I'll be round in a few minutes. Bladesey. He's fuckin rubbish. Me, hanging aboot wi that nae-mates trash? Huh! I think not. I'm starting to hyper-ventilate as I look down on him. – I wish I could believe you . . . I wish I could fuckin believe you . . . I'm fuckin oot ay here! I storm out the room knocking over a chair and I hear Bladesey crying, – Brooosss . . . as I depart.

Outside, I regain my composure. I thumb back towards the interview room. – Damaged. In the fuckin nut. Don't give that spastic any fucking coffee, I hiss at the poor uniformed spastic who's a little shaken.

– Right gaffer, he says meekly.

I like this officer. I like being called 'gaffer'. It's a term some spastics around this nick are going to have to get used to when that promo comes through! I kid you not! I say tatty-bye-byes to the tatty-muncher McLaughlin, thanking the Romanist for his assistance and confirming that, yes, retrospectively, I should have seen that we were dealing with damaged goods in the form of Brother Blades. I drive back to HQ. I'm soon at my desk study-ing Monica from Sheffield's full paps, each little goose-pimple on them clearly defined. The photographer's done the business with this one. A keen student of the game.

The phone goes. External. I skip a heartbeat and then feel a long tense drawing in my chest. I pick it up.

– Hello?

It's Bunty.

– Bunty, I state.

– Have they got him?

–Yes. I've just been down there to see him.

– Still denying everything, I'll bet.

–Yeah . . . to be expected. They all do it. Not a particularly pleasant experience, it has to be said.

–Yes . . . it must have been . . . Bruce, when can I see you?

– I've been giving that a bit of thought Bunty, and I think it's for the best that we keep a low profile with our relationship, at least until this mess is cleared up.

— What . . .

— Bunty, this could cost me dearly. I'm a detective. I should have picked up that Cliff was suspect. I knew what he was like through the craft, with the videos and stuff. We . . . I could be a laughing stock on the job! There's a promotion coming up. You get my drift?

— Bruce, I'll be discreet about us until the time is right. I promise I won't say anything. But you must come and see me Bruce . . .

— Of course I will, I say softly down the phone. — We've got something special, haven't we?

I'll be round to fuck you soon you big fat hoor.

— I think so, she says, her voice breaking, — but I'd never get in the way of your career, I'd never do anything to foul that up.

— Bunty, you don't know how much it means to hear you say that to me. All my life I felt that I was meant for greater things but there was always something holding me back, some missing piece in the jigsaw. That missing piece, I can see now, is the love and understanding of a wonderful woman. That's what you are Bunty, a wonderful woman. And you've suffered so much . . . I want to put that right . . .

— Oh Bruce . . .

— Just keep mum my darling, and I'll be round to see you soon. That's a promise.

— Okay Bruce.

— I'll see you soon.

— Bruce . . . I love you . . .

Fuck off fatso. The moment Bladesey was banged up, that was you and me in the death throes of our relationship. Mind you, I might string this cow along for a bit longer; asks no awkward questions and keeps a good, clean hoose. She'd get a formidable crease oan a collar, that yin! — I love you too Bunty.

There's a silence.

— I have to go, I tell her. I've got another call coming in. I

325

have as well. It's Shirley. Fuckin hell. I've heard ay the expression fanny comin oot the fuckin waws, but it's certainly comin oot fae the receiver. I see Gillman over in the corner by the sink and he's holding up my Hearts mug and guesturing at the kettle with his free hand.

— Shirley, I say curtly. I check for the Kit-Kats in my drawer. Still a few left.

— Bruce . . . I need to see you. I need to talk. I give Dougie the thumbs up sign.

— What about?

— I need to see you! Pleeeassssse . . .

This cunt's gaun fuckin loopy oan ays here. — Alright, alright! Jeannie Deans, in half an hour!

— Be there Bruce, please don't let me down . . .

— I won't, we tell her. I won't what: be there or let her down? Then, thinking of Bunty, not of how we feel about Bunty, but what we said to her, we say, — I love you.

— You mean that?

The even-handed approach. It enhances credibility both in policing and in relationships! — I said it. I'm on my way. See you soon.

— See you.

I put the phone down. What is that spasticated cow wanting from me? We have enough fucking trouble on our plate as it is. I go over to the kettle, where Gillman and Ray Lennox are in conference. — Gascoigne was right, and Best even said it as well. Thir's never been a man, a real man, who hasnae slapped his missus. Aw that liberal airy-fairy bullshit. She steps oot ay line, she gits a bat in the mooth, that's it.

Lennox is shaking his head slowly in disgust. — We investigate crimes ay domestic violence. That's assault and it's against the law ay the land.

— Phah, Gillman sneers, and nobody sneers quite like him. If someone told me, in sincerity, that I girned like Gillman, I would die a happy man. I can tell it's draining the blood from Lennox's face at five feet. — Ah git enough fuckin mooth oan the

job withoot takin it fi some cunt in the hoose. He looks to me,
— Put this cunt right Bruce.

— I have to fly. I'm having woman problems, I smirk.
— But this is a subject which needs further discussion. The bar
ton *(OOOOOOOOOOOOIt's just you and me now BruceOOOOOOOOOOOOO*
OOOOOOOOOOOOOOOOOOOOOOOOO just us OOOOOOOOOOOOOOOOOO)

They nod affirmatively, Lennox with reluctance, and I, we, I
. . . we're all here . . . jump in the motor and speed towards the
Jeannie Deans pub in the South Side. We decide to drive through
Queens Park and we marvel at Salisbury Craigs' imposing face
which towers above us. This city of ours is truly beautiful and we
like this part where there is not a scheme in sight. Why could we
not simply move all the scum to the middle of nowhere, like
Glasgow, where they would blend in more effectively? Come to
think of it, that's exactly what we did do, when we built the
schemes. Sent them far, but not far enough.

We still have a wrap of coke on us and there must be a good
half a G left and we rub a load of it into our gums and our face
goes numb. We need it for this Shirley hoor, we know that she is
going to make demands on us. We are not to be entrusted with
the demands of the weak. It is not in our character.

Shirley is sitting on her own at a table in the corner of the empty
bar. She looks like a hopeful hoor on a day shift. When we get
closer we can observe her distress through her red, puffy face.
Apparently our sister-in-law has been crying.

— Bruce . . . I had a smear . . . a cervical smear . . . there was
something there . . . I have to go back for more tests . . .

— I'm sorry, we tell her, — but that's just one of those things.
No sense in getting all steamed up until you see what the other
test results tell you.

— But I can't cope . . . I've nobody since Danny left . . . I
need you Bruce. I need somebody . . . I need support Bruce . . .

Just looking at her there, at her distress, just for a second,
we wish we were stronger. I wish I was somebody else, the

327

person she's mistaking me for, the person whom she *wants* to mistake me for. The person who gives a fuck. — Sorry, we tell her. — I don't see what I can do. You'll have to sort it out.

I've been licking her diseased fanny. Oh my God.

Then I, we, start to think: no way should Stronach be getting his game in the middle of the park with that young boy languishing in the reserves, what's his name, him that played towards the end of season. He's fit now, so there's no excuse for such poor selection.

— Bruce, please, she says, and grabs our hand in hers. We brush her away. — Sorry Shirley, we say, rising, as she starts the waterworks. — Nothing we can do. Urgent case, eh. Sort it out and keep me posted. Chin up! Ciao!

We dance across the floor in the pub, slipping deftly past two chairs and as we turn can see her round, dark, black hole of a mouth and she's bawling something but we are spinning away out the door and she rises to follow us but we nash like fuck across the car park, humming the closing credits tune of *The Benny Hill Show*.

She's still in hot pursuit screaming Brooosss and we realise that we're running in the wrong direction, away from the car. We look back and slow down, regaining breath and then turning round, standing still and smiling as she approaches us breathing heavily. We then do a quick shuffle and sell her such a Charlie Cooke-style dummy that had she been a defender, she would, indeed, have had to pay to get back in the park!

Gotcha!

Emulate that Stronach!

She falls on to her knees howling in frustration as we, I, we dive in the car and start up the motor and we head down the road, watching her broken figure receding from us in the mirror.

Shirley brought it on herself. A disease of the fanny, divine retribution for her infidelities. We have our rash, that is our penance. We do not inflict our misfortune on others. We are not made that way.

Daft cunt.

Our, my, head is spinning but I feel euphoric and sick at the same time. There is no way that I can go back to the office and be harassed by hoors. It's hoggers the morn: oot wi the old, in wi the new. Same rules for fanny as for everything else. We, I, radio in to Toal, telling him that we are following up several leads. I then head home, via stopping at the offie for more supplies, then driving out to Hector The Farmer's place to pick up some books of a specialist nature which will be used to provide our, my, evening's entertainment.

Hector's buoyant when I get to his. He's smoking that pipe, which always gives him an even more contented air. —You know Bruce, the best thing ye ever did was tae pit me in touch wi wee Claire. I've turned intae a right auld sugar daddy. Fantastic wee lassie.

My fuckin . . . I feel a surge of jealousy and remember that she's just a hoor and it's all commercial transactions. I have a quick malt with Hector and head off. As he shows me out that fuckin collie tries to jump me again. — Down Angus! It's just Bruce!

He hauls the dug away and I drive off, still annoyed at Claire for going with that old bastard.

Women.

I can't

Carole

Shirley

I can't

Shirley, find somebody strong. This job, this life, it's drained my strength. I don't need a lame duck in tow.

Some bastard beeps me on the bypass and I think about giving chase but I don't feel up to it.

Our coping capacity is low.

I binge on the *00eat0000000eat00000eat00* **don't binge on the coke Bruce** niggling voice is telling me to eat *00don't binge on the coke00* charlie's fucked our appetite and all I want is more of the same, fuck eating anything now.

Coke for fuel, coke for energy. Have a coke and a smile. Coking coal. This is white, not black; clean, not filth. You never eat coke. You just snort it up.

Snort the whole fuckin lot of it up.

I've done the lot, so I try to have a wank to Hector's vids in order to distract the coke craving, but I can't concentrate. My whole body wants the blood my cock needs and I head up to Ray Lennox's. I'm tanning it in the car, giving a daft spastic the V-sign as I cut him up. Cheeky cunt. Polis. Priority. I come upon Ray's gaff and I batter the door polis-style until his dressing-gowned figure appears on the doorstep. — Ray, I smile, — sort me out with some posh. Pronto mate.

— Bruce . . . I can't . . . he says.

— Sort ays oot Ray! Hogmanay the morn! I snap, grinding my bare teeth at him. The night is but young.

I hear a voice coming from inside the house. — Who is it Ray? What's wrong?

— It's nothing! he shouts back into the gaff.

That voice. It sounded like Drummond. I suppose plenty hoors have those irritating whingy tones. Maybe it's that Trudi bird.

— Company Ray? I smirk.

— Wait there a minute, he says shaking his head before moving back in. Ootside in this cauld? My fucking arse. I step into the lobby. He's gone for a second or two and returns, producing a gram. — That's it Bruce, that's my lot.

— Aye, you'll ken, I say, then I head away, leaving him looking like fuckin Noddy. Cheeky cunt.

I get into the motor and I want to snort a line on the dashboard, but there's too many cunts around. Desperation takes over and I do it anyway. It's as strong as fuck. You have to test the stuff, save wasting police time putting it through the labs. One big snort. I'm trembling as I drive through the city back towards Collie. I don't know what I want to do. I'll probably hit the piss in a bit. I need to take the edge off this coke. Now. I need a drink now. I stop off outside a bar I used to frequent years ago, before we went to Oz. It'll have to be one: we realise that our bank cards are at home.

FUCKEN STUPID SHITING CUNT!

Our fist slams the dashboard repeatedly until our hand is swollen and almost too sore to hold the wheel. Then we exit and go into the pub. A pocket of shrapnel: barely enough for a pint of lager. I feel like a fuckin jakey as I walk into this tiny dive of a public bar. There's a small lounge separate from it next door, partitioned by a wooden panel and some frosted glass. From behind it I can hear the hee-hawing laughter of a four-bacardi slag, when I don't even have enough to stand the cow one. I get the pint of lager up and throw two-thirds of it back in no time. There's a party of auld cunts playing dominoes in the corner and a nae-mates fucker reading the *Evening News* at the bar. I recognise him as polis, Drylaw I think. I finish the pint quickly and exit the dive, getting in the motor and driving swiftly back to Collie. I'm focused all the way on the bank cards which are in the inside pocket of our jacket over the chair in the front room.

With great despondency we, I, we (we're all here now) clock a car parked outside our house. It looks vaguely familiar. We consider double-backing, but we need our cards and our money. We ignore the occupant of the car, even now we recognise it as Chrissie and storm down the path. But she's straight out after us.

— Bruce . . . I've tried to call you at work, she says. Her swine-like nostrils flare at me.

Why pick on Bruce all the time, there's others too, why can't they fuckin well dae anything . . . — She's ill you know, she could be dying, we tell her. We produce our keys and put them in the lock.

—Who?

— Shirley, my sister-in-law. She's ill. Same rules apply, we say, turning the lock.

—Too bad, she says, pushing in the door after me.

We try to repel her but she's all over us like a cheap suit and she's shouting, — C'mon, I want to turn off the gas for you, come on, and her hands in my flies. — God, this place stinks . . . c'mon Bruce . . .

It's only fuckin well me, only me . . . I'm on my fuckin ain here . . .

I pull away, but she's still coming on, this fucking cackling witch, her mocking, vicious hoor's eyes; and I'm pulling her hands away, but I'm stiffening against my will. — Leave me . . . leave me . . .

— C'moan . . .

She's got my cock out and she's sucking me off and we are crying, crying for Shirley no no no crying for ourself and she's got my belt off and I'm saying, — Naw naw but Chrissie, wait a minute, wait a minute Chrissie, and she's diving out of her clothes and she gets the cord from her bag and wraps it round her own neck.

I'm shivering and trembling and I need my charlie, it's in my pocket, and I need to see Shirley or Carole . . . she's the one I need . . . and she's tightened the belt around my neck before I can speak and her sharp painted nails dig into the foreskin of my semi she's pushing me back on to the couch and it's horrendous and she's pushing her cunt on to it against my will and thrusting on to me and the friction's hurting me and she's choking me harder and I can't breathe or speak as the grip tightens . . .

— Git fuckin harder ya silly wee poof! C'moan! Get it in! She's rubbing and twisting harder and I'm getting harder and it's going up, she's enclosing me, and I want to fuck this bitch to pieces but there's no way, cause although I'm hard now she's fucking the life out of me, throttling it out of me and she's screaming: —Turn off ma fuckin gas! Fuck harder! Move! Move! Turn oaf ma fuckin gas!

I'm choking and blacking out as I convulse and she's screaming and growling and her teeth bite my bottom lip as she roars
and bucks and crashes before she pulls away gasping and I watch
my cock disintegrate.

She lies back and lights a cigarette. – Mmmm. That was
great. What's wrong Bruce? You okay? You're greeting like a wee
laddie!

– Shirley's ill, I say. – My sister-in-law. She's no well.

I'm crying for myself.

She looks at me and shakes her head. – You're no fun any
more Bruce.

– We hear voices Chrissie. Aw the time. Do you ever hear
them? All our life we've heard them. The worms.

– What? What are you on about?

– We say this, they say that. We turn the records on loud. It's
like the messages in the records when they play them backwards.
Like me and her. We're together still, you ken that? It's all of us
. . . I, we, I hear myself singing in a low, tuneless voice, – Why
not take all of me . . .

– I have to go, she says, pulling her clothes on. – Whatever
it is that you're on, you should lay off it.

We say nothing, we're just willing her not to be there.
Depart depart depart naebody asked you tae come

When she goes, we binge on the coke we got from Ray.
After a few hits we wish the cow would come back cause I'd
really show that cunt, but naw, my cock's still as limp and sad as
Ray Lennox's that time with

with Shirley.

Cause it was me and Shirley and I let her down and I can't
blame the others.

I go to phone, but decide against it. I try to light the fire, but
my hands are trembling. A bit of Toal's manuscript has been pre-
served, brittle and dry.

[ANDERSON]
This psycho, you reckon he'll strike again?

[TEALE]
What makes you so sure it's a he?

[ANDERSON]
C'mon Bill. They usually are.

[TEALE]
I think that our mystery lady may have more
to do with this than we imagine.

ANDERSON looks visibly flustered.

[ANDERSON]
What makes you say that?

[TEALE]
Basically, there's two things. One, she's
vanished off the face of the planet which
means someone's covering up for her,
someone perhaps, who knows a lot about
this investigation, and secondly

What the fuck . . .

What the fuck does this cunt Toal know? I should have read
that script. Fuckin Carole!

Daft fucking cow.

Fuck.

I should have read that script. Knowledge is power, or so
they say. But fuck it. Keep your head down and your heart hard
and you'll be okay. Slow breathing.

Slow breathing.

Easily done.

Our hearts are hardened in this business. They have to be as hard as our sponsors' heads and that's what fucks us up. They can afford to be hard because they can abstract it all and they can do that because they are removed from it all.

We, on the other hand, must pay the physical and psychic price so that these pampered rich cunts can flounce around unperturbed.

Naw, there isnae such a thing as a free lunch. *We* always pey.

I get the ban then hit the Royal Scot via the se and Bernie the insurance ma k pies in the oven behind the ba ting.

— I'm goin me, — Brisbane, he adds.

— Right, I n can't swallow much of this shite ling down my face and I'm charl ae even notice.

—You spent a b

— Eight years in Sy hasing pimps round Kings Cross sta derous Greek bastards and I manag s family were moving in on the a the suburbs. I was shot at in Sydn as in the Met or up here. Don't let bollocks about Australia. It's a vio ll of murderous convict bastards. st like here. He's looking at me lik some kind of nutter and I tell pas that poofs like you can sell on the fuckin line. Remember th and leaving the bemused idiot

Home and to t that I'll never sleep until it gets the filth and dirt and games.

00000000000000000000000000000
0000000000000000000eat0000000
000000 thank you 0000000000
0000You. You were your parents' first born. But something was wrong. Your father had no time for you. Outside, the people in the village seemed to glance at you as if you were a freak. Parents would tell their children not to play with you. At home you would look at yourself in the mirror, and try to see what it was they saw. All you could see was an ordinary young boy. Stevie always played with you though. You and Stevie, Stevie and you. Stevie was bubbly and enthusiastic. He did the same things as you did but people responded differently; indulgence to him, impatience with you. Sometimes though, when you hung back, you seemed to get through on Stevie's slipstream. But you and he were inseparable.

Your dad loved Stevie and he didn't like him playing with you. He thought that Stevie should play with his normal friends. The ones at school who were the same age, not two and a half years older. At night in your bed you could hear your father and mother arguing, his voice rising, your mother crying. You wanted to stop it. But after a while you started to see it differently. You started to become aware of the words he used that would make her cry. You studied him. At first it was daunting. He seemed an impregnable fortress of power, of fearful omnipotence in your child's world. But then eventually, under your critical eye, the cracks started to appear. You learned what got to him, although you **knew that you could never exercise that knowledge. Yet.**

But we did. We d___ ___ crippled in the armchair to hideous ___ trembling, try to haul ourselves into a ___ n, sick day where the demons are waiting for us.

This morning they come in the thin and miserable shape of Drummond. I am out on patrol with her. Why? I don't know why. I can't think straight. She is going on about the case: victims, suspects, scenes of crimes, reports, forensic, analysis, politics and I want to scream: SHITE. I DON'T FUCKIN CARE ABOUT THIS. I'M FUCKIN WELL DYING HERE!

Cause I am.

I can't breathe in this fuckin car. That fuckin coke flares up my sinuses, my bronchitis. I'm coughing and shaking and the smell of her perfume is unbearable. She must be on the rag dousing herself like that. A pathetic cover-up job. It's stinking like a hoor's cubicle in the red-light district on a Saturday night at the height of the tourist season back in the Dam, this fucking motor.

This isnae Hogmanay . . . this is fuckin Halloween . . .

Out with her of all people. Cruising them. Looking for Ocky. Her. Never fuckin polis.

But we are fuckin polis.

We are sick and shivering and frightened. Lennox tried to poison me with that coke. It was full of shit. He's trying to kill us. We feel like shouting at Drummond: SEE IF WE DIE IT'S RAY LENNOX'S FAULT, RAY DRUG ADDICT LENNOX, THE SAME RAY LENNOX YOU THINK THE SUN SHINES OUT HIS ARSE BUT YOU DON'T KNOW WHAT HE'S LIKE. HE WILLNAE FUCK YE LIKE THE WEY YE WANT, WE'VE SEEN HIS FUCKIN COCK AND IF WE DIE IT'S LENNOX THAT'S THE MURDERER

I'm hyperventilating. We are hyperventilating. I'm I'm I'm smelling that muthafuckin bacon fry . . .

Somebody phone the police. Help. Please.

— Are you okay Bruce?

— Yes. Okay I certainly am.

— Look, you can say it's none of my business . . .

— I'm fine . . . honest. I've just been having a bit of a bad time, we tell her, gaining control of our breathing as sweat pours from our brow. We roll down the window and a frozen blast of air comes in.

— If you want to talk about it . . . she lowers her voice, adopting the Miss-Hunter-in-good-cop-mode-stance. Miss Cunter. I'd fuck her eyes oot now if I had the chance. Probably an arid-fannied spinster whose vagina tastes of Arizona soil.

But who does she think she is, to think that I'd take her into my confidence? — Don't put on your Personnel hat Amanda. This is real poliswork. You have to cope, to get on.

My heid's nippin tae fuck and I'm shivering. Polisworkpolisworkpolisworkpolisworkwhatwouldyoukena-bootthathehhnnnnn

— It's not my Personnel hat. I'm concerned about a col-league, that's all.

— Is that all it is? I smile at her, trying to compose myself.

— Please, don't flatter yourself. I think you're a silly, pathetic man and I've no interest in you other than us having to work together.

I've heard that line before. Usually mouthed by a cow with a wide-on who wants it filled. – You fancy me. That's all there is to it. I can tell.

– Bruce, you're an ugly and silly old man. You're very possibly an alcoholic and God knows what else. You're the type of sad case who preys on vulnerable, weak and stupid women in order to boost his own shattered ego. You're a mess. You've gone wrong somewhere pal, she taps her head dismissively.

I'm seething in my seat. I start to speak, but the cow raises her hand and cuts me off. – You were out of order that time with Karen. She was on a low and drunk and you took advantage.

– You've really got a problem, you ken that? That was none of your business. Consenting adults, I tell her.

– She wasn't in any state to consent or not to consent, Drummond clucks. – You think if she had been sober she would have went with you?

Cheeky fuckin hoor . . . – Fine, well she shouldn't have fucking well drank then should she? You gaunny stop people fae daeing that next? She wanted a drink, so she had one. After she had a drink, she wanted a shag so she had one. Don't talk to me like I'm a fuckin rapist. Why all this interest in Karen? You fuckin jealous? Is that it?

– Oh God, she tuts, rolling her eyes, – I'm not a lesbian Bruce, before you start with any more of your silly predictable responses. I have a boyfriend. He's far better looking, more intelligent, sensitive, stronger and younger than you. In the sexual marketplace you're not even Poundstretcher or Ali's Cave to his Jenners. You're a sad creature. I certainly don't fancy Karen in any way shape or form, but I fancy you even less. You repulse me. Can I make it any plainer?

This isnae . . . this isnae . . . – Well why aw the fuckin concern for me . . . I hear myself bleat. This cow . . . – I'm not like that . . . I'm not like that ah'm no ah'm no ah'm no ah'm no . . .

– Because you're my colleague and you're a human being. You have to get yourself straightened out, and then you might just become the kind of person you imagine yourself to be, although God knows what that is.

What the fuck is this . . .

kens nowt *00000eat000000000000eat0000000000* kens nowt
0000000000 **all you need** *0000000000000*
00000000000 **is love***00000000000000*

– I'm . . . I'm not so good at my job now . . . not so good . . . I've been in it too long . . . in Australia I was the best . . . my family don't talk to me . . . cause of the strike . . . they're a mining family . . . Newtongrange . . . Monktonhall . . . they don't talk to me. They don't let us in the house. My father. It was my brother. It was the coal, the dirt, the filth. The darkness. I hate it all. They won't let us in the hoose. Our ain fuckin hoose. We tried. We really fuckin well tried . . . ah wis only daein ma fuckin job . . . polis eh. It was only the strike.

She turns to me, her teeth grinding together like she's been up all night on the charlie as well . . . – Accept it. Deal with it, she snaps. – You have a wife, a daughter . . . don't you?

– That's all gone . . . I'm shaking my head, – she told lies . . . stupid lies . . .

– Who did?

– Both of them . . . stupid lies, we laugh, – It's all gone wrong. Same rules apply. We used to be good at the auld police-work. I'll bet they told you that. Eh?

– Yeah, they told me, she says disinterestedly.

Well how would she know cause she's never fuckin polis but if she could help us, if she could just try to understand like Carole used to . . . if we could explain . . . – There's something wrong with us now. Something bad. Something . . . inside.

– Have you been to a doctor?

– He can't do anything for us. Nothing. That's it over, I tell her. Now I realise that I can't talk to her. Her! Her of all people. I was weak, weak to start. – Same rules. Look, stop here. I'm getting out and I'm staking out Setterington and Gorman.

– Bruce, I don't think you're fit to work at the moment . . .
she says.

I turn in the seat and look at her in a grim, tearing focus.
That nosey cunt. Get a fuckin life of your own instead of nosing
into other people's. – I'm heading up this investigation
Drummond! Don't you ever forget that! GET ON WITH
YOUR FUCKIN JOB AND STOP PLAYING THE AMATEUR
PSYCHOLOGIST! I roar with violence and she cowers under
the impact of my words and my hot slavering breath, stopping
the car abruptly, her face crimson and her eyes watering. I jump
out. She starts off at pace. Once she's out of sight I get a taxi
home and go to my bed where I see more demons forming in the
swirling patterns of my artex ceiling.

The bed we used to share.

Time we acted.

It's Hogmanay, and I'm going out tonight. Going out with
Carole.

More Carole?

I've had a lot, in fact maybe too much, but it's that time of year. It's freezing and I'm glad I've put my big coat on. I'm carrying my nice new handbag, the one Bruce got me for last Christmas, well that should now be the Christmas before last, but I've not really used it yet. The Tron is sectioned off and the city is heaving. This used to be a traditional Scottish affair but now it's just the Edinburgh Festival at New Year, another tourist thing. I'm sick of it. I head away from it all, down Leith Walk, passing crowds of jeering youths, couples and tourists who are all making their way up the town.

I turn off a sidestreet and see the glowing light of a bar. I'm heading towards it but I'm aware that there's a car cruising alongside me, as if I was a hooker or something. One guy's hanging out the window making signs. I ignore him. Then it stops a little bit in front of me and two young men get out. They approach me and one blocks my path. My grip tightens on my handbag.

– Happy New Year doll! he says.

– Ye comin fir a wee ride sweetheart? the other asks.

– No . . . I . . . I start, then stop. I don't like talking. To strangers. Not when I'm out with

They start to laugh. I start to laugh. We start to laugh.

Then one man gets out from the back of the car and pushes us into the back seat as another pair of hands grab hold of our wrists. We're in the back seat of the car crushed between two men and the other two have got into the front and we're speeding off. It's strange, but we never thought of reacting: resisting or running off, although we had time to do both. This seems the right way.

– You're a fuckin sick fairy. Ah'm gonny fuckin cripple you, one young man says, turning around in the front passenger seat. We know this albino-skinned boy to be Gorman. We know the record of this thug.

– Ye shag guys like that . . . darling? a guy next to us is laughing. He is big. His hands are like shovels. His head is as chunky as Darth Vader's mask. This man we know to be Setterington.

They can't talk to us like that. – Listen! we tell them, – Police! We're working undercover!

They laugh. They just laugh at me. We pull off the wig we have been wearing. We still hold on to our handbag. Carole's handbag. My present. Last Christmas I gave you my heart. The car seems to be moving so slowly, and there is a sickness in our stomach, a sickness which makes us feel as if we have eaten too much candyfloss at the fairground and gone on the waltzers. Stacey liked the waltzers. Us and her, her tucked in the middle. The nuclear family, spinning, twisting, disorientated, but still huddled together.

Still . . .

– Sexier oan but, eh, one guy's laughing. He's laughing at us. We do not recognise him.

Spinning, twisting out of control. The wig. It cost two hundred pounds from Turvey's on the Glasgow Road. Made specially to look like Carole's hair, long and black. I told the guy it was for my wife. Her hair fell out after chemotherapy. How terrible, he said. She smokes too many cigarettes, I told him.

– Any keks you wear may be taken doon and used in evidence, another one smiles; Liddell, this one is called.

– I'm Detec . . .

I'm

We're a family . . . we knew a fam . . .

– Detective Se . . . we start to tell them, but Setterington has punched us hard on the nose with his anvil fist and the tears are filling our eyes and there is a sharp noise of pain spreading across our face and hitting the centre of our brain and an irregular pattern of breathing fits, a heaving in our chest, half a sob, half a puke. The only thing we can react to is the pain. We can see or feel nothing else.

How did it make you feel

We're different to what they think

Where's the fuckin back up team? We are fuckin polis! Police.

They put a plastic carrier bag over our head. We are now unable to see where we're going. We're remembering how this all started: that when Carole first left with the bairn we used to set the table for two and then we started wearing her clothes and it was like she was still with us but no really . . . Carole . . . Carole, why did you dae it, with that fuckin nigger, those whores they meant nothing tae me . . . you're fuckin big-moothed hoor ay a sister . . . fanny like the fuckin Mersey tunnel . . . and the bairn . . . oh God . . . God . . . God . . . we want to live . . . all we're asking for is some law and order . . . it's the job . . .

we want tae make it up . . .

we're not like the scum they put in the prisons . . .

we want tae make it right . . .

. . . we don't know where we're going. We don't know at all. This is Edinburgh. It's winter but it's hot and sticky under this plastic bag and we can't fuckin well breathe here.

We've lost the handbag.

And their voices.

— Need a bag ower that cunt's heid before ah'd fuck it, Gorman's voice.

— Get away! It's a fuckin guy ya poofy cunt! another is telling him.

— Ah'm no gonnae fuck it wi ma cock, ah'm ah ya daft cunt, bit we'll see what we can find tae stick up this queer erse, see how much the cunt can take.

— Barry.

We're bundled out of the car and pushed up a set of stairs. Stairs. We can see the steps under our feet. Pushed. The coon. They make us move too quick and we go over in our heels, stumbling, but they're stopping us from falling and they are shouting obscenities at us.

— Move yir queer erse ya fuckin buftie!

— C'moan ya fuckin daft twat!

This place is derelict, we can see the broken glass under our feet. It's abandoned, no noise but our own. We reach the top of the stairs and they throw us into a room. Then there's more voices. A girl's voice. I recognise it.

— Ah kent ah had seen him fae somewhaire.

Estelle.

— Did eh huv a plastic bag ower ehs heid at the time?

— Wide cunt!

I feel a sharp pain in my testicles. I cover them with my hands. My fingers knead the material of the skirt.

— Nice one Ocky!

Ocky. I've been kicked by Ocky.

— The thing is boys . . . and girls, it's Lexo's voice, — we have tae go aw the wey wi this pig. Ye ken what that means.

— Ye cannae waste a pig man, the other guy, I think his name's Liddell, is saying.

There's a nervous laugh from Estelle. She thinks those cunts are joking. — Ah'm no wantin nowt tae dae wi this, she says.

— Dinnae be daft Lexo, Liddell's saying. — Ye cannae waste a pig. End of. That's it fucked eftir that.

Another voice cuts in, gasping, frightened. — It's nae fuckin joke . . . c'moan boys . . . ye cannae kill the boy . . . no a polisman . . . My assailant Ocky.

—You shut yir fuckin grassin wee mooth, Ghostie says, and I can sense Ocky trembling from here. — We'll see tae you later. We ken aw aboot you pal.

— Ah'm no a grass . . . Ocky pleads.

Poor Ocky. Always between a rock and a hard place.

— Lexo's right, Ghostie says. — This cunt kens the score. We did the boy.

— We dae him n aw, Lexo's mocking voice continues, — Deid cunts tell nae tales. We can torch this place wi the cunt in it. Or what's left ay the cunt in it.

One of them whips off the bag. There is a sharp light in our face and we blink. We look at them. Yes, there's the four of them, the same four, plus Estelle and Ocky. Liddell is holding an old anglepoise lamp in my face.

The handbag is on the shelf. Setterington is mincing around with it.

But we are starting to get in control now. They shouldn't have taken off the bag. Our face is throbbing and sore, our eyes still water, but we're thinking again. We see them. The lamp does not bother us. They look at our unflinching gaze.

We see them.

— Look at him, what a fuckin tube, Ghostie Gorman the evil-looking little albino twat spits. He then smiles, and produces a wrap of charlie and starts rubbing it on his gums. — High grade mate, high grade. Took it oot ay yir bag thaire. Nab it fae D.S. duty, aye?

I say nothing.

— Should've joined the polis masel! he laughs, and the others chorus him.

345

I'm looking at Ocky, then at Estelle. Her face is pinched and angry. She looks at me with a raw hate as if she's blaming me for putting her in this position. Ghostie sees me staring at her. — Like the bird here, dae ye? Sexy eh? No as sexy as you bit, eh no mate?

He pulls Estelle to him and kisses her, pushing his tongue into her mouth. She's awkward and stiff, resisting slightly then complying. He stops and turns to me. Estelle rubs her lips. — French kissin, Ghostie explains. — That's me gittin intae practice for the World Cup. The nosh as well. Ah went tae this French restaurant last summer there. Ye like French grub?

— No bothered, I tell him.

— The posh one off the Royal Mile, he urges. — A real French job. Ah like the garlic, me. Garlic snails.

He puckers his lips and makes a slurping sound.

— You ever go tae that place mate, Le Petit Jardin? Ghostie pronounces the restaurant name with an affected French accent.

— Naw. I never went there, I tell him.

Me and Carole never went there. I never liked French food. I always preferred going out for a curry. The Raj doon at the Shore in Leith. Tommy Miah's place. That was always my favourite. A windae table if we could get yin. The Anarklia in Dalry Road. Carole liked the vegetarian options there.

— It wis durin the Festival, Ghostie tells me, tarrying leisurely. This cunt's worse than Toal. — Ah goes in, in a resturant in ma ain city. The waiter comes up and sais: Do you have reservations? Ah just looks aroond . . . he twists his head haughtily around the derelict room, — and ah goes: Aye, ah do. The decor, then he looks contemptuously at me like I was the waiter, — the service, and probably the food. But I'd still like a fuckin table.

The others smirk and smile sycophantically as he goes through the pantomine. Ocky and Estelle's grins conceal death-masks of terror, and only Lexo is unmoved, looking out the window.

Ghostie shakes his head grimly. — But naw. Nae table. No room at the inn, he shrugs. — But Le Petit Jardin shut doon for a month eftir that. Within a few hours ay us gittin bombed oot, some wee mob had steamed the place and turned it ower. Terrorised the clientele. Now ah nivir huv any bother findin a table. Treat ays like royalty, so they dae. Even wi this Edinburgh's Hogmanay, wi aw they tourists, ah could walk in any time and they'd sort ays oot straight away.

There will be no pleading for forgiveness. They are rubbish, they are criminal scum. They are different from us. There is now no fear in us. They are weak.

— You think that impresses me, we laugh, shaking our head, — that you can get a mob ay daft wee bairns tae dae a stupid frog restaurant over? It doesnae, we shake our head mockingly, glaring into his dark eyes.

— Shut yir fuck . . . Liddell starts, putting the lamp down and moving forward.

Ghostie raises his hand. — Shut up. Let the cunt speak.

I look around at them all, then back at Ghostie. — Ah ken you mate. You hide in the mob. You are one shiting cunt. Me and you then . . . I'm staring at his cold, cold eyes. — Ah'd take you. We look round at them. — Ah'd take any one ay yis in a square go! Fuckin shitin cunts! we snarl at them.

We can see this pushes the right buttons in their spastic psychology. They are shocked. Laughing, incredulous, but taken aback. They know that they are going to have to work for what they thought would just be sport. To have to put themselves on the line in some way. We've cracked their fuckin code and we are challenging them to prove to us that they are what they think themselves to be. One of them, Ghostie Gorman, goes, — Right, this cunt dies. Ah'm takin um.

— Lit's jist fuckin dae the cunt now n stoap fuckin aboot, Lexo says.

— Naw. Ah want him. Gorman looks at me and laughs loudly. — You die, he says softly.

He signals for the others to depart, and they file out tentatively. He has an old key, which he uses to lock us in this room. — The key to the house of love, he smiles, putting it on the mantelpiece.

It's just him and us, the fuckin donkey. Without announcing our intentions, we fly at him, but he catches us with a punch to our face and it hurts and he's all over us and we feel weak and broken under his raining blows and it shouldn't have been like this and he's laughing at us and the fear is here now and our despondency rises as we realise we've got nothing to give, we are just static. His head crashes into us and our nose explodes much worse than in the car because it's crunched into our face and we're choking on our own blood and we can't breathe and there are more digging blows and our arms feel so heavy, we can't even fuckin well lift them to hit back or block him.

We're on the ground. Only Bruce is taking the blows, the boots. He is protecting me, protecting Stevie, all the rest . . . no . . . no . . . Carole isnae here. Stevie isnae here. It's just me. Bruce. Bruce and the Worm.

— Mind ay that auld disco song? Doctor Kiss-Kiss? That's me, he says strutting around. He offers his hand. I take it.

He pulls me to my feet. His arm is around our shoulders. We can't move.

— Ah've always fuckin hated cops, he explains. — No in the normal way everybody hates cops. Ah've eywis hated the cunts in a special wey. You're different though sweethert. You kin be saved. Ah'm gonny make an honest woman ay you yet!

He yanks our head back and he's looking at us in the eye. His long tongue licks his lips.

— Fuckin wide poof polis! He smiles. — Now it's time for you to learn something . . . He sticks his tongue in our mouth, mingling his saliva with our blood.

He probes for a while, then withdraws and we hear his voice, — Sexy! Whoa hoah! You thought ye could take *me*, ya fuckin sick poof! Ye liked that, eh sexy, he pants softly. — Ye liked it, eh?

Yes. We know that we want him to do this again, this is our last wish. We want to say, Please, let us be together like that again, just one last time, but we can't shout, only think, only hope that he can somehow sense this wish.

He does.

He pushes his tongue into our head again, but now we raise our weary arms to embrace him. Our hands lock together behind his back to celebrate our own joining, our own communion, our brotherhood. A grip nothing can break . . . it's Carole . . .

Oh Carole

we embrace her and bite hard into her tongue and she's squealing and trying to push us away like she did when we just wanted to hold her after we confronted her about the nigger, but no my darling, you cannae get away this time, no, cause we're hugging her tight and as she tries to pull free we're moving forward, no no my darling, we can't let you go, not now . . . because we need to be together Carole, you know that . . . it's just how it always has to be . . . our eyes have shut but through the membrane of our eyelids we can still see the light and we move towards it.

Move in tae the light Stevie . . . Carole . . . away from the filth, intae the light . . .

But this isn't Carole. This is excrement. What is this thing doing here, doing here with us instead of Carole!

It has to go.

At the right time we release our grip and push and watch him falling backwards, crashing through the rotten window panes, still holding on, but unable to pull himself back in, and trying to grab the old, worn curtains but the material just tears in his hands and he looks at us with hate and incomprehension, his own blood spilling from the severed tongue in his mouth, as he slides out the window and crashes down on to the concrete court below. We look out and down and we can tell by the way he's bent and broken that he's gone, and then, as if to confirm our suspicion, a huge heart-shape of blood forms around his head.

The spastics are banging on the door screaming threats. Ha ha ha.

I go to shout at them but there's something in my mouth. I put my fingers in and take it out. A piece of his tongue. I reach down and see Carole's handbag and put it in her purse.

I'm screaming back at them through the door: — Who's fuckin next spastics! We are the Edinburgh polis! We kill spastics! WE HATE NIGGERS! ESPECIALLY THE WHITE ONES THEY CALL SCHEMIES!

Then it stops.

It seems like an age.

Then we smell burning. They have set the building on fire. We go to the window and see them running out of the stairway. They scream a death threat up at me as they clock their spastic pal and we shout back: — Youse die! Youse git the same as that fuckin spastic! YOUSE DIE!

We get the key from the mantelpiece and open the door. There is a surge of heat and the flames are everywhere, tearing up from floor to ceiling along the old papered walls.

We are trapped. The thick, filthy smoke is filling our lungs.

Our only option is to go to the kitchen and climb out on to the back drainpipe. When we get outside the wind is flapping in our ears and we feel that we are so high. The sky above us is a lovely pale blue with a cloud formation the shape of a twisted beggar. The pipe is slippy, but we hold on. Then it wrenches from its brackets and we lose our grip and fall, and there is no time for us to brace for impact and we are crashing down into something which takes our weight as it cuts and rips all around us and we're sinking into a filthy green brittle tomb, which is where we come to rest, in this fucking hedge and we are unable to move. The hedge grows over a spiked fence and one spike has missed our head by inches. We can't move, all we can do is think of Carole and sob. We cry for ourselves, not for her. It is important to remember that we always cry for ourselves.

Oh Carole, I am but a fool

Carole is nothing you see, I am the fool. Poor me.

Then we hear voices. First we half-see the blurred figure of a uniformed spastic, asking us who we are.

Darling I love you, though you treat me cruel

You treat *me* cruel.

At some point one of the voices becomes familiar: — Well Robbo, you've really fucked it up this time.

We are torn to pieces in a woman's dress, stuck in a hedge and we hear Toal talking to us, and in our present circumstances it has to be conceded that he may have a point.

You hurt me, and you make me cry

All we can say is, —You should see the other cunt.

— We're still scraping that particular piece of shit off the pavement at the front.

But if you leave me, I will surely die.

— Boss . . . I . . . don't leave me . . . stay with me . . . we whine in a voice that is not our own.

— Don't try to talk Bruce, later. I'm here, Toal squeezes my hand. A good man Toal, I've always said it. He's got a look in his eye, like my mother had when she was dying in that hospital bed. When we were trying to tell her that we were sorry for all the fuck-ups. Sorry that we were not somebody different. Sorry that we werenae like Stevie. A look like she understood. But she still pitied me.

Toal's alright, but I can see the pity in his eyes, a pity I detest more than anything.

351

I'm taken in an amb *0000I'm worried about you* ward with
only minor cuts and b *Bruce. I have to; we are one. The* told that
we are very lucky to *survival of the parasite depends* like fuck.
They did somethi *on the continued existence of the host.* to do wi

*But things are not going at all well for you
my friend, while I'm becoming more
ambitious, thinking about multiplying the Self
and bringing some more significant Others into my
life. Even though this will mean competition for the
precious few nutrients you deign to provide me with
your food intake. Such irony Bruce, me worrying about you,
you who took away the Other, that most beautiful of souls
that was ever housed in a living organism, even one as primitive
as my own. The lines have been drawn. On one side we have
my bonnie Bruce and his friend Doctor Rossi and on the other
my good Self. I feel the intensification of the chemical
onslaught and the vigorous contractions of the bowel,
signifying renewed zeal in the attempt to cast me into
oblivion. Well my friend, my solex is firm and I am
determined that I will not pass through your bonnie
wee arsehole into the twilight zone of the
plumbing system of fair Edina city. Scotia's
darling lavvy seat00000000000000must
try not to move0000000000000000
000000000000000000000000000000*

whizz in m *0000000 wakey wakey Bruce 00* quacks are aw the
fuckin s *000000000can you eat? No, I don't* ble nurses at any
rate. *think you can 00000000000000000000000*

A *00for the rest of us in here Bruce 000000000* y are hospital
issu *000000000000000000000000000000000000000000* 's at my side.
000000000000000000000000 eat 0000000000000000 edative.
*0000The fairest and most liberal of Scotia's sons our bonnie
laddie Bruce might not be, but fate has decreed that I set up
house in his bowels and if I'm honest, I have got used to it
here. I shall not be moved. No sir. Even less moved than you
Bruce. Less moved than the time of the first great coal*

strike of recent memory, from 1972 to 1974. The power cuts,
when your father sent you and your wee brother Stevie to
steal the coal from the byng in order to heat the house. Coal
that he had earlier dug from the ground by his own hand,
but which was the property of others OOOOOOOOOOOO

Stevie

OOOOOOOOOOOOOOOOOOYou were older. You were supposed
to watch out for Stevie, this was understood. It's the way things
always have to be. The pair of you were just kids, and you both
saw it as a big adventure. For you there was the added incentive
of perhaps being able to do something that would please your father.
It was easy enough for the pair of you to slip in through the overlap
of the corrugated iron fence. You gasped as you looked up at the
big mountain of coal in front of you. Let's climb the mountain, you
said, or was it Stevie who said it? Who charged up first, and who
followed? Does it matter? It was just wee boys playingOOO
OOOOOOOOOOOOOOOOOOOOOOOOOOOOOOOOOOOOOOOOOOO
OOOOOOOOOOOOOOOOOOOOOOOOOOOOOOOOOOOOOOOOOO

Just a game for boys. Games. For silly wee boys.

OOOOOOOOOOOOOOOOOOOOOOBut you hear him shouting,
Ah'm the king o' the castle and you're the dirty wee
rascal! Stevie bawls that at you, looking down on you, his
face set in a caricature of a cruel and despotic monarch. The
wee boy's faster and he's beaten his older brother to the top.
The wee boy is better at everything. He's more outgoing, has
more personality, everybody says, than the quiet, brooding boy,
than the other laddie. That was how they referred to you both
in the village: wee Stevie Robertson and the Other Laddie.
You are angry at this humiliation. Another one, another
reminder that even here, on your own, away from the glare
of the adults and the other kids, he is still Wee Stevie
and you are still the Other LaddieOOOOOOOOOOOO

Fuck off

OOOOOFuck off, you curse as you push Stevie back
down the hill, and the wee lad loses his balance and falls.
Picking up momentum down the steep, loose pile of coal

353

he slides down the other side of the mountain to the bottom; right down into the open hatch to the bunker which usually stores all the coal, but now it is chronically over-stocked, and he's trying to climb out but he can see the mountain above him, being shifted by your movements. You don't mean to move the coal, but you still experience a strange elation as well as a crushing fear as it starts shifting and comes sliding down on Stevie, sealing him in. Now you are falling as well, riding down on it, but you're not going into the hole with your brother because it's been sealed by the coal which has rushed in ahead of you, and you come to rest only partially buried in the pile of stinking dark fossil fuel which has entombed him in the bunker. You can see nothing though. You try to gather your senses as you scramble out from the coal, towards the light. It seems to fill your lungs, that thick, black dust, but you scream STEVIE! The night watchman comes as you emerge blackened from that pile of coal. He shouts at you, but you stand your ground and tell him that your wee brother's in there. You are back into the pile, digging, screaming: Move intae the light Stevie!OOOOOOOOOOOOOOOOOOOOOOOOOOOOOOOO

Move intae the light . . . the filth . . . it's so fuckin dark man, just so fuckin dark . . . . . .

OOOOOOOOOOOOThe night watchman is digging as well. More people come. There is talk of getting a pipe for oxygen. People keep digging. Time passes. The mood darkens. Your father arrives. He arrives as they pull Stevie out, battered, broken, lifeless and blackOOOOOOOOOOOOOOOOOOOOOOOOOO

Battered, broken, lifeless and . . . Carole!

OOOOOOOOOOOOOOOOOThe man you knew as your father. He is crouching, crying, beside his son's body. Your mother has not yet arrived. Your father looks up at you and points. The villagers fall into a silence as if to accommodate his words. You know what he is going to say so it doesn't shock you, or maybe you are already in shock because everything seems in slow motion and the people slightly further away and their voices more detached than you are used to.

This thing killed him, your father screams, this bastard spawn
ay the fuckin devil killed ma laddie! You look straight at him.
You want to deny and affirm his assertions all at once.
You're no ma son! You've never been ma fuckin son!
You're filth!
He stands up and moves towards you.
You feel a hand on your shoulder. A man leads you away as
your father is restrained and comforted. You will later work with
this man, know him as Crawford Douglas. He takes you to your
grandmother's, where you will now stay. You know at this point
that the man you believed to be your father is not. This does not
bring you comfort. All you ever wanted to do was to belong.
Now Stevie is gone.
*You can't feel a thing for him*OOOOOOOOOOOOOOOOOOOOOOOOO
OOOOOOOOOOOOOOOOOOOOOOOOOOOOOOOOOOOOOOOOOOOOOOO

That is not true

That is not

true.

The Tales
Of A Tapeworm

The hospital discharge procedures. The discharge in my pants. In my flannels. I wait for the taxi for Robertson in the A&E.

— Is there nobody who can take you home? a concerned nurse asks.

— No . . . I say.

She looks at me with a sick pity and then leaves to attend to her duties. She's replaced by a jakey who sits sucking on a purple tin. He hands it to me. I take a swig, expecting to wince as the sickening, syrupy liquid hits my gullet, but I feel nothing.

— I've been comin here for ages, he tells me. — Got off the skag, but I was straight on this stuff.

Tennents never advertise the purple tin. It's not a recreational drug; they know it's as strong a drug as heroin or crack. They know that you don't need to market hard drugs like those. The desperate will always find them. Scotland's greatest export next to whisky. The white man cometh. He take your land. He give the whisky. Just when you think it safe to go back in water he give you old purple tin. The white Caledonian Ku Klux Klan are coming.

— Taxi for Robertson.

I'm going home.

The nurse is back. She has a nice smell. Not like the

hospital. Not like the jakey. Not like me. – I wish there was someone you could stay with, she says, touching my wrist.

I'm never really alone, but the voices are silent. For now.

I smile and follow the cabbie. I wish there was someone I could stay with ... ike real people do. Like I was a ... funny woman. If only ther ... 't cold on her.

00000000 You went to stay with your granny in Penicuik. She did not tell you much about your real dad, other than that he had not been well and that he was dead now. The man you once tried to call Dad, the one who gave you your name, you became happy to think of as Mister Robertson. He was not your dad, not your real dad in any sense. He was the man who married your mum00000000000000

The purple tin will destroy America once they import it over there . . . those Russian jakeys begging in the streets under capitalism, we'll do those cunts as well.

Obliterate surplus labour!

Obliterate them with the old purple tin!

Don't give em Ecstasy! We don't want them dancing! Keep them dulled, staggering and incoherent as they die! Make it glamorous. Put it on celluloid, put it on hoardings. Just keep the real thing as far away from us as possible.

000000Life was better for you out in Penicuik. Your granny was eccentrically kind through her alcoholic stupor and your mum would sometimes come and visit. On occasions she would bring your new half-sister. Mister Robertson was never to hear of this, she insisted, although that omnipresent look of pity on her face began to disgust you so much that you often felt like maliciously informing Ian Robertson that you had seen the new baby0000

And the white race of Caledonia will stalk the Earth as juggernaut superbeings . . . like from that album by that shite heavy-metal band . . . who the fuck was it . . .

00000000000000As your half-sister grew from infant to child, your mother stopped bringing her. She had another son and her visits became less frequent. Eventually, they all but ceased,

> *by which time you scarcely noticed. At school you were quiet.*
> *You worked hard and the teachers liked you. While you enjoyed*
> *their approval, you had difficulty in forming relationships with*
> *the other kids. Peer friendships made you suspicious.*
> *You couldn't wait to grow up.*
> *You wanted to be bigger, stronger.*
> *The night held terrors. You would sleep with the light on. Always.*
> *Once you went to church with your reluctant granny where you*
> *made up sins for a grateful priest. She loved you, in a strange and*
> *twisted way, and she did not get on with her daughter, your mother.*

Carole, you standing there and me bending your fingers back, loaded up with cocaine and alcohol and you looking at me with your large eyes in a weird state way beyond fear and me trying to think of why I should stop and trying to feel something that will make me stop before that crack

that crack

and your scream changing now; more broken and desperate than ever before, me making *you* feel but me still feeling

nothing.

How did it make you feel?

But it wasn't me that did it. We all have to take our share of the blame.

We can cope with this nothingness. We know it too well to be disabled by it. But it's so cold. The central heating seems to have broken down. The pilot light has blown out. Carole knew how to fix it. We, I, we consider getting a fire together, but it all seems too much: the fetching of coals, the finding of firelighters (is there a new pack?), the kindling, the lighting.

No.

We have knocked on Tom Stronach's door a couple of times,

but there is no reply. We once heard the television, so we know that Julie is in. The New Year's Day game. Stronach will be playing in that. But no, the papers said that he was dropped. I would think that he would attend though. Surely. We venture out to Safeway's for food.

We cannot move our head as we walk.

We hear our breathing in the cold air: rhythmic, deep. It puts us into a kind of a trance. We are still alive. We are in the supermarket. Breathing.

The tins and packets on the shelves are just colours and shapes to us. We cannot recognise the products, cannot read the labels. If we take one of each then the chances are that we will have enough of the right things.

This one.

That one.

This one.

– Detective Ser . . . Mister Robertson . . . I hear a voice at my side.

I turn round to see her, a woman. She looks . . .

. . . she has a large smile on her face. Her hair is nice and her teeth are so white. She wears jeans and a beige polo-neck sweater under a brown lined leather jacket. There's a sadness in her eyes.

Who is she? I'm befuddled and besotted by lack of sleep and all those voices in my head, clamouring for attention . . . for recognition . . .

All I can say is, – How have you been doing?

– Not bad . . . not good, her face screws up and she laughs bitterly. I really want to see her smile again. She looks so beautiful when she smiles. – I'm really missing him. Why is it only the good die young? she asks me, and she asks it in a *real* way, as a *real* question, looking at me as if she thinks that I might know the answer.

– Eh . . . I . . . eh . . .

Now she's seeing me for the first time. She sees my surgical support collar from where I hurt my neck in the fall. She sees the six-pack of the old purple tin in my shopping basket. I hadn't realised it was there. It was like they just jumped in of their own accord. She's seeing me now. She's seeing a jakey with a four-day growth, a manky overcoat, stained flannels and old trainers.

– Are you alright? she asks.

– Eh? Oh, *this*, I laugh, looking down at myself. – Undercover, I whisper conspiratorially.

– Isn't it a bit extreme for shoplifting?

– Ha! This isnae shoplifting. This is huge-scale corporate fraud I'm investigating. I nod over to the staff offices at the back of the supermarket.

– I see, she says vaguely, as her son comes over to her side. –You remember Mister Robertson. The policeman. He tried to help your dad.

– Hiya, the wee guy smiles, but as he clocks me he takes a step back. I smell my flannels. Wafting up the inside of my coat under my nose.

– It's okay Euan. Mister Robertson's doing detective work. He's dressed up as a tramp. It must be exciting being undercover, eh Euan?

The wee guy forces another smile.

– Hiya, I smile back. I look at his Hearts tracksuit. The new one. A Christmas present. I point at the crest. – So you're a jambo eh? Did you go yesterday?

– Naw . . . he says sadly.

– Colin used to . . . his mother begins.

– Who's your favourite player? I ask, expecting a Neil McCann or a Colin Cameron.

– Tom Stronach, I suppose, he says, then smiles doubtfully, – but he's no as good as he used to be.

– My next-door neighbour! I'll have to get Tom to sort us out with some special tickets for Tynecastle. Would you like that?

– Aye, that would be barry.

– Speak properly Euan, his mother says. She looks at me. – You're really kind, but I couldn't let you . . .

– It's no problem. Honestly.

We exchange addresses and phone numbers.

– That's a really kind man. Mister Robertson. A good man, I, we, hear her tell the kid as they depart.

Our hands are almost cut in two by the handles on the plastic bags, but we are unaware of this until we reach home.

Who are we?

Who are we?

How did we feel?

We put the hands under the warm tap to help our circulation, but the water is boiling from the electric immersion. We flinch with the scalding pain and shed tears at the iniquity of the situation: that transgressors are living better lives than we are currently able to. More festive television, and a load of fuckin

OOOOOOOOOOOOOOOOOOOOOOOO why not fix us a snack Bruce?

I'm getting a little concerned OOOOOOO at your lack of eating.

Think of me, if not you. All those noises in your head, voices
clamouring for your attention.

Well, as I'm getting no response from you, I might as well carry
on with your story. You were brought up by your grandmother,
a drunken, bitter, kind woman. There was a gap in her life since her
husband, your grandfather, had departed, which was on occasion
inadequately filled by various men who didn't quite measure up.
Crawford Douglas had been one such man.

Sometimes, in that house, you think about her and your grand-
father. You think about him being there, sharing it with her. You
think about the gap he left, how there were still traces of him every-
where. You think about how much she hates this man. – He must
have been horrible for ye tae hate him so much Nan, you once
ventured to ask her as she sat on the couch stroking her cat. She
looked at you for a couple of seconds, then gazed off into space.
In a slow, whimsical voice which seemed not to belong to her,
she said, – No son, he was a lovely man. He went away though,

the good ones always do. It's the trash that stick aroond. But ye always hate the good one who goes more than the bad one who stays.

The current bad one who was staying was Joe Caughey, who worked as a night watchman at the supermarket. Joe would come back to your grandmother's at closing time on Friday and Saturday nights. He smelt of aftershave and alcohol, but you always associated him with the smell of shite as he would wipe his arse with the towels in the bathroom, which were always streaked with it. Whether he did this deliberately or whether he didn't wash his backside properly when he had a bath on Saturday and Sunday mornings, you would never know.

You were fascinated by this, because as a child, you were very interested in urine and faeces. You would spend ages on the toilet, withholding your shit, forcing it back into your bowel before letting it go. You would pish under the fireside rug and wait until it dried out, the smell of urine stinking out the house. Your granny blamed the cat and put sheets of the Evening News under the rug which were stained yellow. It excited you watching the rug absorb that lake of pish, wondering whether or not you'd be detected. Eventually, she was to throw the rug out, after having the cat put down. – Billy's gone feral, she explained. – He was a dirty animal. She threw out Joe Caughey as well. She suspected him. But not you. She'd never throw you out.

Your grandmother had had a son, who died as a child. You didn't know how this had happened. You knew that she blamed God and had tentatively renounced her Catholicism. On vulnerable occasions, when badly hungover, she'd return to the church, wracked with guilt. Later she would drunkenly sneer that she would never set foot in that place again. If he's there, he disnae stop the badness. If he's no, then we shouldnae worry about him, she would say. Alcohol and bingo, once complements to marriage and religion, expanded to take their place in her life. Your granny hated the devout qualities of her daughter, your mother. But, in her own way, she loved the son her daughter left her OOOOOOOOOOOOOOOOOO _____ hat we can do.

So we watch television. At some point Toal comes tae the hoose. My first foot. At least he comes here, rather than compelling us go in *there*. That evil, evil place. Some of them would have, Niddrie would have. We have been officially on the sick, our neck in a surgical support collar.

— It might no really seem appropriate Bruce, but Happy New Year.

— Happy New Year Bob, I hear a voice coming from my stiff, cold, numb lips.

Toal explains to us that we are now suspended following an inquiry of the internal variety, the type of all our inquiries.

— Don't worry, we'll do what we can, he tells us, looking aroond our hoose. He's not taken his expensive-looking camel coat or his leather gloves off. He looks like a football manager. Like the guy who manages Wimbledon, him that played for Spurs. Steaming breath comes from his mouth. A few feet away in our fireplace lie the ashes of his manuscript.

We cannot nod while we are wearing our support collar. — Appreciate it, we say meekly.

Toal is trying to be firm and compassionate at the same time. He must make us aware of the gravity of the situation, but also offer hope that things will improve. We cannot even feel sorry for ourselves any more. This is a bad sign. We think.

— Listen Bruce, we've obviously had to withdraw your application . . . for the promotion. Now is not the right time for you to meet with the promotion board. You see that, don't you?

We understand what Toal is saying. We cannot be bothered responding. They've now taken the job we coveted, the one which was ours by right, but the sense of loss that we feel is strangely negligible.

Toal's looking around the house with distaste. It's a mess: aluminium takeaway cartons, chip-shop wrappers, beer cans (purple? aye, it's found us at last!), plates with rotting scraps of food on them, even a pile of dried sick in one corner. — Listen Bruce, Toal's face pinches as he allows his nostrils to acknowledge the stench we have long been oblivious to, — you can't live like this. Is there nobody we can get in touch with, to make sure you're being looked after?

—No . . .

BUNTY

SHIRLEY

CHRISSIE

CAROLE

Carole. The only one who could give us anything. The rest would just take. We have nothing to give them. But Carole will never return.

—You sure?

— I'll sort it out boss, we tell Toal. His face looks sourly down at us. — Honest, I try to force a smile.

— I want you to Bruce. The police welfare people will be round to see you soon. They'll be able to offer professional help. I know things seem pretty bleak at the moment, but you're not the first officer on the job who's lost it and you won't be the last. Busby's had his problems. Then there was Clell. He seems on the mend now. Bruce . . .

Toal looks a bit sheepish. He's rubbing his gloved hands together.

—Aye?

—You've got friends you know, he says softly. Then he smiles slightly. — We're no as daft as you think. Your wife. We know she was having an affair with a black guy. It's no a big city Bruce, and it's a very white one. Things like that get noticed, no matter how discreet the parties are. But, as I said, you've got friends. We look after our own.

His words hit me in a slow, stupefying flood. I feel like a test-crash dummy on low impact. I'm trying to work out what he means. —You mean you knew . . . all time . . . you . . .

— Don't say anything Bruce, Toal says sternly, — Don't say a word to me.

He turns and pulls the net curtains and looks out the window. Then he faces me, keen-eyed: — Sometimes things are best left the way they are. There's reputations, morale and careers at stake. In some ways, aye, it's penny wise and pound foolish. We're a bit short-termist in our thinking. But then again, we're burdened wi this wee problem of three score and ten. Needs must, he grins.

Same rules apply. I try to smile but I feel my face frozen, as if all the muscles and nerves in it have been severed.

— You know, all this stuff about a mystery woman? I wasted a lot of time on her, he laughs and shakes his head looking at me, slightly embarrassed. — I overheard Bob Hurley saying to you in the bar one time: They're all fucking Jackie Trent. You know, I thought that this Jackie Trent girl was involved and was having it off with most of the guys on the investigation in order to get them to cover things up. I spent ages looking for a Jackie Trent to run checks on. Then I realised it was all just some canteen in-joke, a bit of silly rhyming slang.

— Yes . . . Jackie Trent, I hear the words reverberate in my head and parrot mindlessly out from between my lips.

— Anyway, I'm sick of it all. Funny Bruce, I misjudged you. You see, somebody half-inched a private document of mine. From my office. The bastard stole the hard copy, erased the file and the back-up disk. I had my suspicions, he looks at me and shrugs.

We know that our face is too blank to register anything.

— I got a bit paranoid for a while. I was testing out everyone, trying to find cracks. I mean, all that stuff I was giving you about poor Inglis, as if I care who he shags. You were good though Bruce, I'll give you that. Anyway, I was daft to have this stuff at the work. I was doing some private stuff, during breaks you know, maybe when I had a spare minute. Sometimes I'd stay late and work on it, it's quieter at the office than at home. I thought that perhaps you knew, well . . . what we knew. You see Bruce, I was writing a screenplay based on the case of a racist murder. I based it loosely on the Wurie murder, with my own fictive embellishments of course. In my screenplay, the murder is being covered up by a racist cop who has a motive . . . not to solve the crime.

— How does it end . . . I ask too quickly.

— Oh, we fit up some thugs. A happy-ever-after story.

I nod. The sort of ending people like.

—Yes, I got a fright when the document was stolen and the files erased. At first I suspected . . . certain parties. But I knew that the person would have had to have read it, and I would have been able to tell. Of course, I had another copy on the hard disk at home, so it wasn't too much of an inconvenience. You can't be too careful, eh! I still might finish it and send it off to a production company. A pipe dream, but nothing ventured, eh?

— Aye . . . that's good . . . that you've done it . . . I mean that you have an interest . . .

— Aye. I'm fed up on the force. Had it up to here, a leather glove salutes his forehead. — Clell's right. The law spends too much time demonising ordinary people who're just trying to get on with their lives. Society's changed and the law hasn't kept pace; so it's us, the mugs, who have to enforce them, who get it all in the neck. I'm sick of it. There's enough genuine bad guys to lock up without sending some daft kids on a H.M.P. University of Crime course for smoking weed or selling pills. You can't criminalise people for a consumer preference. Might as well jail them for preferring Cornflakes tae All Bran. A load of fuckin nonsense, he shakes his head. — Anyway, I have to go.

I feel an anxiety rising in my chest. I want him to stay. No. I want him to tell me something. I have to ask.

— Boss, one thing. What happens to the guy in your script . . . the, eh racist cop?

— Not got to that bit yet Bruce. Maybe you could help me! he smiles. — Anyway, the welfare will be round soon. As I said, try to hang on in there.

Toal departs.

A good man.

We are alone. We switch on the television. There is nothing on.

(*000000you loved once000000before Carole00000*)

No. We love only ourselves.

(*000000you loved once000000surely everybody does000000*)

No. This is not us. We are thinking of somebody else.

(*000000Rhona000000Rhona000000Rhona000000*)

Rhona.

We have to think of Rhona. The mob of hate reminded me, always the mob of hate. There were the pit villagers and then Gorman and Setterington's thugs. In between them, another mob. Who?

No, it does us no good to think of that.

(*000000000000000000000000000why not 000000000000000000*
000000000000000000000000000why not 0000000000000000)

because it's done and it's in the fuckin past

(*000000000000think of food then 000000000000000000000000*
000000000000000000000000000000000lovely, lovely grub 000000)

I can't even eat a thing

000000000000you're becoming hard work Bruce. Too much of the 'I', not enough of the 'we'. You're eating for two now! If you can't think of Rhona, I'll remind you.

Rhona.

Rhona was the wee lassie you never really knew but who was your first love. You first saw her in the playground at the secondary school. Can you still see her standing there, in front of the art block with her pals? She did art as well, but she was the year below you. You were a fifteen-year-old virgin with your hormones all over the place. She had a copy of a Mott the Hoople album: Mott. You thought that this was cool, her being into that. You wanted to speak to her. Everybody probably did, but no one had the bottle.

Yes, it was the way she looked that made you want to talk to her, but the way she moved repelled and embarrassed you. Embarrassed you for you and embarrassed you for her. Then you said to Dermott, your friend at school, that you were going to talk to her and

that was that. As you approached her you could feel your face
going red, your eyes starting to water. You said something stupid like:

– That yin's no as good as All The Young Dudes.

– It's better, she replied, looking at the sleeve.

– Naw it's no, you inanely retorted, a prisoner of your own inarticulacy.

– Aye it is, she insisted, and things were going nowhere until she added,

– It's jist cause you've no heard it right.

– Ah've no goat it yit, you said.

You still couldn't even move in Bruce, could you? It took her
friend to say, – We're playin it the night, up at her bit, eh Rhona?
Rhona looked embarrassed, but you took your chance then.

– Can ah come up and have a listen?

She told you, – Come if ye want OOOOOOOOOOOOOOOOOOOOOOOOOO
OOOOOOOOOOOOOOOOOOOOOOOOOOOOOOOOOOOOOOOOOOOOOOOOOOO
OOOOOOOOOOOOOOOOOOOOOOOOOOOOOOOOOOOOOOOOOOOO

— Come if you want, I'm telling her on the phone, – just
come if you want.

I put the receiver down on the cradle and I realise that I
don't even know who I was talking to. It was a her though. But
I don't know who it was. Bunty? Chrissie? Shirley? The polis
welfare woman? Carole?

Naw, it wisnae Carole.

I'm sitting here inspecting the rash on my thighs. I've taken
a felt-tipped pen and drawn the border around the extremity of
the infected skin. This way I'll be able to calculate the rate at
which the infection spreads. If I could calculate my entire skin
surface, I could work out how long it would take for me to be
completely covered in the rash.

I'll fuckin well tell Rossi. I'll have the information before
that useless quack can get it. In three years, four months, twelve
days and six and a half hours from now, your patient, Detective
Sergeant, no, not now Detective Inspector, Detective Sergeant
Bruce Robertson will be just one, big festering scab.

Is that news?

You question my method of calculation? My methods are my
methods are my methods. I do not give an Aylesbury Duck.

I rise and go to the window. Those are snow storm clouds gathering.

*OOOOOOOOOOOOOOOOOOOOOOOOOOOOOOOOO*You were in the clouds Bruce, but part of you was unsure as to whether or not she was setting you up for more of the same ridicule and humiliation that had been yours ever since you were aware of breathing air. But you went. Hormones are a powerful force, more so in Bruce Robertson than in most young men. But you were scared Bruce. You went down to her place on the edge of your scheme, down by the river and the farms.

When you got there, everything was fine. It was great just sitting in the warm and talking about music, and especially to girls. You went home and masturbated about her. As much as you tried to avoid thinking about her caliper, as much as you tried to erase it in the image you formed of her in your head, it almost always resolutely reappeared, in all its cold, gleaming, metallic, leathery splendour. You felt guilty afterwards, but why? Every young man masturbates.

You wanted to kiss her though Bruce, you wanted to kiss her so badly.

The next day you went to her house alone. You listened to the album with her again. You said, – Would it be alright if I kissed you, like just on the cheek?

She laughed and said, – Nup, no oan the cheek. I want a real snog.

You trembled and said, – Awright well . . .

It was strange at first, your lips and hers. They felt tight, different to how you imagined. Then you considered the saliva and germs. But soon you relaxed and got into it, both of you, your mouths and tongues started to disappear. Your cock got hard and your head went dizzy.

A couple of days later you met her in the playground. She smiled at you and one of her friends said something. You came over. You always got a

*red face when you talked to her in front of her mates, in fact
any time you talked to her at the school.*

*But it passed. After a while you grew comfortable and the jealousy
and aggression you felt from the other young men whom you knew
were looking at you and her, it stopped bothering you. You knew what
they were, for all their tough talk and posturing: virgins to a boy.
They talked incessantly about all the lassies they had fucked but you
never saw any of them with a bird. You confronted them with that
inadequacy, that way you strutted around with Rhona. After a while
you fed off their outrage. You felt yourself getting stronger and them
getting weaker. It was satisfying. You started to thrive on this
difference. You had always felt different but inferior, but now you
were coming to feel yourself to be different but superior. This was
how you were coming to be seen as well. All you needed to do
was to assert that difference and accept the consequences.*

*Rhona made you strong. She was so proud as she lurched along with
her twisting, loping stride, her head raised in a defiant serenity. There
were some people around who felt themselves to be at the bottom of
the economic and social structure, who had nothing to look forward to
but more humiliations. They loved the idea of this beautiful young
lassie in a caliper. You remember the term they used, that word which
came out of their mocking, pinched, sneering mouths: spastic.*

*Soon you weren't a virgin any more. You nor Rhona. You couldn't
do it in her house or your granny's place so you did it up against
the pillars of the old bridge down by the river.*

*It was dark and quiet and a sweet smell was rising up from the
river as you manoeuvred through the broken railings towards its
bank. Rhona stalled and gave you an accusing look as you turned
back to face her. – C'moan, it's awright but, eh, you urged.*

*– Ah cannae, she spat, entangled and irritated. You freed her
calipered leg from its entrapment of wire and shrub. You shifted*

your weight and, putting your arm around her, pulled her to you. You let her momentum, as Mr Conroy in science used to say, pull her through the gap towards the verge. She panicked, tensing and letting out a scream, but you held her tightly and swang her on to her feet. You felt so proud that you were so strong and that she was so light.

You liked it when you could get close to her like that. That warmth of her next to you, the smell of her hair, the scent she sometimes wore, her mother's probably.

You had to sort of wedge her up against the old bridge to stop her from sliding down the bank into the river. She was not too pleased, tutting away, so you moved quickly, hiking up her skirt and getting her knickers down to her ankles so that she could step out of them using her good leg. You pulled them up her gammy leg and wedged them in between the thin flesh and the straps to stop them from getting dirty on the ground.

Your trousers and pants are down next, but you both freeze as a car makes its way over the single-lane bridge above you, crunching at the gravel as it goes. You push up against her and she helps you to get it in, using her hand. She is gritting her teeth and you are as well because it's sore and you realise that you should have touched her up first, to make it juicy and easier to get it in but you are desperate, worried that she'll change her mind at the last minute or that somebody will disturb you.

The second time is like the first time, but it was the time after that, or the next one, the third or fourth you can never remember, that was the last. Why can't you remember? Your mind plays such tricks on you.

The last time. Just like the other two or three.

You are thinking that one day it would be great to shag in a bed, although this would do for now. Yes, you put your hands over the cheeks of her arse to stop it from grinding against the stone wall as *you fuck her. She is into it now as you are getting right up and she's whispering, – Gie's it . . . gie's it . . . and you have your tongue in her mouth and she has hers in yours and you are making love now, it has gone way past the sordid, uncomfortable entry into a state of sheer fucking brilliance.*

You finish first and cannot carry on. Just like the first three or four times. You feel her frustration. You think that you should take your time. Now that it's over you have a powerful urge to run away and leave her. She now seems like what they call her, a cripple, a spastic. But your pal Dermott says that it's normal to feel this way after you've had your hole. Chemicals are exhausted in you and they take a while to build up again. No way would you have ever ran away though, with her having a caliper. You think you love her. You lie awake at night not thinking of Stevie and the filth, but about how good it would be if you and she were married. No just for the sex, but so that you could have a house together and you could take care of each other. You know that her mum and dad would not agree to that. You think it is daft and soft to feel like this but this is how you feel.

Your grandmother found out. Her friend Agnes saw you kissing Rhona on a park bench in town. You come home one evening and she is sitting up with a half-bottle of whisky and a few cans of Carlsberg Superlager, in front of the telly. By this time she is in an advanced state of alcoholic disintegration. – Aye, they tell ays that you've goat a wee girlfriend now, she said, – one that cannae run away fae ye! One wi a gammy leg! You ignore her witch's cackle and head up to the refuge of your room.

Outside they all play the same game. They call you a pervert. The Son of the Beast and The Spastic. Rhona never wears make-up to school, so she looks younger. Like a first year instead of a second year.

But back to that night, the night of your fourth time. You take her home. Then you see them ahead, Brian Meldrum and his crowd. They are there with some bigger guys. You don't mind them calling you the Cripple Shagger. You can handle that. You know that it is just jealousy because your girlfriend is so gorgeous. The best looking girl in the school, easily, in spite of the caliper. You can handle what they say to you, but you don't want them saying anything to her. She doesn't deserve it, and you love her. – Mibbee cut acroas the golf course, you tell her.

– Aye, she replies, knowing what you mean straight away. She squeezes your hand and looks down. Your heart feels heavy and you wish that you were strong enough to destroy them all, to destroy anybody who would hurt her. But they hadn't seen you, they seemed out of their heads on glue and cheap wine. So you go back down the road, through another wire fence to the golf course.

Elated at having escaped at best a bad taunting, you pick up the pin from one of the holes on the course and throw it like a javelin. You are showing off to Rhona, but she is saying, – Dinnae Bruce . . . dinnae . . . as she moves over to the lip of a bunker.

Then there is a rumble in the sky and the rain comes teeming down. Then you see a large flash, followed by another rumble. Then you hear Rhona let out a strange yelp like a small dog that has had its paw trod upon and you turn to see her briefly shrouded in an electrical glow as she is struck by a bolt of lightning.

You run the fifty yards or so towards her in the semi-darkness, the rain lashing down on you. All you can hear is the halting sob in your chest and you can't even call her name0000000000000000000000000 000000000000000000000000000000000000000000000000000000

Rhona!

Carole!

Stacey!

I take out her picture and stick it back on the sideboard. She used tae wear braces on her teeth, the wee yin. They really straightened them out. A good thing, though I was against it at first. She never wore anything on her leg though.

The kitchen is smelling bad. Something has died in here. I open the back door. It's cold and I'm wearing only my boxer shorts and my dressing gown, which hangs open but it's good to see the snow fall again. Like the Bing Crosby and Danny Kaye film *White Christmas*, where they open the patio doors of the General's holiday inn in Vermont and the snow tumbles down and they burst into song and the closing credits come up. I sip on another purple tin as I watch the snow cascade down. I sing to myself: I'mmm steaming, it's a shite Christmas . . .

There's something on the ground, in the garden . . .

OOOOOOOOOOOOOOOOOOOOO*you look down at what is on the ground and then you have turned and are crossing the fence again, walking over into the scheme from the farm. They are shouting at you but you can hear nothing distinct. You stop and look at the pink blossom trees, the ones Rhona always pointed out to you. She loved their fragrance.*

Then Brian Meldrum is barring your way. – Robertson, ah'm fuckin well talking tae you!

You are looking at him and thinking how hideously ugly wilful stupidity can make people look. Remember when you used to think those kind of thoughts Bruce? You were thinking how much this boy is letting himself down without really being aware of it.

– Bruce Robertson, the Cripple Shagger! Whaire's yir wee spazzy bird the day?

– She's away . . .

– Tidy wee piece mate, another guy says, – ah'd ride it!

– Fuck off ya pervy cunt, Meldrum laughs.

374

– Naw bit, the older guy says, she's a fuckin wee doll. Jist cause youse cunts huvnae goat the bottle tae ask her oot. Disnae matter aboot a gammy leg, it's the coupon and the tits and the fanny ye huv tae worry aboot. That wee Rhona, wee honey man . . .

Meldrum's still staring at you. – What's up wi your face Robertson? Ye git a knock-back? His winey breath is on your face. Not like Rhona's perfume.

You hear the rain crashing off the bus shelter roof above you. – Naw she's away, gone . . . the golf course . . .

– Does she dae line ups? the other guy asks.

– She's on the golf course . . . You are shivering now. Thinking of her. How you did nothing. How it was all because of them. To avoid their ridicule.

– In this weather! Lit's find her!

They drag you out of the shelter into the rain, on to the bridge and over the gate. You take them to the spot where she is waiting.

– It's pissin doon . . . she'll no be here . . . one guy says.

– Aye she will, she's mibbee fucked up her leg. We'll need tae take her hame.

– Where is she? The thunder has stopped but the rain has soaked you all.

– Ower thaire . . . behind the bunker . . . you tell them.

Meldrum runs over. – Hey baby . . . hey . . . he stops on the lip of the bunker. – What the fuck . . . fuckin . . . he turns back to rest of you, – GIT THE FUCKIN POLIS!

He punches you hard in the guts, knocking all the wind from you and spreading a sickness throughout your body. – What did ye fuckin well dae tae her! Ya fuckin perve!

You are aware that he has you down and is booting into you, they all are. You are crying, but not for yourself. You are crying for her.

The police come and take you down to their station. They tell you it was silly to throw away the pin on the course as the lightning strikes the highest point. So it was you that killed her. No. An accident. Another accident. But the police are good to you. Kind. Understanding.

Sometimes you can still see her face, so cold and stiff, her freckles like they had been painted on. Not like Rhona, not like when she smiled and you talked and kissed and shagged.

She was your first love but you never really knew her as well as you wanted to. She liked music and she looked and ~~e liked~~ *smelt nice and she wore a caliper and your heart* ~~e these~~ *used to and still does break, if you're honest* ~~mindless~~ *with yourself, every time you think of her.* ~~use like this~~ *Sometimes you can't help yourself but the* ~~games are no~~ *games help. Or at least they used to. Now they are no longer enough.*

Sh\[...\] days l\[...\] when \[...\] vandalis\[...\] sort of sh\[...\] longer en\[...\]

What is it? A sack of coal. A find.

I drag it into the cold, dark room. I slowly build up the fire and light it. It catches on quickly. I sit transfixed by the lapping flames which provide the only light in the room, except for a small, annoying flash on the sideboard next to me, which throws a dull, sick red tint over Stacey's picture.

I switch on the answer machine to play back my messages:

— Bruce, Bunty. Please call me.

Beep.

— Bruce, Bunty. I'm worried about you darling. They said you were sick. I called but you weren't in. Call me.

Beep.

— It's Chrissie. Call me sometime sexy!

Beep.

— Hello Bruce. It's Gus here. Hope all is well and that you'll soon be fighting fit again. Gie's a wee tinkle!

Beep.

— Mister Robertson, it's Heather Sim here. Euan's mum. It would be great if you could get tickets for Tynecastle for the Celtic match on the twenty-first. I don't know if that's convenient or not. If you could get back to me on six-one-two-seven-double-four three. Thanks again.

Beep.

— Brucey baby, it's Chrissie from-be Hynde here; the last of the great Pretenders! You haven't been answering either your calls or your callers. I was round yesterday. I know you're in. There are roadworks outside. Your gas needs turned off. What's the matter big boy? Can't you stand the heat? Call me if you just happen to rediscover your bollocks!

Beep.

— Anybody home? Oh well . . .

Beep.

— Bruce . . . please, please, please call me. It's Bunty. Please Bruce.

Beep.

— Bruce . . . it's Shirley . . . Bruce . . . call me . . . call me!

Beep.

— Bruce. Gus. Ah didnae git it Bruce. They didnae gie me it. Phone me Bruce, I want to take this up wi the Federation. Ye ken who they gave it tae!

Beep.

— Hello . . .

Beep.

Enough of it. I disconnect the phone. More television, that's what I need.

More television.

No. The channels, the voices, always the fuckin voices . . .

Then a knock on my door. I can't be bothered but the knock's getting louder and louder and it's just like whoever it is is going to kick the door in, polis-style. I'm opening up and he's here, standing in front of me in the doorway, and I'm looking over his shoulder, watching Tom Stronach's BMW pull out and head down the road. The winter sun glints in my eye. The snow-storm. It's gone. It's just away. Fuckin hell.

— I had to come Bruce, he says to us. — I was worried about you. You've been through the fucking mill. I had to come, he repeats.

We want to close the door, but it seems easier to let him in. We say nothing, but we go through to our kitchen and sit down. We look outside at our garden, a dead mess. It was once so lovely. Carole liked working in it, I never did. I appreciated her efforts though. Liked to sit out there with a can of lager. Simple pleasures. Stacey's swing . . . got that a few summers ago now. How many?

Ray follows me in and sits down opposite us. A concerned visitor.

— Of course Bruce, ah dinnae need tae tell ye that while I was chuffed aboot the promotion, it's been a bitter-sweet experience for me. If you hadnae had that . . . well, the problems you've been huvin . . . well, you'd've walked it mate. Hus tae be said.

— Aye Ray, that's the way it goes, we nod. This is what it's about. This is what Gus's message was about.

Lennox's face is set in an evaluating smile, tight round the mouth, eyes searching but strangely dead and mechanical, the polis way. — Ken what your problem is, he laughs coldly, — ye dinnae practise what ye preach.

We can say nothing.

Lennox is talking to us in the manner that pretends it's all for our welfare, rather than his gloating benefit. — You telt me Bruce. Mind what you says: You need to suss out what the party line was and then spiel out the script.

— Aye, I mind, we tell him.

— You see though Bruce, you have tae learn a new script. It's like all that equal opps bullshit: just spout that at the cunts and do it with conviction. It's just another wee code you rely on. That's why the likes of Gillman . . . he shakes his head in a condescending smile. He's rehearsed this speech alright. — Your behaviour has to be non-racist and non-sexist. You ken the score; all this equal opps stuff started when mass unemployment took its toll. You couldn't have upwardly mobile schemies taking jobs from the sons and daughters of the rich! So you bring in a handful of overprivileged coons as a Trojan horse sop to equal opps, while making sure you keep the good salaried jobs for the educated bourgeoisie. You start to introduce minimum qualifications, make a uni degree essential where it had never been needed in the past. That way you weed out people that cannae bullshit your script. Of course, fuck all changes. In London coons just get to be truncheoned by a member of their own race once in a blue moon. You know the score.

Lennox gives me an I've-got-it-sussed wink.

— Yeah. This is true Ray.

— I'm no saying you're a dinosaur Bruce, but you've allowed these cunts to paint you that way. Keep the cards close to yir chest mate.

— Close to the chest Ray, like I always told you.

— That's what you told me, he says cheerfully. He looks around the room and he can't hide his distaste. He stands to his feet. Lennox the victor, Robertson the vanquished.

Who would have thought it. Lennox perhaps.

— Anyway, Bruce, got to nash. There is just one thing, and I suppose it's something that everybody feels when they get a promotion, you know, how to relate to the old mates and all of that.

He looks closely at us to see as if we understand. We are looking at him blankly. We have nothing to say.

— I can say this because we're both law enforcement professionals Bruce, but your methods and mines are very different.

Now I ken that we've pulled some shit in the past, but that's finito now, all the coke and that shit. He looks hard and searchingly at me with an authority he's never shown before. The authority of the man who knows he has the state queueing up behind him, on his side. — Savvy?

— Sure Ray, we say.

— Just as long as you realise how the old song goes: 'These days are gone now, and in the past they must remain', okay?

— Okay . . .

— And Bruce, nae hard feelings, eh mate?

— Naw Ray, you know me, I'm not one for living in the past. I'm sure you'll do a great job as inspector.

Ray grips our shoulder harshly. — Thanks mate. Right, I'd better nash. See ye. Things to dae, people tae see.

— Aye. Cheerio Ray.

— Cheery bye bye Bruce . . . oh . . . Bruce, I saw that Bladesey the other day, doon the club at Shrubhill. We all gave him the cold-shoulder treatment. He looked a bit sheepish. Then Gillman went up and put him in the picture, in Dougie's own inimitable style. So I doubt whether our Mister Blades will be showing his face in the craft again. Cheers then, Ray winks, making a clicking noise from the side of his mouth as he departs.

Click click click

Channel hopping.

Clickity c[l 00000000000000]*You grew up and started* sick as a fuckin dug *working in the same pit as the man you thought* estroy me. They to[ld] *was your father. You could sense his hatred. But* all the tapes we[re] *you had your friends now. There was an old miner, a* with sex an[d] *man from Skye named Crawford Douglas. You remember him from when you were a child. He was the one who led you away from the coal byng and Stevie's broken body, down the street and on to your granny's house at Penicuik. You got on well with Crawford. Your gran also did at one time. But no longer. He had lived in Newtongrange for a long time. Crawford did not get on with your stepfather, Ian Robertson. That was a strong enough basis for you to befriend him*

380

and he inducted you into the ancient and noble craft of freemasonry.
One night, when drunk, he told you the true story of your blood father.
He wasn't dead OOOOOOOOOOOOOOOOOOOOOOOOOOOOOOOOOOOOOOOOOO

I'm hearing the voices and I'm pressing the buttons on the handset to change the channels but it's the voice in my head. That same, insistent soft voice, eating me up from the inside . . .

. . . I change channels . . .

OOOOOOOOOOOOOOOOOOOOMolly Hanlon's family originated from
Ireland and via Edinburgh's Old Town found themselves working in
the pit villages of Midlothian. She grew up in Newtongrange and
found herself in love with a local lad, a young miner named
Ian Robertson, who worked with her father.
Ian did not understand the need to be married in a Catholic church,
but agreed for Molly's sake. After all, he loved the girl. Then
something terrible happened, something which would test that
love to the fullOOOOOOOOOOOOOOOOOOOOOOOOOOOOOOOOOOOO

. . . I change channels . . . a Bond film. This time it's Roger Moore . . .

OOOOOOOOOOOOOOOOOOOOOOOOOOOOOwhen she was putting
flowers on the grave of her dead brother, Molly was attacked by
a man. She was beaten and raped. Molly gave a description and the
man was apprehended. He was tried and convicted of a number
of rapes and sexual assaults on women and men. It was revealed
at his trial that this man suffered from mental problems: acute
schizophrenia, depression, anxiety attacks.
This terrible tragedy was compounded when it was established
that Molly had become pregnant by this man. She asked her local
priest for guidance. Father Ryan told her that, as a Catholic, it
was her duty to bring this life into the world. Ian Robertson,
though devastated, stood by her. The wedding was brought
forward and the child bore the name of BruceOOOOOOOOOOO
OOOOOO OOOOOOOOOOOOOOOOOOOOOOOOOOOOOOOOOOOOOO

I change channels . . . cartoons . . . Walt Disney. *Beauty and the Beast* . . .

OOOOOOOOOOOOOOOOOOOOOOOOOOOOOOOOOIan Robertson stood
by his wife, but every time he looked at the baby he saw the face

of the man from the front page of the Daily Record *and the caption:*
THE FACE OF A BEAST burned in his skull.
You knew you weren't like him. Like that thing. You had
*to prove it*OOOOOOOOOOOOOOOOOOOOOOOOOOOOOOOOOOOOO

I change channels . . . adverts . . . real Scots read the
Record . . .

You came to know that face. The old Daily Record *was on*
the microfiche in the Glasgow Room of the Mitchell Library.
You would stare for hours at that face, trying to find
something in it, some humanity.
That strange pilgrimage you made into Glasgow, it took up
all your free time. Sometimes you would take time off from
your job in the pits. Take time off to look at the face of
The Beast. You had to tell yourself that you were nothing
like him. But the women. You wanted them. You always
wanted them. But so did all the young men. It was normal

I change channels: repeats of *Please, Sir.*

OOOOOOOOOOOOOOOOOOOOOOOOOOOOO*you remember Miss Hunter,*
Bruce. At the primary school in Penicuik. You have to remember
her cruelty towards you. She was the brittle, stick-like woman
who victimised you with a zeal far in excess of the casual
sadism she displayed towards the other pupils. It seemed so
personal. Sometimes she would take you aside and shake you
and hiss softly in your ear, – I know who you are Robertson.
I know everything about you, you nasty, evil little man. The
harder you worked, the harder you tried to please her, the
*worse she would be towards you*OOOOOOOOOOOOOOOOOO

The telly goes off.

I don't know whether it's day or night. Some empty purple tins
lie in front of me. The fire still flickers. A welfare woman called
at some point. I can't remember what she said. I need to do
something.

I pull on some clothes and go outside, making my way

towards Colinton Village. The only person I can think of visiting is my physician, Dr Rossi.

The waiting room is full of smelly old cunts, but I've got the upper hand on them now. I'm minging in this old coat! Take some of that ya snobby auld cunts. I produce a purple tin from my coat pocket.

— You can't drink in here, the receptionist tells me. I flash my ID at her. — Police, I tell her. — Working undercover, I explain to the old wifies. One makes a twisted girn with those old, dried-out lips. I want to grab a syringe and fill it up with the contents of the old purple tin and shoot it right into those old lips, rehydrating them instantly! — Plastic surgery, I tell her, — modern techniques. Everybody can afford it, I raise my can to toast technology.

The receptionist calls me and I go in and see Rossi. His jaw drops as I enter, and if I gave a Luke and Matt Goss, I'd say his lack of bedside manner is unprofessional.

He's the McDonald's of medicine, and it takes him a shorter time to come to a diagnosis than it does for them to serve up a Big Mac.

— You're depressed Mr Robertson. I don't do this lightly, but I'm going to prescribe Prozac.

— Fine, we tell this physician.

Rossi though: something is different about him. It's as if it's just dawned on him that he's approaching middle age and he's never going to reach surgical greatness. This, prescribing pills to sad old cunts and being a glorified clerk, like polis, teachers, social workers all are nowadays, this is as good as it gets. Our normally buoyant physician is giving off the defeated, depressive stink of a man whose own limitations have caught up with him. It's a smell we've grown accustomed to lately. It oozes from every sick pore in my own body, as surely as the stale whisky sweat which accompanies it.

When we, I, we are leaving his surgery and walking through the village we screw the prescription into a ball and sling it in the Water of Leith at Colinton Dell. Then we go to the Royal Scot

383

for a pint. This is the only fuckin drug we need: peeve. It was that fuckin coke that fucked us up, that cunt Lennox. Brought us down to his level then nipped in and stole the job that was ours. We should have picked that up, should have seen the signs. But we were weak.

We must now be strong.

Sleep fails to take us during the night. Thoughts are flying through our head like an endless merry-go-round. We can see the merry-go-round, our wife and child waving to us from the stupid horses as we sit and drink our tea in the Piazza of Princes Street Gardens, always distracted, lost in our own thoughts, our dreams of revenge against those who transgress the laws of the state.

We cannot break the cycle by having a fuckin wank cause every time we conjure up a picture of a woman we see the yobs' faces or those of Lennox or Toal, and arousal, to our relief, is impossible under those circumstances.

Terror's grip on us seems physical; sometimes it slackens but it never lets go.

We are walking again, through the Dell, through the long passage, which is like an old railway tunnel. There is one point in this tunnel, the point we have now reached, where it bends and you cannot see the light ahead, nor can you see it if you look back. A couple of steps forward and the light shines, a couple of steps backward and a glance over your shoulder and it's the same story. But here, just at this point: this is limbo. There is the sense that if you stay at this point for too long, stop at this point of oblivion for a certain amount of time, you will just cease to exist.

And we cannot move.

OOOOOOOOOOOOOOOOOthe air blowing from the polar regions across the inhospitable sea and directly into your tobacco ravaged lungs is so frozen that it feels like an Arctic core in your body. I can feel it here Bruce, and I do not like it. You feel that warm mammal flesh wrap around it like layers of blanket assimilating it, allowing its goodness to flow to the organs of your body. Breathing.

(Breathing. I don't like it. Get out of the tunnel Bruce000000)
(00000000000000000000000000000000000000000000000)

The tunnel swirls around us, the stone configuration visible, starting to spin through the filthy, bruised darkness. We hear voices, but we are not tense.

Then we are sadly not in oblivion. We have no sensation of leaving the tunnel or the wooded glen, but know that we have somehow gone back up on to the main road through the noise of the occasional car and its lights.

Then, the Napier University and the rise of twilight and the chirping of birds up towards the gardens at Gilmore Place and then we are at the King's Theatre.

Stacey and Carole and Stacey's wee pal Celeste with us at the pantomine, to see *Mother Goose* featuring Stanley Baxter and Angus Lennie out of *Crossroads*.

We saw it.

Oh no we didn't.

Oh yes we did.

It's light and we are cold; our teeth chatter together. A jakey coughs an insult at us, or it could be a request for money. We look in our pockets and there is a twenty-pound note and some change.

We take out the twenty-pound note and hand it to the jakey who sees the pain in our eyes and his own eyes focus in a grateful then fearful sobriety as he takes the note and mumbles something *00000000000000000000000000000* nd is off down the road. W *0000000000000000000000000000*

The fig *000000Shortly before the miners'* but how, that's what's g *strike, on hearing this news of your true* heid. *father, you left for London and joined the police. You poured over the press cuttings from the Scottish Library. You thought of your own conditions, your own problems and related those to your natural father's. This man, the most feared and hated in the prison system, kept isolated for his and others' safety. The man who became known simply as The Beast. You*

needed to keep going, to keep busy, to shut out thought.
You were normal. You left the pits and joined the force.
Then got married. You settled down. You had a child.
You were normal. Only, there came the anxiety attacks.
The depressions.
The desires.

We travel in the opposite direction, back the way we came. In a shop window we see our thick, dark growth. We should have shaved.

What is there to do but go home.

Home.

Home Is The Darkness

I don't have any photographs. Only memories. I can still vividly recall the time I went in to see him.

My own father. The one who never abused me, never forced me to eat coal, never called me the spawn of the devil. But he was still the one I hated most.

I'd got used to places like this with my work. I'd started not to notice them. But not this place. You had to notice it, had to feel the omnipresent, sickening bleakness of it on your approach to it. That huge perimeter fence, seeming to run the length of the ugly void of shitehouse towns, schemes, industrial estates, factories and old mines which spread between Edinburgh and Glasgow.

Inside, the smell. The disinfectant. No other smell like it. Similar to a hospital but staler and more rank.

I was shaking as the screw Josh Hartley opened the cell for me. All my data of him was gleaned from that one twisted photograph in the *Daily Record*. I thought he would look like the most evil thing I had ever seen. It was anticlimactic. My anxiety fell away but I felt loathing and contempt rise as I looked at this slight, old figure. Could this really be The Beast? His eyes. They were not the eyes of a killer, but the eyes of an auld sweetie wife, privvy to some malicious gossip. His nose, hooked, not like mine, mines is like my mother's. I wanted to haul him down on to the floor and stomp on his head, to crush the life out of him, to take his just as he'd given me mine. I thought of my mother. I resented her weakness. How could she have let this pathetic thing do that to her? How could she have not fought him off?

Did she want it? Did she want *him*? Did she want *that*? No. Never.

How could she have grown the seed of this scum inside of her for some fuckin stupid church run by cunts who dinnae even get their fuckin hole? Or urnae fuckin *supposed* tae at any rate.

It's against regulations.

It's against regulations for a prisoner in this category to be left alone with one officer, let alone a visiting cop, but the screw was a craft stalwart. He gave me time alone. Just five minutes. More than enough when you've been schooled in the discipline of the slippery stairs. I thought that I would have wanted to say something. To accuse, or to question. But I never spoke. There was no point. I just moved towards The Beast.

– What de ye want! What dae ye want! he cackled at me, picking up the hatred and the focused intent.

When the officer returned my hands were round The Beast's neck and his split head was bouncing off the wall.

The screw stopped me. Hauled me off. The Beast still rots away in the psychiatric prison. He is used to being assaulted by prison staff, but I hoped that he remembered that one as a little bit special. But probably not.

Everyt 0000000000listen to me Bruce, you're different waste
it all. The to him. He made his choices, you made yours. You rple.
chose to protect people from predators like him.
You chose to uphold the law. You are too hard on
yourself Bruce. You had a family. You were different to
that monster. They wanted you to be the same, right
from the start, you were the one thing an isolated,
terrorised people could kick out at. That was the role you
took on. But you're different Bruce, you're different from him.

Never mind Rhona. There was Carole. You had Carole.

> *Carole was the Other. You fall in love and after you have returned from London, where you were working with the Met, you get married.*

I change channels. A documentary on Margaret Thatcher.

> *But the impulses are still there. The impulse to hurt and control, in order to try and fill the void inside. You think of the man who sired you. You are repulsed and proud. The urge to hurt, demean and control is great in you. To somehow get back at them. You consider politics as a career. How wonderful it would be to start a war. To send thousands of people to their deaths. You idolise Thatcher over the Falklands. You try to imagine the buzz she must have felt when the word 'rejoice' came from her lips. It makes you feel like you did when you were a child. While other children fantasised about killing in wars, you wanted to be in the position to send others to their deaths from the safety of an oak-panelled office. In your head you practise speeches condemning the enemy.*

> *You look at the job and curse your own limitations and the ones set upon you. From circumstances like your own you know that you cannot achieve power without going through interminably boring processes. But you must have protection, because the normals will incarcerate you in order to protect themselves. So the police force always seems the best bet.*

I change channels. *Holiday*. Judith Chalmers explores the Great Barrier Reef . . .

> *You are restless, however. Australia beckons. The New South Wales police, with its reputation for petty corruption, greatly appealed to you.*

> *But you were not a bad man Bruce. Whatever you did, you always came home to Carole. You had Carole.*

I switch off the televison.

I had Carole, but I fucked every other woman I could get

389

my hands on. Didn't matter what they were like; prostitutes, relatives, birds on a night out who were up for it, workmates. If I'm being honest, I liked quite a few of them, although it was always easier never to admit that. I did it all the time, at any opportunity.

Carole only did it once.

Carole got back at us through shagging that coon. She said she loved him. That was all I knew about him: he was black and she said she loved him. We couldn't help it, finishing that cunt off. It was when we were with her, dressed in her clothes. In that club wearing her clothes with the specialist large shoes we ordered from the shop in Newcastle. These yobs had set upon the cunt, kicked him unconscious. We just had to finish him, we didn't know whether or not it was the guy Carole was with. We did him with the claw hammer we used for our protection on the streets. We bought it in Chelmsford, on the way back from Tony and Diana's. Drummond could search all over Scotland. We needed to have it; there were people who would try to hassle us. We needed to have it, Carole and I.

Aye, we were in Jammy Joe's and we saw Efan Wurie dancing, drinking. We tried to talk to him but he was dismissive of us. We thought he was the same guy that Carole was with. We just wanted to talk to him, to find out if he knew her. But he dismissed us. Rejected Carole and me. He never loved her, he just used her. It was the principle of the thing. Fuck it, any one will dae. We wanted to hurt.

That Estelle Davidson lassie was looking at us all night, she had seen us in the women's toilet. She had pointed us out to Gorman and Setterington and the other thugs present. That was when we had to leave.

We had to leave and wait on them. We had to do this in order to pay them back.

But they got the coon. They got him first. I finished him, but they got him first. I don't know why, I don't care why, probably just because he was there, perhaps he was chatting up their birds. I don't care. I only care about me. Even that is a lie.

{ *Don't do this Bruce000000000000000Don't do this00000*
000000000000000000000000000000000000don't do this00000
000000000000000000000you're better than this 00000000
0000000000000000000000000000000000don't do this00000000
00000000000000000there's more0000000000000000000 *}*

I only care about me and about why I don't care about anybody else.

She thinks that she can do what she likes, well there's no fuckin way, and she's poisoned the bairn against us with these silly stupid lies that she tells, the festering hoor, and it's all gone wrong and she has tae be shown, has tae be made tae pey cause this is nae fuckin use.

When we call her at her mother's all we can say is that we want to see the bairn again, that we want to talk. Sort out the divorce.

Her voice is not the voice of the Carole we know. There is now no room for the words that she had waited for for so long, the words we were not capable of speaking, the ones that might have made a difference. In the absence of the words she became meat, a repository for my come. To be fucked, to be wanked over. To be made to do things she would not otherwise have done. In the sex clubs we joined. Bent by the will of my . . . need? It's not her voice. I almost like this woman. She sounds like Carole before

Enough.

Now that we've told her to come, all we can do is sit and wait. And prepare. Prepare to do the cow.

For good.

{ *00000000000 be reasonable Bruce00000000000000000000*
000 nothing is so bad that it can't be made better0000000
000000000 maybe not with her, but you have your whole
life ahead of you00000000000000000000000 please00
00000000000000000000 please 000000000000000
00000000 don't do this00000000000000000000
0000000000000 it's not fair000000000000
00000000000 don't000000000000000000 *}*

I've made the t-shirt we are wearing. It has YOU CAUSED THIS on it in big, black letters. The noose feels tight around our neck. We look up at it, strung on the rafters of the attic and we're now just waiting, ready to drop out of the hatch as soon as she turns the key in the lock and pushes the door open. We'll land right in front of her in the hallway, so she'll have that on her conscience for the rest of her fucking life the fuckin whore and liar.

{
OOOOOOOOOOOOOOOOOO**Bruce**OOOOOOOOOOOOOOOOOOOOOOOOOOOO
OO**Bruce**OOOOOOOOOOOOOOOOOOOO**Bruce**OOOOOOOOOOOOOOOOO
OOOOOOOOOOOOOOOOOO**Bruce**OOOOOOOOOOOOOOOOOOOOOOOOOOOO
OOOOOOOOOOOOOOOOOOOOOOOOOOOOOO**Bruce**OOOOOOOOOOOOOO
OOOOOOOOOO**Bruce**OOOOOOOOOOOOOOO**Bruce**OOOOOOOOOOOO
OOOOOOOOOOOOOOOOOO**Bruce**OOOOOOOOOOOOOOOOOOOOOOOOOO
}

We wait and think and doubt and hate.

How does it make you feel?

The overwhelming feeling is rage. We hate ourself for being unable to be other than what we are. Unable to be better.

We feel rage.

The feelings must be followed. It doesn't matter whether you're an ideologue or a sensualist, you follow the stimuli thinking that they're your signposts to the promised land. But they are nothing of the kind. What they are is rocks to navigate past, each one you brush against, ripping you a little more open and there are always more on the horizon. But you can't face up to that, so you force yourself to believe the bullshit of those that you instinctively know to be liars and you repeat those lies to yourself and to others, hoping that by repeating them often enough and fervently enough you'll attain the godlike status we accord to those who tell the lies most frequently and most passionately.

But you never do, and even if you could, you wouldn't value it, you'd realise that nobody believes in heroes any more. We know that they only want to sell us something we don't really want and keep from us what we really do need.

Maybe that's a good thing. Maybe we're getting in touch

with our condition at last. It's horrible how we always die alone, but no worse than living alone . . .

(*ooooooooooo***DON'T BRUCE***ooooooooooooooooo***DON'T BRUCE***oooooo*)

Now I'm ready and I hear the key. I jump and I'm falling, then I feel myself rising, I hear a crash, but there's no pain and there's a figure at the frosted glass of the door but it's not her it's too wee it's Stacey no Stacey for fuck sake don't open the door . . . don't . . . and I care . . .

. . . I want more than anything for Stacey not to be there and see this and I'm trying to shout No go away and I hear her screaming Daddy and I want to live and make it up to her and Carole, I can hear her now too, screaming BRUCE because I care and I've won and beaten the bastards but what price victory

STACEY PLEASE GOD BE SOMETHING ELSE SOME-ONE ELSE . . . (*ooooooooooooooooooooooooo*
ooooooooooooooooooooooo

I feel myself slipping out of my Host in a large pile of his excrement and sliding down his leg inside his flannels. Then I'm away from him. There's a piercing scream . . . somebody's in pain . . . like the Other was when the Host was disposing of it . . . the Other I loved . . . now the Host is gone and I cannot sustain this any longer. I can't sustain life outside of the Host's body . . . like the Other I am gone, gone with the Host, leaving the screaming others, always the others, to pick up the pieces
ooooooooooooooooooo
ooooooooooooooooooo
ooooooooooooooooo
ooooooooooooooo
ooooooooooooo)

Irvine Welsh is the author of
Trainspotting (1993), **The Acid House** (1994),
Marabou Stork Nightmares (1995)
and **Ecstasy** (1996).